THE RED DUKE

VAMPIRE AND KING stared at one another across the battlefield. Infernal hatred, pitiless and cruel, blazed in the eyes of the Red Duke. Those of the king became solemn and sad.

'You could not content yourself to be king,' the vampire spoke, his voice low and venomous. 'You had to be Duke of Aquitaine as well.' The Red Duke's face pulled back in a feral snarl, exposing his sharp fangs. 'Now you will be neither.'

The king drew no terror from the Red Duke's words. Tears were in his eyes as he gazed upon the monster. 'The man I knew is dead. It is time he found peace.'

The Red Duke's face contorted in a sneer. 'I will make you immortal, Louis, so that I may torture you and kill you every hour of every day. Then you may speak to me of death and peace!'

A WARHAMMER NOVEL

THE RED DUKE

C. L. WERNER

BLACK LIBRARY

To Sir Christopher Frank Carandini Lee.
The very name has a malevolent ring,
like a secret snarl....

A BLACK LIBRARY PUBLICATION

First published in Great Britain in 2011 by
The Black Library,
Games Workshop Ltd.,
Willow Road, Nottingham,
NG7 2WS, UK.

10 9 8 7 6 5 4 3 2 1

Cover illustration by Cheoljoo Lee.
Internal illustration by Neil Hodgson.

A CIP record for this book is available from the British Library.

UK ISBN: 978 1 84970 073 3
US ISBN: 978 1 84970 074 0

See the Black Library on the internet at
www.blacklibrary.com

Find out more about Games Workshop
and the world of Warhammer at
www.games-workshop.com

Printed and bound in the UK.

THIS IS A dark age, a bloody age, an age of daemons
and of sorcery. It is an age of battle and death, and of the
world's ending. Amidst all of the fire, flame and fury
it is a time, too, of mighty heroes, of bold deeds
and great courage.

AT THE HEART of the Old World sprawls the Empire, the
largest and most powerful of the human realms. Known for
its engineers, sorcerers, traders and soldiers, it is
a land of great mountains, mighty rivers, dark forests
and vast cities. And from his throne in Altdorf reigns
the Emperor Karl Franz, sacred descendant of the
founder of these lands, Sigmar, and wielder
of his magical warhammer.

BUT THESE ARE far from civilised times. Across the
length and breadth of the Old World, from the knightly
palaces of Bretonnia to ice-bound Kislev in the far north,
come rumblings of war. In the towering Worlds Edge
Mountains, the orc tribes are gathering for another assault.
Bandits and renegades harry the wild southern lands of
the Border Princes. There are rumours of rat-things, the
skaven, emerging from the sewers and swamps across the
land. And from the northern wildernesses there is the
ever-present threat of Chaos, of daemons and beastmen
corrupted by the foul powers of the Dark Gods.
As the time of battle draws ever nearer,
the Empire needs heroes
like never before.

PROLOGUE

The clamour of the battlefield roared like thunder across the plain, the pounding of hooves, the crash of blades, the screams of the dying and the ghastly croaking of the eager vultures circling overhead melded into a single diabolic din. The sky was black, choked with dark clouds, the sun hiding its face from the carnage below. Fields that had been green the day before were now a crimson morass of blood and mud, a bone yard of mutilated bodies, the carcasses of the dead and the twice-dead littering the landscape as far as the eye could see.

The strength of the two armies was not yet spent, though battle had raged since the early hours of morning. The pride of Bretonnia made their stand against the debased horrors of a blighted realm, the unliving legions of the vampire, the beast they had ridden to war against.

The Red Duke.

Isabeau the prophetess had warned King Louis that he must face the vampire in the clean light of day, that he must force the fiend to fight him in the sun when the Red Duke's profane powers would be at their weakest. The king had heeded her advice, avoiding contact with the undead legions until he could be sure of the time and place when battle would be joined. Ceren Field offered open ground over which his knights could charge the rotting warriors that marched under the Red Duke's tattered banner. A bright dawn had heralded the day, as though the Lady herself were smiling down from the heavens and encouraging the king's attack.

What horror did the king feel when the dawn faded into blackness, smothered behind dark clouds that grew from nothingness in the empty sky. In a matter of minutes, the bright new day had become as black as midnight. Across the field came the marching skeletons and shambling zombies of the Red Duke's horde. King Louis knew that if he allowed his army to retreat now he would never regain their confidence, not after holding them back for so long, forcing them to watch as the Red Duke ravaged the land.

Into glory or disaster, the king knew he must lead his army now or never. Praying to the Lady that his decision was bold, not foolish, he brandished his lance, letting the royal pennant snap taut in the wind. As he lowered the lance again, he spurred his steed forwards. The earth shook as two thousand knights followed their liege into battle.

Any mortal army would have reeled from the impact of that charge. Hundreds of the enemy were shattered as the knights drove their attack home, skewered upon the lances or crushed beneath the iron-shod hooves of warhorses. But the silent legions that served the Red Duke had no souls to stir with fear, no hearts to quiver with sympathy for their fallen comrades. The undead simply closed ranks about the embattled knights, heedlessly marching over the smashed bodies of their fallen. It was then that the real fighting began.

The king fought alongside his knights, smashing rotted faces with his lance, breaking fleshless bones with his armoured boots and the flailing hooves of his steed. For hours he fought beside his men until a fresh surge of *undead warriors swept him away. Like a mariner cast adrift, he struggled to win his way free from the hostile waves that engulfed him. For each wight he cut down, three seemed to take its place; for every skeletal spearman he broke, a dozen stabbed at him. Against such numbers, the king's courage began to break.*

It was in his moment of doubt, the instant when his deathless foes looked certain to overwhelm him, that King Louis was granted a respite. As though all their vicious energies had been spent, the wights and zombies fell still. Lifeless eyes stared at the king as fleshless arms lowered rusty swords and splintered spears.

A flicker of hope swelled in the king's heart, but was quickly stifled as a cold horror crawled across his skin. The king could feel the vampire's presence before he could see the Red Duke galloping through the putrid ranks of his ghoulish army. The vampire wore heavy armour of steel stained to the colour of blood. The steed that bore him was a spectral thing of bone and witch fire, its corruption swathed in a black caparison. As the vampire advanced, the undead warriors parted before him, opening a path between the Red Duke and the king.

Vampire and king stared at one another across the battlefield. Infernal hatred, pitiless and cruel, blazed in the eyes of the Red Duke. Those of the king became solemn and sad.

'You could not content yourself to be king,' the vampire spoke, his voice low and venomous. 'You had to be Duke of Aquitaine as well.' The Red Duke's face pulled back in a feral snarl, exposing his sharp fangs. 'Now you will be neither.'

The king drew no terror from the Red Duke's words. Tears were in his eyes as he gazed upon the monster. 'The man I knew is dead. It is time he found peace.'

The Red Duke's face contorted in a sneer. 'I will make you immortal, Louis, so that I may torture you and kill you every hour of every day. Then you may speak to me of death and peace!'

Even in that moment, the king felt neither fear nor hate for this thing that had once been his friend. Sombrely, he lowered his lance and spurred his horse towards the Red Duke. The vampire bared his fangs in a vicious grin, gripping his own lance, a barbed thorn of steel already caked in the blood of a dozen knights. With a wolfish howl, he charged his spectral steed at the king.

In that moment, as man and monster bore down upon one another, the evil darkness the Red Duke had conjured to cloak his army faltered. A single shaft of daylight shot down from the black sky, enveloping the king. The king's silvered armour shimmered with sunlight, casting a wondrous glamour into the vampire's hideous countenance. The Red Duke reeled back in the saddle, throwing his arms before his stinging eyes.

An instant, the Red Duke was blinded, but it was enough. The king's lance crunched through the vampire's blood-red breastplate, tearing through steel plate as though it were parchment. The Red Duke was lifted clear from his saddle, writhing upon the end of the king's lance like a bug upon a pin.

King Louis held the struggling vampire aloft, the tip of his lance transfixing the Red Duke's heart. Furiously, the undead fiend tried to cling to life, tried to force his unclean body off the spike that held him. The king felt his arms weaken, the weight of the vampire and his struggles taxing his strength. But he drew deep from his own resolve, forced his fatigued arms to maintain their burden. Sternly, he forced himself to watch the vampire perish. The fiend's pallid flesh began to darken and shrivel, pressing close against *the bones beneath his desiccated skin. The Red Duke's eyes became pools of blood, sanguine tears streaming down his ghoulish face. From the vampire's mouth, a grisly moan arose, a sound at once pitiable and menacing.*

'Not to destroy the monster,' the king murmured to himself whenever he felt his strength waning. 'Not to destroy the monster, but to redeem the man.'

'...FOR SUCH IS the sad and lamentable story of the Red Duke. A song of tragedy and terror that must stir even the tears of the fey by its mournful dirge. Beware, you sons of Bretonnia! Beware the forces of darkness that lie in wait to tempt and trap even the strongest soul! Beware the sad end of that heroic knight, that defender of chivalry and crown! Beware, you children of Aquitaine, lest your wickedness draw down upon you the foul curse of the Red Duke!'

The troubadour doffed his feathered cap, sweeping it across the floor as he bowed to his audience. Hearty applause filled the inn, the floorboards groaning as dozens of feet stamped in approval of the singer's ballad. Jacques le Thorand had recited the epic at the courts of barons and dukes; once he had even performed before King Louen Leoncoeur himself. He certainly found nothing about his current surroundings either opulent or regal. The little timber-walled inn was no different than a thousand others littering the road between Aquitaine and Couronne, a humble place where merchants and messengers could brush the dust of their travels from their boots, where peasants and woodsmen could go to ease the pains of their toils with a swallow of wine.

Jacques had performed the *Last Lamentation of the Red Duke* hundreds of times over the years, expanding upon the ballads of earlier minstrels, combining different versions of the tale until he composed what many Bretonnians lauded as the definitive telling of the tale. The troubadour was proud of his composition, the sort of pride shown by any craftsman who has produced a work he knows is of quality. Jacques, like any true artist, did not measure his success in wealth or privilege, but in the accolades of his audience. It did not matter to him if the applause came from the royal court or from a rabble of grubby peasants. To him, it was all the same.

Even so, Jacques felt an especial sense of satisfaction as he looked out across the crowded common room of the Tipsy Squire. This audience wasn't simply any gathering of Bretonnians. These people weren't Carcassonnian shepherds or Bordelen vintners. These were Aquitainians. They had been raised upon the tales of the Red Duke and the heroes who had stood against him and laid his evil to rest. All the troubadour had to do was step outside the inn's door and turn his gaze northward and he should see the dark shadows of the Forest of Châlons, the place where superstitious peasants insisted the vampire lurked to this day, plotting his revenge upon Bretonnia and dreaming his black dreams of building an empire of blood.

To Jacques, the praise of these people was a coin richer than gold. It was easy to forget his critics, to forget the scornful disdain of crusty historians like Allan Anneau of Couronne. The applause of these humble people, reared upon the legends of their land, was the true vindication of Jacques's talent. Let the historians spew their bitter poison; it was in the hearts of the people that Jacques's ballads would endure.

The hour was late when the crowd finally began to steal away from the inn's warm hearth. They withdrew into the night by threes and fours, some brandishing heavy walking sticks, others nervously fingering little wooden images of Shallya as they went out into the darkness. Jacques smiled at the simple fears of these simple people. Among the lands of Bretonnia, Aquitaine was the most peaceful. The beasts of the forest seldom strayed north, the orcs of the mountains were rarely numerous enough to fight their way across Quenelles and into the meadows of Aquitaine. Even bandits were uncommon, brigands quickly finding themselves beset by Aquitainian knights with no more worthy foes to taste their steel.

It was the grim song of the troubadour that made the peasants nervous as they went out into the night. Jacques had evoked the heroism and tragedy of Aquitaine's rich past, but so too had he conjured up the dark horror of those times. The Red Duke was a name every Aquitainian learned before he left the cradle, a bogeyman called up by mothers and nursemaids to frighten naughty children. Through his ballad, Jacques had made that frightful phantom live again in the minds of the peasant folk. As they left the inn, each one of them imagined the vampire lurking in the shadows, his steely fangs waiting to savage their throats and damn them to join him in his empire of blood.

Jacques shook his head at such credulous beliefs. The Red Duke was gone, destroyed by King Louis the Righteous upon Ceren Field over a thousand years past. True, there had been a second vampire calling itself the Red Duke who had threatened Aquitaine four hundred years later, but Jacques did not accept that this creature had in fact been the same monster. Evil, once vanquished by a King of Bretonnia, did not stir from its grave.

'It is a silvered tongue you have,' chuckled Entoine, the rotund proprietor of the Tipsy Squire. His smiling face shifted between shadow and light as he manoeuvred among the rude tables and timber benches scattered about the room. At each table he paused, inspecting the wooden cups and clay pots his patrons had left behind. Those that had not quite been drained of their contents were carefully emptied into a wooden cask tucked under the innkeeper's arm. Jacques silently reminded himself not to buy the cheapest grade of wine on Entoine's menu.

'Seldom it is that I've seen them linger so late,' Entoine explained, scowling as he noted a long crack in one of the drinking vessels. 'Baron de Lanis isn't the sort to forget when his peasants should be out in the fields. There'll be many a sore head cursing the dawn, I should say.'

Jacques waved the tin tankard he held, an extravagance Entoine normally reserved only for those rare instances when a wandering knight patronized his inn. 'They looked as though they might welcome some sun when they left here. However early the baron wants them working, they weren't too happy to go out into the dark.'

Entoine laughed at the troubadour's words, but the merriment didn't reach his eyes. Jacques had not imbibed enough of the inn's wine to be oblivious to his host's discomfort. 'Come now!' he admonished. 'There can't be any rational reason for them to be afraid. If the farthest one of them has to walk to get home is more than a mile, then I'll accept that you

put no water in your wine!' The troubadour took a
swallow from his tankard, wiping the sleeve of his
frilled shirt across his mouth. 'You'd think my song
had called up the Red Duke from his tomb!'

The innkeeper shuddered at the last remark and
turned away from Jacques. 'As you say, there's no good
reason for them to be afraid of anything.'

'By the Lady!' Jacques exclaimed, slapping his knee.
'That's what you really are afraid of!' He shook his
head in disbelief. 'I admit my ballad is exceptional,
but you can't lose your grip on reality.'

'It was a tale finely sung and none of those people
will regret having heard it,' Entoine told the troubadour. 'But you are a stranger to these parts. You do not
understand the old fears your tale has reawakened.'

Jacques walked towards Entoine, sipping from his
tankard. 'Nursery stories and fairy tales spun to keep
unruly children in line,' he said, punctuating his dec-
laration by pouring the last mouthful of wine from
his cup into the innkeeper's keg.

The innkeeper set down the keg and glared defiantly
at Jacques. 'Is it a nursery story when a shepherdess
goes missing, only to be found weeks later drained
of blood?' He pressed a calloused finger against the
troubadour's chest. 'Is it a child's imagining when a
knight rides through the village, intent on challenging
the evil lurking in the forest, only for his bloodless
corpse to be found floating in the River Morceaux?'

'Beastmen,' Jacques said.

Entoine snickered at the suggestion. 'There haven't
been beastmen in these parts since anyone can
remember. And who ever heard of beastmen leaving
meat on the bones of their victims? There's only one
thing that drinks the blood from a man's veins and

leaves his pallid corpse behind.'

Jacques grimaced, shaking his head at the innkeeper's logic. He had spent years reading every story about the Red Duke's reign of terror, listening to every ballad composed about the vampire and his doom. They were things that belonged to the past. Even if the creature that had threatened Aquitaine six hundred years ago had been the real Red Duke, that monster too had been laid to rest at Ceren Field by Duke Gilon.

Entoine only smiled when Jacques tried to explain all of this to him. It was the sad smile of a man who knows he is right, but wishes with all his heart he was wrong. 'You have your beliefs,' he told the troubadour. 'But what I know, I know. You say the Red Duke died at Ceren Field. I say the vampire still lives, biding his time somewhere in the Forest of Châlons.'

For a moment, Jacques was silent, his eyes roving the deep shadows of a room that suddenly seemed foreboding. It took him some time to free himself from the irrational sense of uneasiness that gripped him. He forced some broken laughter and clapped a hand on Entoine's shoulder. 'You should have been a storyteller,' Jacques said.

WITH ALL THE dignified bravado he could command, Jacques made his way from the Tipsy Squire's common room and mounted the timber stairway leading up to the building's private rooms. Entoine had given his talented guest the best room in the house. Situated at the very top of the inn, the room, like the tin tankard, was usually reserved for wandering knights and other rare guests of noble breeding. The room was uncommonly spacious, its splintered floor concealed beneath an assortment of animal skins and threadbare rugs. The furnishings were heavily varnished to preserve them against the slow decay claiming the rest of the inn, including a bed that seemed large enough for both a knight and his horse. Jacques smiled as he ran his hand across the rough wool blankets and felt the lumpy pillows stuffed with chicken feathers. There was something almost amusingly pathetic about the feeble attempt to recreate the luxury a nobleman might expect.

Jacques sat himself at the edge of the bed and began pulling off his boots. Lumpy and rough though the bed was, he would still welcome Entoine's effort at luxury.

The smile died on the troubadour's face as a clammy chill gripped him. A shudder passed through Jacques's body, a pulse of raw, unreasoning fear that had him back on his feet before he realised it. He licked his lips nervously, his fingers crushing the velveteen surface of his boot as he drew it off the floor, hefting it like a club.

Jacques's eyes peered into the darkness as his breath grew still more rapid. As a child, he had once been trapped in a salt pit with a hungry weasel, forced to spend the entire night with the predator circling him in the dark, waiting for its chance to strike. The memory of that old fear returned to him now, crushing his heart in an icy embrace, sending tendrils of pure terror crawling through his body.

He couldn't see anything in the dark room, but like the peasants who had ventured out into the night, he knew there was something there. He didn't need to see it or hear it to know it was there. He could feel it, feel its menacing presence, sense its lurking evil.

At that moment, silvery moonlight filtered down

into Jacques's room. A further indulgence for visiting nobility, the only window with glass in the entire inn stared out from this chamber. The sudden illumination made Jacques turn his head, made his eyes stare out into the night. He could see the shadowy bulks of the thatch huts of the village and the shimmering waters of the River Morceaux beyond. More, he could see the black, forbidding outline of the Forest of Châlons stretching across the river's far bank, a sinister wall of darkness, a barrier between the realms of men and the domain of Old Night.

Jacques shuddered again and turned away from the nightscape, trying to banish the frightful imaginings it conjured in his mind. As he returned his attention to the room around him, all the colour drained from his face. A dark shape stood in the far corner of the room, a tall shadow that he would have sworn had not been there before.

Jacques tried to look away, tried to tell himself that there was nothing there. He had the urge to dive beneath the woollen blankets, to hide his face and hope the apparition would go away. Stubbornly he tried to cling to reason, to tell himself that there could be nothing there. Yet, the longer he stared at the corner, the more feeble the effort to deny his fear became. With each passing breath, Jacques imagined more detail in the shape. He fancied he saw a head and shoulders covered by a long black cloak. He saw fierce red eyes staring at him from the darkness where a face should be.

Desperately, the troubadour tried to convince himself it was his imagination when the shadow began to stalk outwards from its corner. He choked as the stink of rotting flesh assailed his senses, shivered as he heard the rattle of armoured boots striding across the floorboards. Tears of terror coursed down his face as Jacques cringed away from the ghastly figure. Now he could see the richly engraved armour the apparition wore, archaic in its style, hoary with age. He could see the enormous falchion, its pommel crafted in the shape of a skull, swinging at the figure's side. A face, pale and lean, began to emerge from the darkness, red eyes still trained upon the cowering troubadour.

A cruel grin twisted that inhuman countenance, withered lips retreating from wolfish fangs.

Mercifully, the moon retreated back behind its clouds, plunging the room once more into darkness before Jacques could see anything more. The apparition's red eyes continued to burn in the darkness.

A voice, thin and vicious as the scratch of rat claws upon a casket, rasped from the darkness. 'Be unafraid,' the voice said. 'Sit and be content. This night, at least, you are safer than any soul in all the kingdom.'

Somehow, Jacques managed to find the edge of his bed and seat himself upon it. There was something compelling about that sinister voice, an imperious quality that brooked no defiance. Jacques knew he could no more resist obeying than an ant could resist an ox's hoof.

'I have journeyed far to hear your ballad,' the thing in the darkness said. 'Had it offended me, I should have draped your entrails from the Massif Orcal to the Silent Isle.'

As the voice made this threat, it lowered into an almost animalistic snarl. Not for an instant did Jacques doubt the creature was capable of visiting such a horror upon him. He had learned enough to know what the thing was and what powers a vampire had at its command.

The vampire let the menacing words linger, seeming to savour the troubadour's fear. After what seemed to Jacques an eternity, the creature spoke again. 'The tale was well told,' the vampire conceded. 'I listened to you from the eaves. Even this dead heart was moved by your words.'

Jacques tried to stammer out words of gratitude, anything that might appeal to whatever humanity the vampire might yet possess. A dry croak was the only sound that managed to fight its way up the troubadour's paralysed throat. His visitor ignored the futile attempt to speak. It had not come for conversation.

'There were many things wrong with your ballad,' the vampire hissed. 'The dead have their pride. I will point out your missteps so that you will correct them. When next I hear you sing this tale, I may take some pride in its accuracy.

'To start, Louis Kinslayer did not finish the Red Duke at Ceren Field,' the vampire said, its voice seething with hate. 'That battle was not the end of the Red Duke. Indeed it was, perhaps, only the end of the beginning for him...'

CHAPTER I

The troubadour's song rose above the happy murmur of the crowd, ringing out with its merry cadence, the melody of his lute acting as a serene landscape to his words. Young couples swirled about the green meadow, the rich dresses of the ladies whipping about them as they danced with their noble companions, laughing as they kept time to the minstrel's song. Older lords and ladies stood aside, too sensible to lose themselves in such vigorous celebration, too happy not to join in the laughter.

The marble chapel stood at the centre of the meadow, its plaster ornaments gleaming in the sun. The stone sarcophagus of the knight who had built the chapel seemed to smile down upon the celebrants, his feet buried beneath bouquets of primroses and snapdragons. Garlands of daisies were strung about the walls of the chapel, swaying in the gentle breeze, casting their fragrance across the gathering.

An old man, his raiment richer and finer than those around him, stood at the doorway of the chapel, his wrinkled face pulled back in a broad grin, his eyes misty with tears. He beamed down upon one of the dancing couples, a dark-haired youth dressed in black tunic and hose, his rich raiment edged in golden thread. In his arms he held an auburn-headed woman more beautiful than any frolicking about the meadow. She wore a flowing gown of white, a veil of flowers threaded into her hair.

Only an hour ago she had been the Lady Melisenda. Now she was the Viscountess Melisenda du Marcil, wife of the Viscount Brandin du Marcil and daughter by marriage to the Margrave du Marcil. The old margrave smiled on his new daughter even more than he did his son. He had begun to despair of ever seeing this day, when the bold young knight would set aside his reckless ways and settle down to the more important duty of perpetuating the bloodline. There was a time and place for gallivanting across the realm slaying monsters and rescuing damsels, but it was a pastime that was unbecoming the only son of an ancient and historied name.

The margrave chuckled as he watched the graceful figure of Melisenda glide about the meadow in his son's arms. There would be small need to worry about the du Marcil name now. Unless Brandin had ice water running in his veins, he'd be working on perpetuating the family name as soon as the wedding celebration broke up.

The smile flickered and died on the margrave's face as a sudden chill coursed through his old bones. He cast his eyes skyward, noting the sudden darkening of the sun as stormy clouds swept across the heavens. Aquitaine had been plagued by these sudden storms for months, as though the very elements conspired to cast the land under a pall of perpetual gloom. It was but one of many complaints that afflicted the realm. Peasants spoke of great wolves prowling the countryside, taking whom they would with uncommon boldness. There were whispers of ghouls haunting the old graveyards, rumours of unquiet ghosts abroad in the night.

The ugliest tales revolved around the duke himself. It was said the duke had never really recovered from the *wounds he had suffered fighting the sultan in Araby. It was said the duke's mind was broken, that he was a maddened beast. His court had removed itself from Castle Aquin to a castle at the edge of the Forest of Châlons in order to hide the madness of the duke from his people. Even so, the duke continued to issue edicts that affected every nobleman in Aquitaine. He had instituted a blood tax, requiring each house to send a tithe of knights to the duke's castle. The blood tax fed into another hideous rumour about the duke – that he was going to make war against King Louis!*

Margrave du Marcil shook his head and tried to banish the forbidding thoughts from his mind. He looked again upon Brandin and his bride. This was a day of celebration, to look forward to a bright tomorrow beyond the darkness of today.

The troubadour's voice cracked, his fingers strumming a false note upon his lute. The gaiety and festiveness of the crowd collapsed, replaced by drawn countenances and grim whispers. A pall had fallen upon the celebration, a sense of doom that none was capable of dismissing. Brandin gripped his bride, holding her tight as he turned to cast a worried look towards his father.

The margrave could only shake his head and stare at the darkening sky. There could have been no more ominous time for the weather to take such a capricious turn. The mood in Aquitaine was one of uncertainty and fear, fertile for all manner of superstition. Even the nobility were ready to see omens at every turn.

Margrave du Marcil opened his mouth to compose some amusing words that would dispel the distemper of the wedding guests. 'My friends…'

The margrave's speech went no further. A clamour of hooves thundered across the meadow as a dozen horsemen emerged from the woods, galloping straight towards the shrine. All of the riders were garbed in black – black armour, black cloak, black steed. Only the foremost of the riders broke the sombre appearance of the group, for his armour was a bright crimson, as was the billowing cape flowing from his shoulders and the caparison that covered the huge destrier he rode. Margrave du Marcil recognized the lean, drawn features of the crimson knight. He was the Duke of Aquitaine.

The Red Duke.

The riders brought their steeds to a canter a dozen yards from the shrine and the terrified wedding guests. None of the guests dared to retreat before the advance of the liege to whom they had sworn oaths of loyalty and service, though the heart of each quailed at his approach. There was an aura of power that exuded from the Red Duke, a brooding intensity that made even the bravest knight tremble like a lamb before a wolf.

The Red Duke reined his horse before the congregation. The black knights, silent within their armour, walked their steeds slowly around the celebrants, closing them inside a circle of steel. The duke's pale, stern face swept across the crowd, his intense gaze transfixing each of them in turn.

'A wedding,' the Red Duke observed. 'A festival of which I was not informed.' His voice dropped into a low hiss. 'And to which I was not invited.'

Margrave du Marcil bowed contritely before his lord. 'Only my son and… and… I did not think… to impose… disturb your grace…'

The Red Duke turned his gaze full upon the young Viscount du Marcil. 'Your son should be fulfilling his duty in my army,' he said. 'He should be defending Aquitaine against the traitors and enemies who would destroy her. Instead,' the Red Duke made a dismissive motion with his gloved hand, 'I find him here.'

Brandin stared defiantly at the imposing lord. 'I am the last of the House of du Marcil,' he stated. 'It is my duty to secure the line. I have exclusion from the blood tax.'

The Red Duke leaned back in his saddle, a thin smile upon his gaunt face. 'No one in Aquitaine is excluded from the blood tax,' was his retort. Suddenly he turned his eyes from the defiant viscount to the woman beside him. A hungry quality crept into his gaze that made Melisenda gasp in fright. Brandin put a protective arm around his bride, pushing her behind him.

'It is an old law you have evoked to escape your duty in my army,' the Red Duke told Brandin. 'I shall evoke an even older one.' He lifted his hand and pointed at the viscount's bride. ' I claim droit du seigneur.'

Horror flashed across Brandin's face, quickly replaced by disgust. He glared at the smiling lord. 'The stories are true,' the young knight spat. 'You are mad.'

Margrave du Marcil rushed down from the steps of the shrine, interposing himself between his son and the Red Duke. 'My son… means no… offence. Invoking the old right… it has surprised him. Please, forgive him… your grace.'

Brandin shoved his father aside. 'I can speak my own words. And I say you are mad if you think I'll let you touch Melisenda!' In his fury, the knight reached for the sword at his belt. Instantly the silent companions of the Red Duke edged their steeds towards the outraged youth. A gesture from their master made the grim riders stay back.

Slowly, the Red Duke dismounted, an expression of prideful malignance twisting his features. His cape flowed behind him as he stalked towards Brandin and his bride. 'First you deny me the blood tax, now you deny my right to… examine… the noble qualities of your charming lady. I wonder if you understand who here is lord, and who is vassal.'

Brandin drew his sword from its scabbard, glowering at his arrogant liege. 'Take one more step towards my wife and it will be your last.'

The Red Duke paused. His lips pulled back in a murderous grin, exposing a mouthful of sharpened fangs. The lord's hand closed about the hilt of his own sword. In a single, smooth motion, he drew the blade. Merciless eyes bore into those of the young viscount.

'Prove it,' the vampire sneered.

SIR ARMAND DU Maisne stared up at the massive portrait that dominated Castle Aquin's grand hall. Poised above the yawning mouth of the immense fireplace, anchored into the stone wall by steel hooks, the painting was a masterpiece in the heroic style of Anatoli Bernardo Corbetta, Tilea's most famed portraitist of the sixth century. The subject of the painting was such that was made for the Tilean's brush. King Louis the Righteous, Duke of Aquitaine, seated upon his snowy destrier, Chevauchée, riding through the broken walls of Lasheik to rout the hosts of the Sultan Jaffar. King and warhorse were depicted life-size, a nimbus of light surrounding the sovereign's head and drawn sword. Before him, the swarthy Arabyans cringed in terror, behind him the face of every Bretonnian in his army was filled with awe.

Even now, over four hundred years since Corbetta had captured the magnificence of the king upon canvas, the portrait exerted an aura of magnificence that thrilled Sir Armand's heart.

'It is impressive, is it not?'

Sir Armand only half-turned from the portrait as he heard the question, reluctant to let his eyes leave the radiant figure of King Louis in his moment of triumph. 'It is inspiring,' he said, his voice quivering with emotion. The knight's expression darkened as he remembered who it was he addressed. Hastily he turned away from the hearth and the huge painting, directing his attention completely upon the nobleman who stood beside him.

The other Bretonnian was a stark contrast to Sir Armand. Where Armand was still a youth, the other man was well into his middle age. His hair was dark where that of the knight was fair, his face lined with the stress of power and responsibility where Armand's was marred by the scars won in battle. Dressed in velvet doublet and hosen, the knight's frame still suggested a brooding strength, waiting to be unleashed. Wrapped in the heavy folds of a thick fur cloak, Armand's host moved with the lethargy of an invalid, a man of waning vitality. In the eyes of the two men, however, there was a resemblance, a keenness of mind and temperament.

'Forgive such familiarity, your grace,' Sir Armand said, dropping to one knee. 'I forgot myself.'

Duke Gilon of Aquitaine chuckled at the knight's severe contrition. 'Things are not so grave,' he assured Armand. 'The presence of King Louis the Righteous was such that he inspired men to feats of heroism as have not been seen since the days of Gilles le Breton himself. It is only natural that his influence should still inspire boldness in the hearts of the brave.' Duke Gilon gestured with a beringed hand at the portrait, drawing Armand's attention back to it. 'Whenever my heart despairs, I come here to gaze upon the visage of the king and I am filled with a renewed sense of purpose and duty. King Louis was a true grail knight and never faltered in his quest to defend all things good and honourable. Whether leading a crusade against a foreign tyrant or riding to save this very dukedom from the rule of a usurping monster, the valour of King Louis was never found wanting.'

The duke took a step closer to the portrait, smiling as he admired the work of the famed Tilean painter. 'This was painted shortly before the death of the king, upon his own command. He wanted to leave something for his descendants to remember him, as though his great deeds would not resound down through the centuries.'

'It was King Louis who built this castle, was it not?' Sir Armand asked.

His smile faded as Duke Gilon's gaze lingered upon a space just behind the fetlock of Chevauchée. Here, a hand far less skilled than that of Corbetta had inserted the hindquarters of another warhorse, almost completely obscuring one of the knights behind King Louis, leaving only a single boot and stirrup visible. There was no clue to who the censored knight was, though he had apparently been included at the king's command and then removed at a later time. But Duke Gilon could guess who it had been and why the knight had been erased from the painting.

'This castle stands exactly twelve miles from where the old Castle Aquitaine once stood,' Duke Gilon said. 'The old castle had been foully used by the Red Duke, defiled until its very stones were corrupted with the vampire's evil. After the monster was vanquished upon Ceren Field, King Louis ordered the old castle razed and a new castle built far from where the Red Duke had perpetrated his evil.'

'The Red Duke left many scars upon the land,' Armand said gravely. 'The peasants of my father's fief to this day whisper the most horrible stories about those times. They have a custom that each Witching Night they procure a dead raven and send a delegation to the cemetery on Ceren Field to entreat the god Morr to keep the Red Duke in his grave.'

Duke Gilon nodded as he heard Sir Armand relate the morbid tradition. 'There are many such customs in Aquitaine, and not all of them are practised by peasants.' The nobleman sighed deeply. Directing a last look at the portrait, he withdrew from the hearth and seated himself in a high-backed chair at the centre of the room. Armand followed his lord, taking one of the smaller chairs arrayed in a semi-circle about the duke's seat. A liveried steward hastened away from his post beside a mahogany and brass cellaret, bearing a bottle of dark wine and a pair of silver goblets upon a silver tray.

The two noblemen accepted the refreshments. Duke Gilon waited for his servant to withdraw before resuming his conversation with Sir Armand. 'I did not summon you here only to show you the portrait of King Louis or to share this excellent vintage, though I think you will agree that either would be sufficient excuse to bring a knight to Castle Aquin.' The old nobleman's expression grew sombre. 'It is a more serious problem I need to discuss with you. A delicate matter that concerns Count Ergon's offer to instruct my son in the finer aspects of swordsmanship.'

Duke Gilon raised his hand to forestall any objection from Sir Armand. 'I know that you are renowned as the finest blade in all Aquitaine. The graveyards of one particular fief can attest to your skill and prowess. I do not think your father had any untoward motive when he made his gracious offer. At the same time,

I do not think he appreciates the consequences of merely making such an offer might have.'

'I know that I am young,' Sir Armand said, 'but Sir Richemont is a fair-minded man...'

'It is not your age that is at issue,' Duke Gilon said. 'I have taught Richemont to respect ability wherever he finds it. He will be Duke of Aquitaine one day. Any ruler who will not acknowledge the skill of those he rules will not rule long. No, your youth is not at fault. It is your name. It is all those graves your tremendous ability with sword has filled. It is because if I allowed a du Maisne to instruct my son in anything I would lose the loyalty of the d'Elbiqs.'

Armand scowled as he heard the duke mention the long and vicious feud between his family and that of Earl Gaubert d'Elbiq. A feud that had caused Armand to personally take the lives of sixteen men.

'I see you appreciate the situation,' Duke Gilon said. 'I will spare your father any embarrassment. Sir Richemont has left Aquitaine to go on a pilgrimage to Couronne. While he is away, he will receive instruction from the king's own fencing-masters. When he returns, there will be no need for Count Ergon to renew his offer.' The old nobleman frowned as he saw the disappointment on Sir Armand's face. 'I am sorry, but it is the only way to proceed without slighting either the du Maisnes or the d'Elbiqs. If your two families would only end their feud...'

'Earl Gaubert would never let it go,' Armand stated, bitterness in his voice. 'He has already lost too much. Pride will not allow him to set his hate aside. My father is the same way. All he can think of are my uncle and my grandfather slain by d'Elbiq swordsmen. The feud perpetuates itself, generation upon generation, like two snakes trying to swallow each other's tail. I don't know if anyone even remembers what started the feud. It is simply something they have grown up with and are too headstrong to set aside.'

'You speak as though you would set it aside,' Duke Gilon said, approval in his voice.

Sir Armand shook his head. 'What I want doesn't matter. I obey my father. That is a son's duty.'

The great iron-banded double doors that fronted the hall abruptly were drawn open. A liveried servant accompanied by a steel-clad man-at-arms strode into the hall, bowing as they approached Duke Gilon. Behind them, flanked by two more men-at-arms, marched a young knight in plate armour, his surcoat dusty from travel, his face flush from too many hours beneath the unforgiving sun.

'An emissary from Earl Gaubert d'Elbiq,' the servant announced. The functionary gestured with a gloved hand at the travel-stained knight. 'He says that he brings most urgent tidings.'

While he was being presented to his lord, the dark-haired knight kept his eyes fixed upon Sir Armand. There was unmistakable, murderous hate in the knight's gaze. His fingers flexed about the hilt of his sword, his thumb drumming against the gilded pommel.

'I compliment Earl Gaubert upon his sources of information,' Duke Gilon told the dark-haired knight, his tone cold and disapproving. 'Sir Armand arrived here only a few hours ago. From the look of you, the earl must have dispatched you as soon as the news reached him. He should not have bothered. This is a private audience and does not concern the

d'Elbiqs.' In his anger, Duke Gilon no longer cared if
the d'Elbiqs felt slighted. It would remind them of
their place.

The knight shifted his gaze away from Sir Armand
and bowed deeply before Duke Gilon. 'Forgive me,
your grace, but Earl Gaubert wanted to inform you
that the Argonian boar he purchased is ready to be
hunted. He seeks your permission to conduct the
hunt at the end of the month and begs your grace and
Sir Richemont to consider being his guests and par-
ticipating in the chase.'

Duke Gilon's smile was thin, not a trace of credu-
lence in his voice when he spoke. 'Earl Gaubert has
been toying with that brute for an entire season. Many
in my court thought he was going to make a pet of it.
Now, suddenly, he decides to host a hunt.' He turned
his head and stared at Armand, noticing the tight set
of the man's jaw, the intense look of his expression.
Turning back, he caught the hostile glower of the
other knight, noted the thumb tapping impatiently
upon the knight's sword.

'You have delivered the earl's message,' Duke Gilon
told the knight. 'I will send one of my yeomen with
an answer.' The old nobleman grimaced when the
dark-haired knight made no move to quit the hall,
instead glaring at Sir Armand. Irritably, the duke
motioned for his men-at-arms to remove the impertinent knight.

Armand saw the soldiers closing upon the messenger. It was he who asked Duke Gilon to call them
back. 'Your grace does not recognize the messenger
Earl Gaubert has sent to find me. This man is the earl's
youngest son, Sir Girars d'Elbiq.'

'His only son,' Sir Girars retorted acidly. 'My brothers

lie buried in the family tomb, alongside their cousins and all the others who have been butchered by your sword.'

Duke Gilon rose to his feet, clenching his fist before him. 'I will have no bloodshed here!' the nobleman swore. 'I don't care who started this feud, but I promise if one of you draws a blade here, I will hang victor and victim both!'

Armand shook his head, the look he directed upon Girars was sympathetic. 'We have all lost much in the name of family pride.'

'The du Maisnes have not lost enough,' Girars snarled. 'You've carved a reputation from the corpses of the d'Elbiqs. I am here to balance that debt!'

Armand sighed, feeling as though a great weight were pressing down upon him. 'Yes, I've killed many men, good men. Whatever your father says, they died fairly and in open combat. Think about that for a moment. Think about your brothers and their skill at arms. Think about how strong their swords were. Then remember that they could not vanquish me.' Armand's tone became almost pleading. 'You've only just won your spurs. Don't throw your life away on a fight you cannot win.'

Girars scowled at his enemy's display of emotion. Coldly he drew off the gauntlet from his left hand and cast it down at Armand's feet.

'I will hang you for that,' Duke Gilon cursed. 'I have told you there will be no fighting in this castle.'

'Then we shall take our duel somewhere else,' Girars said. 'That is, if this cur has enough honour in him to take up my challenge.'

Solemnly, Armand bent down and retrieved the gauntlet from the floor. He stared into Girars eyes and nodded his head slowly. 'Name the place and choose your second,' he told the knight.

'Then think about what you will say to your brothers.'

SIR ARMAND DU Maisne reached down from the saddle of his destrier and took the heavy kite shield his squire lifted up to him, the unicorn and grail heraldry of the du Maisnes displayed prominently upon a field of blue. The knight waited patiently as the squire circled the warhorse and lifted the massive lance to Armand. He nodded grimly as he received the weapon, its painted shaft, gaudily daubed in a swirl of red and yellow stripes, incongruous with the vicious steel head.

Across the plain, Armand watched as Sir Girars took up his own arms. The boar and crescent heraldry of the d'Elbiqs marked his green shield, his lance painted in a pattern of blue and black checks that matched the caparison of his steed. Before Girars lowered the visor of his helm, Armand could see his enemy's eyes glaring at him, the extreme passion of his hatred making his cheeks tremble. Seldom had Armand seen such determination, such unwavering commitment to bloodshed. Never had he seen such emotion upon the visage of one so young.

A crowd had gathered upon the grassy plain above the village of Aquitaine, some few miles from the grey walls of Castle Aquin. Word of the duel had passed through the court of Duke Gilon, filtering down even to the peasants in the fields and vineyards. Before the two combatants had even arrived, a festival-like atmosphere had descended upon the designated battleground. Nobles from the duke's court – their lord notable by his absence – sat comfortably in the shade of hastily assembled pavilions while a great mob of peasants sat in the grass and watched the proceedings with an ignorant kind of excitement. Unfamiliar with the nuances of custom and honour, the peasants observed every motion of the knights and their attendants with rapt fascination.

Sir Armand looked to his second, a knight from his father's court named Ranulf. 'If I fall here,' he told the knight, 'I order you to make no action against Sir Girars.'

Ranulf grimaced at Armand's admonishment. 'There would be no question if you had chosen to face him across swords,' the knight growled. 'This d'Elbiq scum would be dead and there'd be one less of the bastards stinking up the dukedom. Why, by the Lady, do you choose to fight him with a lance instead of a sword…'

'Because that is my decision,' Armand said firmly. He looked across the field, watching as Girars had final words with his own second. There was a definite resemblance between them, though Girars's second was a few years older. A cousin, perhaps. Certainly one who had d'Elbiq blood flowing through his veins.

'Count Ergon will not forgive me if I let some slinking d'Elbiq kill his son,' Ranulf cursed.

Armand shook his head. 'If this man kills me, then it is no murder, but the result of a fair duel. If there is any justice in my father's heart, he will understand.' Armand lowered the visor of his helm, cutting off any further protest from Ranulf. He fixed his gaze across the grassy plain, watching Girars as d'Elbiq's warhorse trotted away from the tangle of squires and attendants that surrounded him. Armand prodded the side of his own mount and made his way onto the field.

For all of his bravado, Armand was disturbed by Ranulf's words. The knight was right, there was a wide gulf between Armand's renowned skill with the sword and his ability with the lance. Was it chivalry or pity that had moved Armand to choose the lesser weapon? As the party offended by Girars's challenge, the choice had been his. Indeed, even Girars had been surprised when Armand had shunned the sword and chosen the lance.

Perhaps it was as simple as an abiding sense of fairplay. Armand knew there was no man in Aquitaine who could match blades with him. Sir Girars was no more than a knight errant, still learning the discipline of a warrior. Crossing swords with Girars would be a despicable act, unbecoming any man of honour and decency. The feud between the du Maisnes and d'Elbiqs had already taken much from both sides, but Armand would not let his personal honour become a casualty of the conflict. If he had to die upon Girars's lance to keep his integrity, then that was in the Lady's hands.

Sir Girars spurred his horse into a gallop, charging down the field towards Armand, his lance lowered, its steel point gleaming in the sun like a daemon's fang. Armand urged his own steed down the field, fixing his gaze upon the armoured figure of his foe.

The sound of iron-shod hooves pounded across the field, clumps of grass and dirt flying as the two knights hurtled towards one another. Even the watching nobles held their breath as the two combatants came crashing together.

Girars's lance failed to pierce Armand's shield, or the man behind it. Instead the steel tip of his weapon was deflected downwards, glancing off the side of the thick steel champron that encased the head of Armand's horse.

Armand's weapon struck the top of his foe's shield with such force that the arm holding it was snapped like a twig. Girars's now useless arm flopped against his side, the smashed rim of the shield folded against the pauldron protecting his shoulder.

The violent impact and red rush of pain that followed sent Girars reeling. His warhorse wheeled about in response to his erratic leg movements, spilling its crippled master from the saddle. Girars crashed hard against the ground, clutching his broken arm against his chest.

Sir Armand turned his steed around and advanced upon the fallen Girars. The enemy knight slowly regained his feet, watching in brooding silence as Armand came towards him. The fallen knight held his ground as Armand pointed the tip of his lance at him.

'Honour is satisfied,' Armand told his opponent. 'Yield and I will spare your life.'

Expectant silence held the crowd. Noblemen leaned forwards in their seats, straining to hear every word. A few bold peasants crept out upon the field, their eyes locked upon both men: victor and vanquished.

Girars sagged before Armand's threat, all the strength seeming to wither inside him. He lifted his head slowly, reluctantly, and stared at his enemy.

'A d'Elbiq yield to a du Maisne?' Girars hissed. '*Never!*'

The unhorsed knight suddenly surged forwards, hurling himself beneath Armand's lance. Acting against all the rules of chivalry, Girars drove the mangled mess of armour and shield locked about his left shoulder into the throat of Armand's horse. The surprised animal reared back onto its hind legs, kicking its forelegs through the air. Girars ducked beneath the flailing hooves, beating his gauntlet against his breastplate and shouting at the animal, oblivious to the jeers and boos of the spectators.

Armand was able to stay mounted the first three times his destrier reared. After that, he lost his grip and was thrown to the ground, crashing to earth in a clatter of armour and bruises. The padding beneath the knight's armour absorbed most of the impact, leaving him merely winded from the brutal fall. Quickly he heaved himself up from the grass, swinging about as his enemy came at him.

Girars's sword slashed down at Armand as he rose, narrowly missing the join between gorget and helm. The crippled knight vengefully kicked at Armand's knee, trying to drive him back to the ground for an easy kill. Armand brought his fist smashing into the younger knight's injured shoulder, pounding against the top of the crumpled shield. Girars screamed as the impact drove a sliver of his splintered shield through his torn forearm.

Armand staggered away, using the momentary distraction of Girars to draw his own sword. He paused as he started to slide the blade from its scabbard. Even now, even after Girars's dishonourable conduct, he felt reluctance to cross swords with a foe whose skill was so far beneath his own.

'Coward!' Girars hissed as he noted Armand's hesitance. 'Don't you dare give me quarter!'

The incensed knight lunged at Armand, stabbing at the join between breastplate and cuirass, trying to sink his steel in his enemy's belly. Armand spun with Girars's attack, instincts honed upon years of duels and battles becoming master of his body, over-whelming the mind that would restrain them. Before Armand was consciously aware of what he had done, Girars was lying at his feet, Armand's blade thrust into the armpit beneath the young knight's right shoulder.

Armand watched as his stricken foe's body shivered and fell still. Coldly, he knelt beside the dead knight and wrenched his sword free. Rising, he turned towards Girars's second. Cold wrath filled Armand's voice as he addressed the remaining d'Elbiq, wrath that drew its fuel not from an ancient feud but from what that feud had made him do this day.

'Put him beside his brothers,' Armand said, his voice trembling with rage. 'But when you commend his spirit to the Lady, do not name me as his killer. This boy should never have crossed swords with me. Not until he was man enough to win such a fight.' Armand slammed his blade back into its sheath.

'I did not kill this boy,' he repeated. 'His killer is the man who made him ride out to be butchered. His killer sits in the Chateau d'Elbiq. When you see Earl Gaubert, tell him what I've said! Tell him to waste no more of my time with challengers that are beneath me! Tell him to murder his own children from this day on!'

CHAPTER II

The Bretonnian's sword flashed beneath the desert sun, carving a scarlet swathe through the dusky raider, slashing through the raider's flowing black bisht and tearing into the quilted armour beneath. The swarthy man cried out in agony, dropping his scimitar as he tried to press his cut belly back together.

Ruthlessly, the Bretonnian drove the pommel of his sword into the maimed Arabyan's face, breaking his nose and knocking the spiked helmet from his head. The nomad toppled, crashing face-first into the sand, a cloud of grey dust ballooning around his body.

The Duke of Aquitaine shook the blood from his sword and glared at his remaining foes. Like a pack of jackals, the black-garbed Arabyans circled him, fingering the curved blades of their scimitars, curses and maledictions rattling off their tongues. The duke was thankful he did not understand the Arabyan dialect so well as his sovereign, King Louis. If he did, he might take umbrage from the words these heathen killers hurled upon him.

El Syf ash-Shml, the Arabyans had named him in the crude patois of the bedouin. 'the North Sword', often shorted simply to 'El Syf', the sword. It was a title the duke had earned through a year of bloody fighting to liberate *the kingdoms of Estalia from the Sultan Jaffar. It was a name the Arabyans had come to whisper in terror after the Bretonnian armies came to the deserts of Araby to take the crusade into the sultan's own lands.*

El Syf made for a grim sight, surrounded by the barren sand dunes the raiders had chosen to hide their ambush. The knight was encased in full battledress, every inch of him sheathed in steel armour, bare now that an Arabyan's blade had slashed his surcoat. The platemail was rendered in the finest Bretonnian fashion, each piece of armour richly engraved, the edges gilded. El Syf had always maintained that death should be grandly appointed when it came for a man, and he ensured that those who fell in battle against him would know their slayer was no simple yeoman or knight of the realm.

The finery of the Bretonnian's armour was now caked in the filth of battle. Blood dripped down the breastplate, blood from the knight's own steed. El Morzillo, the brave warhorse gifted upon the duke by the King of Magritta, had died nobly, refusing to fall while it still had the strength to shield its master with its body. An Arabyan arrow in its neck had not been enough to finish the horse, it had taken the sharp edge of a tulwar ripping across its throat to make its courage falter.

El Syf felt the loss of his powerful steed as keenly as he would the amputation of his arm. The death of such a noble animal moved him to a cold fury that sowed fear in the hearts of his foes. There had been over a dozen Arabyans when they had set upon him. Now six of them lay at his feet and the others faltered in their attack.

It was, perhaps, in their minds to retreat, to find easier prey to fall upon. Certainly the black-robed leaders of the ambush were sore-pressed to maintain command over the nomads. El Syf listened to them as the two cloaked

*Arabyans argued with each other, each with his own idea
about how to still claim victory from catastrophe. The duke
turned his head, studying the positions of the other raiders
in the brief respite their broken courage had offered.*

*As he did so, the duke felt his eyes drawn to the crest
of a distant sand dune. A lone rider stood atop the dune,
watching the battle play out. From so great a distance, El
Syf did not recognize the rider, though he could tell from
the style of his armour that he was no nomad, but a knight.
A chill ran through the Bretonnian's body as he stared at
the distant figure. Veteran of a hundred battles, hero of the
Siege of Lashiek, slayer of the wyrm Nerluc, the duke had
never felt such a sense of doom and fear as when he gazed
upon the sinister knight.*

*The duke turned his eyes from the strange spectator,
forcing his attention back to the Arabyans around him.
'Sufficient for the moment were the evils thereof' was an
old piece of peasant wisdom that had somehow impressed
itself upon the nobleman's mind. Whatever menace there
was in the black-armoured knight on the dunes, whatever
was the cause of the evil the duke had sensed, it was of
little concern to him if he was to die upon the blades of his
present enemies.*

*The two Arabyan leaders continued their argument,
each trying to shout down the other. The other nomads cast
anxious glances over their shoulders at the two chieftains,
unsure which of them would prevail, reluctant to press the
attack upon El Syf until they were given the order.*

*El Syf regarded the violent tones of the chieftains. There
was certainly no love between the two. They seemed a
pair of bandits who had temporarily united their gangs
and were now having a falling out because of the toll the
knight had taken on their followers. That thought faded
as he noted a familiar quality about the voice of one of*

the cloaked nomads. A familiarity that brought the duke's blood to a boil.

At least one of the Arabyans was no Arabyan at all!

The duke's mouth opened in an inarticulate roar of rage. Every virtue he held as a knight was repulsed by the treachery he now suspected, his stomach clenched in a tight knot of sickness. Clenching his blade in his fist, ignoring the slight wounds his dead foes had managed to inflict upon him, El Syf hurdled the dead carcass of El Morzillo and rushed the startled circle of his enemies.

The Arabyans were unprepared for the sudden attack, surprised like hunters whose prey suddenly turns upon them. One of the raiders fell with a shattered collarbone, another crumpled in a screaming heap, his arm shorn off at the elbow. Before any others could move to intercept him, Elf Syf was running along the side of one of the dunes, maintaining his footing despite the sand shifting beneath his boots.

The duke's enemies cried out in panic, thinking the Bretonnian meant to escape them. They scattered, racing to encircle the armoured knight. But flight was the furthest thing from El Syf's mind. As soon as he was certain the nomads had accepted his feint, the duke turned, charging straight at the two leaders. He prayed to the Lady, begging her to let him visit justice upon the traitor whose voice he had heard.

The two leaders staggered back in alarm when they saw their victim turning towards them. One of the black-robed men drew a curved scimitar from the sash girding his waist. The other, the man who was the focus of El Syf's outrage, slid a very different sort of weapon from the scabbard hidden beneath his bisht. It was the straight blade of a Bretonnian knight. It was natural that the man should have such a sword. When, in the emotion of his argument with the Arabyan chieftain, the man had slipped and started speaking Breton, there had been an Aquitainian accent about his voice.

El Syf came upon the two conspirators with the marauding strength of a lion. The genuine Arabyan moved to confront him first, striking at him with a lightning-fast flourish of his scimitar. The duke matched each stroke, parrying the curved blade from his sword, biding his time until the sheik made a mistake. When that fraction of an instant came, the duke was ready. A mistaken twist of the sheik's hand, a poor angle of his blade, and the duke's sword was past his guard, stabbing into the Arabyan's chest.

El Syf pushed the dying sheik from his sword and spun to meet the blade of the other conspirator. The Bretonnian traitor had lingered back during the duke's duel with the sheik. There was a look of terror on what little of the man's face could be seen through the folds of his cheche. To the Arabyans, El Syf was a warrior of mythical status, endowed with all manner of mystical abilities. The Bretonnian knew the Duke of Aquitaine better. He knew there was nothing mystical about his skill with the sword, but he also knew better than the Arabyans how great that skill truly was.

The duke met the traitor's attack, catching the conspirator's sword upon the guard of his own, twisting it aside with a practised roll of his own weapon, then following through with a thrust that skewered the renegade knight's throat. The sword fell from the stricken man's hand, his body slumping to its knees. El Syf reached forwards, tearing the cheche from about the knight's face. He glared into features he recognized, those of Sir Bertric.

The duke stood silent a moment, stunned by the discovery. Sir Bertric was the vassal of Baron Gui de Gavaudan, father of Queen Aregund! A servant of the queen's father engaged in conspiracy with Arabyan brigands, a conspiracy

*that could only have been intent upon the duke's murder!
But who would dare order such villainy? With King Louis
upon the throne, who would dare strike in such a fashion?
And why?*

*In the grip of his horror, the duke did not notice the
stricken sheik crawling painfully towards him across the
sand. He was still staring into the lifeless face of Sir Bertric when the Arabyan's knife stabbed out, piercing him
in the back of the knee. El Syf swung around, kicking the
dying sheik with his armoured boot, shattering his face.
This time, the duke made certain of his enemy, stabbing
the point of his sword through the Arabyan's heart.*

*Even as he struck, the duke swooned. The wound the
sheik had visited upon him was minor, the poison edging
the Arabyan's dagger was not. He found that he lacked
the strength to withdraw his sword from the sheik's breast.
A moment later and he could no longer stay on his feet,
but crashed to the sand. His breath came only with effort,
his blood seemed to grow sluggish in his veins. It was with
bleary vision that he saw the other nomads circling him,
wary of him even as death reached out to snatch him into
its talons.*

*The duke could see the sand dunes in the distance. As
his vision began to darken, he noted that the sinister rider
was gone.*

*Perhaps that figure had been an apparition after all, the
duke thought. An omen of his doom.*

THE TENSION IN the *salle haute* was like a living thing,
predatory and lurking, waiting to pounce upon its
prey. Even the lavish appointments, the marble
caryatids which flanked the immense hearth, the long
mahogany tables polished to a mirrored sheen, the
colourful tapestries cloaking the walls and the stained

glass window that reached from floor to roof behind the laird's seat and allowed the noonday sun to stream into the hall in a brilliant rainbow, could not mask the intense emotion slowly building to a boil.

Upon his high-backed chair of oak trimmed in ivory, his hands clenched about the clawed armrests of his throne, Earl Gaubert d'Elbiq stared in silence at the body laid out upon the floor before him. The old nobleman's cheeks trembled, his eyes were moist, his right leg twitched as though from an ague. None of the servants, none of the knights and courtiers dared intrude upon their lord's sorrow, standing as still and silent as statues throughout the high room of the Chateau d'Elbiq.

For the better part of an hour, Earl Gaubert looked down at the body of his son, Sir Girars. His eyes never shut, never so much as blinked, as though he were trying to burn the image of his slain son upon his brain. He had reacted similarly to the death of each of his sons, but this time was different. This time, he looked upon the last of them. As a father, Earl Gaubert wanted nothing but to die and still the misery he felt, the unendurable horror of seeing all of his children dead.

As head of the House d'Elbiq, another purpose gripped the nobleman's heart, a purpose that at last caused him to raise his eyes from the body of his son and fix his gaze upon Sir Leuthere d'Elbiq, eldest son of his brother, the Comte d'Elbiq.

'My son was murdered by Sir Armand du Maisne,' Earl Gaubert's voice was little more than a dry croak as he spoke. 'How is it that you return to me and allow my son's murderer to walk free?'

Sir Leuthere could not hold the vicious gaze of Earl

Gaubert, lowering his eyes and staring at the floor as he addressed his uncle.

'It was not murder,' the knight said, his voice low but firm. A murmur of astonished disbelief rippled among the earl's courtiers. 'Sir Girars fought Sir Armand in a fair duel.'

Earl Gaubert's lip quivered with rage. 'Liar! Coward!' he snarled.

'Sir Girars fell in open battle,' Leuthere persisted. 'He was killed fighting his opponent in a just duel. He showed boldness and courage the equal of any knight of Bretonnia, never showing fear before his enemy, never faltering in his purpose, however great his injuries.'

'My son was murdered!' Earl Gaubert roared.

Resentment filled Leuthere's heart, giving him the courage to raise his face and meet the irate gaze of his lord. 'Sir Girars died the death of a knight,' he said, his voice stern. 'Unhorsed, his arm broken, his enemy offering him quarter, Sir Girars refused to yield. He fought to the last with valour. If heart and conviction alone were enough to win a battle, he would stand before you now.' The knight's voice became solemn. 'But his enemy was better than he with lance and sword. There is no shame in falling before a worthy foe.'

Earl Gaubert sank back into his throne, his face livid. 'A worthy foe? The du Maisnes are the scum of the earth! Ratfolk! Vermin! The lowest bitch in my kennel is more honourable than Count Ergon's daemon-spawned assassin!'

Leuthere listened to the hate in the earl's voice, saw the mindless fury that set upon his lord. The mania of the feud was strong upon him, causing the nerves in his maimed arm to writhe like the coils of a serpent.

'Have we not lost enough already fighting this senseless war?' Leuthere dared to ask. 'Your father dead beneath the hooves of a du Maisne stallion, my father crushed by a du Maisne mace. Your sons and all the others dead upon du Maisne swords. Yourself crippled by a du Maisne lance. By the Lady, where will it end?'

Earl Gaubert's mouth split in a hateful smile. 'Where it must end!' he spat. 'With the taint of du Maisne blood scoured from the realm or the last of the d'Elbiq line fallen in the attempt!' The nobleman lifted himself from his seat and pointed a trembling finger at Leuthere. 'You should not have come back! You should have avenged my son! You should have returned with Armand's head on a spike!' Furiously, the earl swept his hand through the air. 'Be gone from my sight! Let me not see you again until the villain be slain!'

'I have seen Sir Armand fight,' Leuthere said. 'My skill with the sword isn't enough to overcome his. You send me to my death, my lord.'

A cold fanatical gleam entered Earl Gaubert's eyes, a cunning curl twisted his smile. 'If you are afraid, fall upon him in the night. Cut him down when he is asleep, strike at him from a dark alley, set upon him when he is bowed before a shrine. I care not how you do it, but bring me the swine's head!'

Leuthere staggered back as though from a physical blow when he heard his uncle's frenzied rant. He cast his eyes across the hall and saw that, noble and peasant alike, all within the high room were shocked by their lord's scurrilous words. 'I am a knight, not a murderer,' Leuthere protested.

Earl Gaubert slumped back into the chair, for the first time appreciating the magnitude of his outburst. 'Leave me,' he sighed, sorrow beginning to rout fury from his face. 'Leave me alone with my son.'

Leuthere led the exodus of servants and courtiers from the high room, leaving their lord alone with his grief. The knight lingered in the hallway beyond, casting one last look at the solemn earl before servants drew the heavy oak doors shut.

Mixed among the muffled sobs rising from Earl Gaubert, Leuthere thought he heard a word woven amid the weeping, a word that was spat out as though it were the most poisonous curse.

Not a word, a name.

Du Maisne.

A COOL BREEZE rustled through the long grass, making the plain below the hill resemble a strange sea of green waves. The peasants of Aquitaine held that the ground of Ceren Field was tainted, cursed by the monstrous things that had spilled their rancid blood there. No lord had ever been able to get a peasant to work the land or bring his herds to pasture there. Even the tomb of Duke Galand, Aquitaine's greatest hero, a knight who had sipped from the grail, failed to quiet the superstitions. Duke Galand's tomb had been built that his holy spirit might watch over Ceren Field and sanctify it against any lingering evil.

Sir Armand saw nothing to be afraid of, felt only a sense of serenity and peace as he stared down at Duke Galand's tomb from the larger cemetery atop the little hill. It was a broad mausoleum, its walls of white marble rising into a sharp archway above the heavy stone doors which sealed the entrance into the crypt

within. Walls and doors alike were richly ornamented
with carvings of the grail and the fleur-de-lys, sacred
symbols to the knights of Bretonnia. Strands of ivy
crawled across the tomb, their red flowers and green
leaves forming a stark contrast to the cold, pristine
stone. The knight could sense an aura of peace emanating from the hero's grave, a comforting impression
that seemed to tease the tension from his mind. He
did not understand the peasant fears, finding the old
battlefield a place of quiet solitude where a man could
be alone with his thoughts and forget for a few hours
the onerous burden of position, honour and family.

Armand sat upon one of the graves, listening to the
wind writhing through the overgrown weeds. If Ceren
Field was shunned, then the cemetery on the hill
was absolutely forsaken. The narrow ranks of graves,
the cromlechs of knights who had fallen in battle
against the Red Duke, had been abandoned. No comforting hand had tended the graves, only the cruel
attentions of wind and rain. Most of the headstones
were just disfigured lumps of rock, any names upon
them consigned to oblivion by the elements. Larger
monuments had toppled, lying sprawled among the
weeds like broken giants, whatever grace and beauty
had once been theirs lost to history. Sometimes, the
whirl of a fleur-de-lys or the cracked stem of a stone
grail might be recognized upon the weather-beaten
stones, stubbornly defying the corrosion that sought
to destroy them.

One monument alone had withstood the ravages
of time. A great column of white marble that towered
above the graveyard. At its top was a bronze statue of
a knight upon a rearing horse, the stallion's long tail
acting as a third support for the massive statue. The

style of the knight's armour was ornate and somewhat archaic, the visor of his helm lowered, obscuring his face. The knight's right arm was raised high, a bare sword gripped in the statue's hand. His other arm was locked about a huge kite shield. The shield was without device, instead bearing the names of battles, among them Lasheik and Magritta. The last battle written upon the shield was Ceren Field.

There was some enchantment upon the monument, some magic woven into its construction that allowed it to withstand the caprices of the elements. Armand could feel the strange vibrations exuding from the monument like a dull hum at the back of his head, an icy finger poking against his chest. It was a magic unlike the serenity of Duke Galand's tomb, but it was magic of kindred purpose – to soothe and ease the tranquil repose of the dead.

Armand had first started coming to the cemetery when he was a young lad, hiding among the gravestones as he and his cousins played at war. The strange power of the place had impressed him then; it impressed him now. He had been given to forgetting his games and just sitting and staring at the marble monument for hours. It was a habit he still found himself susceptible to.

Who was the knight honoured with such a monument? That was a question Armand had often wondered. There was no inscription upon the column to give the statue a name, only a stylised sword carved into the face of the pillar itself. Sometimes Armand wondered if the statue represented anyone at all, perhaps being nothing more than an abstract creation of the sculptor.

Somehow, Armand could not shake the conviction

that the statue had a living source. Gazing up at the bronze figure on his stocky warhorse, Armand could almost see the knight leaping forwards into battle, bringing righteous death to the enemies of Bretonnia. Some fanciful creation of a sculptor couldn't have such a semblance of life about it. There had been a man, once, who had fought in all those battles, making war against the despotic Sultan Jaffar and the armies of Araby. He had continued to serve King Louis the Righteous when he returned from the crusades, riding with the king's armies against the monstrous Red Duke. The last battle inscribed upon the shield made it clear that Ceren Field had been the knight's last battle. Whoever he had been, he had not survived the destruction of the vampire.

Armand felt the old childish curiosity upon him again. He rose from his seat and walked to the column, pressing his hands against the cold marble. He smiled and shook his head as he started to lean forwards. When he had been a child, he had sometimes been convinced he could hear sounds when he pressed his ear to the column. Sometimes he had whispered questions to the statue, pressing his ear against the stone, hoping to hear an answer.

The sound of an armoured boot clicking against one of the gravestones made Armand spin away from the column. The bloody feud against the d'Elbiqs fresh in his thoughts, Armand's hand instinctively closed about the hilt of his sword. Having left his retainers behind at Count Ergon's castle, he appreciated how tempting a target he would make for any killers Earl Gaubert had dispatched.

A single knight stood among the graves, a knight in black armour and grey surcoat. He carried no shield, though a massive iron club was tethered to his belt. The visor on the knight's great helm was lowered, hiding his features. Indeed, the only identifying feature on the knight was the black raven embroidered upon his surcoat. There was an aura of brooding power that exuded from the black knight as he slowly approached Armand. It was a strange sort of sensation, at once comforting and sinister. Armand kept a ready hand upon his sword.

'Forgive the intrusion,' the black knight's deep voice rumbled. He gestured with an armoured hand at the plain below. 'I was praying before the crypt of Duke Galand when I thought I saw someone moving among the graves on the hill. I was fearful some grave robber or ghoul was disturbing the dead. I do not take such things lightly.'

'You need not have feared, sir knight,' Armand replied, suspicion yet in his voice. 'I came here only to enjoy the solitude of this place. I meant no disrespect to the dead.'

The black knight bowed his head in apology. 'I meant no offence, Sir Armand du Maisne. Once I saw who was among the graves, I realized my mistake.'

Armand took a step back, his eyes glancing at his surroundings, wary of enemies who might have remained hidden while the black knight held his attention. 'You know who I am?' Armand challenged the stranger.

'Indeed, and you know me, though it has been many years since you last set eyes upon me. I am Sir Maraulf.'

'Sir Maraulf?' Armand nodded as he dredged his memory for the name. Recollection was slow in coming, but he did finally remember a marquis of that name. His fief had been devastated by a plague long ago, when Armand was still in swaddling. The plague had killed the marquis's entire household. The marquis himself had been one of the few to survive. In the aftermath of the tragedy, he had set aside his title and his lands to take up the grail quest. Armand had not heard that Sir Maraulf had returned to Aquitaine.

'It is a long time since you were in these lands,' Armand observed.

'Not so long as you might believe,' Maraulf said. 'I have made my abode in the village of Mercal these past ten winters.'

Again, Armand nodded. He had heard there was a strange hermit knight dwelling with the peasants and tending the grail chapel of Mercal. He feared the impertinence of his next question, but no knight of Bretonnia could restrain his curiosity when meeting a man who had taken up the search for the grail. 'Your quest, it was successful, Sir Maraulf? You have seen the grail?'

The black knight touched his hand to his chest, his steel fingers brushing the embroidered raven. 'I found what the gods deemed me worthy to find,' he answered. 'What of you, Sir Armand? What is it that you seek here among the dead?' He nodded his head, indicating the marble monument. 'I was watching you for some time. It seemed to me you would have made obeisance to that shrine. Why?'

Armand suddenly felt very ashamed at the childish compulsion that had come upon him, doubly embarrassed by the importance Sir Maraulf placed upon such a whimsical impulse. 'It was nothing,' he assured Maraulf. 'Only a foolishness from my childhood. I was going to ask the spirit of the knight a question. When I was a child, I would press my ear to the stone and sometimes, I imagined, I could hear a ghost whispering to me.'

Sir Maraulf's attitude became stern. 'One should be wary of asking things of the dead and even more cautious of such answers as they might give. Do you know whose monument that is? It honours a noble knight of Aquitaine who fought alongside King Louis the Righteous in the crusades. When he returned to Aquitaine, many great deeds were attached to his name and he had earned the title "El Syf", which in the tongue of the Arabyans means "the Sword".'

'He sounds like a formidable warrior,' Armand commented. 'If his ghost could speak to me, then it would surely tell me what I wished to know.'

'And what was that?' Maraulf asked, a note of demand in his tone.

Armand's pride bristled at the interrogatory tone with which Maraulf addressed him. At the same time, he felt an unaccountable eagerness to unburden himself to a listener who was made of flesh and bone rather than marble and bronze.

'Three days ago, I killed a man,' Armand said. His face became pale and he shook his head violently. 'No,' he hissed. 'I give myself too much credit. I killed a boy, a fresh-faced youth still earning his spurs. Oh, it was a fair fight and I offered the boy every quarter possible. But in the end, my sword was sheathed in his flesh and he was as dead just the same.

'I had no good reason to kill that boy,' Armand told Maraulf. 'Only the excuses of family honour and family pride. That is a feeble reason to kill a knight so far beneath my own station. Another martyr to a feud so old none really remembers how it started. I have killed and killed again in the name of ancestors who are nothing to me but glowering faces in old portraits and names on plaques.'

Armand turned and stared up at the bronze statue. 'I spoke to my father about my feelings, my desire to see an end to the feud. Count Ergon is a proud man, and in him the hate has taken root too deeply to listen to reason. He could not sympathize with my guilt, trying to console me by saying the boy had been only a d'Elbiq. When I would not be comforted by the reasoning of hate, my father berated me as a coward, a traitor to the family name. His curses drove me from the chateau, drove me to the only place I have ever known where the burden of feud did not rest upon my heart.'

Slowly, Maraulf advanced to Armand, placing his gauntlet upon the younger knight's shoulder. 'What was it you thought to ask your ghost?'

'I would have asked him how to make the faces of the men I have killed fade from my dreams,' Armand said. 'I would have asked how to make the guilt and shame I feel go away. It is one thing to slay a foe who is your equal in a fairly fought contest, but how can any man of conscience live knowing he has done little more than murder upon a boy who didn't have a chance?'

'El Syf was a renowned swordsman in his day,' Maraulf said, lifting his helm to join Armand in staring up at the statue. 'No blade in all Bretonnia could match his. He made it a practice that any man of any station, noble or peasant, might cross swords with him at any hour. If they could but scratch him, a purse of gold would belong to the challenger. Many came to test El Syf, but when he departed Aquitaine to make war against Araby, the purse of gold still sat unclaimed in his castle.' The black knight crossed his hands, making the fingers resemble the wings of a bird. It was a custom Armand had seen peasants perform when consigning their dead to the grim god Morr.

'I think I know what El Syf would say,' Maraulf told Armand as he turned away from the monument. 'He would say "kill without regret and ask no quarter from your foe". For it is by such words he lived... and died.'

'If I could do the same...'

'Regret and guilt serve to remind a man that he is a man,' Maraulf cautioned. 'Without these to bring pain to his memories, a man becomes a monster.' The black knight began to make his way back among the graves. 'If you ever feel the need to ask a question of El Syf again, perhaps you should ask him which side he died fighting for at Ceren Field.'

Armand's mind was troubled by Maraulf's last words. He would have pursued the black knight, to ask him the meaning of that enigmatic advice, but the sound of hooves on the field below arrested his attention. He turned his head to observe Count Ergon and five of his attendants galloping across the field towards the hill. The visor on Count Ergon's helm was raised and there was such a look of anguished concern written across his features that Armand immediately forgave his father for the harsh words that had driven him from the castle.

Before making his way down the hill to join his father, Armand looked for Sir Maraulf to thank him for his advice and for listening to his troubles. But there was no trace of the black knight, only the wind rustling among the weeds.

* * *

'MY LORD?'

Earl Gaubert d'Elbiq lifted his head and squinted in the darkness of the high room. Night had fallen and no servants had come to light the torches, obeying the desolate man's order for solitude. Upon the floor, at the foot of the throne, he could still see the pallid, lifeless features of his son's face, though it had been a day and better since Sir Girars's body had been removed to prepare for burial.

'My lord?' the feeble, nasally voice asked again. This time, when the earl peered into the darkness, he could see a crouched figure standing to one side of his seat. Earl Gaubert recognized the broken posture of Vigor, one of his footmen. Vigor had once been the earl's stable master until a horse had kicked him and broken his back. It was a sense of charity that made the earl keep him on despite the way the crippled peasant depressed his spirits and reminded him of his own infirmity.

'What do you want, slinking about in the dark like a hunchbacked cat?' Earl Gaubert demanded, hurling a goblet of wine at Vigor's head.

Vigor tried to duck, but his broken body wasn't equal to such agility. The peasant whined as the goblet smacked against his skull. 'I meant no disrespect, my lord,' the cringing man pleaded.

'Then explain yourself and be quick about it,' the nobleman snapped.

Bowing, scraping the floor with his grimy hands, the crooked footman presented himself before the throne. 'The servants have been speaking... about what you said to Sir Leuthere.'

'I have forbidden that coward's name to be spoken within these walls,' Earl Gaubert snarled. 'He is afraid of that du Maisne scum that killed my son. I am not. If I was whole, I would take up my own sword against him! I would make Count Ergon mourn for his child as I have mourned for mine!'

A sympathetic smile was on Vigor's face as he heard his lord's pained fury. 'That is what they said,' he continued, nodding his head eagerly. 'They said you wanted Sir Girars's killer slain and did not care how.'

Earl Gaubert scowled at the peasant. 'What are you about?' he asked. 'You think that you can kill a knight! Even when you weren't a crook-back, Sir Armand would have flayed you alive without breaking a sweat.'

Vigor bowed his head still lower, wincing at his master's scorn. 'I did not mean to suggest that I…'

'Then what did you mean to suggest?' Earl Gaubert growled, quickly losing patience with the peasant's timidity.

'Magic, my lord,' Vigor said, his voice lowered to a whisper. 'Use magic to avenge Sir Girars.'

Earl Gaubert shook his head and chuckled. 'Magic? Witchcraft? That is your advice?'

'Jacquetta could do it…'

The nobleman snorted derisively. 'That witch kill a knight? Her spells are fine for hexing crops and spoiling milk, maybe drying out a field or two! But kill a knight? The hag wouldn't know how and wouldn't dare even if she did.'

Vigor nodded his head, but his words were not quite in agreement with those of his lord. 'Jacquetta has worked only small magic for you because you only offered her small things,' Vigor said. 'If you promised her more, she would be able to make better spells.'

'It is too bad you did not have enough to offer her to fix your back,' Earl Gaubert scoffed, but the mockery rang a bit hollow. There was something to consider in the peasant's suggestion. Though it offended every knightly virtue he possessed, Earl Gaubert wondered if magic might prevail where cold steel had failed him.

'Go and find the witch,' Earl Gaubert told Vigor. 'Tell her I want to meet with her.'

CHAPTER III

Baron Gui de Gavaudan paced anxiously along the battlements of Castle Aquin. Sometimes the baron would pause, looking out across the night sky, staring at the stars and the sleeping landscape they shone upon. The green pastures and lush fields of Aquitaine, the finest vineyards in all Bretonnia, these were things worth fighting to protect. Worth killing to keep.

Why wouldn't the fool just die already? If he recovered, the king would restore the dukedom to the sickly wretch, forsaking the title in favour of the great El Syf!

He should be dead, how the old duke had managed to cling to life these many months was a mystery to Baron de Gavaudan. Any other man with the poison of the Arabyan Deathstalker in his veins would have perished in a few minutes. The Arabyans had practically deified a janissary who had lasted a fortnight after being stung by one of the scorpions. Yet here was the Duke of Aquitaine, El Syf, still refusing to let the poison finish him eight months later!

The baron fingered the pectoral about his neck, the silver talisman that marked him as the king's steward. De Gavaudan was effectively master of the dukedom while King Louis was away at the royal court in Couronne. It was more power than the baron had ever known, certainly more than he could claim as father-in-law to the king.

But it was not for himself that he had taken such chances, that he had fouled his honour with murder and poison. It was to secure the position of his line, to make certain the position of his descendents. The title of King of Bretonnia would not pass on to the sons of King Louis and Queen Aregund. When King Louis died a new king would be crowned by the Fay Enchantress, chosen from those who had sipped from the grail.

The Dukedom of Aquitaine, however, was another matter. That title would pass to de Gavaudan's grand-children, ensuring the power and prestige of his line. His grandson would lord over the most prosperous dukedom in the realm, inherit wealth and power second only to that of the royal throne itself. What greater honour could the baron claim than making such a future possible for his descendents?

There was only one thing standing in his way: the sickly mass of broken humanity that had finally been brought back to Aquitaine from the wastes of Araby. El Syf was already more than half dead when he was brought within the halls of Castle Aquin by his retainers.

Half dead wasn't quite dead enough to ease the baron's mind. A man who had survived the poison of the Death-stalker for such a long time might manage a recovery. That was something the baron couldn't allow to happen.

He didn't like what circumstances had compelled him to do, but the baron was a practical man. His enemy was in his grasp, lying sick and helpless in one of the castle's chambers. He did not think the Lady would lower her-self to smiling upon this enterprise, but certainly the gods could not have made a neater gift of El Syf.

No, the baron thought, a cruel smile twisting his face, the old duke will not recover.

The assassin he had sent to visit the sick man would see to that.

What troubled the baron was the time it was taking his killer to do the job. He had ordered all attendants away from the duke's room, leaving the way open for the assassin. The victim himself was already at death's door, helpless to defend himself. All his man had to do was place a pillow over the duke's face, hold it there for a few minutes, and the deed would be done.

Why was it taking the assassin so long to return and report that El Syf was dead?

Baron de Gavaudan stalked along the battlements for another hour, his unease growing with every step. Somehow something had gone wrong. It was a conclusion he didn't want to make but it was the only reason why the murderer didn't come back to let him know the task was finished.

Unable to wait any longer, the baron made his way back through one of the castle's watchtowers, descending into the tapestry-lined gallery that opened upon the guest chamber he had designated as the duke's sick room. He would see for himself why his assassin had failed to return. Had the fool faltered at the last? Some pang of guilt or conscience kept him from doing his duty? If such were the case, the baron intended to have the knave quartered and his innards fed to the crows!

A single candle burned in the musty room, an icy draught rushing through it from the broken window set high upon its outer wall. A shapeless heap of unused furniture cloaked against the dust and damp huddled against the inner wall. The only other appointment in the room was a large four-poster bed, a thin sheet hanging from the engraved tester suspended above the mattress. The baron could see the figure of his enemy through the almost transparent curtain, *a black huddle sprawled across the few blankets de Gavaudan had allowed for the sick man's comfort.*

For a long moment, the baron stood at the threshold of the room. As much as he had been infuriated by the thought that his assassin had faltered in his purpose because of conscience, de Gavaudan found his stomach turning at the prospect of doing the deed himself. He cursed himself for such cowardice, such weakness. Had he not killed a hundred of the heathen at the Siege of Lashiek? Was it not his sword that had cut down Mustafa Amar, the castellan of Magritta before the eyes of the Arabyan's pleading wives and children? Why should one more death weigh any heavier upon his conscience?

Steeled to his purpose, reminding himself that what he did was not for himself but for the future of his family, Baron de Gavaudan crept towards the sick bed. He paused again beside the ominously silent bed. He wondered if perhaps the deed was not already done. The killer might have gone to dull his conscience with wine after finishing the job, too wracked with guilt to remember to report back to his master. Or, maybe, the duke had already been dead when the assassin had entered the room, succumbing at last to his fever.

Cautiously, Baron de Gavaudan reached out and drew back the thin curtain masking the bed. He stared in shock at what he saw.

The body lying upon the bed was not that of El Syf, it was that of the baron's assassin! The killer had himself been slain, slaughtered in a most brutal fashion, his neck snapped with such force that the man's chin rested upon his spine.

Baron Gui de Gavaudan stumbled away from the gruesome scene, his mind reeling with horror. How could such a thing happen? Who had done it? And most importantly, *where was the Duke of Aquitaine?*

A crawling terror rippled through the baron's flesh. The stink of death struck his senses, the cold chill of the grave closed upon his heart. Slowly, tremulously, he turned away from his murdered assassin. His eyes went wide with terror as he saw a shape standing between himself and the door.

The apparition wore the semblance of El Syf, but the once handsome features were pale and drawn, sharp and cruel as the edge of a dagger. The figure's eyes were like pits of darkness, smouldering embers of hate and hunger burning in their depths.

The baron did not have the chance to scream before the deathly figure fell upon him, its mouth open, its sharp fangs tearing into his throat. He flailed against his attacker, trying desperately to free himself from the vampire's clutch, but he was like a lamb in the jaws of a wolf.

Baron Gui de Gavaudan was a long time in dying.

SIR LEUTHERE D'ELBIQ walked his horse slowly down the grassy slope towards the crystal waters of the isolated lake. Lake Tranquil, the site had been named, and a more appropriate name the knight found impossible to imagine. Everything about the lake and its environs conspired to create an impression of peace and beauty, from the way the oaks and willows leaned out over the waters to the manner in which languid waves rolled across the surface. Legend held that the Lady herself had risen from the waters of Lake Tranquil, appearing to Duke Galand and allowing the valiant knight to sip from the grail. Leuthere was inclined to believe the legend. The atmosphere around the lake was such that he could easily imagine the lingering touch of the divine.

Leuthere left his horse to crop the grass around the

lake and advanced to the edge of the water. Carefully he dipped one hand into the crystal mere, drawing a few drops from the lake and making the sign of the grail with his dampened hand. The waters of Lake Tranquil were held to be sacred because of the Lady's manifestation. Even the noblest traveller was forbidden to drink from the lake without first paying honour to the Lady and begging her indulgence. It was a capital offence to fish the waters of Lake Tranquil; many a reckless peasant had ended his life upon a rope for daring such sacrilege.

The knight bowed beside the lake, waiting for some sign from the Lady that she would indulge his thirst. For many minutes, Leuthere listened to the waves lapping against the shore, the dryness of his mouth increasing with every passing moment. The temptation to rise and slake his thirst nagged at him, but the knight maintained his humble pose, refusing to falter in his faith.

A sharp cry sounded overhead, drawing Leuthere's gaze skyward. He watched a large hawk with brilliant golden plumage wheeling through the azure heavens. As he looked, the bird suddenly swooped downwards, landing upon the shore a hundred yards from Leuthere. The hawk cocked its head at him, blinking its eyes in curiosity. Then, with stately stride, the bird marched to the lake, dipped its beak into the clear waters and took several quick sips. The hawk turned its head back towards Leuthere and then leapt back into the air, its powerful wings bearing it once more into the cloudless sky.

Leuthere bowed his head and closed his eyes, thanking the Lady for this sign of her largesse. When he finished his devotions, the knight cupped his hand

and drew a mouthful of water from the lake, feeling the cool purity of its taste flow down his parched throat and course through his body. Leuthere could liken the sensation only to the soothing flush of a fine wine, but even this comparison seemed crude and improper.

Again, the knight thanked the Lady for her beneficence. He turned away from the lake, sitting down upon the soft grass of the slope. He stared out across Lake Tranquil, watching the wind swaying through the trees that clothed its far shore, observing the smoke rising from peasant villages hidden among those same trees. He saw, perched atop a hill overlooking the lake, the tall spire of the Tower of Wizardry, its tile roof and marble gargoyles gleaming in the sunlight.

Leuthere had never been to the tower. Few men had, for it was a holy place where the idle did not tarry. He was uncertain why it was called the Tower of Wizardry, unless in some time lost to legend a wizard had dwelt there. Now it was a shrine to the Lady; for centuries it had been the home of her prophetesses, holy damsels gifted with the ability to pierce the veil of time and gaze at things yet to pass.

He would have given much to have the mystical power of a prophetess just now. The altercation with his uncle weighed heavily upon Leuthere's soul. In his grief, Earl Gaubert had exposed the ugly malignance that festered in his heart. For sake of the feud, Earl Gaubert had sacrificed everything; now he pursued his hate of the du Maisnes not out of family pride or duty, but for spite's sake. His hate had made him blind to both honour and reason. Leuthere did not like to think how far his uncle would go to have his revenge. He did not know where his own duty lay. Should he follow his uncle, his lord and liege, no matter where that path would take him, or must he remain true to the oaths of chivalry and honour? Where did his obligation to lord and family stop and his duty to himself begin?

If he could but peer for a moment into the future and see the road ahead, Leuthere would know which way he must turn. To help his uncle find revenge or force him to make peace with his enemies for the good of the dwindling d'Elbiqs.

Leuthere returned his gaze to the Tower of Wizardry, staring at the grey granite edifice and its lofty spire. He might seek an audience with the current prophetess, a damsel named Iselda. She might be able to answer his questions.

As if bidden by his thoughts, a tiny figure appeared upon the small balcony near the roof of the tower. From this distance, Leuthere could make out little more than a tall, slender shape in a flowing blue gown and wearing a long, conical hat. He watched the distant woman for a moment, then saw her suddenly stare across the lake. Though there was no way he could be certain, Leuthere could not help the impression that the woman was looking directly at him.

ISELDA, TWELFTH PROPHETESS of the Tower of Wizardry and Guardian of the Lake, strode out onto the tile floor of her balcony, watching as the sun began its slow decline towards the west. The damsel studied the celestial flame for a moment, monitoring its progress, watching for the moment when it would be time to perform the ritual. The simple folk of Aquitaine believed that the mystical properties of Lake Tranquil had been endowed upon it by the manifestation of the Lady in its waters long ago. Even if they were told, they would little understand the real power that coursed through those still waters and which was in turn harnessed by the tower. They would not understand the careful rituals and spells needed to maintain the enchantment, the aethyric mechanism that allowed the tower to act as a focal point for the unseen magical energies flowing across Aquitaine.

The dark wizard who had built the tower would have understood, but he'd been driven into exile, banished to the Grey Mountains, by the Fay Enchantress long ago. Under his terrible influence, the tower had been a thing of evil, but the Fay Enchantress had redeemed it, sanctified it with the light of the Athel Loren. She had reclaimed it for the forces of good and entrusted its powers to her wisest students, those whose talent for magic had allowed them to tap into that most sacred of powers, the power of prophecy.

Iselda's delicate lips drew back in a bitter smile. Prophecy. It was as much a curse as a gift. To know when calamity would strike, to see it as plainly as the tiles beneath her shoes, and unable to prevent its coming. Sometimes, even a warning did no good, for there were some catastrophes from which there was no escape.

Even more troubling than clear visions were the many presentiments that insinuated themselves upon the mind of a prophetess. Far more nebulous in nature, these impressions, good and ill, were as elusive as phantoms, as intangible as the wind. They would burn brightly within the mind of the prophetess, blazing with the glamour of the brightest star, then fade into nothingness before the prophetess could even be certain of what she had seen. All that was left behind was an emotion, a feeling of excited anticipation or a cloud of despairing dread.

Fate had chosen Iselda for the role she bore, marked her from birth to the service of the Lady. It was the only life she had ever known, but even she appreciated the strangeness of it. Sometimes she admired the humble peasants with their simple ways and their simple beliefs. Sometimes she pitied them that they could not see the world as it really was, that they would never know the magic that flowed through their land. More often, she felt a tinge of envy that they could exist in their world of ignorance, fearing the future but unable to *see* what there was to fear.

For many months, Iselda had been troubled by presentiments of doom. Nightmares had wracked her sleep, visions of burning villages and crumbling castles, a forest of impaled bodies stretching from mountain to sea, the soil of Aquitaine churned into a crimson mire of blood. At the very edge of her nightmares, in that elusive borderland where dream collapses into wakefulness, she sensed an ancient evil stirring, mocking her with its venomous voice. However hard she concentrated, it eluded her, always keeping to the shadows of her mind.

In all the decades since she had become Prophetess of the Tower, Iselda had never been so disturbed by her gift. She feared to stare into the tower's reflecting pool, was reluctant to gaze at the stars and read the portents written in the heavens. Perhaps it was her fear that kept her blinded to whatever menace threatened Aquitaine, or maybe the evil she feared was subtle enough to hide from a direct confrontation. But there was no denying that the evil was there, lurking and waiting to strike. Iselda knew a ghastly doom threatened the dukedom. Unfortunately, she knew nothing more than the fact that it existed.

The prophetess suddenly felt a compulsion to turn away from the purification ritual she was just beginning to perform. A chill crept down her spine as she turned away from the sun and cast her gaze across the calm waters of Lake Tranquil. Her sorcery allowed her to see the knight watching her from across the lake as clearly as if he stood beside her. He was a young, good-looking man, a storybook image of a Bretonnian knight. She did not sense any evil in him, yet there was something about him that caused her face to turn pale with dread.

Iselda quickly turned her face from the young knight and withdrew back behind the walls of the tower. She felt her body shivering with fear, nausea boiling in her stomach. It was as though some unseen fiend had torn open the door between worlds and allowed her a glimpse of the daemonic realms.

Whatever was threatening Aquitaine, it was drawing nearer and the young knight was associated with it somehow. In some way he was connected with the doom Iselda had sensed hovering over her.

The prophetess struggled to compose herself. Whatever her fear, she was not one of the peasants. She could not afford the luxury of ignorance. She had to face this evil and unmask it while there was still time.

Iselda rushed back onto the balcony, intending to beckon the young knight to come to the tower. Talking to him would be a quicker and more direct way of learning who he was and where he had come from than relying upon her magic. If she knew more about the man, she might learn something about the evil she had sensed.

When Iselda looked back across the lake, however, the young knight was already gone, riding off into a twilight that seemed darker than any the prophetess had seen before.

EARL GAUBERT D'ELBIQ scowled in disgust at the squalid mess around him. The cave was bad enough, dank and dreary, its ceiling so low in places that a man was forced to crawl to make any progress through its narrow tunnels. Dirty liquid that was more mineral than water dripped from the walls, each drop echoing wildly as it splashed into the stagnant pools that pitted the floor. Rats and pallid cave frogs scampered about the nobleman's feet, deranged bats flittered through his hair, cobwebs clutched at his face and the tiny bones of vermin crunched beneath his boots.

Yes, the cave was bad enough on its own, but the noxious accoutrements collected by the witch were worse. Heaps of dried stinkweed, strands of mouldering hensbane and poison oak, the rotting carcasses of birds and beasts strung up by their heels. Skulls, human and animal, arranged in little piles throughout the hideous maze. A grotesque idol that looked like it was made of swamp moss and smelled like cattle manure squatted at the centre of the witch's lair, welcoming the earl with a smile made from eggshells and eyes crafted from the fangs of panthers.

The earl glared at the offensive sculpture, crushing a pomander against his nose to fend off the smell. One of the knights he had brought with him stomped forwards to pull down the hideous thing. Vigor moved to stop him, but quickly remembered his place, instead muttering fearfully to himself, terrified of what the witch would do if the earl's man touched her god.

A sharp cackle arrested the knight as he reached to grab the idol. The startled knight looked around in surprise. Finding no one, he angrily returned his attention to the grotesque statue. This time, however, he noticed something different about the thing. A long black tongue had appeared between the idol's teeth, a black ribbon of scaly flesh that stared at him with beady eyes and hissed as his fingers came near it.

Cursing loudly, the knight leapt back, recoiling from the odious serpent that had so suddenly materialised.

'Your man is wise to keep his distance.'

Earl Gaubert and his attendants turned at the sound of the voice. They watched as a woman entered the cavern, stepping out from a tunnel each of them would have sworn hadn't been there but a moment before. Despite the uncouth surroundings, she presented a striking figure, every graceful curve of her nubile body exposed by her scanty raiment. A black skirt slit to the waist, a black bandeaux about her breasts, a tangle of necklaces about her throat and a set of bone sandals upon her feet composed the entirety of her costume. Her hair was a sombre mane framing her face with wild confusion. There was a cruel beauty about the witch's face, a glamour that at once aroused and repulsed.

'That is a Moussillon marsh adder,' the witch informed her guests. 'Had it devoted its attentions to your man, he would have died a most excruciating death.' Jacquetta swept her defiant gaze across each of the visitors, baring her teeth in a cold smile. 'You all would have. My pet has made its nest somewhere inside Onogal's head.'

'I did not come here to play with snakes or stare at strumpets,' Earl Gaubert snarled. He pointed his fist at the witch. 'The only reason I suffer you and your filthy cult, Jacquetta, is because you are useful to me. Stop being useful, and I'll see every last one of you burn.'

Hisses sounded from every corner of the cave. The earl turned about as he heard the angry sounds, watching as a motley variety of scruffy figures emerged from the shadows. Some wore filthy cloaks and hoods, looking as though they had come fresh from the fields. Others were naked as babes, their skin pale beneath the layers of dirt that were caked onto their bodies. Many of these troglodyte creatures bore the stigma of mutation upon them, their faces twisted by bestial snouts, their hands disfigured by feline claws and bovine hooves. The knights drew their swords as Jacquetta's followers surrounded them.

'I will forgive this rudeness because I know you are distressed by your recent loss,' Jacquetta told the earl.

'How dare you, a peasant, speak to me in such fashion!' Earl Gaubert roared.

Jacquetta smiled at him coldly. 'I dare because I know why you have come here. I dare because I can give you what you want.'

Earl Gaubert held the witch's gaze for a moment, then scowled at his attendants. 'Lower your swords,' he told them. If it would help him be avenged upon the du Maisnes, then he would suffer the witch's impertinence.

'A wise choice, my lord,' Jacquetta cooed, not bothering to hide the mockery in her voice.

'Do not toy with me,' Earl Gaubert warned. 'You say you know what I want and that you can help me.'

Jacquetta strolled casually across the cave, her

movements as lithe and sinuous as those of the marsh adder, each provocative swing of her hips drawing the gaze of Earl Gaubert's knights. 'You want Sir Armand du Maisne. You want him dead, but not simply dead. You want him humbled, humiliated upon the field of honour. You want his reputation as the finest swordsman in Aquitaine cast into the dirt alongside his bones. You want to destroy more than just a man, you want to destroy his very name.'

'Yes!' Earl Gaubert gasped. All thoughts of position and propriety were gone now. The nobleman struggled to maintain the scepticism he had felt when crawling through the tunnels, but Jacquetta's words had so fully expressed his desire that he felt his very soul trapped by her voice. 'That is what I want!'

'There is a price,' Jacquetta told him. 'Are you willing to pay it?'

'Anything,' Earl Gaubert answered, not even bothering to consider what such an agreement might mean.

Jacquetta smiled at the nobleman's reckless offer. She stepped over to the smelly idol of Onogal, holding her hand to its mouth and letting the snake slither across her fingers, careless of the death that lurked in its fangs. 'Anything,' she mused. 'Very well. I and my followers are not without our sensibilities. We tire of lurking in the shadows, hiding in filthy caves and deserted hovels. We desire a certain… respectability, accommodation more befitting our hedonistic proclivities. We want to leave the shadows behind us and step out into the light. To do that, we would need your protection, Earl Gaubert d'Elbiq.'

The price was one that made even Earl Gaubert hesitate. It was scandalous enough to have dealings with the witch and her cult in the dead of night where no one could see them. But to have the witch operate out in the open, and with his protection, to allow her to worship her obscene gods and spread her foul beliefs among his peasants…

'You shall have everything you ask,' Earl Gaubert said, deaf to the shocked protests of his knights. 'When Sir Armand du Maisne has been ruined and destroyed more thoroughly than any knight of the realm, then shall I order a great temple built for yourself and your followers.'

The witch nodded her head, pleased that the earl's hate had been great enough to forego any quibbling over her price. 'I know that the word of a nobleman is the one thing he will not violate. But know that there are powers I serve who will visit untold horrors upon you should you break faith with me.'

To illustrate her point, Jacquetta lifted her hand. The serpent twined about her fingers suddenly became rigid. With a violent motion she dashed the adder to the floor, its petrified body shattering like a clay vessel.

Earl Gaubert went pale at the cruel display of the witch's power, intimidated by forces he did not understand and which he had been taught from the cradle to loathe and despise. At the same time, the display of black magic crushed the last of his reticence. However mighty Sir Armand's skill with the blade, it could not defy such sorcery.

'How will you destroy him?' the earl asked, staring down at the broken snake.

Jacquetta came closer to the nobleman, her soft hand caressing the maimed lump of his arm. For an instant, Earl Gaubert felt strength flow through him once more. Then the witch withdrew her touch and he was a cripple once more.

'Living in the shadows, I know others who have hidden themselves from the prying eyes of the ignorant and the blind. There is a man I know of who has some talent for evoking the spirits of the dead. My followers have helped him collect... materials... for his researches. More importantly, he knows and fears my powers. He will help us achieve your purpose, Earl Gaubert.' A cold light crept into Jacquetta's gaze. 'Your enemy is reckoned the greatest living swordsman in all Aquitaine. With magic, we shall evoke the spirit of the greatest swordsman Aquitaine has ever known!'

CHAPTER IV

King Louis stared out across the bloody battlefield, watching as peasants armed with torches drove off the hungry crows and vultures. The carnage was unspeakable, the noble dead of Bretonnia laid out in ghastly rows, their lifeless eyes gazing up at the uncaring sky. Smoke rose from the great bonfires where the corpses of the Red Duke's vanquished army were being consigned to the flames. This odious chore had fallen to the few living knights who had served the vampire and survived the battle. King Louis was at a loss what to do with these men. Part of him wanted to simply exile them from the kingdom, allow them at least the chance to redeem their honour in some foreign land. Then, as he considered the horrors the vampire had visited upon Aquitaine, the king found himself wanting to cast these men into the flames alongside the husks of zombies and wights.

So much misery. It would be generations before Aquitaine could recover from this carnage, be more than a shadow of the land King Louis had known and loved. History would say he had won a great victory upon Ceren Field, but he did not feel like a conqueror. All he felt was tired and old, his heart filled with a sadness that tore at his soul. So much had been lost at Ceren Field, things that no victory could restore. The Aquitaine he had known was gone, as dead as the knights of Cuileux and the dragons of Tarasq.

The king lowered his eyes and looked upon the body laid out at his feet. The crimson armour shone like a mantle of rubies in the blazing sun, the jewelled necklace about the corpse's throat was like a burning star. There was no cruelty or malice in the lean face of the dead man, only an expression of peaceful repose. How hard had that face fought to have that look upon it, all down the Estalian peninsula and out across the sea to the desolate shores of Araby and the thorny walls of Lashiek. The dead knight had fought so terribly hard to find peace. In the end, it had taken the king's lance to bring it to him.

'Sire, it is time.' The words were spoken with reluctance by the armoured knight standing beside the king. Sir Thierbalt was one of the king's generals, a knight who had drunk from the grail and who had campaigned alongside his king in the lands of the heathen. Sir Thierbalt found his current duty the most onerous of all the trials he had ever endured.

King Louis stared at his old friend, a blank expression in his eyes. Sir Thierbalt felt tempted to turn away, to leave his king alone with his sorrow. The knight knew he couldn't. Sometimes even a king needed to be reminded where his own duty lay.

'Sire, he must be burned with the rest,' Sir Thierbalt said.

King Louis turned away, watching as the rotting carcasses of the Red Duke's army were tossed into the bonfires. The sickening stink of burning flesh and the putrid juices of mortification struck the king's senses. He cringed at the obscene sound of bones cracking in the flames. Even in the worst years of the crusades, he had never seen such a ghastly sight.

'No,' the king said, his voice low but firm. 'He will not burn like a piece of rubbish.'

'The Red Duke must be destroyed,' Sir Thierbalt repeated. 'The Prophetess Isabeau has warned that every trace of the vampire must be annihilated.'

King Louis stared down at the body, studying the peaceful expression on the corpse's face. 'The Red Duke has been destroyed. There is nothing left of the monster, only the man remains.' The king quickly wiped his eyes. 'I will not see the Duke of Aquitaine burn with the rest of the vampire's carrion! He shall lie with our own dead. I will build a monument to the heroic deeds of the man and shall forget the horrors of the monster!' King Louis saw the uncertainty on Sir Thierbalt's face. 'This is my decree,' he said sternly. 'Not the prophetess, not the Lady herself shall make me alter my decision.'

The king's will was law. The body of the Red Duke was not consigned to the flames, as Isabeau had ordered, but was instead borne from the field of battle. A great column of marble was erected upon the hill overlooking Ceren Field and into this pillar the vampire's body was placed. A bronze statue depicting the Duke of Aquitaine at the height of his heroic glory was set atop the pillar and rich engravings chronicled the life of the noble warrior before he had descended into darkness.

The Prophetess Isabeau warned against honouring a thing that had turned to evil and visited such wickedness upon the land, but her words fell upon unheeding ears. The king's grief was great; only by paying tribute to his dead enemy could he ease the burden of his heart.

Isabeau did prevail upon the king to allow her to place enchantments upon the monument, spells that would protect the tomb and hold it inviolate against all manner of evil. King Louis never recognised the import behind her *magic, never suspected that Isabeau's purposes were other than those she had professed to her king. So certain was he that death had cleansed the body of the Red Duke's evil that he would have resented it had Isabeau confessed her fears to him.*

The damsel's spells would protect the tomb from the ravages of wind and rain, but they would also protect the land from that which lay within the tomb. For in the vampire's body, Isabeau sensed a seed of evil, an evil that must never be allowed to rise again.

In the darkness of the first night after Isabeau's spells sealed the tomb, something stirred within the marble pillar. Something engorged by the darkest of magic. Something that ripped the broken lance from its heart. Something that sneered at the foolish compassion that had prevented King Louis from destroying its body. The king would suffer for his mistake. All Bretonnia would suffer.

Then the vampire attempted to leave his tomb. The unseen power of Isabeau's wards drove him back. The vampire found it impossible to even approach the walls of his crypt, repulsed by the enchantments that saturated the marble column. The Red Duke could only turn within the small interior of his prison and curse at the walls that confined him, the walls he couldn't even touch.

Alone in the eternal darkness of his own tomb, the Red Duke passed the long years, tormented by the bloodlust that consumed his corrupt body. Hour by hour, his ravenous hunger swelled, torturing him with pangs of longing he was powerless to satisfy. Vainly he cast his thoughts upon the past, trying to forget his hunger by reflecting upon his deeds, losing himself in moments heroic and infamous with equal abandon.

Once, twenty years after being imprisoned in his tomb, the Red Duke heard banging sounds against the walls.

Desperately he cried out, little caring if those who assailed the marble walls brought rescue or destruction with them. The louder he cried, the faster the banging sounds came. For the better part of a day, the vampire listened to the walls of his prison being struck by hammer and chisel. But never did the enchantments which held him falter, never did a single ray of light or wisp of new air creep into the darkness.

The vampire could not know that King Louis was dead and that with his death, Isabeau had ordered workmen to visit the Red Duke's tomb and efface it of all trace of the vampire's name lest it become a shrine to his evil. Only one mark did the workmen forget to remove before they left, a single stylised sword, a tribute to the knight whom the Arabyans had named 'El Syf'.

When the workmen left, the vampire was abandoned once more to the silence and the darkness. His only companions though the years his haunted memories and his eternal hunger.

Sometimes, the Red Duke would imagine he heard again the sound of hammers cracking against the walls of his prison, shrieking out in desperation to these mocking phantoms of memory, begging them for the release that would end his hunger.

AN ICY NIGHT wind slithered through the weeds, making it sound as though a phantom army was marching through the cemetery. It was an impression Earl Gaubert d'Elbiq found particularly disturbing. With only the feeble light of Morrslieb, the sickly Chaos moon, shining down upon the hilltop, any number of goblins and ghouls might be hidden among the gravestones.

Strangely, it was the thought that human eyes might

be observing him from the darkness that worried Earl Gaubert the most. Ghosts and fiends could only kill him. A man could do much worse to him. If word reached Duke Gilon and his fellow lords about this midnight excursion to Ceren Field, far worse would befall Earl Gaubert than mere death. He would be disgraced, condemned for consorting with followers of the Dark Gods. His lands would be stripped from him, his house abolished. He would be executed with a noose, killed like a peasant, denied the headsman's axe which was the proper death for a nobleman condemned by his lord.

Earl Gaubert cast a defiant scowl across the long shadows of the graveyard. He was willing to risk even such disgrace and ruin in order to avenge himself upon Count Ergon and the cursed du Maisnes. What tortures could Duke Gilon visit upon him that were worse than the pain of burying his sons, of watching their murderer roam free?

The earl pulled his bearskin cloak tighter about his body, fending off the chill of the night. He nodded to his companions, Sir Aldric and Sir Jehan, two of his most valiant and loyal knights. Men who could be trusted to obey his every order without question and who would keep their mouths shut about anything they saw or heard. Slowly, the three men made their way through the maze-like confusion of headstones and crypts, the overgrown weeds clutching at them as they forced their way among the tombs.

After a few yards, a grey mist began to rise from the earth, clinging to the headstones like ghostly cobwebs. The deeper the men penetrated into the cemetery, the thicker the mist became, at last becoming a smothering blanket of fog. Natural fogs seldom penetrated so far inland as Aquitaine, and Earl Gaubert knew this cloud did not belong to the natural world. It was some magical veil conjured up by Jacquetta to cloak her activities in the graveyard. The witch was nothing if not cautious. It was one of the reasons Earl Gaubert had tolerated her foul little cult for so long. It was easy to harbour evil in one's fief if the evil in question was discreet.

A green light suddenly shone within the fog, beckoning Earl Gaubert and his knights onwards. The nobleman motioned for his men to precede him and advised them to keep their swords drawn. The witch might be their partner in this enterprise, but it was imprudent to trust her too far. Whatever her occult powers, she was still only a peasant and therefore a creature without any understanding of honour.

Through the grey veil, the three men marched, following the witch light as it manoeuvred among the tombs. Earl Gaubert lost count of the twists and turns the beckoning light demanded of them, certainly it was impossible to tell where in the cemetery they were. With the stars and moon hidden behind the fog, there was no way to determine even which direction they were moving. The nobleman accepted the annoyance of this circuitous journey with a grudging tolerance. Jacquetta was being careful, leading her lord on such a confusing path in the event that there had been spies lurking in wait. There wasn't a man born who could make sense of the route Earl Gaubert and his knights had taken. Even one of the fay would have been lost in the witch's fog.

When the witch light finally flickered and died, Earl Gaubert proceeded towards its last position. The fog began to grow thin, the night sky once again stretched across the heavens, and the nobles could once more see the dark bulks of crypts and tombs looming all around them. Their course had led them to the centre of the graveyard, to a spot where a great column of marble thrust upwards from the ground. The earl could feel the soft, subtly disturbing aura of the column, a feeling somehow owing some kinship to the divine atmosphere of a grail chapel where the relics of those who had seen the Lady were enshrined. It was not quite the same though. Where a grail chapel evoked a sense of peace and purpose, what Earl Gaubert felt emanating from the column was more visceral, more aggressive. There was a sense of alarm, of warning attached to the enchantment.

Almost, Earl Gaubert allowed the ancient magic to sway him, to make him forget the sinister purpose that had brought him to the graveyard in the dead of night. Then the earl saw the laughing faces of Count Ergon and Sir Armand flash before his eyes. Hate swelled his heart, stifling the fear that had moved him. The du Maisnes would pay and the spells of a long-dead damsel were not going to keep him from his revenge.

Black candles were arrayed about the base of the column, their flame writhing in the darkness like a living thing. Before the candles stood a grisly altar, its surface cloaked in the flayed skin of a woman, and upon this unspeakable symbols had been written in blood. Tiny grinning skulls, the fleshless heads of murdered children, rested in each corner of the altar, their empty sockets staring accusingly at the three noblemen. Sir Jehan, offended beyond endurance by the sight of the obscene altar, began to draw his sword. Only the reprimanding hiss of Earl Gaubert restrained the knight from casting down the loath-some tabernacle. He shared his knight's disgust, but unlike Jehan, he understood the necessity behind the abomination.

From the shadows, cloaked figures shuffled into view, the diseased shapes of Jacquetta's cult. The witch herself emerged from behind a headstone, smirking at Earl Gaubert's disgust. She caressed one of her long, sinuous legs as she stepped into the light.

'You came,' Jacquetta said. 'I half imagined you would be too timid. Knights seldom have the stomach for sorcery.'

Earl Gaubert scowled at her. 'Do not mock me, you peasant trash,' he hissed. 'Witch or whore, I'll see you quartered if you trifle with me!'

Jacquetta shrugged, the gesture causing her black cloak to slip and expose a milky white shoulder. 'You need my magic to have your revenge, my lord. It would be wise not to forget that.'

'You spoke of some other warlock whose magic we also needed,' Earl Gaubert reminded her. 'I trust you have found him?'

The witch nodded, gesturing with her hand towards one of the tombs. From the recessed doorway, a tall, cadaverously thin man stepped into view. He wore a long black coat, bone buttons running down its front in double rows. A battered, almost shapeless hat was crushed about his greying hair. The man's face was gaunt, with a wide forehead and a square jaw. There was a sneaky, calculating quality about his eyes that reminded Earl Gaubert of a rat or a goblin.

'You are the warlock?' Earl Gaubert asked.

The man in the black coat bowed at the waist. 'Renar of Gisoreux, your subject, my lord,' he said, his voice

surprisingly stentorian and with a cultured inflection
about it. It still bore the accent of a peasant, but a
peasant who had come from a more affluent setting
than some rural village.

Renar did not wait for the earl to acknowledge
him, but instead pointed to the grisly altar. 'You
have brought the goblets, my lord?' He nodded as he
watched one of the knights remove three silver cups
from a bag tied to his belt. 'Place them upon the altar,'
he said, walking towards the monument as the knight
moved to carry out his command.

Renar rounded the altar, studying the three goblets.
After a time, he nodded once more and drew a small
leather pouch from one of the pockets of his coat.
Even Earl Gaubert cringed at the suggestive shape
of the thing and tried to tell himself the pouch had
been crafted from the paw of a monkey. Renar opened
the bag where it had once been attached to a wrist.
Carefully he poured a dark powder from the pouch,
dumping an equal measure of the substance into each
of the cups.

When he was finished, Renar drew a curved dagger
from beneath his coat. Setting the edge of the blade
against his palm, he directed his gaze at Earl Gaubert.
'Do you understand the purpose of this ritual?' he
asked, a note of demand in his tone.

'I understand it will avenge my sons,' Earl Gaubert
growled back. 'Now be about your spell, warlock!'

'This is the tomb of the Red Duke,' Renar told
Earl Gaubert. 'The greatest monster and the greatest
swordsman to ever spill blood upon the soil of Aquitaine.' He smiled as he saw that revelation unsettle
the arrogant nobleman. Like all knights, Earl Gaubert
understood nothing of magic and had never imagined

he would be brought to the resting place of the spirit he would have invoked. 'This monument was erected to imprison the Red Duke's spirit, enchanted by the magic of the prophetess. For nearly five hundred years the old magic has kept the essence of the Red Duke trapped inside this pillar of marble. That is the power we have set ourselves against, the power of the grail. It is what stands between you, my lord, and your vengeance.'

Earl Gaubert looked at the ground, shame filling his heart. Renar had driven his words like a dagger into the earl's heart, cutting to the last of his pretensions. If the nobleman thought he could call upon the black arts and remain true to his beliefs, remain a respectable knight of Bretonnia, Renar left him with no room for doubt. What he was calling upon were the forces of evil, the powers against which the Lady and the knights who served her were opposed.

Even now, Earl Gaubert knew he could still turn back. He saw the entreaty on the faces of his companions, begging him to break faith with these villainous wretches and return to the chateau while they still had something left of their honour. Then the old hate came crawling back into his mind, the bitter spite that would be satisfied only with bloodshed.

No need to fear the misgivings of his men. They were loyal knights who would die before defying the lord they had sworn their oaths to.

'If the Lady will not grant me revenge,' Earl Gaubert said in a low voice, 'then I shall treat with those gods who will.'

Jacquetta smiled at the nobleman's words. Renar greeted them with a grim nod.

'Jacquetta's magic will undo the wards placed upon

the tomb,' Renar said. 'Then I shall evoke the spirit of the Red Duke. His skill with the sword shall be drawn out, channelled into the receptacles prepared to receive such power.' Renar winced as he brought the blade of his dagger slicing across his palm. Blood dripped from his injured hand, trickling down his wrist. Cautiously, he held his hand above the silver goblets, allowing a few drops of his blood to fall upon the dark powder.

Immediately, the powder began to boil as the blood struck it, bubbling and foaming with almost volcanic violence. The goblets began to fill with a stagnant crimson liquid, the magical fusion of Renar's blood and the dark powder.

'Evil begets evil,' Renar pronounced. 'The blood of a necromancer and the ashes of a sorcerer. United they form a compact with the forces of Old Night and the Lord of the Black Pyramid. Through this tether to the netherworld, the power you seek will flow. Your bodies are weak, inured upon virtues and morality repugnant to the dark powers.' Renar tapped the blade of his dagger against the silver goblets. 'This potion will rectify the balance and prepare you to receive the strength of the Red Duke.'

Slowly, reluctantly, the three knights approached the altar. The symbolism of this profane rite was not lost upon them. It was a blasphemous mockery of the ultimate ambition of any knight, a foul parody of the grail quest. They stared in undisguised horror at the crimson filth slopping over the lip of each cup.

'Drink,' Renar told them. The necromancer's eyes narrowed with scorn as he saw them hesitate. 'Drink,' he repeated, his voice a commanding snarl.

Earl Gaubert seized his cup, bolting its obscene

contents. The nobleman staggered back, struggling not to gag upon the vile stuff. One after the other, his companions followed his example, choking and coughing as the potion slithered down their throats.

Jacquetta laughed openly as the last of the knights drank from the cups. She clapped her hands and her cloaked cult gathered about the altar, each taking a black candle into his left hand. The cultists began to chant, their voices raised in a repugnant cadence of obscenity and blasphemy.

The witch herself took Renar's place behind the altar, the necromancer retreating once again into the shadows. Cackling, she cast aside her cloak, exposing the pallid nakedness of her body. With an almost boneless sinuosity, she swayed before the monument, her voice raised in a semi-human howl.

'I call upon the Fly Lord, Grandfather Nurgle of the Ten Thousand Poxes, raise forth your leprous hand!

'I cry out to the Blood God, Great Khorne of the Ten Thousand Terrors, raise forth your bloody axe!

'I implore the Wise Raven, Mighty Tzeentch of the Ten Thousand Lies, raise forth your feathered talon!

'I beseech the Dark Serpent, Prince Slaanesh of the Ten Thousand Torments, raise forth your burning lash!

'I command all the nameless powers and principalities, cast down this holy place! Rebuke the old enchantments and break the ancient wards! Erase the sacred signs and open the door that was shut!

'By Zuvassin and Necoho and fiery Phraz-Etar do I compel the daemons of sky, earth and flame to heed my bidding! By the black name of Be'lakor do I command the ruin of this sacred place!'

As Jacquetta's voice rose to a shriek, a deep rumbling

sounded within the hill. Headstones trembled, tombs shivered, the witch's cultists were thrown to the ground. A peal of thunder crackled across the night sky, its echoes booming across the land.

Earl Gaubert expected to see the marble column burst apart, to be cast down like a fallen tree. Instead, the monument stood as proud and tall as ever, defying the black magic that had been unleashed upon it. The nobleman cursed, his hand dropping to his sword. He had risked so much, made so many sacrifices, even suffered the indignity of drinking the necromancer's abominable potion – all for nothing!

As the earl drew his blade and stalked towards the shrieking witch, he did not notice the gilded sword fixed to the face of the column suddenly crack apart and crumble into the weeds.

Sometimes, he would imagine he heard again the sound of hammers cracking against the walls of his prison, shrieking out in desperation to these mocking phantoms of memory, begging them for the release that would end his hunger.

Then, into the eternal darkness there came light, a light black and terrible. He could feel the unholy energies rippling through the air, scorching him with daemonic claws, tearing at him with phantom knives. The pain was intoxicating, luxurious, invigorating. After the long centuries alone, his only sensation the insatiable hunger burning through his veins, even the agonies of hell were a pleasant respite.

Slowly, he felt another change in the air. He could feel the ancient wards shattering beneath the hammers, evaporating into nothingness. The marble walls had become simply things of stone. The magic of Isabeau was gone.

* * *

ISELDA AWOKE WITH a start, her hand clutching at her heart. Sweat drenched her body, her bed sheets coiled about her legs in a tight knot from the violent uneasiness of her slumber. She stared at the darkness of her room, almost afraid of what she might see staring back at her. The certainty that something evil and obscene was lying in wait became unbearable. Firmly she collected her thoughts, exerted her will and evoked a nimbus of icy blue light into being above her bed. The faerie light drove back the shadows, illuminating the wood-panel walls and richly tiled floor of the room. Nothing more menacing than her wardrobe and a heavy chair stood exposed by the light.

Still, Iselda could not shrug off the sinister feeling that oppressed her. She felt like a doe that hears the unseen wolf stalking her through the forest. A terrible danger hung over Aquitaine, her premonitions had warned her of the lurking malignance. Now, however, her nightmares had become even more intense. She had seen a black crypt standing open and empty, the casket inside ripped open. She had watched a red shadow rise from the tomb and stretch its hand across the land. Whatever the shadow touched withered and died, only to rise again as a decaying husk.

She had seen the shadow grow more distinct, transforming into the figure of a pale man dressed in red armour. She had gazed upon the man's face, seen the evil etched upon his features, the madness burning in his eyes. Then the man had seemed to notice her. His pale lips pulled back in a smile, exposing his sharp fangs...

Iselda kicked her way free from the sheets and rose from her bed. She hurried across the cold floor, snatching a fur-trimmed gown from her wardrobe and

tossing it about her shoulders. This was no hour to be
tended by servants, even if Iselda was of a mind to
tarry. The last of her dreams had possessed a sense of
immediacy that brooked no delay. Something monstrous had happened, something that announced the
beginning of the calamity she had been sensing for
so long.

The prophetess hurried along the dark halls of the
tower, gliding along the galleries with all the noise
of a ghost. She wanted to consult the reflecting pool,
that basin of enchanted waters drawn from the Crystal Mere deep within the forest of the fay. The future
could be seen within those waters, if one had the sight
to see.

The oracle chamber was situated at the very heart
of the tower, many levels below that of Iselda's private rooms, yet she reached the chamber in only a
few minutes. The sense of immediacy she felt caused
her to regret every second wasted hurtling down stairs
or racing along halls. Every passing moment brought
the menace nearer, she could feel that fact in her very
bones.

When she stepped into the oracle chamber, Iselda
immediately shuddered. The room was absolutely
frigid, so cold her breath turned to mist before her.
Even in the dead of winter, the room could not be
cold. Only the taint of black magic could leave such
a chill in the air. Whispering a quiet invocation to
the Lady, asking for her protection, Iselda cautiously
approached the reflecting pool.

What she saw made her cringe away in revulsion.
The basin, shaped in the semblance of the grail, was
cracked, the floor around it drenched. But it was not
the enchanted waters of the Crystal Mere that stained

the floor. By some occult force, the waters had become viscous and thick, darkening to the colour of blood. Despite the gory puddle around the basin, there was still enough within the pool to fill it nearly to the brim.

Iselda could see things writhing in that basin of blood, maggot shapes that crawled and slithered with mindless life. There was something more though, something within the very depths of the pool. Only by ignoring the revulsion that wracked her body and the fear that clawed at her heart was she able to gaze down into the pool, to peer into its depths.

She saw an image staring back at her, the hideous countenance from her dreams.

Iselda knew now the menace she had sensed for so long. She knew the evil that loomed over Aquitaine, the evil that would besiege the Tower of Wizardry as it had once before.

What the Prophetess Isabeau had feared throughout her long life, the dire warning she had passed down to her successors, had come to pass.

The Red Duke was free!

THE FACE OF the column split open, ancient masonry crashing to the ground. Earl Gaubert and the cultists watched in amazement as the crack spread, entire blocks of stone falling away from the monument, smashing to the ground with such violence that clouds of dust rose into the air. Jacquetta's incantation trailed off, ending on a note of uncertainty. The witch backed away from the damaged column, crossing her arms defensively over her chest, fear beginning to crawl across her face.

A jagged opening gradually appeared where the

marble had broken away, exposing a black hollow within the monument. A stagnant gust of wind billowed from the lightless depths, its smell rank with the stench of death. Weeds turned yellow and brittle, withering before the stunned eyes of the onlookers. Jacquetta's cult backed away from the monument, their twisted faces trembling with fear. Earl Gaubert made the sign of the grail as a feeling of unspeakable dread came over him.

A tense silence settled upon the graveyard as the last of the crumbling blocks fell from the fissure. It was a menacing silence, pregnant with the promise of horror.

The silence was broken as a gangling shadow burst from the hollow column, flinging itself upon Jacquetta with inhuman speed. The witch's soft flesh was savaged by steely claws, her body trapped by the shrivelled arms that encircled her. She cried out as the withered, skull-like face of her attacker leered at her, desiccated lips pulling back to expose long sharp fangs.

The vampire's head darted forwards, his jaws locking about Jacquetta's throat, worrying her flesh with the savagery of a starving dog. Bright blood streamed from the wound, coursing down the witch's breast, staining her milky skin with the colour of death. She struggled to scream as the fangs slashed her veins, but all that escaped was a croaking whimper.

The cultists took up Jacquetta's scream, giving voice to the terror she could not express. The black-robed peasants and mutants scattered, fleeing in every direction, retreating into the labyrinthine darkness of the graveyard. Jacquetta reached out to them, imploring her faithless cult for help.

The sight of a helpless woman begging an uncaring mob for aid was too much for Jehan. He had set aside many of his vows and virtues for the sake of his lord, but the knight would not ignore the obligations of chivalry. Grimly, he gripped his sword and lunged at the creature savaging Jacquetta.

THE VAMPIRE NOTED the knight's approach, tearing his mouth from the wound on Jacquetta's neck. The creature hissed wrathfully at the man, his face shrivelled and pale where it was not smeared with the witch's blood. Angrily, he threw the dying witch aside, flinging her across the altar with such force that her spine broke upon impact with the stone obstruction.

Jehan received a good look at his foe for the first time. The vampire's body was withered, but from its desiccated husk there was fastened the armour of a Bretonnian lord, armour stained as red as the blood smearing the creature's fangs. A thick-bladed sword hung from a chain about the vampire's waist, the golden pommel cast in the semblance of a grinning skull.

In a blur of steel, the vampire drew his blade, springing towards the knight with bestial fury. Contemptuously, he swatted aside Jehan's guard, crumpling the edge of the man's blade with the superhuman power of his blow. Jehan reeled, staggered by the violence and suddenness of the attack. The monster allowed him no quarter. The serrated blade he held licked out, smashing through the knight's arm, slashing the chainmail as though it were cheesecloth. Blood bubbled up from the mangled flesh beneath the armour.

Snarling, howling like a beast of the wilds, the Red

Duke fell upon the wounded Jehan. The powerful warrior was crushed by the vampire's clutch, held as helpless as the witch had been while undead fangs tore at his mangled arm. Struggling, kicking, screaming for help, the knight could do nothing as the vampire engorged himself upon the man's lifeblood.

It was a drained, lifeless husk the Red Duke let fall to the ground minutes later. He wiped the back of his hand across his mouth, licking the blood from his fingers, savouring the intoxicating tang of fear trapped within the sanguine liquid. After so many centuries, there was nothing like the taste.

He would never suffer such privation again, the vampire promised himself. He would gorge himself, fatten himself, stuff himself until the hunger was sated, until he was acquitted of the long centuries of starvation and torment.

The Red Duke bared his fangs in a ravenous snarl. There was more blood nearby, he could smell it coursing through terrified hearts, thundering through shivering veins.

All of it would be his, a feast of blood to drown the years of deprivation and agony. Not a man, not a woman, not a child would leave the graveyard. Peasant or noble, they were people no longer, but cattle to be tracked down and slaughtered. Fodder for their dread liege, the Red Duke, rightful master of Aquitaine.

EARL GAUBERT HAD fled along with the rest, dragging Aldric with him. The nobleman's heart pounded with terror as he blundered through the maze-like darkness, uncaring of direction so long as his steps took him away from the monument and the monster his madness had set free.

Yes, the earl admitted, it was his fault, the responsibility was his alone. In his insane lust for revenge he had allowed himself to treat with the forces of darkness and the unholy powers had betrayed him. Instead of evoking the Red Duke's spirit, instead of stealing from that spectre its skill with the blade, Jacquetta and Renar had resurrected the vampire himself in all his terrible glory. Earl Gaubert felt his skin crawl as he remembered the sight of the undead gorging himself upon Jacquetta's blood, of the vampire tossing about one of his bravest and boldest knights as though he were a child.

'My lord, we must hurry,' Aldric advised him when the crippled nobleman's endurance faltered and he leaned upon the cold back of a headstone. There was fear upon the knight's face, only his sense of duty and obligation kept him by the old man's side.

Screams rippled through the night, obscene cries of agony that pierced the very stars with their horror. The vampire was hunting the members of Jacquetta's cult, stalking them among the tombs, battening upon their diseased blood.

Earl Gaubert crumpled beside the headstone, the strength deserting his legs. He covered his face with his hand, tears falling from his eyes. What had he done? What kind of monster had he set loose? The enormity of his shame turned his stomach and he retched into the weeds.

'My lord,' Aldric grabbed his master's shoulder and shook the sick nobleman. 'That thing is still out there, killing everyone it can find! We have to get out of here before it finds us!'

The earl turned bitter eyes on his vassal. 'I deserve to die,' he said. 'For hate's sake, I sent my sons to their deaths. For hate's sake I spat upon my oaths to the Lady and the blessings of the grail. I have committed an unforgivable sin. Without the promise of my protection, the witch and the necromancer would never have dared such an outrage. I am the guilty one. I am ready to pay for my crime.' Earl Gaubert smiled weakly at the knight. 'You have been loyal to the last, Sir Aldric. Run now, escape while you can. Consider your oaths fulfilled and leave an old man to meet the doom he has brought upon himself.'

Aldric shook his head. 'It would be the craven act of a knave to abandon my lord.' The knight helped Earl Gaubert back to his feet. 'We will return to the chateau and muster your knights. Even the Red Duke does not have the power to stand alone against the might of your soldiers.'

His knight's words of martial pride stirred some hope in Earl Gaubert's heart. There was still a chance to undo the evil he had unleashed. They could return with a company of cavalry and scour the graveyard until they brought the vampire to ground. They would destroy the monster and hide the shame Earl Gaubert had brought upon the name d'Elbiq.

A sudden chill gripped the nobleman. He watched as the weeds around the headstone began to wilt. Turning his head, he gasped as he saw a grisly shape standing atop one of the tombs. It was just a dark silhouette, a shadow framed by the sickly light of Morrslieb, but Earl Gaubert could feel the creature's malignant gaze fixed upon him.

'Behind me, my lord!' Aldric shouted, pushing his master around the back of the headstone. The knight brandished his sword, shaking it at the watching shadow. 'Hold your ground, fiend! Sup upon the peasants, but think not to touch my master or I shall send your rotting carcass back to its grave!'

No sound came from the menacing shadow, the creature seeming content to crouch and watch the two Bretonnian nobles. Then with the speed and abruptness of a lightning bolt, the vampire leapt upon his prey, lunging at Aldric with the ferocity of a pouncing lion. The knight's sword was knocked from his grasp as the vampire's shrivelled body smashed into him, the force of the undead monster's impact bearing him to the ground.

The Red Duke's claws gripped either side of Aldric's head. With a single twisting motion, the vampire broke the man's neck. A hiss of satisfaction slithered through the Red Duke's fangs as he rose from the twitching corpse and fixed his fiery gaze upon the cowering figure of Earl Gaubert.

Frantically, the earl tried to draw his sword, in his terror he forgot the infirmity of his crippled arm and tried to grip his weapon as he had before his fateful duel with Count Ergon du Maisne. The palsied fingers refused to close around the sword, the trembling arm refused to draw the blade from its scabbard.

In two steps, the Red Duke reached the pathetic cripple. A sweep of his hand ripped the sword from Earl Gaubert's feeble clutch. The nobleman screamed, stumbling across the graves, trying to keep a line of headstones between himself and the vampire.

Before he had gone twenty feet, the earl collapsed, grabbing at his chest, trying to ease the burning pain that pounded through his body. An old, sickly man, he was not equal to the ordeal he had been put through. Now the earl's terrorized flesh failed him, his weak heart sending waves of pain and weakness through his body.

The Red Duke stared down at the panting, wretched figure of Earl Gaubert. There was no pity in the vampire's eyes, only the merciless hunger of the damned.

CHAPTER V

Screams intruded upon the duke's unquiet sleep, the shrieks of dead and dying men mingling with the fevered night-mares that tormented his mind. El Syf concentrated upon the anguished voices. He used their horror to draw him out from the black borderland of fever, the poisoned world of weakness and slumber that had held him for so long.

By Herculean effort, the knight opened his eyes, blinking as the dim light of his surroundings stung his eyes. He could see the canvas walls of a large pavilion, could smell the wood burning in the belly of a bronze brazier. He was laid out upon a richly appointed bed, thick furs wrapped about his weakened body. The air was hot and arid, yet lacked the fiery malignance of the Arabyan desert. Could it be that he was back in Estalia?

Screams continued to rise from beyond the walls of his tent, mingling with the clash of steel and bestial, chittering cries. The knight recognized the sounds of battle when he heard them, though who or what was fighting, and why, he had no idea. Whatever the nature of the conflict, though, it was not the way of a knight of Bretonnia to sit idly by while there was need of his sword.

El Syf struggled to raise himself from his bed, but even the act of moving his arms from where they were folded across his chest was beyond him. He sagged wearily against his pillow, tears of frustration rolling from his eyes. He tried to focus upon what had happened to him, remembering the poisoned dagger the sheik had stabbed him with, remembering the sinister knight with the dead face who had loomed over him as he lay stricken upon the sand.

Memory was banished from his mind as the duke became aware that he was not alone in his tent. A furtive rustling sound arrested his attention. Wincing against the strain, he managed to tilt his head enough to gain a view of the boxes of supplies stacked in one corner of the tent. Two repulsive figures were crouched over the boxes, their scrawny bodies draped in ragged cloaks, their furry hands rummaging through the contents of each chest as they forced it open.

One of the creatures lifted its head, listening attentively to the screams and sounds of battle raging outside. The cloaked shape turned, cackling to its comrade in a thin, snivelling voice. As it turned, the duke could see its monstrous countenance, the verminous visage of an enormous rat!

The other ratman chittered with amusement as it heard the words of its comrade, then the sharp ears on either side of its head tilted back, flattening against the sides of its skull. The ratman spun about, its beady eyes fixing upon the prostrate figure of El Syf. Black lips pulled away from chisel-like fangs as the skaven hissed angrily. Its furry hand dropped to its waist, pulling a rusty dagger from its belt.

El Syf fought again to move his leaden limbs, his mind screaming as the two ratmen warily crept towards him, blades in their clawed hands. To fall victim to such abominations was enough of an indignity but to lie helpless before them, to be slaughtered like a pig…

The duke struggled to turn his gaze away from the

murderous ratmen. He saw the flap of his tent open. His heart swelled with relief as he watched Marquis Galafre d'Elbiq slip inside the tent. The nobleman's armour was stained with the black blood of skaven; fur and gore caked the sword gripped in his mailed fist. A look of loathing coloured the handsome features of the young marquis as he noticed the skaven creeping towards his prostrate lord.

The duke could have wept with joy as he saw his vassal steal towards the monstrous ratmen. Hope filled the nobleman's breast as he saw his rescue near.

Horror gripped the duke as a change suddenly came over the expression on his vassal's face. From loathing, the face of the marquis fell into an attitude of miserable sorrow. He turned his gaze from the ratmen to the sick bed of his lord. There was pain in the marquis's eyes as he met the duke's imploring stare.

Silently, before the ratmen were aware of his presence, Marquis Galafre d'Elbiq withdrew. He cast one guilty look at the duke before retreating from the tent.

The duke's final hope had been dashed. The man who should have been his rescuer had abandoned him.

Abandoned him to the skaven!

THE RED DUKE stood before the shattered ruin of his monument, staring up at the bronze statue atop the column. Hate shone in the vampire's gaze, a cruel smile spreading across his face. Engorged upon the blood of his victims, the vampire's body was no longer shrivelled and leprous, but flush with the ruddy glow of the life he had drawn from his victims' veins.

The vampire paced back and forth, admiring his handiwork.

Upon the column, the crippled body of Earl

Gaubert d'Elbiq twitched and shuddered, the last of the nobleman's life dripping into the weeds below. Impaled upon the statue's raised sword, Earl Gaubert had taken a surprisingly long time to die. Long enough to satisfy even a vampire's vengeance.

The Red Duke sipped from one of the silver goblets scattered before his tomb and enjoyed the macabre spectacle of the impaled man. Even five hundred years had not been enough to erase the familial resemblance between Earl Gaubert and the man who had betrayed the Red Duke so long ago. The vampire had vowed to scour Aquitaine of the d'Elbiqs, root and branch. Now he was one small step closer to achieving that purpose.

A sudden sound trespassed upon the deathly silence of the graveyard. In a blurring flash of movement, the Red Duke leapt across the grisly altar and the broken husk of Jacquetta, his sword in hand before his feet again touched the earth. The vampire's fangs glistened in the sickly light of Morrslieb as his fiery gaze swept across the tombs.

A man stepped from the shadows, cadaverous in build, the stamp of peasant ugliness about his features. The Red Duke knew this intruder was something more than a humble peasant, however. Only magic could have hidden the mortal from his sight for so long. Only magic could have kept the man safe while the starving vampire had feasted upon the witch and her cult.

'Halt!' the peasant said, his voice deep but betrayed by a tone of trepidation. 'You will do my bidding.' The man raised a grisly talisman, a candle crafted from the hand of a murderer, each of its fingers bursting into light as he evoked its power. 'I, Renar, master of the dark arts command you in the name of Nagash him-self…' The necromancer hesitated as the Red Duke's malignant stare transfixed him. He raised the corpse-candle higher, almost as though to hide behind its feeble light. 'In the name of the Supreme Lord of the Damned…' Renar began again.

The Red Duke threw his head back and laughed, a sound that more resembled the hungry howl of a wolf than anything human. There was no merriment in the vampire's laugh, only malevolence and pitiless hate. Renar cringed as the terrible laughter swept over him.

'Master of the dark arts indeed!' the Red Duke scoffed. With a gesture, he drew upon his own occult powers. The fingers of Renar's corpse candle flickered and died one by one, snuffed out by a spectral wind. The necromancer gasped in terror, recoiling into the doorway of the tomb behind him. The vampire felt a surge of contempt for this craven mortal, this slinking peasant who had the audacity to think he could com-mand the Duke of Aquitaine! For such temerity, the cur should be torn limb from limb! His blood should sate the hunger that yet raged through the vampire's veins!

The Red Duke waved his hand, motioning for his black knights to seize the impudent wretch. He glanced aside, puzzled when his warriors did not answer his command. He raised a hand to his breast, feeling the jagged rent in his armour where the lance of King Louis had pierced his heart. His knights were gone, destroyed upon Ceren Field. The Red Duke fixed his mind upon that fact, trying to dredge it up from the confusion that afflicted his brain.

Only he had survived the battle, and then only because of the foolish sentiment of the king and the occult power of the jewel he wore about his throat. The vampire's hand closed about that jewel, a blood-red stone that had been wrested from the bony fingers of a liche. Its power had sustained the undead horse lords in their barrow mound for a thousand years. Now that power served the Red Duke alone.

The vampire's grim gaze considered the terrified necromancer grovelling before him. The Red Duke's Kingdom of Blood had been shattered, but he would rebuild it. To do that, he would need slaves, even such slaves as this cringing peasant. After all, Renar's magic had played a part in destroying the enchantments that imprisoned him. That spoke well of the necromancer's abilities, if not his good judgement. A true master of the black arts never summoned anything he could not control.

No, the Red Duke decided. It would be rash to kill the peasant out of hand. He could prove useful while the vampire regained his strength.

Renar noted the vampire's indecision and he began to hope that the monster might grant him a reprieve. 'I... I freed you,' Renar said, tossing aside the useless corpse-candle. 'My... it was my magic... that called you back...'

The Red Duke sneered in contempt at the necromancer. 'Your magic? No, mortal, all your magic did was to break the seals that bound me! Know this; for five-hundred years I have endured my prison. Locked inside my own tomb. Unable to escape. Unable to die. Unable to feed!'

'Then... then you must... be grateful...' Renar stammered.

'Perhaps, a few centuries ago,' the Red Duke considered. 'Now I only wonder why a man of your talents did not come sooner to free me.' The vampire's hand clenched about the sword he held, a mad gleam in his eyes.

'I… we… did not know!' Renar insisted. 'Everyone… they said… the king destroyed you!'

The Red Duke advanced towards the necromancer. 'Then why did you disturb my tomb?' he demanded.

Renar blanched at the question, but knew only the truth would possibly save him. 'Earl Gaubert d'Elbiq!' he shouted. 'It was the earl! He sought revenge upon Count Ergon du Maisne! His sons have all been killed by Sir Armand du Maisne, the finest swordsman in Aquitaine. The earl thought that by evoking your spirit, one of his knights might gain the skill to defeat Sir Armand.'

The vampire laughed again. He glanced up at the now still body impaled upon the statue's sword. The Red Duke mockingly saluted the dead Earl Gaubert.

'It would be ungracious of me to ignore my benefactor,' the vampire said. 'And I have my own debt to repay. The d'Elbiqs for trying to kill me. The du Maisnes for letting me live.'

'But Count Ergon has an entire army!' Renar protested. 'He would have accepted a challenge from d'Elbiq, but no knight in all Bretonnia would trifle with the Red Duke! If you show yourself at the Chateau du Maisne, they will send to Duke Gilon for every soldier in Aquitaine!'

The Red Duke scowled at mention of another duke, another pretender to the title that was rightfully his. 'You are right, peasant,' the vampire snarled. 'I shall need an army to do what I must do.' The vampire sheathed his sword and stretched forth his hand. Renar could see the dark energies gathering about the

Red Duke as he drew upon the black arts at his command.

'I shall have my army,' the Red Duke hissed. Renar could see the body of Earl Gaubert's dead knight shiver, the crushed head lolling upon its broken neck as the corpse began to rise. Empty, staring eyes gaped in the knight's bloodless face as he shuffled across the graves. Stiffly, with awkward motions, the zombie bowed before its master.

Other shapes moved among the tombs now, blundering through the graveyard, drawn by the inviolable summons of the vampire's sorcery. The broken, pallid shells of Jacquetta's cult stumbled out from the darkness, their ragged cloaks draped about their bodies like burial shrouds. Last of all came Sir Aldric, his head draped against his shoulder, his eyes unfocused and glazed.

The Red Duke watched the zombies assemble before him. His powers had grown weak after so many centuries of inactivity, sufficient at the moment only to raise the freshly dead. But his strength would return, restored by the blood of innocents. Then, even the ancient dead entombed in the barrows of the horse lords would not be beyond his ability to summon and command.

Renar shook his head as he moved among the zombies. 'We will need more than these,' the necromancer advised. 'Many more.'

'There will be more,' the Red Duke said. An angry look crossed his face and he turned from the necromancer, stalking back towards the monument that had imprisoned him for so long. He glared down at Jacquetta's shattered corpse. Fury twisted the vampire's face out of all human semblance.

'Attend me!' the Red Duke snarled at the lifeless body, enraged that Jacquetta had not risen with the others. 'I am your lord and master! You will attend me!' he clenched his fists above the woman's body, focusing his hideous will upon the defiant corpse.

Dark magic saturated the witch's body, causing it to writhe and jump. A cold light began to shine from the pores of her skin, a spectral luminance that caused the soil around her to blacken. Renar gasped as he watched the furious vampire direct still more power into the corpse, horrified by the amount of magical energy infusing Jacquetta's body. He expected the entire cemetery to be reduced to ash by the forces the Red Duke was drawing upon, both awed and horrified by the magnitude of the vampire's power.

The cold light began to seer away the flesh from Jacquetta's body, exposing the bones within. Even these began to shrivel and blacken, reduced to reeking mush by the arcane forces that engulfed them.

From this liquefied mess, a radiant figure slowly took shape. It was as ethereal as a moonbeam, too fluid and graceful to share the crude stuff of flesh and bone. Renar thought of the Lady venerated by the nobles of Bretonnia and of the mysterious fay who haunted the forest of Athel Loren. But where such visitations had always been described in terms of beauty and warmth, the apparition he gazed upon was hideous and terrible. It was the withered ghost of a woman, her face a leering skull, her black hair flowing behind her like a nest of oily serpents. A nimbus of spectral malignity clung to the phantom, an aura of murderous envy towards the living.

Jacquetta's ghost stared at Renar and her mouth opened in a keening wail. The necromancer screamed as the sound pierced his brain. He could feel the unholy power of that screech draining his vitality, siphoning years from his soul with each passing heartbeat. Hairs fell from Renar's head, wrinkles crawled across his hands as the banshee's wail savaged him.

'Enough!' the Red Duke snarled. At his command, the banshee fell silent, ending its magical assault upon Renar. The necromancer breathed uneasily, horrified by the nearness of his escape. Jacquetta had been a capricious, dangerous woman in life. In death, she had become a baneful harbinger of doom.

The Red Duke stared at his new minion, curious that the witch's spirit had been strong enough to use his magic to restore itself in such a formidable fashion. But her will was not her own. Like the zombies, she would obey without question the commands of her master.

Obedience was the duty of a peasant, whether living or dead.

THE HEAD OF every patron inside the Broken Plough turned as the tavern's ramshackle door was kicked open, several planks being knocked free from their fastenings. They quickly lost interest in the violence of the intruder's entrance when they saw that he was a knight. Nothing good came of inquiring into the business of the nobles and it was the smart man who kept his curiosity tempered by a pot of ale or jug of wine.

The taverner wrung his hands at the damage done to his door, but didn't even think about raising his voice to the armoured warrior who stood in the doorway. Instead he rounded the log he used for a bar and hurried to place himself at the service of his noble guest.

'Sir Leuthere d'Elbiq!' the taverner exclaimed with more exuberance than he felt. 'It is indeed an honour for so noble a personage to visit my humble establishment!' The fat little man tried to be discreet as he wiped his sweaty palms on his apron, mentally calculating just how much money he would owe Earl Gaubert if his lordship had learned how large the tavern's real revenue for the past year had been.

The knight didn't take any notice of the taverner, sweeping his gaze across the common room, studying the peasants huddled on their benches. None of the commoners cared to meet Sir Leuthere's inspection, being careful to keep their faces focused on their drinks. Their attitude didn't bother the knight. He could find the man he was looking for without needing to see his face.

'I fear my humble establishment is too humble to have the fine provision to which you are accustomed, my lord,' the taverner continued to sputter. 'But if you will allow…'

Sir Leuthere marched past the proprietor, leaving him to blink in confusion as the knight made for one of the rear tables. A peasant wearing a grubby cloak that looked to have been cut from a horse blanket was huddled over a clay pot of brackish-tasting wine. He didn't look up until the knight set his hand upon the man's crooked back.

The peasant flinched away from Leuthere's touch, a curse snapping from his lips. The oath died half-finished when he saw that the man accosting him was a knight. His face turning pale, the peasant shrank away until his crooked back was pressed against the wall.

'The kitchen staff told me I might find you here, Vigor,' Leuthere said. 'They also said that five days ago

Earl Gaubert left the castle with you and two of his knights. My uncle and his bodyguards haven't been seen since. Where did they go, Vigor?'

Vigor winced at the question. He reached for the pot of cheap wine on the table. Leuthere's armoured hand slapped the cup from the peasant's trembling fingers, dashing it against the wall.

'Where is he, damn you!' Leuthere snarled.

'I didn't go with him!' Vigor insisted. Seeing his words increase the anger on the knight's face, he quickly abandoned the pretext of ignorance. Vigor glanced across the tavern and lowered his voice. 'I took him to see Jacquetta the wise woman,' he said in a low whisper.

'You mean the witch?' Leuthere gasped, shocked that a lord of Aquitaine would treat with such a vile creature.

Vigor nodded his head. 'I didn't know what Earl Gaubert wanted from her. By the Lady, I swear I didn't! When I found out... I left him... I slipped away when his lordship wasn't looking...'

The knight's face became livid. Turning away from the trembling Vigor, he fixed his furious gaze upon the taverner. 'Your establishment is now closed, Pierre! Clear every filthy peasant from this pig-sty, and that includes you and your staff! I want to speak to this worm alone.'

Ashen-faced, the peasants did not need Pierre's encouragement to vacate the Broken Plough, fairly falling over one another as they quit the premises. Soon, Leuthere had the solitude he had demanded. Discussing the dishonour of his uncle was not the sort of subject for prying ears... even those of mere peasants.

Leuthere grabbed the front of Vigor's tunic, pulling the blubbering man to his feet. 'A peasant can be hanged for abandoning his lord!' he snarled.

'Mercy!' Vigor cried, grovelling at the knight's feet. 'I did not want to abandon his lordship! If I had known why he wanted to see her... why he needed the witch...'

'Why did Earl Gaubert go to see Jacquetta?' Leuthere asked, inwardly dreading the answer he might hear. For a knight of Bretonnia to stoop so low as to employ black magic to avenge himself upon his enemy was a stain that would impinge not only the earl's honour but that of the entire d'Elbiq line. Leuthere considered that his uncle must be mad to set upon so infamous a path.

Vigor shook his head, an inarticulate moan rising from his trembling body. 'I cannot tell you! I cannot tell anyone! Do not make me, my lord!'

Leuthere jerked the peasant back to his feet, glaring into Vigor's face. 'You'll tell me if I have to drag you to the dungeons of the chateau!' He felt a tinge of sympathy when he saw the effect mention of the castle's torture chamber had upon Vigor. It was almost as if the man's twisted body were already stretched out upon the rack.

'No! No! I'll talk, my lord!' Vigor whined. 'Hang me, take my head, but don't send me to the Black Room!' The peasant glanced guiltily about the tavern. He didn't want to betray the confidence of Earl Gaubert. He had enough loyalty to his lord to spare Earl Gaubert that indignity if he could.

Vigor's voice dropped to a feeble whisper, forcing Leuthere to strain to catch every word. When he heard what the peasant had to say, the knight understood the reason for Vigor's hushed tones.

'Earl Gaubert seeks the tomb of the Red Duke,' Vigor said. 'He hopes to use the Red Duke's power against the du Maisnes.'

Leuthere released his grip on the peasant's tunic. Icy horror ran down his spine. First a witch, now a vampire! The thirst for revenge had driven his uncle insane!

'The Red Duke was destroyed by King Louis the Righteous,' Leuthere stated. 'The vampire burned with the rest of his unholy army.'

Vigor shook his head, staring guiltily at the floor. 'Jacquetta said that a monument was built to the Red Duke, a place to trap his spirit. That is where she took Earl Gaubert.'

The knight glared down at the crook-backed peasant. 'Then that is where you are going to take me,' he told Vigor. Inwardly, Leuthere prayed to the Lady, prayed that he would be in time to stop his uncle.

After five days, however, he knew he would be too late. Barring a miracle, whatever evil could come from Earl Gaubert's madness had already been set into motion.

THE AFTERNOON SUN did not brighten the gloomy atmosphere of the graveyard overlooking Ceren Field. Sir Leuthere could feel the clammy fetor of the place oozing through his armour, seeping through his skin and into his very bones. The feeling sickened him, made his flesh crawl in a way he hadn't felt since he was a headstrong knight errant scouring abandoned villages for ghouls and dereliches. The sensation of inhuman evil and dark magic was something a man did not forget.

Leuthere glanced back down the grassy slope of the hill to the old tree where they had tethered their mounts. The animals had refused to be led any closer to the graveyard, forcing Leuthere and Vigor to hike up the side of the hill. Such timidity from Vigor's burro wasn't especially surprising. Like the peasant, a burro was not endowed with a sense of courage and valour. But for Leuthere's magnificent destrier Gaignun to show fear was something that shocked the knight. Gaignun had been his steed for five years, had fought with him against orcs and beastmen many times and never shown a moment's hesitation when charging headlong into the enemy.

The mounts were not the only animals repulsed by the unnatural taint surrounding the graveyard. Entire stretches of the hillside were black with crows, the scavenger birds drawn to the cemetery by the stench of death but too frightened to descend upon the tombs. It was an eerie sight that did nothing to ease Leuthere's nerves or quell his fears for his uncle. Whatever doubts he had that Jacquetta had really led Earl Gaubert to the secret grave of the Red Duke were quickly fading away.

The two men marched into the sinister silence of the graveyard, the last warmth of the afternoon sun abandoning them as they moved among the graves. Leuthere felt his pulse quicken as he noticed a dark splotch splashed across one of the headstones. Vigor hurried to the grave, setting his hand against the discoloured stone. He rubbed his fingers as a crusty substance adhered to his skin. His face was grim when he announced his discovery.

'Blood, my lord,' Vigor said. 'About three, maybe four days old,' he added as he considered how dry the material was. Before his injury, Vigor had been one of Earl Gaubert's most trusted servants and had often been called upon to attend the nobleman on his hunts. Leuthere was ready to trust Vigor's estimate regarding time.

The knight looked hard at the graves around him. All of them seemed somehow too ignominious to be the tomb of the Red Duke. He didn't know what to expect the secret grave of a vampire to look like, but somehow he felt he would know it if he saw it.

'Let's press on,' Leuthere said, pointing deeper into the maze of tombs. Vigor blanched at his words, but the peasant's contrition was genuine. He did regret setting Earl Gaubert upon this path and would make amends if he could. If that meant following Sir Leuthere straight into a vampire's lair, then so be it.

The sun was just beginning its descent when the two men finally reached the marble column at the heart of the graveyard. Throughout the afternoon, they had followed a winding course among the graves, sometimes finding more evidence of old violence, sometimes even discovering a discarded sword or broken dagger. Vigor had identified one of the knives as belonging to a man named Perren, one of Jacquetta's followers.

As soon as he set eyes upon the column, Leuthere knew they had found what they were looking for. Intuition, foreboding, whatever strange humour worked upon his mind, the knight knew that it was here the vampire had been entombed. It was here that Earl Gaubert had come to seek vengeance upon Count Ergon and Sir Armand. It was here that the honour of the d'Elbiqs had been shattered. As shattered as the broken face of the column.

'Shallya's mercy!' exclaimed Vigor, pointing in horror at the statue atop the monument. Leuthere followed the peasant's gesture and felt his blood grow cold. There was a body impaled upon the statue's upthrust sword, a body that he recognized only too well.

Earl Gaubert had found what he had sought, and it had destroyed him. Leuthere, like all the children of Aquitaine, had been reared on tales of the Red Duke's evil. He could still remember accounts of the forest the vampire had erected around Castle Aquin, a forest made from the impaled bodies of those who had resisted his murderous rule. Five hundred years in the grave had not lessened the vampire's appetite for horror.

'I have to get him down,' Leuthere said, his voice a sullen growl. Whatever his uncle's crimes, it offended his very soul to see the earl's body treated with such disrespect. Leuthere knelt before the column, beginning to remove his armour so that he might climb the monument more easily.

'It would be wiser to leave him where he is,' a sepulchral voice intoned from among the graves.

Leuthere swung about, his sword at the ready. Vigor worked a dagger from his belt and positioned himself where he might guard the knight's flank. Both men glared defiantly at the dark figure standing between two granite tombs. How long the other man had been standing there, neither of them could guess.

The stranger strode out from the shadows, revealing himself to be a powerfully built man dressed in black armour, a dark surcoat marked with the figure of a raven billowing about him in the breeze. Both Leuthere and Vigor breathed a sigh of relief when they saw the knight was dressed in black and grey. They had feared the stranger would be clad in crimson.

'That is my uncle up there,' Leuthere challenged the black knight. 'Spitted like a snail upon a stick!'

'Kin or liege, you would do well to leave him up there,' the black knight warned. To illustrate his point, the knight reached down and grabbed a rock. He cast the stone at the monument, striking the leg of the impaled corpse. Earl Gaubert's body thrashed into motion, pawing and scrabbling wildly.

For an instant Leuthere believed his uncle might still be alive, but the ghastly way in which Earl Gaubert's body had been mutilated and the even more horrible way in which he now moved made the knight realise the hideous truth. His uncle was dead, and his body had been abused in a manner more foul than Leuthere could have imagined.

'If you will leave him until midnight, I shall bring him down myself,' the black knight offered. 'I know a ritual that will banish the corruption that infests your uncle's remains. Then, perhaps, his spirit can know some peace.'

'You would have my gratitude, if you can do what you say,' Leuthere told the strange knight.

'I can. I am Sir Maraulf, Custodian of the Chapel Sereine,' the knight said, bowing to Leuthere. 'The dead have few secrets I do not know.'

Sir Leuthere shook his head. He had heard dim rumours of a knight who had taken residence in a village called Mercal, but he had never given them much credit. 'If you know so much, then perhaps you can tell me what did this to Earl Gaubert d'Elbiq?' he demanded.

'You already know what did this,' Sir Maraulf said.

'By accident or design, your uncle has unleashed an evil that has not been seen in these lands for centuries. That evil has gone, for now, vanished into the darkness to bide its time and gather its strength. In the past months, I have come often to this graveyard, drawn by a fear I could not place. But at the last, I was too late to prevent the doom I feared.'

Sir Maraulf fixed his stern gaze upon Leuthere. 'Three nights ago, my premonition grew too great to ignore. I rode here from Mercal in the dead of night, but I was too late. The evil had already been unleashed. All that I could do was remain and bring peace to the poor soul who had been left behind by the monster he had released.'

Leuthere replaced his sword in its sheath, casting a forlorn glance at the scrabbling thing atop the monument. 'On behalf of my lord, I thank you for your vigil,' Leuthere said. 'But would it not be better to track down the thing that did this?'

'The "thing" you speak of has a name, though now you fear to use it,' Maraulf said. 'There are any number of shadowy places to which the Red Duke may have gone. Too many for one, or even two knights to search. And there is no guarantee that the knights would succeed in their quest. Few things are more dangerous than a vampire fighting on its own ground.'

Leuthere clenched his fist. 'Then we just allow the Red Duke to escape?'

Maraulf shook his head. 'That would be an evil even greater than releasing him. No, we prepare ourselves. The Red Duke will not hide for long. He will strike when his hate and his madness grow too strong to deny.' The black knight pointed at Leuthere. 'You must ride to Duke Gilon and warn him of the menace that is abroad in his lands. It will be hard to convince the duke that this evil has returned to again plague Aquitaine, but you must prevail.'

Leuthere nodded in agreement. 'I will seek an audience with Duke Gilon, but what will you do?'

'I will return to Mercal,' the black knight stated. 'I will return to the Chapel Sereine and prepare it to withstand the Red Duke's attack.'

'How can you be so certain the Red Duke will come to you?' objected Vigor, his doubt causing him to forget his place and trespass upon the conversation between the knights.

Maraulf fixed his cold gaze on the peasant. 'The Red Duke will come to Mercal,' he said. 'He will come because he left something there five hundred years ago.'

CHAPTER VI

It sat upon a lone hill at the edge of the Forest of Châlons. The River Morceaux knifed its way around the western approach to the hill, ripping a deep fissure through the limestone, a great canyon hundreds of feet deep. The river curled away to the north, continuing its winding course to its headwaters high in the Massif Orcal.

The hill was a rocky, lifeless mound of stone, its soil swept away into the river by the merciless violence of wind and rain. Even the most desperate shepherd could find no pasture for his flock upon the barren hill. Only vultures and panthers made their lairs among the dead rock, using the higher vantage point to sniff out prey in the valley below.

If not for the accident of its location, the dead hill would have been left to crumble into the river roaring at its feet. However, the hill presented too valuable a position to be ignored. The vantage it offered was something valuable to more than vultures and panthers. From the hill, sentinels could observe the high passes within the Massif Orcal and watch the borders of the sinister Forest of Châlons. A vigil maintained upon the hill could pass warning quickly to Aquitaine about enemies mustering to raid into the pastures and vineyards of the dukedom. The threat of goblins and orcs descending from the mountains was an ever present one and the presence of beastmen deep in the interior of the forest was not to be discounted.

So it was, in the earliest days of the dukedom that a stone tower had been erected upon the hill, entrusted to a margrave whose fief was close to the site. For many generations, the tower was maintained, but as years passed without the feared incursion of marauding monsters, the margraves began to neglect their duty. From a garrison of knights and archers, the tower's defences dwindled to a single man-at-arms whose chief duty was to collect tolls from peasants seeking to shelter from storms within the decaying fort.

Looking upon the hill from the plain below, the Red Duke did not see its crumbling walls and broken gate. He saw what the old dukes of Aquitaine had seen: a position that could be fortified and held against almost any army. Bordered on two sides by a sheer precipice and the River Morceaux, an attacking army would find its options for siege limited. Anyone doing so would be forced to put his back to the Massif Orcal and the danger of having a horde of greenskins set upon him from the rear. The longer such a siege went on, the greater the likelihood of drawing out the goblins and orcs who infested the mountains. A prepared defender could do more than withstand his enemy here. He could break them.

The vampire smiled, running his armoured hand along the fleshless neck of his steed, forgetting that El Morzillo no longer had a mane to stroke. The Estalian warhorse had died in Araby, his bones bleaching under the desert sun. It was the phantom of his faithful steed that served him now, conjured from the shadow world beyond death by the ghastly powers now at the vampire's command. El Morzillo had answered his master's call, returning to the Red Duke as a grisly nightmare of bone and sinew, balefire burning in the depths of its skull, smoke flaring from its jaws.

The Red Duke turned in his saddle, glaring at those who followed him. The mortals trembled as his gaze fell upon them. The undead simply stared back at him with their lifeless eyes, waiting for their master's command.

The vampire's eyes lingered upon the twisted face of Baron de Gavaudan. The baron had been the first victim of the Red Duke's bite – the assassin sent to kill the rightful Duke of Aquitaine had been fortunate to have his life choked out of him. The Red Duke had not intended Baron de Gavaudan to rise as a vampire. Perhaps that explained the grotesque results of the baron's resurrection. The baron's skin was split and decayed, looking as though it had been six weeks in the grave. His arm was a shrivelled lump cradled against his chest, one of his legs as immobile as a lump of steel. One side of the baron's face was paralysed, a stream of treacle dripping constantly from his slackened mouth. When the baron looked at something, only one eye moved, the other frozen into a vulturine stare.

Moreover, Baron de Gavaudan sported another debility. He was utterly without a will of his own, a thrall completely dominated by the demands the Red Duke made upon him. The Red Duke had exploited the baron's unresisting nature, at least when he had tired of torturing the wretch. Under interrogation, the thrall had eagerly confessed the plot against the man who had been El Syf – at least as much of it as the baron's broken mind could remember.

'Bring the cattle forward,' the Red Duke snarled at his drooling lieutenant. The lesser vampire giggled inanely as he set spurs into the decayed sides of his undead steed and moved back down the trail.

The Red Duke regarded Baron de Gavaudan for a few seconds, then turned to face one of his mortal retainers. Many knights had flocked to the Red Duke's banner, *drawn by tales of his martial prowess and the cowardly attempt to usurp his domain from him. The vampire was more than willing to make use of such men, but he knew the strict codes they lived by. Whatever oaths they swore to him, there were other vows that might make them falter in his service. Fortunately, he had found other servants who were not so strict about matters of honour.*

Sir Corbinian was such a man, a refugee from the dukedom of Moussillon. He was a wanted man, declared outlaw by his own father for an outrage perpetrated against a Shallyan priestess. Corbinian had escaped custody, killing his brother in the process and fleeing to Aquitaine. Whatever chivalry the knight had ever possessed had died inside him long ago, replaced with a brutal sadism that made him a perfect vassal for a vampire.

The Red Duke addressed the grim-faced knight. 'You will take your men-at-arms and surround the hill. Let the scum know that if so much as one worker leaves the site, I will send ten of them to take their place.' The vampire glanced back at the hill, noting the sharp precipice that bordered it on two sides. 'If any of the workers want to leave, they are free to choose the river.'

Wailing cries and the sharp snap of whips heralded the return of Baron de Gavaudan. The vampiric thrall led a motley crowd of terrified Aquitainians flanked by decayed zombies and grinning skeletons. There were several hundred people in the column, the ragged tatters of their clothes ranging from the shawls of farmers to the cloaks of vintners and the bright tunics of merchants. Even the royal colours of the nobility could be seen clinging to the shivering bodies of several of the Red Duke's 'cattle'. As the crowd marched, half-drunk mercenaries urged them forwards with vicious snaps of cow-hide whips.

The Red Duke raised his hand and the column came

to a stop. He closed his eyes, savouring the stench of fear and despair that rose from the wretched throng. His mind revelled in the sobs of the women and the cries of the children. It was right that these vermin should suffer, it was right that they should know the pain and hopelessness that burned in his breast. These scum had stood aside and allowed Baron de Gavaudan's plot to unfold, believing his lies and supporting the king's claim upon Aquitaine.

How many of them had watched his wife fling herself from the parapets of Castle Aquin? How many of them had seen her broken body lying sprawled upon the flagstones? How many of them had listened to her wailing in despair night after night, weeping for the husband liars had told her was dead?

The vampire's hand clenched about the hilt of his sword. He could cut them down, all of them. He could butcher them as he had butchered the Arabyans at the Battle of Magritta. He could leave their carcasses strewn across Aquitaine, fodder for the wolves and ravens. Yes, he could kill them all, but then their suffering would be over.

And for these vermin, their ordeal had only begun.

'There is an old quarry at the base of the mountain,' the Red Duke stated, pointing at the craggy feet of the Massif Orcal. 'First you will tear down the ruin standing on this hill. Then you will bring stone from the mountain and build a new castle for your rightful lord. Day and night, fair weather and foul, you will work and you will build my castle. Forget the gods and the Lady, their words mean nothing to you now. The only words you will listen to now are the directions of my engineers and architects. Fail them, and discover what suffering really is.'

Murmurs of horror swept through the crowd, wails of anguish rose from the women, the elderly fell to their knees and began to pray. One of the slaves, the rags of a *nobleman's tunic draped about his shoulders, pushed his way forwards.*

'Please, your grace, we beg you for mercy,' the man sobbed. 'We have given you no offence, your grace. We will serve you loyally, as loyally as we did when…' The spokesman caught himself.

'When I was alive?' the vampire asked, finishing the nobleman's thought. There was no forgiveness in the Red Duke's eyes.

The spokesman turned, clutching at the stirrup of Baron de Gavaudan's decayed steed. 'At least spare the children and the women!' he begged. 'Show them some pity!'

The baron's reply was another mad giggle. The half of his mouth that worked pulled back to expose a gleaming fang. The vampire reached down to seize the impertinent slave.

'No,' the Red Duke's stern voice froze his thrall, allowing the spokesman to scramble away from the baron. 'This man does not deserve the mercy of a quick death. He will stay here and be spared the labour of his friends and neighbours. He will watch them slave to build my castle, will watch as they die one by one. And when the last stone has been laid and the castle is complete, he will be tied to a horse and sent into the mountains for the goblins to make sport of.'

The vampire's pallid face spread in a malignant grin. 'Before death finds you, you will wish I had let you build my castle.'

THE CRAC DE Sang still stood upon its hill overlooking the River Morceaux and the Forest of Châlons. Time had eroded the cliffs, casting some of the old hill down into the precipice. The castle itself had fallen into ruin, razed by the victorious armies of King Louis after the Battle of Ceren Field, looted by orcs and goblins after the Bretonnian army rode away.

The vampire stared up at the spiked battlements of his castle, the thick walls of granite, the soaring towers riddled with arrow slits, the thick gates of oak banded in steel. The road leading up to the hill was paved in the bones of those who defied him, flanked to either side by the twitching husks of his enemies impaled upon tall stakes. At night, the husks would be soaked in pitch and set alight, an avenue of corpse-candles to light the Red Duke's domain.

King Louis would never break him, not in a thousand years. The Red Duke would defy the treacherous usurper. He would not rest until he had broken the hypocrite, until he had brought ruin upon all the realm. The king would live only long enough to see Bretonnia become the Red Duke's Kingdom of Blood. Louis would know the price of evil then, the wage paid by all those who betrayed the blood.

Renar stared anxiously at the vampire upon his spectral steed, unnerved by the strange way the Red Duke stared at the ruins upon the hill. There was an almost fanatical intensity in the vampire's gaze. Renar quietly shifted away from his gruesome master, watching him carefully as he made his retreat.

'Go to the castle and announce me,' the Red Duke declared, waving his hand through the air.

Renar glanced at the hill and the pile of collapsed walls and broken towers. Nervously he looked about him. The animated bodies of Earl Gaubert's bodyguards and Jacquetta's dark cult stood in a double file behind the Red Duke's horse. The zombies made no motion to obey the vampire. Renar cast a hopeful eye towards Jacquetta, but the ghostly banshee continued to flit aimlessly along the path, muttering to itself.

That was when his heart sank, because he knew the Red Duke intended his command for the only living thing among his grisly retinue.

'My lord,' Renar said, bowing before the vampire. 'The castle is in ruin. There is nothing but rats and spiders living up there now.'

The Red Duke glared at the necromancer, his fingers closing about the hilt of his sword. 'Do as you are told, peasant,' the vampire snarled. 'Sir Corbinian will be eager to receive me.'

Renar scratched his head as he studied the wrecked fortress. One look at the Red Duke convinced him that whatever his opinion of this fool's errand, there would be decidedly unpleasant consequences if he delayed any longer. Unless Sir Corbinian was a rock lizard, Renar didn't think the vampire was going to find anyone waiting for him.

The necromancer sighed and began the long march across the rubble-strewn path that climbed up from the valley to the top of the hill. With every step, with each desolate pile of broken masonry he passed, Renar felt more perturbed. Surely the Red Duke understood there was nothing here.

Halfway to the shattered castle gates, Renar heard a scuttling sound rising from the darkened halls of the fortress. He hesitated, feeling his skin crawl as he felt unseen eyes watching him. Nervously, the necromancer looked over his shoulder and cast an imploring gaze towards the Red Duke. The vampire was unmoved by Renar's anxiety, waving his hand impatiently, gesturing for the man to hurry about his errand.

A low hoot echoed from the ruins, followed by more scuttling footsteps and the clatter of falling stone. Renar licked his lips, his mind turning over the spells he'd spent his life learning and considering which of these magics would be the most beneficial should something suddenly lunge at him from the darkness.

Renar was still trying to remember the full incantation that would cause a man's skin to blacken and shrivel when something suddenly lunged at him from the darkness.

A charnel stink struck the necromancer first, a stench so foul that even the grave-robbing sorcerer was sickened by it. Then a wiry body smashed into him, pitching him to the earth. Renar landed hard, his bony arse slashed by a sharp piece of stone. He yelped as the rock cut him, but the exclamation was quickly stifled when a set of fangs snapped at his face. Renar quickly forgot about his bruised backside.

The necromancer crossed his arms and tried to push away the slavering thing that crouched atop him. Its build was thin and emaciated, even more so than the necromancer's sickly frame, but there was a ghastly strength in the creature's limbs, more than enough to defy Renar's efforts to shove it off of him.

Other creatures came scuttling out from the shadows, some loping on all fours like starveling jackals, others creeping about in a hunched, manlike fashion. The things were hairless and naked, their pasty skin blotched with sores and scabs, their faces pinched and distorted. Their hands ended in long black claws, the teeth in their mouths were sharpened like fangs. There was little in the way of intelligence in the beady, hungry eyes that fixed upon Renar's struggling frame.

The necromancer recognized the creatures in an instant. Many times he had encountered their like, slinking about graveyards, trying to gorge themselves upon freshly interred bodies. They were ghouls, debased men whose bodies and souls had been corrupted by the hideous provender they had gorged themselves upon. Renar had driven their like from a dozen cemeteries, routing the cowardly ghouls with a display of magic, driving them back into the shadows and leaving the necromancer free to conduct his own morbid researches in peace.

This was different, however. The necromancer had done more than disturb these ghouls at their dinner. He had trespassed into their lair, the decaying ruin they called home. There was just enough of a man lurking within their diseased brains that the ghouls would fight for their home.

With a moment to prepare himself, Renar might have driven the ghouls back, but the necromancer had been taken by surprise, his thoughts on the distemper of the Red Duke rather than the ruins and what might be hiding within. That was a mistake that had left the Bretonnian helpless before his feral attackers.

The ghoul atop his chest snarled something that sounded horribly like the word 'Supper' in a glottal sort of debased Breton. The cannibal's mouth spread impossibly wide, displaying the rows of sharpened teeth. A string of drool spattered onto Renar's cheek as the ghoul leaned over him.

Suddenly, the ghoul's hideous face was wrenched away, the creature's hungry leer dissolving into an expression of shock. Renar could hear the other ghouls wailing and shrieking as they scurried back into the darkness, abandoning their fellow to the malignant force that had seized him.

El Morzillo's spectral hoofs clattered about the broken tiles of the courtyard, the skeletal warhorse cantering in a wide circle through the ruins. Upon the horse's back, the Red Duke towered, his right hand closed about the scruff of the ghoul's neck, effortlessly holding the struggling cannibal off the ground. The vampire scowled at the rancid creature, his face pulled back in an attitude of noble disdain.

'You dare foul this place with your filth?' the Red Duke hissed. 'The Crac de Sang is my refuge, my bastion against traitors and usurpers! By what right do peasants trespass in my domain!'

The ghoul continued to flail about in the vampire's grip. The Red Duke dashed the creature to the paving stones, its skull cracking open as it struck the ground. A pool of blood began to form around the ghoul's twitching body.

The Red Duke dropped from his saddle in a fluid dismount any knight of Bretonnia would envy. Instantly the vampire marched towards the dead ghoul. His breath was ragged, at once violent and excited. He paced towards the pool of blood, his eyes staring longingly at the crimson liquid pouring from the corpse. The Red Duke's face crinkled in disgust and he turned his back to the vile carcass. He started to walk away, then turned back towards the gory scene. Three steps towards the pool of blood and the vampire reasserted control over himself. Angrily he turned away from the ghoul's body.

'De Gavaudan!' the Red Duke bellowed. 'The stupid peasant bitch has spilled the wine!' The vampire's words boomed through the ruined courtyard. 'Pull the fingers from her hand one by one and feed them to her!' The vampire glared up at crumbled walls and broken battlements. 'De Gavaudan! Attend me you faithless coward!'

Renar rose from the ground and watched as the Red Duke roared at the ruins, his fury mounting with each moment. A horrible thought occurred to the necromancer: if the vampire did not find the men he was calling for, then he might direct his rage towards the only person around.

Discreetly, Renar crept away from the courtyard and back down the winding path. He'd decided it might be safer to wait in the valley below with Jacquetta and the zombies.

The Red Duke prowled through the corridors of his castle, feeling the rich carpet sink beneath his armoured feet. His long crimson cape billowed out behind him, brushing against the bare stone walls at either side of the hall, sometimes upsetting the vibrant portraits and rich tapestries adorning them. The vampire had liberated these heirlooms of his ancient family from the galleries of Castle Aquin where they had hung undisturbed for generations. He had brought them to Crac de Sang not simply as plunder or for the greedy pleasure of hoarded wealth. He had kept them with him because they were a link to his past, something that allowed him to remember who his family was.

Who he was.

Daily, the Red Duke could feel the hungry darkness inside him growing, devouring his identity with cancerous persistence. The hate within his heart remained strong, but the sorrow that had fed that hate was fading away, vanishing a little more with each dawn. It was an effort now for the vampire to recall the smell of his wife's hair, the feel of her fingers clasped in his. The thought that one day he would lose even the memory of her voice tormented him like a hot iron pressed against his skin.

The Red Duke's sweeping march down the corridor came to a stop. He turned and faced the wall, his eyes staring keenly at a pair of portraits hanging above a cherrywood table. The portrait on the right was that of a stern young knight, proud and bold in his expression. There had been a time when the vampire had seen this face looking back at him from any mirror he held. Now there was only a grisly shadow that glared back at him from the single looking glass he had allowed to remain within his castle.

Swiftly the vampire turned his face from his painting, his eager eyes racing to the canvas upon which the smiling face of his wife would beam down upon him, shining some light into the darkness that had become his soul.

THE RED DUKE'S armoured hands reached towards a pile of rubble, passing through the empty space where had once hung the most precious treasure in all Crac de Sang. His desperate eyes scoured the desolation, fighting to deny the terror that threatened to crush the vampire's shrivelled heart.

An anguished howl echoed through the ruins of the vampire's castle. The Red Duke fell to his knees beside the collapsed wall, his fingers clawing at the ground, gouging furrows in the flagstones. Tears fell from the monster's eyes as he raised his face and stared desolately at the emptiness where once had hung the portrait of Duchess Martinga. Another pained wail sounded from the vampire as he pressed his clenched fists to his eyes.

The face of his wife was gone, lost to the shadows that had devoured his soul. The Red Duke had needed her portrait to anchor her image in his mind, to make her something more than a cold dead memory. As the vampire's tormented cries scattered into the darkness, he knew it was not the woman he mourned, but rather the emotion that time and the curse of the undead had stolen from him. He could remember his love for her, the pain of her loss, the fury of his revenge, but he could not *feel* them now. The last fragile link between the man and the monster had been lost.

The Red Duke rose from the dusty floor, rage replacing sorrow upon his drawn features. His armoured fist cracked against one of the standing walls, dislodging a stream of debris and causing a ten foot section to crash to the ground. The vampire stalked away from the cloud of dust that rose from the wreckage, his wrath growing with each step. All of his treasures and riches were gone, his great fortress cast into ruin. Those responsible for such destruction would rue the day of their birth and beg for the mercy of death before the vampire was done with them.

The great hall stretched before him, its marble floor carpeted in the bloodied tabards and surcoats of fallen knights. A line of tall columns flanked the room; upon each face of each pillar was chained the dead and dying wreckage of those who had dared to oppose him. Rats gnawed at the captives, worms writhed in their open wounds. The despairing moans of the wretched shuddered through the hall. Some called out to the Lady for mercy, others cursed their oaths and tried to swear allegiance to their captor. One knight, more stalwart than most, had tried to end his suffering by swallowing his own tongue. He had been caught before he could die, restored to life by the vampire's dark arts. Now the knight could only cough curses on the Red Duke with the ragged stump of tongue left to him.

The vampire found the glottal noise soothing as he sat at his table and supped among the dying. It was a particular delight to bring the daughters of his enemies to his table, to fete the ladies with a sumptuous feast before the famished eyes of their tortured sires. Those who had been the Red Duke's prisoner long knew how the dinner would end, watching with mounting horror as the vampire spurned all meat and wine placed upon the table. The Red Duke would watch them as he leaned back in his claw-footed throne, savouring every exquisite twinge of despair on the faces of his prisoners.

In the end, the vampire would tire of his entertainment. Then he would slake his hunger. A clap of his hands would bring the decayed husks of his servants lumbering into the great hall. The zombies in their immaculate livery would attend the Red Duke's table. First they would seize his dinner guest, stripping from her whatever rich gown the vampire had drawn from his wife's wardrobe to accentuate the appearance of his victim. There would be a moment of shocked horror when the zombies seized the girl, followed by the impotent threats and pleas of the knightly prisoners. Then a moment of outraged disbelief as the clumsy cadavers ripped the clothing from the struggling girl's body.

Trembling and naked, the Red Duke's guest would be laid upon the table. Tethers would bind her flailing hands, chains would be locked about her kicking feet. A living servant would attach the chain to the hook hanging inconspicuously from the ceiling while a brawny zombie worked the wheel set into the rear wall. The girl would be pulled upwards, her terror mounting with each shuddering creak of the wheel. Inch by inch, she would be pulled towards the ceiling, but only far enough to suit the Red Duke's needs.

With a grandiose flourish of his cape, the Red Duke would rise from his seat and draw a steel dagger from his belt. He would never use the edge against his victim, instead employing the sharp point to stab a delicate-seeming cut in the side of her neck. The cut would just penetrate the artery

*beneath the sobbing girl's smooth skin, allowing blood to
flow freely and copiously from the wound.*

*The Red Duke always used a crystal goblet to catch the
dripping blood, and always remembered to toast his captive
audience as he drank his late dinner guest dry.*

THE RED DUKE shook his head to clear his thoughts,
staring in confusion at the empty hand that a
moment before had held a goblet of blood. He cast
his gaze across the sad wreck of his great hall. The
pillars had been cast down, the long table and claw-
footed throne rotted away into ruin. He could see the
iron wheel set into the back wall, now corroded into
a lump of crumbling rust.

Crac de Sang had been destroyed. The vampire
remembered that now. An enemy had breeched the
walls, sacked and plundered his mighty fortress. The
question remained. Who had done this, and how?
When he had departed to drive the usurper's army
from Aquitaine, the Red Duke had entrusted the safe-
guarding of his castle to Sir Corbinian.

*'Have mercy, my lord!' Corbinian's shout echoed through
the damp confines of the dungeon.*

*The Red Duke turned away from the sinister device he
had been hovering over. It resembled a long wooden table,
its surface covered by barbed hooks. At either end of the
table, a great winch was fastened. Dried blood coated the
table and the floor beneath it. The flickering torches set
into the walls of the dungeon illuminated every ghastly
inch of the rack, the device its sadistic Arabyan creator had
named 'the fingers of hell'.*

*The vampire approached the wall to which his errant
vassal had been chained. He paused just beyond reach of*

the imprisoned knight. Corbinian knew it was useless to try to reach his tormentor, but that did not stop him from trying. The Red Duke sneered at the man's futile effort to push his body away from the wall and get his hands around the vampire's throat.

'I am the one who disobeyed you!' Corbinian pleaded. 'She's done nothing to you! Let her go!'

For a moment, the Red Duke smiled at Corbinian, almost as though considering the knight's entreaty. Then the vampire's lips parted, exposing his cruel fangs. 'The wench was marked to die the moment I took her from her father's castle. You knew that, yet you chose to defy me.'

'Please, your grace, spare her!'

The Red Duke scowled at his captive. 'Love is a poor thing to own,' the vampire hissed. He gestured with one of his gloved hands. Henchmen shuffled out from the darkness, their faces hidden beneath leather hoods. Between them, the torturers held the limp body of a young woman. The Red Duke watched his men lead their prisoner towards the table, then turned to glare at Corbinian. 'Everything a man loves dies,' the vampire said. 'Everything he values must turn to dust. It is only the things inside a man that he can keep with him always. Things like loyalty and honour.'

'I admit I broke faith with you!' wailed Corbinian. 'I know I have wronged you! But punish me, not her!'

The vampire turned away again to watch as the torturers lifted the unconscious woman onto the table. Her body flinched as the barbed hooks jabbed into her skin. The men had been quite thorough in their earlier attentions to her, but she would regain consciousness soon enough. The fingers of hell would see to that.

'Do you know this device?' the Red Duke asked Corbinian. 'It is an Arabyan invention, used to punish those who violate the harem of a Caliph. The offender is placed *upon the table, the hooks latch themselves upon her skin. Then her arms are tied to the pulley at the head of the table. As the winch turns, she is dragged across the hooks and the skin is flayed from her body. It takes a long time. Sometimes the Arabyans will pardon the offender if they endure the pain well enough. But I think I shall ignore that tradition.'*

Corbinian lunged at the vampire again, his chains rattling as they wrenched him back against the wall. 'I will kill you!' the knight swore. 'If I have to claw my way back from the pits of Morr, I will kill you!'

The Red Duke smiled at the knight. 'Pay particular attention to her suffering, because you will be next. And after you die, I shall help you claw your way back from the pits of Morr. I think you will serve me much more faithfully once you are beyond the distractions of the flesh.'

'CORBINIAN!' THE RED Duke shouted, his commanding voice booming from the shattered halls of his castle. Bats fluttered from the broken windows of the remaining tower, frightened by his voice. A scrawny wolf loped away from a pile of masonry, a whining pup clenched in its jaws. 'Corbinian!' the vampire shouted again.

The clatter of disturbed rubble was the only sound to rise from the ruins. As the Red Duke's attention was drawn to the rubble, his supernatural senses told him he had located the long-dead knight. With a hurried stride, the vampire marched to the pile of debris. He could see the outline of steps protruding from under the rubble. Once, this stairway had connected to the dungeons beneath the castle. The irony that Corbinian had been imprisoned in those dungeons a second time was not lost upon the vampire.

'Corbinian!' the Red Duke hissed. 'Attend your master! This I command!'

The rubble continued to shift. Soon stone blocks were tumbling from the pile of debris, clattering about the flagstones at the vampire's feet. After many minutes, a tunnel-like opening was exposed. A dark, spindly shape lurched out from the hole, its face a fleshless skull with green witchlights burning in the depths of its eye sockets. A rusty, bat-winged helm encased the skull and about the skeletal body decaying strips of armour were draped.

The wight stared silently at the Red Duke. Its bony hands closed about the sword sheathed at its side. Without a sound, the wight drew its blade.

The Red Duke regarded the skeletal horror with a cold gaze, making no move to defend himself against the wight's sword. The vampire knew that there was no independent will left to the undead creature. If there had, it would have dug its way free long ago.

Still without making a sound, the wight stabbed the blade of its sword into the ground and sank to one knee, bowing its head before its ancient master.

Five hundred years had not been enough to free Sir Corbinian from the grip of his monstrous master.

CHAPTER VII

From the hilltop, the Bretonnian commanders watched the relief column march across the open desert. Despite the blazing Arabyan sun, the knights shivered with dread as they saw the seemingly endless tide of men and beasts advancing across the burning sands. The steel of their spears and spiked helmets glittered in the sun, making the entire procession resemble a winding river, an elemental force ripping its way through the wastes.

Instinctively, the knights looked to their leader, wondering if the indomitable Duke of Aquitaine had finally found something even he could not fail to fear. The duke's face was grave as he squinted through the strange bronze cylinder and swept its glass eye across the Arabyan army. It was many minutes before he lowered the device from his eye and nodded grimly.

'A remarkable invention,' the duke said, handing the telescope back to Baron Wolff, one of the knights from the Empire who had ridden to join the Bretonnians in their crusade against Sultan Jaffar. 'The craftsmen of your country are talented indeed to create such a wondrous device.'

The Imperial knight bowed his head as the telescope was returned to him. Most of the men from the Empire who had joined the crusade showed little deference to the

145

Bretonnian nobility, whatever their rank. The Duke of Aquitaine, however, was one Bretonnian who had earned the respect of every man in the crusade.

'It is of dwarf make,' Baron Wolff confessed. 'The engineers of the Empire have not learned the precision to recreate them for ourselves.' The baron's voice grew firm. 'But we will,' he vowed.

'What did you see through the glass, your grace?' asked a tall Aquitainian knight with mouse-coloured hair.

The duke turned and raised his voice so that all could hear him. 'The enemy is led by Mehmed-bey. They march under the standard of the Black Lizard.' His statement brought anxious murmurs from the gathered knights. Mehmed-bey was one of Sultan Jaffar's most efficient and brutal generals. He had earned the sobriquet of 'Mehmed the Butcher' after the Battle of the Nine Jackals. A crusader force had been sent to capture the Oasis of Gazi. Mehmed had allowed the knights to seize the oasis, but only after the magic of his fakirs had changed the water into wine. Despairing of thirst, the knights had been forced to fend off the repeated assaults of Mehmed's akincis, fast nomad lancers and horse archers. Wearing down their resolve, the Arabyans forced the crusaders to drink the magic wine – a liquor of such potency that neither man nor horse could withstand its properties.

With the crusaders now helpless, Mehmed-bey attacked the oasis one last time, employing his armoured sipahis to massacre the defenceless Bretonnians. The Arabyan knights took the oasis without a casualty. Those crusaders he captured alive Mehmed ordered hung by their feet from the palm trees, their mouths filled with salt and their lips sewn tight with twine. One man alone did the brutal general spare, allowing him to ride away and bear the tale to his countrymen, and this messenger Mehmed ensured would never bear arms against the sultan again by chopping off his hands before setting him on his horse.

'Leave my land now, or stay forever in your graves.' Such had been the fearsome warning sent by Mehmed-bey to the invaders of Araby.

There was no general among Sultan Jaffar's armies whose mere name could have intimidated the crusaders as that of Mehmed the Butcher. However, the Arabyan's villainous reputation could be used against him. Once battle was joined, the crusaders would fight to the last man, only too aware their horrible fate if they should fall alive into Mehmed's hands.

It was the Duke of Aquitaine's responsibility to see that when the fighting started, it was fought upon ground that favoured the Bretonnians, not their enemy.

'Mehmed-bey has roused the whole of the western caliphates,' the duke told his knights. 'This army numbers in the tens of thousands, more than enough to break the siege at El Haikk if it is allowed to reach the corsair city. Much of the Butcher's army is mameluk slave-soldiers, but armoured janissaries and sun-blackened dervishes march under the Black Lizard as well. Nomad riders guard the flanks and sipahis on strong desert horses make up the vanguard. Through the Imperial glass, I have counted no less than fifty war elephants.' The duke swept his gaze across the ranks of his followers. 'There can be no question. Mehmed-bey means to smash through the forces of King Louis and rescue his villainous master from El Haikk. If he succeeds, the crusade is over. Jaffar will be free to continue his reign of evil. Our own army will be broken, the survivors cast into slavery or forced to slink back to their homelands in shame.'

The duke saw the doubt and fear on the faces of his men. It was the emotion he had wanted to provoke. The *best way to instil courage in a man's heart was to draw out his worst fears and force him to confront them. He gazed out across the band of warriors, knights from royal Couronne and fey-haunted Quenelles, from the mountain reaches of Montfort and the wind-swept coast of Lyonesse, from the dark forests of Artois and the verdant plains of his own Aquitaine. Foreign knights from every corner of the Empire looked upon the Bretonnian duke with the same expectant, longing expression as the men of his own land. Even the dusky Tilean mercenaries, sell-sword adventurers who had joined the crusade not to free Estalia and Araby from a wicked tyrant but from the promise of plunder, even these honourless soldiers looked to the duke for hope and guidance.*

The duke smiled. These men expected him to lead them to victory. They might doubt their ability to stop Mehmed-bey and his vast army, but they did not for an instant question the duke's command. Such unwavering trust, even in the face of their fear stirred the duke's heart with pride. With men such as these, he would break Mehmed-bey.

'To us has been entrusted the greatest honour. To us has been given the hour of glory. Before us marches the enemy, wicked and abominable, arrogant in his strength, proud of his tyranny and evil. In the mind of the heathen, the war is already over. With a host of slaves who have never known any life but war, the Butcher would break our righteous cause. He would save the corrupt throne of Jaffar and extend to the lands of Bretonnia and Estalia and Tilea and the Empire the same cruel chains that imprison the men of Araby. He would make of our sons and daughters, of the sons and daughters of all free men, a legion of slaves to feed the cruelty of his sultan.'

The Red Duke's pallid face pulled back in an expression of pitiless hate. 'All that stands between Mehmed-bey and his victory is us, this small company of knights and yeomen, this small gathering of free men who will not submit humbly to the chains of a foreign despot, who will not meekly cast aside their freedom and end their days as a mameluk slave-soldier!'

The vampire's hand clenched into a fist of steel. 'We noble few, who stand against the tide of oppression and tyranny this day, to us belongs the greatest glory the gods have seen fit to bestow upon mortals! We will not step aside and allow the enemy to continue his cruelty! We will not let fear make us forget duty and honour! We will stand and we will fight!' The Red Duke threw his armoured fist into the air. 'And we will be victorious!'

Fleshless skulls stared back at the vampire with their empty sockets, the Red Duke's words failing to stir the blood of the dead as they had once fired the hearts of the living. The ranks of the decayed skeletons in their rusty armour and tattered surcoats stood in mute silence as their master addressed them. The rotting bodies of the Red Duke's more recent victims maintained the same unmoving formation, the dead minds of the zombies unable to draw emotion from the vampire's speech. Only the slavering ghouls, drawn from their holes by the vampire's aura of sinister power, reacted to his words, howling like beasts and beating their feet against the flagstones.

One other reacted to the Red Duke's words. The peasant necromancer Renar. The thin man grimaced as he listened to the vampire address the grisly host assembled in the crumbling courtyard of Crac de Sang.

'Your grace,' the necromancer said, coughing as a fit of nervousness held him. 'Mehmed-bey was killed five hundred years…'

The vampire spun about, glaring at Renar. The Red Duke blinked in confusion as he continued to stare at the man. It took a moment before he remembered who the peasant was, another moment to recognize the spectral figure of Jacquetta and the bony husk of Sir Corbinian. His face twisted in a pained snarl, his clenched fist smacking against Renar's jaw, knocking the necromancer to the ground.

'Do not be impudent, peasant,' the Red Duke hissed. 'I know who I march against. Du Maisne will pay for his sins… and those of his fathers.' The vampire gestured at the decaying undead mustered in the courtyard. 'It is a poor general who does not inspire the hearts of his men with a few stirring words. If those words are drawn from the past, of what consequence is it to soldiers such as these?'

Renar dabbed at his split lip with the cuff of his coat, nodding his head in servile agreement. The necromancer, however, was anything but reassured.

If the Red Duke noted Renar's misgivings, he gave no sign. The vampire swept his cloak about his powerful frame and stalked through the shattered gates of his fortress.

'We march upon the Chateau du Maisne!' the vampire growled.

THE NIGHT RIDE from Ceren Field to Castle Aquitaine was one that would have daunted even the best horseman in all Bretonnia. Sir Leuthere could only credit the grace of the Lady and the enormous import of his errand for keeping him in the saddle and not lying beside the road with a broken neck. The knight did not feel much concern over the danger of his reckless ride, only the danger that he would be unable to warn Duke Gilon made his heart tremble with fear. A hideous evil had been set loose upon Aquitaine. It was vital that Duke Gilon be made aware of the threat so that he could muster the knights of Aquitaine to stop the monster Earl Gaubert d'Elbiq had unleashed from its tomb. If they acted quickly, there might still be time to stop the Red Duke before the vampire had the chance to regather his terrible strength.

Sir Leuthere reached Castle Aquitaine sagging against the neck of a shuddering steed, its muzzle flecked with foam. The knight nearly fell from his saddle when grooms and servants came to attend the nocturnal visitor who had so dramatically and alarmingly raced across the castle's drawbridge. In any other dukedom, Sir Leuthere's feat would have been impossible, for the other provinces of Bretonnia were under constant threat from orcs, beastmen and marauders from the sea. But Aquitaine was a largely peaceful land south of the River Morceaux and its lords, secure in their sense of safety, often left the gates of their castles lowered and unbarred at night.

Leuthere gave praise to this uniquely Aquitainian custom, thankful for the time it saved him. With each passing moment, he felt a growing anxiety that his warning would be given too late, that already the Red Duke was calling a new army to him, an army resurrected from restless graves.

The risks he had taken and the mounting sense of urgency he felt made the interminable delays that followed tortuous to Leuthere. In spite of his insistence, none of the castle servants would awaken their lord at such an unseemly hour, and as Leuthere's pleas became more demanding the night steward threatened to have the knight confined. Leuthere subsided, contenting himself to wait in a draughty parlour until he was allowed an audience with Duke Gilon.

It was well into the morning, after Duke Gilon's ablutions and breakfast, before the frustrated young knight was presented to the ruler of Aquitaine.

Duke Gilon sat at the head of a long table in the castle's dining hall, his closest advisors, retainers and relations flanking him along the table's wings. An empty seat to Duke Gilon's right denoted the continued absence of his son Sir Richemont, but otherwise the hall was filled to capacity. It was the duke's habit to confer with his advisors after breakfast and many of the courtiers resented the interruption of this meeting by a brash young knight, the dust of the road still soiling his armour, the stink of horse still clinging to his clothes.

Duke Gilon turned a stern eye towards Leuthere, studying the man as he was conducted into the hall. He remembered Leuthere as the knight who had acted as second to Sir Girars d'Elbiq. The memory of that ugly event was not one to leave a favourable impression.

'My steward tells me you have ridden all night to bear me news of dire importance to my domain,' Duke Gilon said.

Leuthere wisely decided not to mention the many hours he had awaited Duke Gilon's convenience. 'That is so, your grace,' the knight said, bowing before his lord. 'I have come from the cemetery at Ceren Field. I bring horrendous news. The Red Duke has risen from his grave. He has returned to once more ravage Aquitaine!'

Gasps of alarm spread through the hall as the councillors and retainers reacted to Leuthere's words. The emotional response quickly collapsed into incredulous sneers as the assembled noblemen considered the likelihood of Leuthere's claim.

'King Louis the Righteous slew the vampire almost five hundred years ago,' one balding councillor objected.

'The Red Duke was destroyed at the Battle of Ceren Field,' grizzled old Sir Roget, captain of the Castle Guard, declared. 'It can't have risen from its grave, because it was never given one!'

'That's right!' chimed in a third retainer. 'They burned the vampire to ash along with his army! If he's come back as anything, it is as soil for our vineyards!'

Leuthere's face turned crimson as he listened to the jeers of the retainers. They had quite overcome their initial horror at the suggestion that the Red Duke had returned. Now they found the subject a thing of absurdity to be mocked and scoffed at.

Only Duke Gilon remained objective. He lifted his silver flagon and brought its base cracking against the tabletop, the loud report of metal against wood ringing through the hall. The councillors grew quiet as their lord motioned them to silence. The duke's gaze was piercing as he focused on Leuthere.

'It is a bold claim you bring before me,' Duke Gilon stated. 'Some might go so far as to call it audacious.'

'On my honour, what I have told you is the truth,' Leuthere replied. 'The Red Duke has returned.'

'You have seen him?' Duke Gilon asked.

Leuthere shook his head. 'No, but I have seen the Red Duke's sign. A coven of witches violated Ceren Field and through their dark arts restored the vampire to the world of the living.' The knight hesitated, unwilling even now to admit the shameful truth behind the cult's actions. 'My uncle, Earl Gaubert d'Elbiq, learned of what the witches intended. He... tried to stop them, but it was too late. The witches succeeded in their profane purpose. My uncle was slain by the Red Duke, his body impaled upon the crusader monument overlooking Ceren Field. Through the foulest sorcery, the illusion of life was returned to Earl Gaubert's corpse. When I found him, my uncle's body was writhing like a bug stuck upon a pin.'

This elaboration upon his report made more than a few of the retainers reconsider their mockery. There was a hideous veracity about Leuthere's words.

Again, Duke Gilon remained unemotional, weighing the young knight's account against the history handed down by tradition and the songs of the troubadours. Was it possible the Red Duke's body had somehow escaped destruction at Ceren Field? Was it really possible the vampire lived again? The possibility was too dire to dismiss out of hand. At the same time, it was too calamitous to accept blindly.

'Did the Red Duke remain at Ceren Field?' Duke Gilon asked.

'No, your grace,' Leuthere answered. 'It was evident that the vampire had left sometime before I discovered my uncle's body.'

'Then where do you think he has gone?' the duke's words were spoken in a strangely soft voice.

'I do not know,' Leuthere confessed. 'Someplace to gather his strength and marshal his forces. But I think I know where he will strike first when he does start his attack.'

'And where would that be?' Duke Gilon wore a thin

smile as he thrust the question at Leuthere.

The knight was oblivious to the baiting words. 'I think the Red Duke will attack the Chateau du Maisne.'

Duke Gilon's face grew red with anger. 'If he does, then I swear by the Lady that the d'Elbiq's will be stripped of title and lands! Does Earl Gaubert honestly believe I am such a fool that I would accept this nonsense! He plots a massed attack against the du Maisnes to avenge the death of his last son. Then he concocts this absurd story about the Red Duke rising from his grave in an attempt to cover the dastardly massacre he intends!'

Leuthere could not hold the duke's gaze, his suspicions uncomfortably close to the truth of what Earl Gaubert had planned to do. The knight could only hang his head in shame as he considered the dishonourable wickedness his uncle had sanctioned in the name of feud.

Duke Gilon took Leuthere's silence for an admission of guilt. 'Sir Roget, remove this lying cur from my sight,' the duke rapped at the captain of his guards.

The grizzled Roget rose from the table, marching solemnly towards Leuthere. One of the old knight's hands was coiled around the hilt of the dagger hanging from his belt. From the expression on Roget's gruff face, it seemed he wanted nothing more than an excuse to draw his weapon.

'I have told you the truth,' Leuthere insisted, but his words sounded feeble even to himself. 'The Red Duke is free! He has returned!'

Roget's fist cracked against Leuthere's chin, sending the knight staggering back. 'Hold your lying tongue or I'll cut it out and feed it to the hogs!' the old warrior snarled. He nodded his head and a pair of men-at-arms seized Leuthere by the shoulders, dragging him from the hall.

'Next time Earl Gaubert wants to try something, tell the varlet to think up a better lie!' Sir Roget warned as the doors closed behind Leuthere's departure.

THE AFTERNOON SUN found a disconsolate Sir Leuthere sitting beneath a cherry tree a league from the outskirts of the village surrounding Castle Aquitaine. The warmth of the sun did nothing to ease the cold, deathly dread that coursed through Leuthere's veins. He could only think of the awful doom that threatened the dukedom, the horror his own uncle had unleashed upon the land. Sir Maraulf had entrusted him with the duty of warning Duke Gilon and mobilising the knights of Aquitaine against the Red Duke before the vampire grew too powerful to stop.

Shame at his abject failure to convince Duke Gilon that the warning he had brought was genuine stung Leuthere like the burning kiss of a viper. The insane, generations-old feud between d'Elbiq and du Maisne had done more than twist the minds and souls of the two families. Like a pestilent infection, it had polluted the attitudes of everyone in Aquitaine, making them believe the two houses had no thought beyond perpetuating their ancient hate. It was a burden every d'Elbiq and du Maisne carried with him, whether he was aware of it or not. Leuthere had seen today a dramatic example of the prejudice hundreds of years of strife and hate had left behind. Even Duke Gilon saw only treachery and feud when a d'Elbiq spoke of a du Maisne.

What would he do now? Leuthere agonized over this question. He could ride back to the Chateau d'Elbiq, marshal the knights of his house and ride for the Chateau du Maisne. He smiled sadly at the image. No, he was even more likely to be greeted with hostility by Count Ergon than Duke Gilon. Count Ergon would never believe him if he claimed he had gathered an army in order to protect the lands of his ancient enemies. There would be fighting, and whichever side prevailed they would be easy pickings for the vampire when he came.

Perhaps he should seek out Sir Maraulf, try to use the strange hermit-knight to track the Red Duke to whatever lair the vampire had hidden himself? Leuthere was under no delusion that such an effort had any great chance of success, but if he died in such an attempt, at least he could die with honour, trying to atone for the evil his uncle's madness had loosed upon the world.

Leuthere stirred from his repose beneath the tree, watching a lone rider galloping down the road to Aquitaine Village. The knight recognized the dappled pony and the cloaked rider. Vigor had tried to match Leuthere's pace during the night, but neither peasant nor steed were equal to the knight's determination. Somewhere along the way, Vigor had fallen behind. Now, it seemed, the peasant was desperately trying to rejoin the knight.

At almost the same moment that Leuthere saw him, Vigor turned in his saddle and waved at the knight. With a sharp pull on the reins, he turned his pony towards the cherry tree.

'Your loyalty is appreciated,' Leuthere greeted Vigor, 'but I fear your effort has been wasted. Duke Gilon will not listen to me. No one in the court will believe the Red Duke has returned.'

Strangely, the peasant only gave the slightest of nods when he heard Leuthere's dire news. 'She said that they would not listen,' Vigor said, his voice solemn and not without a trace of awe.

Leuthere stared hard at Vigor, puzzled by the peasant's tone and demeanour. 'Who told you they would not listen?'

'After I lost all hope of catching up to you, I set my pony to a less gruelling pace,' Vigor explained. 'I saw no purpose in breaking the animal's leg or my neck, so I just walked along the road, thinking to join you once the sun was up and I could see where I was going. It was thirsty work walking a pony all through the night, so when dawn came, I went looking for a stream.' The peasant's expression became even graver and he repressed a slight shudder. 'What I found was a little pond of the clearest, bluest water I have ever seen. As I knelt down and cupped my hand to draw water from the pond, I became aware of another reflection beside my own gazing up at me from the pool.'

A thrill of wonder coursed through Leuthere's body. 'You don't mean to say… You don't mean you… A simple peasant… You're telling me you've seen… the Lady!'

Vigor shook his head. 'At first I thought she was the Lady, my lord, for she was so young and beautiful and wondrous. But as I grovelled in the mud and apologised to her for setting my common eyes upon her face, the vision in the water told me to rise. She said that she was not the Lady, merely one who served the Lady. She knew the errand you had set yourself, my lord, and she said that it would be for naught. She said that Duke Gilon would not believe you.'

Leuthere felt the religious fervour drain from his heart when Vigor confessed that the vision had not been the Lady herself, though he knew he should feel honoured that one of the Lady's servants had shown interest in his quest. 'What else did she say to you?' the knight asked.

'She said I was to find you and bring you back to the pond as quickly as I could,' Vigor said.

Leuthere nodded. The knight walked to where his horse grazed and pulled himself into the saddle. 'Let us be off then,' he said. 'Perhaps there is still hope that we can undo this evil before it grows too strong to stop.'

SIR LEUTHERE DID not need Vigor to tell him when they reached the pond. The knight could feel the change in the air, the tingle of magic flowing against his skin, prickling the hairs on the back of his neck. For the first time since he'd brought the body of his cousin back to Earl Gaubert, a sense of peace filled him. Despite Vigor's insistence that the vision he'd encountered wasn't the goddess, Leuthere found a thrill of expectation surge through him. Would the Lady reveal her true self before a mere peasant? No, she would not. That was an honour reserved only for the knights who devoted their lives to defending the realm.

As they dismounted and walked their horses towards the pond, Leuthere found the sense of tranquillity grow, dulling the immediacy of his fears, clearing his thoughts of the doubt and guilt that tormented him. No longer did he agonize over what he could have done to stop his uncle from conceiving such a dastardly plot. No longer did he torture himself with the question of how he, alone, could stop the monster who had nearly destroyed all of Aquitaine. It was enough that he was here, now, in the presence of the divine.

The little pond was just as Vigor had described it – clear and pure, unmarred by reeds and slimy growths. Gazing upon the surface of the pond was like staring at a silver mirror. No natural water could possess such purity. Leuthere felt his pulse quicken. He turned, motioning for Vigor to stay back, resentful that he should share this experience with a mere peasant, the treacherous rat who had helped Earl Gaubert dishonour himself.

Vigor kept his distance, holding the reins of the horses while his master walked to the edge of the pond.

Leuthere leaned over the water, staring down at his own reflection. He was at once reminded of the placid waters of Lake Tranquil, though he could not say exactly why. Perhaps all places touched by the presence of the Lady shared a certain kinship to one another.

A moment more, and the memory of Lake Tranquil was thrust even more forcefully into the knight's mind. Another reflection appeared in the water beside Leuthere. It was the image of a beautiful young woman dressed in a rich gown of sapphire, her golden tresses wound inside a casque of silvery wire. With a start, Leuthere realized he recognized the woman. Though he had never seen her so close, he knew he gazed upon the image of the Prophetess Iselda, Guardian of the Tower of Wizardry.

'Do not be saddened that I am not the Lady,' the image in the water told Leuthere, guessing immediately the thoughts churning within the knight's head. 'It is her power which flows through me, her magic which allows me to speak with you. Your cause is known to me and I have made it my own. Through me, you may know that the Lady favours your quest.'

Leuthere bowed his head in contrition. 'Forgive my audacity, prophetess. It was not my intention to offend one of the Lady's grail damsels.'

The reflection of Iselda smiled benignly at the young knight. 'There is no offence to be forgiven,' she assured him. 'It is I who should apologize for not reaching you sooner. Time grows short for Aquitaine and I fear the delay has already cost us dearly.'

'Duke Gilon would not credit my warning,' Leuthere said. 'His advisors would not believe me when I told them the Red Duke had returned.'

'They will not listen to you,' Iselda said. 'There is only one voice who will make them listen. You must ride to the Chateau du Maisne and warn Count Ergon of his peril. Earl Gaubert evoked the power of the Red Duke to strike down the du Maisnes and it is the vampire's intention to honour that compact. Count Ergon must be warned. Duke Gilon will listen when he hears the same tale from both a d'Elbiq and a du Maisne.'

Leuthere shook his head. 'I do not know that I can make Count Ergon listen. The feud burns as strongly in his heart as it did in my uncle's. If I ride to the Chateau du Maisne, I am likely to find only death there.'

Iselda's image nodded sadly. 'You must both overcome your hate if the Red Duke is to be stopped. This I have seen within my mirrors of prophecy. Unless d'Elbiq and du Maisne stand together, the vampire will complete the circle of blood and Aquitaine will become a land of the living dead.'

'Then I shall ride to the chateau,' Leuthere said. 'Perhaps I can make Count Ergon listen before his retainers hang me.'

'You must ride quickly,' Iselda urged. 'The Red Duke's power clouds my mirrors, I can see the strand of his fate only when it touches upon those of others. It is difficult to foretell the vampire's actions, only his intentions. He will march upon the Chateau du Maisne, but I cannot predict when and how. Even now, the Red Duke's creatures may be closing upon the castle.'

'I will ride as though the Green Knight himself were hot upon my heels,' Leuthere vowed. 'If it is within my power, I will reach Count Ergon and warn him of his peril.'

Iselda's reflection smiled at Leuthere's vow. Slowly the image began to fade, the pond losing its mirrored sheen. Weeds and scum again clouded the surface, frogs and dragonflies haunting its banks. The sense of peace evaporated from Leuthere's breast, urgency and fear flooding back into his heart.

The knight turned and dashed back to where Vigor stood with the horses.

'You saw her?' Vigor asked as he helped Leuthere mount his horse.

The knight nodded. 'She says I must ride to the Chateau du Maisne and warn Count Ergon that he will be the first target of the Red Duke's wrath. I can only pray to the Lady that he will hear me out before ordering my execution.'

Vigor shook his head and mounted his pony. Leuthere stared at the peasant in surprise.

'You need not accompany me,' the knight said. 'It is likely I ride to my death.'

Vigor's face was solemn as he regarded the knight. 'It was because of me that Earl Gaubert consulted Jacquetta,' he said, his voice heavy with guilt. 'If not for that, none of this would have happened. I am only a peasant, but I must make amends for what I have done. If that means I will end my life hanging from a rope, then I am willing to accept that as the price I must pay.'

'Mayhaps you shall get your wish,' Leuthere said, turning his horse back towards the road and digging his spurs into its flanks. It was many leagues to Count Ergon's lands and Iselda's warning was still ringing in the knight's ears. Time was the enemy now.

If it wasn't already too late.

CHAPTER VIII

Horror filled El Syf's poisoned heart. There was a venom flowing through his body that made the Arabyan poison seem a plaything for children. He could taste the filth on his lips, feel it burning in his throat.

The Duke of Aquitaine had been a fighter all his life. It had been expected of the man who would one day rule the most beautiful dukedom in all Bretonnia. His father had pushed him hard, even more so than his younger brother. As the heir, it had been El Syf's duty to prove his courage and worthiness to rule. Across Aquitaine and far into the hinterlands of Bretonnia, the young El Syf had searched out monsters to slay and wrongs to right. Always he…

No, those days were past now. There was only death's cold embrace to succour him in this time of terror. Yet even death was no easy thing for El Syf to seek out. He could not simply lie in the sand and allow his life to wither away. Every breath, every moment he had to fight to die, fight against the corruption polluting him. As he had struggled to resist the fiery pain of the Arabyan poison, now he bent his will to helping it kill him. If the poison could only work fast enough, there was a chance he could claim a clean death.

Even the thing that had put this curse upon him had told the duke as much.

Bit by bit, the duke could feel himself dying. He longed for the strength to reach out and seize the curved dagger clutched in the sheik's dead hand, but the power to move even a single finger was beyond him. It was a tortuous ordeal simply to blink his eyes, an effort that El Syf found more arduous than his fiercest battles. He could see the vultures circling overhead, drawn by the stink of carrion. Inwardly, he begged the scavengers to descend, to set upon him with beak and talon, to tear from his flesh the taint of the undead.

The first vultures swooped down upon the body of the sheik. Others landed upon the butchered Bedouins. One scraggly bird with grey feathers and a white ruff about the base of its leathery neck came hopping towards El Syf, croaking hungrily as it closed upon him.

Suddenly all of the scavenger birds took wing, squawking angrily as they fled back into the desert sky. The poisoned knight groaned as he watched the vultures flee. The sound of pounding hooves and rattling armour crashed down around him. The duke could not turn his head to see the riders as they hastened to the battlefield, but he could tell from their frantic voices that they were Bretonnians.

Armour clattered around him as knights rushed to his aide. El Syf could hear the frantic voice of Marquis Galafre d'Elbiq. The marquis had ridden hard for the crusader encampment to bring back help after the ambush. Unfortunately, that help had come much too late.

The weather-beaten face of Earl Durand du Maisne filled the duke's vision, staring down at him. Earl Durand had been his vassal for decades, but the duke had never seen a look of such grave concern upon the knight's face before. Earl Durand bent over the duke's body, pressing his ear against El Syf's chest. For many minutes, he listened, straining to hear the sluggish pulse of the duke's heart.

All the torments of hell ravaged El Syf's body as he forced a whisper to wheeze through his paralysed lips. 'Leave me,' the duke commanded his vassal. 'I am already dead.'

Earl Durand rose and stared down at the duke, an expression of shock on his face now. El Syf was certain the knight had heard his plea. He blinked his eyes, trying to reaffirm his command.

Earl Durand turned away quickly. For a moment, he stood there, his back to his dying lord. Then he began shouting orders to the other crusaders who had ridden to rescue the embattled Duke of Aquitaine.

'He is still alive!' Earl Durand cried, relief and triumph in his tone. 'We must get him back to camp and allow the king's physicians to attend his wounds!'

Tears rose up in the duke's eyes, a silent scream howled through his mind.

'Let me die,' El Syf struggled to shout to his men, but not even the faintest moan sounded from his lifeless lips.

'YOUR CHILDREN WILL beg for death, Durand, and I shall not listen.'

The Red Duke sat astride his spectral horse, glaring at the walls of the Chateau du Maisne. He watched the flicker of firelight playing at the castle windows, listened to the sounds of laughter and revelry seeping from the fortress, intruding upon the night.

'My lord.' Renar flinched as the vampire stared down at him, eyes red with anger. 'Your grace,' the necromancer hurriedly corrected himself. 'Is it wise to attack the castle now? Surely we do not have enough men to mount a siege…'

The Red Duke scowled at the gaunt man, exposing his gleaming fangs. 'I do not lead men,' the vampire growled. 'Those days are past,' he added with bitterness in his voice. 'What is left to me are carrion and scavengers.' He extended his armoured hand, indicating the silent ranks mustered in the woods behind him, the grisly formations of bleached skeletons called up from the crypts beneath Crac de Sang and the degenerate ghouls that had infested the vampire's castle.

'We will never get past the walls,' protested Renar. 'We need trebuchets and siege towers, the troops to crew them. It would take an army of thousands to besiege the castle and breach its walls. We have only two hundred.' Renar cringed as he brought his last point up. The way the vampire's mind wandered, it was possible the Red Duke wasn't even aware of the size of his force, believing himself at the fore of a crusader army of a thousand knights ready to break the sultan's army at Lashiek.

Instead of flying into a rage, the Red Duke smiled indulgently at the necromancer. 'I do not need an army to breach the walls of Durand's castle. I need only one slave to penetrate the castle and open its gates for us. Then we shall test the quality of this Count Ergon's steel.'

UNLIKE MANY OF the castles peppered among the green fields and lush vineyards of Aquitaine, the gates of the Chateau du Maisne were kept closed at night. Guards patrolled the battlements day and night, ever on the watch for enemies. The du Maisnes did not need orcs and beastmen to threaten their lives. For their family had the ancient hate of the d'Elbiq's to menace them.

The men-at-arms who patrolled the walls of the castle had served the du Maisne family all their lives, peasants who had been elevated from working in the fields to protecting the lives and property of their noble lords. It was about as prestigious a position as a common-born peasant could aspire to and the gratitude of the soldiers towards their patrons engendered in them a loyalty gold could not buy.

Gaspard was such a man, the son of a swineherd in the village of Bezonvaux. His brawn had drawn the attention of the Reeve of Bezonvaux – a life spent hefting the hogs his father kept had made the young Gaspard the strongest man in the village by the time he was sixteen. Eager to please his lord, the reeve had dispatched Gaspard to the Chateau du Maisne to answer a call for more soldiers. Gaspard had never been back to Bezonvaux and never regretted the life he had left behind. He was content in his new life as a soldier in service to Count Ergon du Maisne, despite the dangers it entailed. He'd been wounded once by a d'Elbiq archer during a skirmish between the feuding families and come close to losing an arm from the injury. It was as close to death as he had ever come.

At least, until the moment Gaspard turned the corner of the castle gatehouse and found himself confronted by a strange figure. The figure was that of a shapely young woman, her voluptuous body scarcely concealed by a diaphanous robe that danced about her body in the cool night breeze. Long locks of coal-black hair waved in the wind, seeming almost to reach out to him.

The guard's first reaction was one of amorous curiosity regarding who the woman was and why she was prowling the battlements at night in such attire. Gaspard's thoughts instantly turned toward fright.

There was something unnatural about the woman, her entire body, even her long black hair possessing a luminous quality that made her almost appear to glow against the backdrop of grey stone crenellations and the black night sky. Goosebumps pimpled the sentry's arms as a chill of terror crawled through his body.

The woman turned towards Gaspard, her face beautiful and lascivious. Then the face collapsed, washed away like a footprint on a beach. Gaspard opened his mouth to scream as he found himself staring into a ghostly skull, but no sound rose from his paralysed throat.

Crippling pain stabbed through the guard's brain as the keening wail of the banshee burned into him, a spectral shriek only the ears of Jacquetta's victim could hear. Gaspard fell to his knees, his halberd falling from his hands. He tore the iron kettle helm from his head, struggled to remove the mail coif beneath. Blood streamed from the sides of his head, dripped from his nose. Crimson tears stained his cheeks as vessels in his eyes burst.

The banshee regarded her victim with the hateful envy of the undead towards the living. She waited until the man's armoured boots thrashed against the parapet, watching as the final death spasm shivered through the rest of his body. Then the spiteful apparition continued on her way towards the gatehouse, flitting along the wall like a scrap of linen caught by a gust of wind.

There would be more guards inside the gatehouse. Jacquetta could feel the warmth of their life-force even through the thick stone walls. The windlass that raised and lowered the castle's portcullis would be there too. One of those guards would raise the gate for her.

Before he died.

'BY THE LADY!' cursed Sir Folcard as he emerged from the castle stables. His prize destrier had been feeling sickly and the knight had taken it upon himself to supervise the ministrations of the stable master and the farriers. He might trust a mere peasant to treat his wife for stomach pains, but he'd be damned if he was going to trust his horse to some low-born wastrel.

The object of the knight's ire was the yawning space below the castle's gatehouse. For some reason, the portcullis had been raised – in direct violation of Count Ergon's orders. With the recent death of Earl Gaubert's last son, the count had imposed strict measure to protect against any vengeful measures initiated by the d'Elbiqs. Foremost among these was keeping the castle gates closed after dark.

Some peasant-soldier was going to be flogged for this oversight, that was the thought smouldering in Sir Folcard's mind as he stormed across the courtyard towards the gatehouse. He started to shout obscenities at the men-at-arms stationed in the gatehouse, his annoyance rising when no one appeared at the narrow windows in response to his tirade.

Then the knight noticed movement in the dark, tunnel-like corridor beneath the gatehouse. He stood for a moment, an unaccountable fear running down his spine as he watched the motion resolve itself into the shape of a rider. As the intruder emerged into the courtyard, Sir Folcard's blood turned to ice. The rider bore only a twisted resemblance to humanity, his feature sharp and hungry, his skin as pale and lifeless as that of a corpse. Red armour enclosed his monstrous frame, a black cape billowing about his shoulders. Beneath him, the steed he rode was a thing of glowing bone and rusted armour, witchfires smoking in the pits of its skull.

The Red Duke smiled at the frightened knight. Slowly the vampire raised his finger and pointed at Sir Folcard. A pack of slavering things rushed out from the darkness of the gateway, falling upon the knight before he could take more than a few frantic steps back towards the stables. The ghouls bore the man to the ground, rending his body with their sharpened fangs and poisoned claws.

Sir Folcard's screams brought startled men rushing to the doors and windows of the castle. They stared down in stunned horror as the ghouls feasted upon the shrieking man. Cries of alarm, shouts of terror spread through the castle, replacing the merriment that had so lately echoed into the night.

The Red Duke waved his armoured fist, motioning the silent ranks behind him towards the castle keep. The du Maisnes would be there, at the heart of the castle. They would try to make a stand, to defend their home against the undead invaders. That would be their mistake.

'Take the zombies and secure the postern,' the Red Duke snarled at Renar. 'If any make it past you, I can promise you will envy the dead before I am through with you.'

The necromancer bowed his head in reluctant obeisance. Renar was no warrior, no battlefield commander. He was an evil wizard who tried to steal the secret of immortality from the dead. He knew nothing of war and command. But he did know it was unwise to question the draconian edicts of the Red Duke. Reluctantly, Renar led the decaying ranks of his troops towards the postern gate.

'Sir Corbinian,' the Red Duke hissed. 'Take your men and hold the escape tunnel.' The vampire closed his eyes, recalling the details of the Chateau du Maisne when his vassal Earl Durand had given him a tour of the fortress. 'You will find the entrance beneath the blacksmith's forge,' the Red Duke said.

The fleshless wight raised its sword in salute and marched away, its skeleton warriors following after it with almost mechanical precision. With the departure of the wight and Renar, the Red Duke was left with the ghouls and fifty skeleton warriors.

The vampire felt a rush of contempt for his enemies as he watched them close the keep's great doors, barricading them against the Red Duke's attack. Even when he was mortal, such a feeble defence wouldn't have held him back. But now, with the powers of darkness at his command, the efforts of the defenders only filled the vampire's heart with contempt. These men were already dead, they just didn't know it.

Arrows stabbed down from the windows and hoardings of the keep, skewering several ghouls on their barbed heads. The remaining cannibals scattered, fleeing back into the darkness, abandoning their own dead and wounded. The archers at the windows cheered as the ghouls fled, for the moment forgetting the imposing figure in red armour seated upon his skeletal steed.

It was their last mistake.

The Red Duke drew the fell energies of Old Night from the air around him, weaving the raw essence of dark magic with an instinctual facility beyond the ability of all but the most powerful sorcerers. His black soul bound the power to his indomitable will, enslaving it to his command. He stretched forth his hand, clawed fingers reaching into the night sky, and with a piercing howl the Red Duke unleashed his spell.

The bestial roar thundered across the courtyard, snapping the archers from their premature celebration. Instantly the dreadful sound became the focus for the keep's defenders, the fearful note shivering through their flesh. Trembling, the bowmen trained their weapons upon the Red Duke, thirty-six Bretonnian longbows with arrows nocked took aim.

Before the bowmen could loose their deadly arrows, a cacophony of shrill shrieks descended upon the keep. The archers retreated as a flood of fluttering wings and verminous fangs filled each window, as a seemingly endless wave of chittering bodies dove upon them. The bowmen were forced to cast aside their weapons, to shield their faces from the slapping wings and slicing teeth of a living storm. Bats, summoned down from the sky in their multitudes by the dark magic of the Red Duke, converged upon the keep by the thousands.

The Red Duke watched as the bats swept the archers from the parapets. Boldly, the vampire spurred his horse forwards, slowly marching his steed towards the oaken doors that barred the gateway into the keep. Skeleton warriors followed obediently in their master's wake. A dozen of them bore a stout log between them, moving with an almost mechanical precision beneath the ponderous weight of their burden.

'Open the way,' the vampire ordered his undead soldiers. The skeletons did not hesitate, but simply shifted their hold upon the log and charged the thick oak doors. The crude ram slammed into the portal with a violent impact, jarring the skeletons with the force of the blow. The skeletons instantly recovered, having neither mind or flesh to be stunned by the attack. They drew away from the doors and, with the same mechanical precision, repeated their assault.

The Red Duke turned from observing the attacking skeletons, fixing his attention instead upon Jacquetta's ghostly figure. 'Go inside and clear the way,' the vampire ordered the spectral witch. Jacquetta's beautiful face corroded, withering once again into the leering skull of a banshee. Obediently, the undead witch drifted across the courtyard, gliding towards the inner wall of the keep. She did not hesitate when she reached the stone obstruction, but instead vanished through the unyielding wall.

The vampire hissed in satisfaction, watching his bats continue to torment the men at the windows of the keep. It would not be long now. Earl Durand had escaped him in the earlier war, but no power on earth would save his descendents from the Red Duke's revenge.

'THEY'RE TRYING TO break through the main hall!'

Sir Armand turned at the sound of the shout, casting aside the rich tapestry he had been using to help corral bats in the upper gallery. He thrust the improvised net into the uncertain grip of a servant and hastened to the landing. The knight could see the main hall below. Men-at-arms and gangs of servants continued to drag benches and tables across the room to reinforce the huge double-doors which opened into the courtyard. While he watched, Armand saw the doors shudder and heard the booming impact of the battering ram.

Men rushed to brace the doors with a heavy bench taken from the keep's chapel. Suddenly the men-at-arms dropped their burden, falling to the floor and clutching their heads in agony. A loud, keening wail filled the hall, reverberating from the stone walls. Armand staggered back as the sound assailed his senses. Even from the gallery above the hall, the noise was almost unendurable.

A ghostly form manifested amid the crippled defenders, the spectral image of a raven-haired woman, her face reduced to a sneering skull. The banshee continued to emit her agonizing screech, letting the sound torture all of the men in the great hall. Jacquetta could only kill with her scream by focusing it upon a single victim at a time, but the vengeful spirit was not stymied by the limits of her power. The banshee reached down and picked a discarded sword from the floor, her bony fingers closing about the bronze hilt. Still screeching, keeping the defenders disoriented and helpless, Jacquetta closed upon the nearest of the cringing men and stabbed the point of her stolen sword into the man's skull.

Armand's blood boiled as he observed the callous murder. Tying a heavy scarf about his head to at least soften the banshee's wail, the outraged knight drew his sword and leapt over the gallery's balustrade. He landed on his feet, taking only the briefest pause to recover from his jump before dashing off to confront the murdering ghost.

The banshee turned away from the liveried groom she had just killed, the man's blood dripping from her sword. Jacquetta stared at Armand, her skull-like face filling out, becoming once more the stunning visage of the witch in life. She smiled invitingly at the young knight, beckoning to him with a crooked finger. Armand responded to the banshee with a grimace and a snarled oath.

Instantly, Jacquetta's face decayed back into a leering skull. The banshee streaked forwards, gliding across the hall to meet Armand's charge. The knight parried her thrusting sword, fending her off with a backhanded slash that should have opened her up from shoulder to breast. Instead, to the knight's horror, his sword passed harmlessly through the banshee's ghostly body.

Jacquetta pressed her attack, pushing Armand towards the cross-wall that bisected the lower floors of the keep. The knight struggled to keep his focus, to prevent panic from overwhelming his mind. He had to remain calm, let instinct and battle-hardened reflexes carry the fight. The banshee might be spectral, but her sword was a thing as solid as his own. That was what he had to attack.

Another boom and the cracking of wood sounded from the entryway. A few men-at-arms struggled towards the failing barrier, but the tormenting scream of the banshee kept the others writhing on the floor. If the barricade was not reinforced soon it would fail.

The greater plight of the keep galvanized Armand, his duty to father and family vanquishing the last of his fear. He mounted a furious attack upon the banshee, this time focusing solely upon the physical sword gripped by the spectral hand. The greater strength of the knight prevailed, battering the blade, swatting it aside like a child's plaything, the insubstantial banshee knocked about as she refused to lose hold of her sword.

Armand could have broken away, fled back into

the gallery while the banshee reeled from his assault. Doing so, however, would not help the keep's defenders. Armand was determined to hold his ground, to press Jacquetta so sorely that the ghost forgot about the other men and concentrated solely upon him. Without the banshee's wail stabbing their brains, the soldiers would be able to at least defend the barricades if the doors were broken.

Another powerful strike from the knight's sword sent Jacquetta spinning across the floor, whirling like a crazed goblin fanatic. For the first time, the banshee showed fear, recoiling with a hiss as her spin brought her close to the cross-wall and the row of torches bolted to the bare stone.

Armand was quick to seize upon the banshee's display of weakness. Another mighty blow drove her away from him long enough for the knight to lunge across the hall. The banshee guessed his intention, rushing at him in a frantic charge. Her sword struck sparks from the stone floor as Armand narrowly rolled away from an overhanded sweep of the ghost's sword. Before Jacquetta could try again, Armand had his objective in hand, pulling a torch down from its iron sconce and driving its flaming end into the banshee's skull-like face.

The banshee's spectral wail fell silent as the ghost emitted a different sort of shriek, a scream of pain. Her face was sizzling as she retreated from Armand's torch, ghostly steam rising from her morbid visage. Jacquetta's sword clattered against the floor as she clutched at her smouldering cheekbones.

Armand rushed the wounded banshee, intending to finish her before she recovered from the shock of her injury. But even as he started his lunge, he knew he was too late. Jacquetta lowered her skeletal hands and fixed him with a malignant stare. Her fleshless jaw dropped open and from the banshee there sounded a different kind of shriek, a shriek only Armand's ears could hear, a shriek that would not simply torment, a shriek that would kill.

The knight crumpled to his knees, his face contorted into a mask of agony. He could feel the banshee's scream like burning fingers digging inside his skull. Armand tore the rag from his head, crushing his hands against his ears, trying to block out the ghostly wail.

Through the spectral shriek, Armand could hear the clamour of the great doors splintering, bursting open as the battering ram worked their ruin. He watched as the few defenders at the barricade were driven back, forced to retreat by the silent, grim march of the skeletons pouring into the keep. Then the knight's vision collapsed into blackness and he slumped to the floor.

A moment later, the killing shriek of Jacquetta was silenced. An enraged rider galloped across the hall, smashing down the few soldiers who stood in his way. Armoured in crimson, his black cape flowing behind him, the Red Duke charged across the hall towards the cross-wall. His gauntlet closed about the neck of the screaming banshee, the ghost's essence becoming solid beneath the vampire's touch. Savagely, the Red Duke ripped her from the floor, flinging her away like a sack of rubbish.

'No!' the vampire snarled. 'This one is mine!' The Red Duke bared his fangs in a venomous display of hate. 'Durand du Maisne, know that death is the price of treachery!'

The Red Duke pulled back on the reins of his steed,

the skeletal horse rearing back, its hooves kicking out above the prone knight.

Before the Red Duke could bring his steed's hooves smashing down, a challenging voice rang out through the hall.

'Monster!' Count Ergon shouted down from the gallery, his face torn and bloody from the fangs of bats. 'Coward! Leave my son alone and face me!'

The Red Duke glanced in confusion at the knight lying on the floor and the nobleman hurling abuse at him from the gallery above. The vampire shook his head, trying to clear the muddle of thoughts and images. Finally, he focused his burning gaze upon Count Ergon.

'You should have let me die in Araby,' the vampire hissed, his fingers tightening about the hilt of his sword. 'Now I will scour you and all your line from the land, Durand du Maisne. I will strike your name from the records. I will pull down this castle stone by stone. I will open the tombs of your fathers and their fathers. I will make it so your family is not even a myth told among peasants.'

Count Ergon blanched at the vampire's threat, a horrible suspicion rising inside him. This was no nameless monster from the night. This was the most infamous creature in all Aquitaine's long history. This was the Red Duke himself.

The vampire sneered at Count Ergon's sudden fear. Forgetting Armand, the Red Duke turned his horse and galloped towards the timber stairs leading up into the gallery. A pair of men-at-arms, attendants of the count, broke away from their master, running down the steps, trying to block the vampire's progress. Desperately they tried to hold the Red Duke back with their spears, jabbing at the armoured vampire, driving the points of their weapons into the fleshless neck and empty belly of his steed.

The Red Duke hissed in annoyance. With one driving sweep of his blade, he splintered the spears of his foes. A second sweep of his sword, with the inhuman strength of the undead behind it, claimed the heads of both men, flesh and bone and mail parting like butter before the vampire's sword. The valiant soldiers collapsed upon the stairs, their heads rolling obscenely down the steps.

The Red Duke drove his spurs into the flanks of his deathly steed, driving the spectral beast to mount the stairs, climbing up to the gallery in a series of stumbling jumps. Arrows clattered against the vampire's armour and lodged between the ribs of his skeletal horse as a small group of bowmen tried to fell the monster.

Gaining the gallery, the Red Duke charged the nearest of the bowmen. The vampire's sword crunched through the man's kettle-helm, splitting the skull beneath the iron hat. The stricken soldier crashed against the balustrade, already dead when his body pitched over the side to fall into the great hall below.

The courage of the other bowmen faltered as they saw the gruesome demise of their comrade. Some threw down their bows and fled in abject terror, a few others rallied about their lord, begging Count Ergon to escape. The count waved them off. It was not that he did not share the terror of his men, if anything he had more reason to fear the Red Duke than they. But he knew that only by keeping the vampire here could he give his family any chance with their own escape. While the Red Duke fought him here, the countess and the rest of his household would be slipping through the postern gate and on their way to the sanctuary of Castle Aquitaine and Duke Gilon's protection.

The last of Count Ergon's men, shamed by their lord's display of courage, set aside their bows and drew their short swords. Count Ergon called out to them when he guessed their intention, knowing such a reckless attack was nothing but suicide. The Red Duke cut each of them down, barely even glancing at each man as he brought his blade slashing down. Soon, Count Ergon was alone upon the gallery with the vampire. Even the sounds of battle in the gallery below had fallen silent, the triumphant undead standing in rigid ranks awaiting their master's next command.

'You are brave, Durand,' the Red Duke grinned. 'It warms my heart that you have not forsaken all your knightly virtues.'

Count Ergon glared at the vampire. 'You have no heart, monster! If there was anything human inside you, it withered into dust centuries ago!' The count lifted his sword, pointing the weapon at the Red Duke. 'Before I put you back in the grave, at least know I am not Earl Durand du Maisne. I am his descendent, Count Ergon du Maisne. You have butchered my kin and my servants. For that, Lady willing, I will send your spirit back to the hell that spawned it.'

The Red Duke sneered down at the nobleman. 'I was going to kill you, Durand,' the vampire hissed. 'But now I think I shall do much worse to you.'

With no further warning, the Red Duke dropped down from his saddle. The code of chivalry under which he had once lived yet lingered in the vampire's mind, sometimes continuing to guide his actions. Commoners and beasts might happily be butchered from the saddle, but the code of arms demanded that an unhorsed knight be fought on foot. Not that the Red Duke expected Count Ergon to benefit from the discarded advantage.

Count Ergon did not charge the Red Duke. He had seen to what effect such attacks had profited his soldiers. The nobleman instead awaited the vampire's advance, thinking that by fighting defensively against the monster, he might surprise the fiend and cause him to make a mistake the count could exploit.

Like some slavering wolf, the Red Duke stalked towards Count Ergon, an inhuman hunger burning in the vampire's eyes. The vampire slashed at Count Ergon's side, capitalizing upon the nobleman's lack of shield. Count Ergon spun his body in time with the attack, bringing his own sword around to block the Red Duke's blade. Too late did Count Ergon realise that the vampire's attack was only a feint to draw him out.

The Red Duke smashed the flat of his sword into Count Ergon's shoulder, sending a pulse of numbing pain down the nobleman's arm. The superhuman strength of the vampire's blow caused the sword to fall from his enemy's paralysed grasp.

Instantly, the vampire was upon his unarmed foe, seizing him by the throat, pressing him back until his spine was crushed against the balustrade. Count Ergon cried out in pain as the Red Duke increased the pressure, the nobleman's fists smashing uselessly against the vampire's armour.

'I will break your body,' the Red Duke hissed, his face only inches from the terrified eyes of his victim. 'I will snap your spine like an old rotten twig, leave you a crippled, crawling thing.' The vampire's lips pulled back in a feral grin, exposing the sharp fangs. 'Then I will make you immortal, one of the eternal undead.

You will pass eternity slithering on your belly, creeping in the shadows, sucking blood from the veins of rats and vermin! I will be avenged upon you, Durand, avenged throughout eternity!'

Count Ergon screamed as the vampire began to carry out his threat. He could feel the mail he wore digging through the padding underneath, the iron rings cutting into his flesh.

Suddenly, the pressure was gone. An expression of surprise came across the vampire's pallid countenance. The Red Duke looked down in surprise at the stream of sickly treacle leaking from a gash in his side just below the rim of his cuirass. Torn links of mail dangled about the edge of the vampire's wound. Slowly, the Red Duke turned to face his attacker.

'Let my father go!' Armand roared at the vampire. He wagged the tip of his sword at the Red Duke, spattering his breastplate with the stagnant treacle that had lately coursed through the vampire's veins. 'You are brave against an old man or a knight knocked senseless by the shrieks of your hag. Let's see how you fare against the greatest swordsman in Aquitaine!'

The Red Duke shook his head, blinking in confused rage. He could smell the blood of Durand du Maisne in this bragging fool. The vampire glanced contemptuously at Count Ergon. With a snarl, he threw the nobleman over the balustrade.

'Father!' Armand screamed. The knight's first impulse made him want to rush to the great hall, to help his stricken father if he could. Other instincts, those drilled into Armand's brain by a lifetime learning the art of war, prevailed. He was a warrior locked in battle. He would not turn his back on his foe, whatever the reason.

'The greatest swordsman in Aquitaine?' the Red Duke scoffed, striding towards Armand. The treacle leaking down the vampire's side had already begun to subside, the fiend's recuperative powers beginning to repair the damage the knight's blade had wrought.

Armand readied himself to meet the Red Duke's attack. He met the vampire's thrust with a skilful parry, compensating for the monster's greater strength by bracing his legs for the bone-jarring impact. As the Red Duke's blade slid from Armand's steel, the young knight thrust forwards with a stabbing riposte. The point of his sword glanced across the vampire's breast-plate as the monster twisted his body in time with the knight's attack.

Savagely, the Red Duke brought his blade whipping up and around the guard of Armand's sword, the edge of the vampire's sword slashing across the knight's fingers. Armand's gauntlet was scoured down to the mail glove beneath the steel plate, his entire hand stinging from the vicious impact. Only by force of will did Armand prevent his blade from falling to the floor alongside that of his father.

The Red Duke did not relent in his assault, driving forwards with a furious series of thrusts and cuts that taxed Armand's reflexes and stamina. Foot by foot, the young knight was forced to give ground before the vampire.

'The greatest swordsman in Aquitaine?' the Red Duke laughed. 'Is that what you call yourself, Durand? Too bad you chose to pit your steel against the greatest swordsman in all Bretonnia!'

The vampire matched deeds to words. With contemptuous ease, the Red Duke mounted a counter-parry as he caught Armand's blade upon his steel. The fiend's sword slashed across the knight's vambrace, splitting the couter guarding his elbow. Mail was shredded by the cruel edge of the Red Duke's sword. Armand cried out as he felt the vampire's blade cut into the tendons of his arm.

Snarling, the Red Duke spun his body around, describing a graceful arc as he brought his sword low. This time it was Armand's knee that was slashed by the inhumanly powerful blow, the fan-plate above the poleyn bent out of shape by the malignant force behind the Red Duke's blade.

'The greatest swordsman in Aquitaine,' the Red Duke hissed, glowering at his bleeding foe. The vampire licked his fangs, hunger burning within him as he saw the blood leaking down the knight's armour. 'I think I will reclaim that title from you, Durand.'

Armand gritted his teeth, forcing his maimed body into motion. 'I am not Durand!' the knight yelled. Locking both hands about the grip of his sword, he lunged at the Red Duke, throwing his entire body behind one last, desperate effort to skewer the vampire upon his sword.

The Red Duke did not seek to dodge the assault. He merely caught the front of Armand's sword in his mailed fist, arresting the motion of both man and blade with his superhuman strength. Terror and despair filled Armand's face as the vampire began to bend the point of his sword back upon itself, the scream of bending steel filling the gallery.

'No,' the vampire hissed as he glared at the bleeding knight. 'You are not Durand. You are dinner.'

CHAPTER IX

The Red Duke glared at the Tower of Wizardry. The vampire shook his fist at the woman staring down at him from the balcony high above the battlefield. The magic of Isabeau had defied every strategy the Red Duke had devised to bring down the fortress and destroy the prophetess who had defied him and refused to recognize his claim on Aquitaine.

Siege towers had been bowled over by hurricane gales that came from nowhere to sweep across the battlefield. Iron picks had bent and buckled when driven against the enchanted masonry of the stronghold. The sappers he had dispatched to undermine the tower had become utterly disoriented, driving their tunnels instead beneath Lake Tranquil and flooding their excavations. Trebuchets and mangonels fell apart as they loosed stones against Isabeau, their mechanisms corroded by the prophetess's spells.

Only main force was left to the Red Duke's army, to break down the walls from sheer strength and obstinacy. At first, the vampire had raged over the failure of his knights to ride down the peasants as they fled into the tower for sanctuary. The bodies of three of the most defiant of his men still swung from a tree outside the vampire's pavilion. Now, however, he looked upon the escape of the peasants

*as fortuitous. With only herself and her retainers to feed,
Isabeau might have rationed the tower's store of provisions
for a year. But with seven hundred starving peasants to
succour, the store would quickly be played out.*

*If he could not smash his way in, then the Red Duke
would starve the tower's defenders out. His own army
could easily outlast Isabeau, almost three-quarters of the
vampire's troops were skeletons and zombies, things that
needed neither food or sleep to keep them going. Leaving
the undead to hold Isabeau inside the tower, the mortal elements of the army could safely forage for provisions in the
abandoned farms and villages.*

The tower would fall. It was only a matter of time.

*The Red Duke turned his back to the Tower of Wizardry
and marched back to his pavilion. Even with an overcast sky
to shield him, the vampire felt discomfort from the unseen
sun. He was eager to slink back into the comforting darkness beneath his pavilion of black silk and crimson banners.*

*A messenger stopped the vampire as he swept aside his
tent's door-flap. The young soldier bent his knee to the Red
Duke, genuflecting before the creature to which his family
had bound themselves with oaths of loyalty. The Red Duke
could not place the boy's name, but he could see the mark
of nobility in his manner and quality of armour. A squire
from one of the northern lords, those men whose ideas of
honour had caused them to prefer their rightful master to
Louis the Usurper.*

*'Your grace,' the messenger began, gasping for breath. The
dust of the road covered his armour and a tatter of bloodied
cloth bound his right arm. 'My father, Count Froissart is
sore beset by the king's forces in the wine fiefs! Castle Aquin
has fallen and Marquis d'Elbiq has betrayed us in the south
and joined the Duke of Quenelles against us!'*

The Red Duke's eyes blazed with fury, his armoured

hand shot out, closing upon the throat of the messenger. A brutal turn of the vampire's wrist and he snapped the squire's neck.

The vampire shook his fist at the Tower of Wizardry. This was the witch's doing! Isabeau had kept his forces occupied here long enough for King Louis and his allies to invade Aquitaine from north and south! Already the western half of his realm was beset by the Usurper's troops!

A cold smile crept across the vampire's dead flesh. Louis had tricked him, but the Red Duke would still win the war. He had always been the greater strategist during the crusade against Araby. Now the king would get a gruesome reminder that he owed his victory against Sultan Jaffar not to the Lady, but to the tactics of the rightful Duke of Aquitaine.

'De Gavaudan!' the Red Duke snarled. His twisted thrall emerged from the darkness of the pavilion, hissing spitefully at the dreary grey afternoon, shielding his eyes with his good hand.

The Red Duke ignored his slave's discomfort. He had a job for the filthy creature, a task the vampire was unwilling to entrust to one of his mortal servants. The example of the Marquis d'Elbiq was reminder enough that the loyalties of his knights might falter when forced to choose between their duke and their king.

'Gather my black knights,' the Red Duke told Baron de Gavaudan. He glanced up at the hanging tree and the rotting bodies dangling from its branches. 'Have the necromancers cut those two down and add them to the company. Ride southward, putting to the torch every village and farm. That will draw out Louis.' The vampire smiled, imagining the king's reaction to the brutal campaign of terror Baron de Gavaudan and four-hundred undead knights would unleash. The king would be moved to protect the peasants, *his advisors would urge him to attack the black knights while they were ranging ahead of the Red Duke's infantry. Like almost all Bretonnians, they would never consider that a commander would use his knights as merely a diversion, that the infantry would be his real weapon.*

King Louis would expect to find the Red Duke with Baron de Gavaudan and the wights. Therefore he would be taken by surprise when the Red Duke flanked the king's army with his infantry. De Gavaudan would draw the king out, the Red Duke would close the trap upon him.

'Stand fast at the village of Mercal,' the Red Duke told his slave. 'If the king's forces reach you, hold them at Mercal. I shall march my troops against the rear of the army, trapping them between us.'

Baron de Gavaudan nodded his head in understanding. The vampire thrall looked askance at one of the mortal men-at-arms bearing a net of fish towards the camp stores. 'The living ones will slow you down,' the decayed vampire warned.

The Red Duke turned his head and watched the man in question labouring under his burden. He intended to keep the mortal knights with him to give him a reserve of cavalry when the black knights rode off with Baron de Gavaudan. But his slave was right, living infantry would tire and slow his force down.

'Have the necromancers attend to them as well,' the Red Duke ordered. 'Warn them to be thorough. I want no man left behind when we quit this place.'

THE SIGHT OF crows circling above the Chateau du Maisne was the first inkling that Sir Leuthere was too late in bringing his warning to Count Ergon. As the knight and Vigor rode towards the castle, the open gate left no question that something was wrong. A mangy wolf came slinking out from the gateway as the two men rode up, scampering off into the brush, a severed human hand clenched in its jaws.

The scene within the courtyard was enough to turn even a knight's stomach. The half-eaten bodies of men and women were scattered throughout, crows picking at what other scavengers had left behind. The corpses of several ghouls, their unclean flesh feathered with arrows, sprawled near the stables, their faces pulled back in a rictus that exposed their sharpened teeth. Oddly enough, the sound of stamping hooves and anxious whinnies rose from the building beyond the ghouls. Apparently the massacre had not spread to the horses.

'We're too late,' Vigor shuddered, turning his face from the ghastly scene. 'The Red Duke has already been here. We're too late!'

Leuthere merely nodded, afraid if he spoke he would find the same panic expressed by the peasant sounding in his own voice. The knight cast his gaze across the bodies, trying to find Count Ergon or Sir Armand among the dead. He felt his gorge rise as his scrutiny found the mangled body of a woman, only the silver band locked about her wrist able to testify that the gnawed remains were those of the Countess du Maisne.

'We're too late!' Vigor cried.

Leuthere fixed the peasant with a stern look. 'Go quiet the horses,' the knight ordered, nodding at the stables. 'I'll have a look inside the castle.'

'They're all dead!' Vigor protested. 'The Red Duke is going to kill us all!'

'Go tend to the horses,' Leuthere repeated, his tone even more authoritative. A lifetime of service overcame

Vigor's rising panic and the peasant responded to the knight's command. Leuthere felt some relief when the crippled peasant dismounted and made his way towards the stables. The chore would give Vigor something to occupy his mind and keep him from letting his fear overwhelm him.

The knight dismounted as well, marching across the courtyard to where the doors of the keep had once stood. They were splintered and smashed now, one hanging limply from its fastenings, another thrown deep into the main hall of the keep. As Leuthere entered the hall, he could see the bodies of armoured men strewn everywhere. Some bore the marks of spear and sword, others had their skulls caved in by maces and hammers; still more bore no mark of violence except for the blood staining their ears and the expressions of abject horror frozen on their dead faces.

Here and there, Leuthere found some sign of the creatures that had visited such destruction upon the chateau. A rusty dagger, the corroded strap of a boot or vambrace, a bit of crumbling armour. Once he stumbled upon a fleshless skeleton draped across a table, its bones bleached by time and the elements, its skull shattered by some blow which had rendered the body beyond even a vampire's power to restore to obscene life.

About the stairway leading up to the gallery overlooking the main hall, Leuthere found the butchered remains of Sir Armand. The knight knew he looked upon the handiwork of the Red Duke himself. Only that monster could have mutilated the great swordsman in such a fashion. Armand's back and neck had been broken, the thumbs cut from his hands and the eyes gouged from his once handsome face. Leuthere was reminded of the inhuman savagery that had left his uncle's mangled body impaled above the cemetery at Ceren Field.

Leuthere tore a tapestry from the wall and draped it across Armand's body. In life, the warrior had been the bane of his family, the terrible swordsman who had fought to such great effect in the centuries-old feud between d'Elbiq and du Maisne. Earl Gaubert had struggled to impart a pathological hatred of the killer of his sons into every man who owed fealty to him. Some of that hatred had lingered in Leuthere's heart even as he rode to warn Count Ergon. Now, all he could feel was a sense of loss. In death, Leuthere could recognize Armand's bravery and honour, he could respect the warrior who had fought so fiercely and so well for his family. Such a man had not deserved to die this way, his body abused by an inhuman fiend.

Moans echoed about the lifeless hall. Leuthere turned, ripping his sword from its sheath. His eyes scoured the shadowy hall, hunting the darkness for any sign of motion. His heart drummed against his ribs, fear coursed through his veins. Perhaps the vampire had not left after committing his atrocities. Perhaps the Red Duke was yet within the walls of the Chateau du Maisne!

Cautiously, Leuthere walked into the darkness, heading towards the source of the sounds. He hesitated as he saw a body lying amid the jumble of a shattered table. He kept his sword at the ready, not knowing if what he gazed upon was man or monster. There was no guessing to what dishonourable deceit a vampire would stoop.

The moaning shape lifted a hand, painfully trying

to pull itself out from the splintered wreckage of the table. As the figure moved, it lifted its head into what little light penetrated the hall.

Leuthere's hand clenched tighter about his sword. The face was that of Count Ergon du Maisne, patriarch of the d'Elbiq's hated enemies!

The instinctive hate slowly drained from Leuthere's heart. There were more important things now than the ancient feud. Besides, Count Ergon was hurt and helpless. Even in the name of feud, Leuthere would not attack a man who could not defend himself.

Leuthere sheathed his blade and moved to assist Count Ergon in extricating himself from the wreckage. The nobleman locked his arm around Leuthere's, using the knight as leverage to kick his way free of the splintered planks. Count Ergon stood unsteadily on his feet and turned to thank his rescuer.

Gratitude withered as Count Ergon's face hardened. His hand clutched at the empty scabbard hanging from his belt.

'That was my reaction when I saw who it was trapped under the table,' Leuthere said. 'I am Sir Leuthere d'Elbiq, at your service, my lord.'

'You are a d'Elbiq,' Count Ergon agreed, making the name sound like an obscenity. 'There's no hiding that weasel-taint in your face. I should not be surprised to see you here! Earl Gaubert sending his jackals out to pick over the monster's leavings! Give me a sword and I'll settle with that villain for once and all!'

'My uncle is dead,' Leuthere said, answering the count's outburst with a voice both low and grave. 'He was murdered by the same fiend who did this.'

Count Ergon shook his head, staring at the carnage around him, wincing as he saw his servants and soldiers strewn about the hall. The impact was enough to make him forget his long nourished hate. For the moment, it was enough that Leuthere was a man, another living soul in this charnel house of destruction.

'It was a vampire,' Count Ergon said. 'A creature in red armour riding a skeleton horse. It claimed to be the Red Duke, vanquished these many centuries by good King Louis.'

'He is the Red Duke,' Leuthere told the count. 'Risen from his secret tomb at Ceren Field. Risen to reclaim Aquitaine for his Kingdom of Blood.'

Count Ergon shuddered, nodding as the knight spoke. Easily the nobleman could believe what Leuthere told him. The ferocious monster could have been no less a horror than the infamous Red Duke.

'I tried to fight him,' Count Ergon said. 'He handled me as though I were a child, ripped the sword from my fingers and seized me by the throat. I should have died, but at that moment my son challenged the monster. The Red Duke tossed me aside, threw me like a rag-doll off the gallery...' Abject terror consumed the nobleman. Frantically, he began rushing to the bodies lifting their heads, staring into their faces.

Leuthere knew what the desperate nobleman was looking for. 'Sir Armand is there,' the knight said, pointing to the mutilated body at the foot of the stairs. Count Ergon ran to the sorry corpse, crying out in agony when he saw the havoc that had been done to his son's body. 'He must have acquitted himself well against the vampire for the Red Duke to do that to him,' Leuthere said.

Tears streamed from Count Ergon's eyes as he knelt beside Armand's body. He leaned over and brushed his fingers across the cold forehead, pushing back a stray lock of hair.

'He was a truer knight than any I have known,' Count Ergon said. A flash of pain passed across his features. 'I never told him that. I never told him how proud I was to call him my son.'

'I am certain you did not need to,' Leuthere said, breaking the mournful silence. The knight shifted his shoulders, his flesh crawling as he considered the unpleasant duty before him. 'Count Ergon, though I am a d'Elbiq, please believe me when I tell you how unwelcome it is to bear such tidings. Sir Armand, I fear, is not the only loss your house has suffered.'

The count clenched his eyes as fresh pain swelled within him, a piteous groan rising from his throat. 'Elaine did not escape?'

Leuthere shook his head. 'The fiends must have been waiting for the countess and her attendants. I saw no evidence that any escaped.'

'Then it is all gone,' Count Ergon cursed, rising to his feet. 'The ancient house of du Maisne is no more.' He glared at Leuthere, and laughed bitterly. 'This is a banner day for the d'Elbiqs. You have finally won the feud.'

'Only a low-born varlet would take any satisfaction from what was done here,' Leuthere said. 'I ride to stop this monster. I swear before the Lady, on the sacred grail itself, that I will not rest until the Red Duke is returned to his grave.'

'A noble purpose,' Count Ergon commented, sarcasm in his tone. 'Sir Armand was the greatest blade in all Aquitaine and here he lies at my feet, broken by the Red Duke. What hope do you have of destroying the vampire?'

'None,' admitted Leuthere. 'Only the knowledge that my purpose is just and my faith that the Lady will not allow this evil to endure.'

The knight's words impressed Count Ergon and the nobleman would have taken back his scorn of a moment before. A hopeless fight was the kind a knight was most obligated to pursue if he were worthy of his rank.

'I will set aside this feud between us,' Count Ergon decided. 'I will help you catch this vampire and bring him low – but remember, mine is the greater claim to vengeance. Mine must be the sword that puts the Red Duke back in his grave.'

Leuthere felt sympathy for the count's emotion, but knew there was a more important duty than revenge before the nobleman now. 'What you wish is impossible,' Leuthere said. 'There is a more important task which only Count Ergon du Maisne may perform. Duke Gilon must be warned of this menace, must be made to believe the Red Duke has returned. He would not believe a d'Elbiq knight, but he will believe Count Ergon du Maisne.'

The count clenched his jaw in anger. 'I will not forget my son and my wife and my servants slaughtered like cattle by grave-cheating horrors. Beside you or against you, I will take up the Red Duke's trail. The vampire will not escape my justice!' Count Ergon reached to the neck of his armour, pulling from beneath it a heavy gold chain. A large signet ring hung from the necklace. 'We will stop at the first chateau we come across and I will dispatch a message to Duke Gilon telling him the vampire has indeed returned. Duke Gilon will not dispute the message when he sees my seal affixed to it.'

Leuthere sighed. 'There is no way to make you change your mind?'

'Only by using your sword and leaving me here with my son,' Count Ergon replied.

'You have set aside the feud, so too shall I,' Leuthere said. 'Until the Red Duke is vanquished, we are comrades in arms.' The knight turned his gaze to the sorry corpse of Sir Armand. 'If you will allow me, I would help you bury your son before we pursue his killer.'

'There will be no grave for my son,' Count Ergon answered. The nobleman turned Armand's head so that Leuthere could see the ugly wounds in the dead man's neck. 'The vampire shattered my son's body, then ensured Armand would share his profane curse. He damned my son to an eternity as a crippled monster crawling on its belly through the shadows.' Count Ergon rose from the floor and shambled towards the shattered table. 'I know such was his purpose because he threatened me with the same fate.'

Count Ergon drew a long sliver of wood from the collapsed table, carefully inspecting the sharpness of its splintered end. 'No grave for Sir Armand du Maisne,' he said, his voice grim. 'A stake through the heart and a bonfire to cremate the bones. That is the only way to spare my son from the curse of the vampire.'

RENAR RAN HIS finger through the long blond mane of his horse, admiring the feel of the animal. Like any Bretonnian, the necromancer appreciated good horseflesh and the graceful, lean-limbed courser he had taken from Count Ergon's stables was among the finest he had ever seen. A peasant, even the most prosperous merchant, could never hope to own such a fine animal. Money could buy one, of course, but the laws of the nobility would quickly settle any peasant who had the audacity to ride such a fine beast.

The necromancer smiled and moved his fingers from the fine mane to the flowing purple caparison covering the horse. Purple was a royal colour, set aside for the higher ranks of the nobility. These trappings had probably belonged to Count Ergon himself, or perhaps his wife. It was an act punishable by the most cruel mutilation for anyone not nobly born to display royal colours.

A spiteful chuckle rattled through Renar's rotten teeth. He had no reason to fear the tyranny of the knights and their laws any longer. Not now, not with the Red Duke as his protector, not with an army of the walking dead to stand between him and a noose. He, a miserable peasant, had risen to the position of advisor and confidant to the most powerful warlord Aquitaine had ever known.

The necromancer patted the saddlebags draped across the flanks of his horse, filled to bursting with plunder from the Chateau du Maisne. Renar's mouth watered as he imagined the things he would buy. There were booksellers and antiquarians in Moussillon who specialized in certain outré subjects. Renar knew of one scabby old merchant who possessed a copy of the *Liber Mortis* written by the Sylvanian necromancer Frederick van Hal. The secrets contained just in that single tome would be enough to make Renar the most fearsome sorcerer in the history of Bretonnia. With his powers enhanced and the Red Duke's army, Renar would be able to carve a kingdom from the bloodied husk of Aquitaine.

Of course, that meant continuing to manage the

vampire and trying to control his capricious moods. Renar wasn't happy about that prospect, but he was confident he would find a way. He needed the Red Duke; the vampire still had the mind and genius of the brilliant warlord he had been in life. At the same time, the Red Duke needed him. There were limits to what even the most powerful among the undead could accomplish. It took a beating heart and a mortal soul to fully draw upon the fell powers of Dhar, the black wind of sorcery, the power that sustained the lesser undead and which fuelled the dark art of necromancy.

Renar looked about him, watching as the silent ranks of zombies and skeletons marched along the little country road, making the long journey back to the Crac de Sang. Now that the Red Duke had shown his hand, it was important that they return to the fortress and fortify it against attack. The nobles of Aquitaine could not be expected to remain idle once they were aware of the vampire's return. The Crac de Sang offered the best stronghold from which to fight a defensive campaign.

If the Red Duke stuck to the plan, they would be able to hold off an army once his old fortress was restored. With a tireless legion of undead labourers, the vampire declared the castle could be made defensible in only a few weeks.

Renar was not convinced. He wanted more bodies marching beneath the vampire's banner. He'd railed against the Red Duke's decree that the corpses of Count Ergon and his retainers be left to rot in the Chateau du Maisne. The Red Duke had decided that Durand du Maisne's descendant and any craven enough to follow him were unfit to serve the rightful

ruler of Aquitaine. Nothing Renar could do would
sway the vampire's decision. He could take some
small consolation that the Red Duke had allowed
Renar's zombies to scavenge arms and armour from
the dead and the castle's stores. The vampire's pride
was not above seizing the resources of a vanquished
enemy. Only the horses had been left behind – too
frightened by the unnatural taint of the undead to be
managed on the long march. Renar supposed they
could have slaughtered the beasts and revived them
as zombified husks, but such a prospect offended
even his pragmatism. In the end, only the horse Renar
chose for himself had been taken, and even that fine
animal had to wear blinders and be soothed by the
necromancer's spells before it would allow itself to be
brought near the undead warriors.

The necromancer turned in his saddle, watching the
shuffling columns of walking dead following behind
him. There were more of the creatures now. Renar
had suggested to the Red Duke that they stop at each
village they passed on the way back – to 'impress soldiers' as he phrased his plan. The peasant inhabitants
fled when they saw the ghastly army coming, but the
inhabitants of their graveyards could not. After passing through half a dozen villages, Renar had created
enough new soldiers for the Red Duke to almost
exhaust the store of weapons taken from the Chateau
du Maisne, doubling and almost trebling the force
that had attacked the castle.

Slavering shapes loped back towards the column,
sharp-fanged ghouls the Red Duke had sent to scout
the terrain ahead. The vampire chose to think of the
slinking subhumans as venerers, but the only game
the loathsome creatures were adept at sniffing out

was carrion. They had been quite useful finding large graveyards for Renar. From their agitation, it seemed that the Red Duke's army would be inducting fresh recruits quite soon.

Renar spurred his horse to the head of the column where the Red Duke and the gruesome wight-lord Sir Corbinian held conference. If the skeletal knight uttered any responses to the Red Duke's words, it was in no such voice as Renar could hear.

'When de Gavaudan returns we shall dispatch the knights to the left flank,' the vampire was telling his old retainer. 'Then we shall deploy the archers behind the dunes. When Mehmed-bey leads his Arabyans down the wadi, the cavalry shall engage him, drawing him deeper into the defile. Then, unable to advance because of our horse, unable to retreat for the press of his own men, and unable to turn right or left because of the dunes, we shall rain volley upon volley upon the heads of the foul Paynim!'

The vampire twisted his head around as the ghouls came loping back. He smiled down at the first of the monsters to reach him. 'Ah, a hobelar bringing word from my noble vassal! You have lost your steed, my good man! Retrieve another from the remounts!'

The ghoul stopped short, his fanged face contorting in confusion as the vampire spoke. Anxiously, the creature backed away from the Red Duke.

Renar grimaced, shaking his head in frustration. What new madness was this?

'It doesn't have a horse,' the necromancer snapped. 'If you gave it a horse, it would eat it. It isn't bringing word back from anybody. You sent it out to look for graveyards so we can steal bodies. We steal the bodies, I use my magic, they come alive and we give them a spear to stick into an enemy.'

The Red Duke turned his skeletal horse about, directing a hard stare at the necromancer. 'How dare you ride your lord's horse, peasant!' The vampire gestured and Sir Corbinian shambled forwards, seizing the courser's reins in his bony hand. The animal bucked furiously, the calming spells unable to soothe away such close contact with the wight. Renar was thrown to the road, landing on his backside. The wight-lord allowed its grip to slacken, the courser pulling free and racing away.

Renar scowled and cursed as he watched his prize run off, gold and jewels spilling from the saddlebags. 'Black bones of Nagash! That was *my* horse! That was *my* treasure!'

'Mind your tongue, varlet,' the Red Duke warned. 'I tolerate your insolence only because I need every man to fight the Arabyans.' The vampire waved a hand towards the galloping horse. 'That fine animal returns to my loyal vassal Baron de Gavaudan. If you came by any of yon plunder fairly, then he will return it to you.'

Rolling his eyes, Renar got back to his feet. 'Baron de Gavaudan is dead! He has been these past four hundred years!' The necromancer spread his arms, gesturing at the tall trees bordering the road, at the green fields beyond. 'This isn't Araby! This is Aquitaine!'

The Red Duke closed his eyes, pain flaring across his face. He raised his hand to his forehead, driving the armoured fingers of his gauntlet into the pale skin as though trying to rip the agony from his skull.

'Where is de Gavaudan?' the vampire demanded when he lowered his hand.

'I told you,' Renar snapped. 'He's dead.'

The Red Duke's expression became one of livid rage. 'I asked where he is, not what became of him!'

Renar staggered on his feet, all thoughts of lost wealth and power driven from him by the fury in the vampire's voice. 'He fought King Louis at the village of Mercal and was defeated.' The necromancer swallowed hard, not knowing how the Red Duke would react to such news. 'The king's men destroyed them all. Not a single one escaped.'

The Red Duke's scowl took on a cunning quality. 'Turn the column about,' he ordered.

'What about the Crac de Sang?' protested Renar.

'We're not going to the Crac de Sang,' the Red Duke hissed. 'We're going to Mercal.'

CHAPTER X

He was more dead than alive as they laid him upon the brass-framed bed and its thick coverings of silk and fur. The standard of Bretonnia's king fluttered over his head, fixed to a stand beside the bed. A squadron of pages decked out in the royal livery circled the bed, creating an artificial breeze with ostrich-feather fans. Squires scurried about the tent bearing jugs of cold water drawn from the wells of El Haikk and chilled by the magic of Imperial wizards. Physicians swarmed over him, examining every finger and toe as they solemnly tried to restore his vitality. In one corner of the pavilion, a dour priestess of Shallya erected a tiny shrine and prayed to the goddess of mercy and healing for his recovery.

El Syf was only dimly aware of all this, his mind wandering back to the ambush in the desert and the strange dark knight who had been both his rescuer and his destroyer.

'He won't survive,' the voice of Baron de Gavaudan was sharp with frustration. 'Every physician says the same thing. They can't stop the poison. Even the Arabyans don't know what kind of venom is in his veins. There's no hope.'

'This is no hero's death,' was the bitter observation of

Marquis d'Elbiq. 'Lying abed, his life drained out of him
by these damn doctors and their leeches! Better he had
died in harness fighting the filthy heathen!'

'A hero's death or no,' Baron de Gavaudan declared, 'we
must accept that the Duke of Aquitaine will not recover.'

'Then if he is to die, let him die on Bretonnian soil!' The
regal voice of King Louis the Righteous was harsh with
fatigue and despair. 'This abominable land has claimed
too much of our blood already. It will not have his!'

'Be reasonable, sire,' Baron de Gavaudan implored. 'He
cannot last much longer. It would be foolish and cruel to
send him back to Aquitaine now. Let his body be borne
back with the other noble dead when we decamp these
damnable deserts.'

'Marrying your daughter does not make you my father,'
the king replied acidly. 'No man in the crusade has
fought as nobly or as well for our cause as the Duke of
Aquitaine. There is no honour we can pay him that could
be too great.'

'But he is dying,' Baron de Gavaudan persisted. 'We
must think of the future. There must be a new Duke of
Aquitaine. You, sire, are the next in ascension. You are
the logical one to assume his duties.'

'Let him return to his home with full titles and honours,' King Louis said, his voice heavy with sadness. 'It is
a knave who would play jackal at such a time.' The king's
voice grew firm. 'This is my decree: the duke's vassals
shall bear him back to Castle Aquin with all dispatch.
An honour guard shall see them through the desert and
the fastest ship in the fleet shall be at their disposal when
they reach Lashiek. Every consideration shall be given for
the comfort and dignity of the duke as he is returned to
Aquitaine. If it is within the power of man, we will return
him to his domain that he may gaze upon the greenery

of Bretonnia before he is taken into the Lady's embrace.'

'As you say, sire,' de Gavaudan said. 'Every considera-tion must be made…'

SIR MARAULF SHOOK the shoulder of the sleeping peasant. The man's hands instantly flew to the spear propped up against the earthen wall. His head bounced about like that of some enormous bird, his eyes struggling to pierce both the darkness and the sleep crusted at their corners.

The knight gave the startled peasant a reassuring pat, urging him to be calm. The attack Maraulf feared had not yet manifested. Even so, he wanted the man to be vigilant. Because the attack would come. Maraulf had never been more certain of anything in his life.

Ironically, it was the thing the knight most desper-ately prayed for that was taking an unmerciful toll on the defenders of Mercal. Time was what he needed, time to strengthen the defence of Mercal, time to convince the local earls and marquises that it was in their best interest to send troops to protect a cluster of peasant hovels and a half-forgotten chapel.

Most of the lords had laughed at Maraulf's entreaty, scoffing at his claims that the Red Duke had returned. Perhaps, had he completed his quest and become a grail knight, they would have listened to him, but Maraulf had been moved to take a different path. Now, more than ever, he understood the gulf that separated him from the knightly classes to which he had once belonged.

There was still some hope that the gods would move the hearts of some of the lords who hadn't laughed at him. Even a dozen knights and a few score men-at-arms might be enough to hold the

Chapel Sereine and the cemetery around it. Enough to thwart the Red Duke's plans and break his evil before it could fully begin.

Until then, Maraulf had to make do with the troops available to him. There had been no shortage of volunteers from Mercal itself – every able-bodied man, and several of dubious health as well, had taken up arms to defend his home. The man he had awakened, Trejean, who now gripped his spear so fiercely, had been nothing more than a chicken farmer a few days ago. He had never done anything more warlike than chasing foxes from his coops with a stout club and a raised voice. Yet there had been no hesitation when Maraulf explained the village's peril to Trejean. The thought of facing the walking dead was something terrifying to the peasant. The thought of seeing his family and his home destroyed by such creatures was more horrible still.

All of Maraulf's peasant-warriors were scared, and as the hours turned into days, that fear only grew. They were unable to eat, unable to sleep, unable to think about anything except the terrible doom that hung over their village. Time was wearing them out, fear eating them away until they dropped exhausted at their posts. These men were not knights or soldiers. They were farmers and swineherds, coopers and leatherworkers, men for whom the thought of war was almost as horrifying as the Red Duke himself.

The knight left Trejean and continued his march along the trench. The peasants had laboured hard to build the defensive earthworks around the Chapel Sereine and its graveyard. Duke Gilon's engineers could have done better, of course, but Maraulf was impressed by the way the villagers had followed his commands. He supposed it was, after all, only a little different than digging a drainage trench or an irrigation ditch, but it would be just as effective against a cavalry charge. The excavated earth had been formed into low mounds, creating a staggered barrier all around the graveyard, tall enough for a man to hide behind but short enough that they would not conceal the enemy's advance.

Maraulf lifted himself up from the trench, looking over the anxious, weary faces of his men. He could see how uncomfortable they were with their improvised weapons – crudely fashioned spears, farm implements lashed to poles, rusty axes and maces plundered from some ancient battlefield. This was all strange to them, the idea of bearing arms and defending their homes. It was strange to Maraulf too. After so many years, the knight had never expected to ever lead men into battle again, be they peasant or noble. He could only have faith in the gods that his leadership and their courage would not be found wanting.

A pang of guilt passed through Maraulf's heart. The knight lifted his eyes from the trench and its defenders to the vast graveyard beyond them. The cemetery was many times the size of Mercal itself, growing with each passing year. Many of those buried here were of the knightly classes, buried here so that they might be beside the Chapel Sereine and the grail knight interred within.

It was the chapel and its holy aura that would draw the Red Duke to this place. The vampire would come for what had been buried in secret below the chapel. Maraulf couldn't allow the Red Duke to violate those hidden catacombs. It was more important than his own life and the lives of the villagers. The Chapel

Sereine had to be protected, to the last drop of blood if need be. To ensure that, the knight had devised a cruel deception.

Maraulf had told the villagers that the safest place for them to seek refuge was within the blessed walls of the chapel. While the men defended the cemetery, their families took shelter in the marble-walled shrine. They never guessed that their safety was an illusion, that they had instead placed themselves at the very centre of the coming storm. True, the enchantments placed upon the chapel would prevent the Red Duke from raising the dead buried beneath it or those buried in the surrounding graveyard. But the holy wards were not so strong as to hold back the vampire or the undead that already marched under his banner.

The knight's fingers traced the raven embroidered upon his cloak. It was a knavish ploy, but there were some things more important than honour and chivalrous vows. The gods would understand. It would be for them to judge his actions.

'You expect them to come tonight, my lord?' The question came from a grizzled old peasant. Despite his age and the lack of teeth in his lower jaw, Jeanot was a powerfully built man, his shoulders broad, his arms knotted with muscle beneath the coarse fabric of his robe. He wore a mail coif, the hood pulled back to form an iron muffler about his throat. Bits of garlic were tied to the cuffs of his sleeves and pinned to his belt. A horseman's mace, its surface pitted with age, swung from a tether lashed about his wrist.

'They are already overdue,' Maraulf told Jeanot. Unlike the villagers, Jeanot understood the ways of war. He was a grail pilgrim, the only man in Mercal who had known the knight interred in the Chapel

Sereine when he was alive. As a boy, Jeanot's village had been attacked by orcs. The brutish marauders had been stopped by the arrival of a lone knight who had given them battle and taken such toll upon them as to send the monsters scrambling back to their mountains. Since that day, Jeanot had followed the knight throughout the land, ringleader of a small cult that venerated the knight as a living saint. The cult of pilgrims had followed their knight throughout Bretonnia, fighting beside him in his many battles. When he had at last died and been interred in the Chapel Sereine, Jeanot and the other pilgrims had remained to watch over his grave.

The original battle pilgrims were all gone, all save Jeanot, but others had come to take their place, men who had heard the tales of the grail knight and sought serenity through serving the holy warrior's spirit. There were only a dozen of the pilgrims in Mercal, but Maraulf considered himself lucky to have them. They were the closest thing to real soldiers he had to draw upon.

Instead of scattering the pilgrims along the trench, Maraulf kept them back near the chapel itself, a reserve to react to the Red Duke's attack. He would have preferred a squadron of fast-moving cavalry, but in the crowded ground of the cemetery, Maraulf thought the dismounted pilgrims might actually prove more manoeuvrable.

Maraulf stared at the battle pilgrims, a ragged group of unkempt men dressed in coarse homespun robes, each bearing some bit of armour on his person. One wore a vambrace suspended from his neck by a leather thong; another had a pauldron tied to his head like a helmet. Each man wore the scrap of armour not for protection but as a talisman, for each piece had been taken from the grave of their grail knight. A dark-haired pilgrim named Girard bore a heavy reliquary box fastened to a stout maplewood staff, the little wooden doors bearing a crude representation of the grail branded upon them. Inside the box itself were the helmet of the grail knight and the splintered skull of his warhorse. For the pilgrims, these were the most holy of relics, as important to them as the grail itself to the knights of the realm. As peasants, they could never hope to see the Lady or sip from the grail; all they could do was pay obeisance to a knight who had.

It was a sentiment Maraulf could appreciate, for the grail was lost to him, though in his case it had been choice not birth that had denied him such a path.

The black-garbed knight watched as the sky began to grow darker. Storm clouds were sweeping across the night sky, blotting out the stars one by one. His flesh crawled as his spirit sensed the workings of foul magic in the air. Grimly, Maraulf drew his sword. 'Get your men ready,' the knight told Jeanot. 'Send the swiftest of them to warn the villagers.'

The knight's voice was like a metal snarl as he spoke through the steel mask of his helm.

'The waiting is over.'

THE RED DUKE'S skeletal steed marched through the muddy lane that formed Mercal's main thoroughfare. Except for a few pigs and some chickens, the village was deserted and as quiet as the grave.

Armoured skeletons patrolled ahead of him, smashing down the wicker doors of each hut they passed, searching each hovel for any hidden inhabitants. *The vampire could smell the rich spices and salty sea air as his*

troops secured Lashiek, scouring the city for the sultan's cor-
sairs. There was no mercy for the heathen pirates; as each
was found he was dragged into the street and beheaded. It
was a kind fate for such loathsome villains.

WHEELING HIS HORSE about, the Red Duke closed his
eyes, forcing his mind to focus. When he turned his
steed back around, the white walls of Lashiek faded
back into memory, the mud huts and thatch roofs of
Mercal springing back into stark relief. The vampire
snarled in annoyance as a pair of skeletons pulled
down a straw shack and began to sift the debris looking for anyone caught inside.

They wouldn't find Baron de Gavaudan and the
company of undead knights he'd used to attack Mercal in a straw shack. The Red Duke knew his thrall
was nearby, he could sense the lingering essence of
the other vampire like a dull ache at the back of his
skull. He wasn't sure how Baron de Gavaudan had
been vanquished, he only knew that he had. It hadn't
even been King Louis or his household knights that
had worked the ruin of de Gavaudan, for there had
been no shortage of cavalry when the Red Duke had
met the king upon Ceren Field. Even as bait, Baron de
Gavaudan had been a disappointment.

Renar came slinking down the street, flanked by packs
of ghouls. Degenerate as they were, the necromancer
and the cannibals were still living creatures, able to operate more freely than the true undead. It took no part of
the vampire's arcane power to spur his living vassals to
greater effort, only a snarled command.

The necromancer's long face was pinched with
dissatisfaction. Renar had considered himself too
important to be employed for mere reconnaissance.

It was both humiliating and humbling for him to be sent ahead of the Red Duke's army, sent to sniff about the terrain with the loathsome ghouls.

The Red Duke little cared for Renar's opinion. A peasant's only purpose was to obey the will of his lord.

'We could have trouble ahead,' Renar informed the vampire. The Red Duke scowled back at the gaunt man, not liking the surly note in his voice. 'The villagers... they've gathered in the cemetery... built earthworks... made spears...' Renar injected a healthy dose of contrition in his tone as he noted the vampire's displeasure. 'There's a chapel at the centre of the graveyard. I could sense power emanating from it... a force antithetical to that which sustains the undead.'

The Red Duke nodded as he digested Renar's report. 'Then it will be your task to secure the chapel and break its enchantments. Take the ghouls with you.'

Fear filled Renar's eyes. 'My magic will be useless!' he protested. 'I won't be able to call a single corpse from ground sanctified by such...'

'Then you will just have to break the enchantment,' the Red Duke snarled. 'Your spells were powerful enough to shatter the wards which trapped me in my tomb. They should be enough to break those protecting the chapel.'

Renar shook his head. 'I had time to examine the spell laid upon your tomb. I have no idea what magic guards this place!'

The vampire bared his fangs. 'Then you will find out, mortal. Take the ghouls and circle the cemetery. I will lead my troops in a frontal assault upon the defences. When the defenders converge upon me to throw back the attack, then you shall fall upon them from behind and strike for the chapel.'

Still dubious, the necromancer squirmed inside his long black coat. 'Master, what if I cannot break the spell? All of this will be for nothing. Isn't it more reasonable to find another…'

'If your magic is not strong enough to serve me, then you are useless to me, peasant,' the Red Duke hissed. He gestured with his hand, beckoning the skeletal Sir Corbinian towards them. The armoured wight stared at Renar with its witch-fire eyes. 'Sir Corbinian will accompany you. He will protect you and see that you reach the chapel in safety. If you fail to break the enchantment, he will remove your wormy head from your shoulders.'

Renar trembled as he heard the vampire pronounce his doom. Gazing upon the Red Duke, however, he saw that the monster would hear no further debate. The fiend's mind was decided. It was the necromancer's job now to serve or die.

Resigned to his fate, Renar led the ghouls away. They would circle around the village of Mercal and strike the cemetery from the thin stand of woods that bordered it to the north. As the necromancer withdrew, the skeletal figure of his protector and potential executioner kept pace with him, one bony fist locked about the grip of its rusty blade.

'LOOSE ARROWS! LOOSE arrows!'

Sir Maraulf waved the blade of his sword overhead, torchlight shimmering across the steel. In the unnatural gloom that enveloped the cemetery, the knight's blade acted like a banner, drawing peasants to his position. He risked a look over his shoulder, trying to penetrate the dark and see how many men were stirring from their positions to reinforce the embattled southern flank.

Too few and too slow, Maraulf decided. Most of the villagers had never even been in a tavern brawl, much less a real life-and-death fight. He could see several paralysed with fear, clinging to the walls of their ditches like babes at their mother's breast. If only the local lords had heeded him. If only they had sent him a few dozen men-at-arms and a handful of knights.

Maraulf chided himself for his thoughts. There was no use wishing for things that would not be and there was no sense berating scared men for their fear. All was in the hands of the gods.

The Red Duke's attack came in silent suddenness. One of Jeanot's battle pilgrims saw them first. The man had quitted the trench to relieve himself and come scrambling back behind the defences, muttering about a company of dead men marching out of Mercal village. A minute later, the first of the zombies had appeared within the flickering ring of light cast by their torches.

Arrows brought down several of the rotting creatures, but even the way they fell, soundlessly and with a peculiar motion more like a broken puppet than a dying man, evoked a sense of horror in the peasant bowmen. With each volley, their shooting became more erratic and imprecise. At first admirably accurate, their archery became as sloppy as that of any giggling goblin lunatic. Maraulf and Jeanot were compelled to maintain a steady stream of orders just to keep the bowmen loosing arrows into the oncoming horde.

Despite the slovenly archery, the ranks of zombies were thinned out considerably by the time they reached the earthen walls. The undead scrabbled clumsily at the barrier, trying to climb over the loose earth. Peasants and pilgrims crouching in the trenches rose up, driving spears into them, transfixing the decayed creatures so that pilgrims armed with clubs and maces might smash in their rotting skulls.

Maraulf had dared to believe they might hold the position until a second wave of attackers appeared behind the zombies. These were the fleshless husks of men, living skeletons drawn out from their ancient graves. They bore heavier armour than the rags and scraps worn by the zombies and in each bony fist was a sword of steel or a spear of iron. In numbers and armament, the skeletons far excelled Maraulf's men.

The knight's blood ran cold when he looked past the marching skeletons and spied their gruesome general. Seated atop a spectral steed barded in crimson, his red armour gleaming in the torchlight, the vampire's face was contorted into a mask of vicious pleasure as he watched his monstrous host converge upon the peasants. Maraulf was no stranger to the undead. Across Bretonnia and beyond he had fought their foul kind in the name of his god. He had penetrated the hidden crypts of several vampires and brought to them Morr's justice. But this creature was different – this was a monster whose exploits had haunted Aquitaine for centuries. This was no nameless fiend of the night, this was the Red Duke, a black legend returned to visit his revenge upon the living.

Maraulf felt fear pound through his veins for the first time in decades. He glanced to east and west, finding neither side of the cemetery under attack. There was, perhaps, still time to escape. He could order the retreat, leave Jeanot and his pilgrims to fight a rearguard while the rest of them escaped.

The thought shamed him. There was much more than his life and honour at stake here. The Red Duke had to be stopped from entering the Chapel Sereine if it cost all their lives. Right now, the vampire was a menace. If he could recover the bodies of his vanquished knights, the Red Duke would become a threat to all Bretonnia.

Maraulf waved his sword overhead, crying out to the peasant bowmen to loose arrows into the oncoming horde. He waited only long enough to hear the first volley, then turned back to the trench. He rushed to support a peasant spearman as the villager collapsed before the combined assault of a zombie and a skeleton. The man cried out in terror as the zombie held him down, its decayed fingers clawing at his tunic. The skeleton raised a corroded bronze axe and prepared to brain the screaming man.

Soundless as the undead themselves, the dark-garbed Sir Maraulf fell upon the monsters. His sword smashed into the skeleton's arm, cutting it in two, sending axe and forearm spinning away in the darkness. In the same brutal sweep, Maraulf brought the edge of his weapon slashing through the zombie's scalp, opening the decayed head like a pot of rancid jam. The creature shuddered and slumped across the peasant, its greasy brains running down its rotten face. Maraulf's finished the disarmed skeleton with a backsweep of his blade that broke its spine and left it twitching on the floor of the trench.

The rescued peasant scrambled out from underneath the unmoving zombie, his face pale with horror. The man did not even glance at his discarded spear, but instead turned and ran screaming from the battle.

Maraulf watched the fleeing man stumble his way across the graveyard. He could not fault the man for his terror, as much as it might doom them all. There was a limit to what could be expected of peasants unversed in the art of war.

The knight quickly forgot the fleeing peasant as he saw movement among the gravestones. It was not the wholesome motion of men, but the loathsome scuttling of inhuman creatures. Maraulf was familiar enough with the ways of the undead to recognize the animalistic scurry of ghouls.

He cursed himself for a fool. He had allowed himself to concentrate upon the Red Duke as a monster, forgetting that he had been a man first, a man who had led armies into battle. The seemingly mindless attack on the earthworks was not the unthinking assault of a monster, it was the calculated feint of a tactician. While Maraulf had concentrated his forces to repulse the Red Duke's attack, the knight had opened the way for the vampire's more nimble slaves to penetrate the cemetery from behind.

'Jeanot!' Maraulf cried out. 'We are attacked from behind! Break away! Fall back to the chapel!'

The knight's orders must have been heard by the Red Duke. At once, the ferocity of the attack increased, a savage vitality infusing the skeletons and zombies trying to capture the trench. A spectral figure with a filmy white gown appeared among the bowmen, her beautiful face corroding into a leering skull as she opened her mouth and emitted a deafening shriek that brought men to their knees.

Maraulf clasped his hands against his helm, trying to block out the banshee's scream. Even with her shriek piercing his brain like a piece of hot iron, the knight would not be swayed. Resolutely, he turned and raced back towards the chapel.

His sword licked out, slashing through the neck of a ghoul feasting upon the body of a pilgrim. The cannibal collapsed across his victim. A second ghoul reared up, her jaws caked in gore, a human toe caught between her fangs. Maraulf kicked out, his boot smashing the creature's face into mush. Like a stricken cur, the ghoul whined and scurried away.

Maraulf turned away from the savage tableau and resumed his dash towards the chapel. He could see a gaunt figure in a shabby black coat standing before the steps of the chapel, his long hands reaching out towards the barred doors. No ghoul, this one, but a man. Maraulf's guts churned with loathing. There was only one sort of mortal debased enough to traffic with vampires and ghouls. As a rule, the knight tried to remain dispassionate about killing, but the destruction of a necromancer was one pleasure no amount of pious serenity could quell.

Another pair of ghouls lurched up from their cannibalistic meals as Maraulf drew near the chapel. He brought his sword crunching through the shoulder of one, leaving the creature strewn across a grave, life-blood jetting from the ghoul's ruptured veins. The second monster pounced at him, long claws spread to rip the knight's flesh. Maraulf twisted aside from the ghoul's lunge, then brought his blade smashing down as the beast swept past. The sword chopped through the ghoul's back, bisecting him cleanly above the waist. The mutilated monster's momentum sent its severed halves rolling among the graves.

Renar spun about in alarm as the grim knight advanced. The necromancer raised his arms before him, almost in entreaty. Maraulf was unmoved. He could sense the power gathering about the evil conjurer. He pointed his sword at Renar, making it clear that the villain could expect no quarter.

The necromancer sneered, then unleashed the spell he had been conjuring. Maraulf felt a sharp burn against his breast as the little raven talisman he wore became red hot, flaring with energy as it absorbed the black magic directed against the knight. Renar's sneer became an expression of terror as Maraulf continued to advance towards the chapel.

Suddenly, a new opponent came before Maraulf, a ghastly shape that lumbered out from the shadows of the chapel. Maraulf hesitated as the armoured skeleton raised its rusted sword and saluted him in the fashion of a knight issuing a challenge. There was no humanity in the witch-fires that glowed in the sockets of the wight-lord's skull, but some element of the man yet lingered in the monster's bones.

Maraulf did not deign to return the wight's salute. Such proprieties were for the living, not the undead. The knight instead charged at the skeletal monstrosity, his sword flashing out in a deadly arc. The sweep of Maraulf's sword passed the shoulder of his foe, the wight displaying unexpected agility as it dodged the attack. The fleshless skull grinned at Maraulf as the wight's rusty sword cracked against the knight's pauldron with such force the armour was almost torn from its fastenings.

There followed a grim duel, man against monster, living against undead. Blow for blow, strike for strike, the two combatants fought with equal skill. But skill was the least of the inequalities of this macabre duel. As seconds stretched into minutes, Maraulf's vigour began to fade. The strain of his muscles, the fatigue of his flesh, the pain of his wounds, these began to sap the knight's skill. Fear of failure plagued his every thought, polluting the purity of his swordsmanship. If he fell, Maraulf knew the chapel would be taken, the Red Duke would restore to hideous unlife his foul army.

The wight suffered no such distractions. Its muscles were dust, its flesh only a vague memory, its wounds no more than gashes stricken upon unfeeling bone. No fear stirred its mind, only the inviolable command issued by its master. Every moment, Maraulf grew weaker but the strength of the wight-lord remained constant.

In the end, Sir Corbinian's blade slipped past Maraulf's guard. The rusty sword passed through the knight's armpit, stabbing deep into the body within the armour. The wight wrenched its blade free as the stricken Maraulf collapsed at its feet. Grimly, the skeleton raised the sword and saluted the mortally wounded knight.

THE RED DUKE watched as his slaves brought bodies out from the catacombs beneath the Chapel Sereine. Renar had been unable to completely efface the magical guards placed upon the tomb, but he had managed to reduce its efficacy enough to allow the undead to trespass within its walls.

The vampire cast an amused look at the emaciated necromancer. It was actually a brilliant idea, one so simple the Red Duke knew he might never have thought of it. Faced with death for failing to break the enchantment completely, Renar had made a desperate suggestion. If they could not raise the black knights from their tombs, then why not remove them from their tombs?

'This had better work,' the Red Duke threatened as his zombies brought the last pile of bones out from the chapel. The vampire glanced about the cemetery, at the fresh bodies strewn about the graveyard. After smashing through the last defences, the undead had been presented with the villagers cowering inside the chapel. Only a few of the peasants had escaped the massacre, fleeing into the forest. The ghouls were tracking them down even now.

'I assure you, it will, your grace,' Renar answered, trying to keep his voice from trembling. The necromancer gestured to the piles of bones laid out across the graveyard, each knightly corpse arranged into its original shape along with the remains of his horse. 'The massacre of the peasants has saturated this place in dark power. Even the sanctity of the chapel cannot protect this place now.'

El Morzillo stamped its hooves as the Red Duke leaned down from the saddle. 'Then be about your task,' the vampire told Renar.

The necromancer almost choked as the foul breath of his undead master washed over him. Nodding hastily in agreement, Renar assembled his paraphernalia: black candles made from the fat of murdered men, the skull of a stillborn, three locks of hair plucked from the head of a hanged man, a vial of dirt from a sorcerer's grave. Renar drew a circle about himself with the crushed bones of a mutant and sat down. His voice ringing across the graveyard, magnified by a force greater than that of fleshly lungs, the necromancer evoked the fell powers of darkness, drawing upon the terrible energies harnessed ages ago by dread Nagash, lord of the undead.

Bodies twitched as dark vapours swirled around them, seeping up from the very earth. The recently slaughtered peasants were the first to rise, their fresh bodies easily absorbing the foul energies of Dhar. Broken and butchered, the mangled bodies began to rise to their feet with awkward, jerky motions. The new zombies were hideous, their gory wounds fresh and crusted with blood, their clothes spattered with the filth of battle and death. Empty eyes stared from lifeless faces as the undead awaited the command of their master.

The ancient bones of the Red Duke's black knights were slower to absorb the fell power evoked by the necromancer, but soon they too began to change. The shattered skeletons began to knit themselves back together, forming complete bodies once more. Men and horses came to their feet with a clatter of fleshless bones and rusty armour. The risen skeletons flexed their limbs, as though testing their restored motion and motivation. A semblance of will remained in the wights and each marched to its steed as its body was restored, mounting into decayed saddles, brandishing corroded swords and lances as they saluted their crimson-clad overlord.

The Red Duke smiled in satisfaction as he watched his army reform itself from its own destruction. Between the peasants of Mercal, the black knights from the catacombs and the buried dead of the cemetery, the vampire now had a force numbering not in the hundreds, but the thousands. He was ready to face this Duke Gilon and remove him from the throne bestowed upon him by a usurper.

Thoughts of his stolen dukedom turned the vampire

away from the resurrection of his army. He focused instead upon the heavy casket his slaves had dragged out from the catacombs. Unlike the black knights, the body of Baron de Gavaudan had not stirred in response to Renar's spell. It took a different kind of magic to revive a vampire.

The Red Duke gestured to a waiting pair of skeletons, armoured grave guard recruited from the ruins of the Crac de Sang. Between them, the grave guard bore a prisoner, the leader of the battle pilgrims who had fought to the last to protect the chapel. As a reward for their persistence, the Red Duke had marked Jeanot for a very special death. At his command, the grave guard bent the struggling man over the open coffin. Jeanot's face stared down into the dusty bones of the vanquished Baron de Gavaudan.

One of the skeletons brought a rusty dagger slashing across the pilgrim's throat, sending a torrent of blood streaming into the casket. The grave guard held their butchered victim over the coffin as his life dripped away. Only when the man was nothing but a dead shell did they let him sink to the ground, his blood-less body already drawing strands of Dhar into it.

Grey smoke erupted from the coffin as a terrible metamorphosis took place. The fresh blood of the slaughtered Jeanot reacted with the ancient bones of Baron de Gavaudan. Flesh and muscle began to grow upon the naked bones, hair began to sprout from the barren skull. In a matter of minutes, the vampire's body had regenerated from the very dust of its dis-solution.

The Red Duke watched impassively as a lean hand clawed at the edge of the coffin. Baron de Gavaudan's twisted countenance leered out from the fading smoke as he pulled himself upright. The baron grinned crookedly at his lord. 'Master,' the creature hissed.

'You failed me,' the Red Duke pronounced. He gestured with his mailed fist and the grave guard converged upon the casket. Baron de Gavaudan struggled as the skeletons tried to push the lid of his casket back into place.

'For four hundred and seventy eight years I have been trapped inside my own tomb,' the Red Duke declared. He stabbed a finger at the twisted Baron de Gavaudan. 'I have suffered because of your failure here. Now you will know the torment I endured. When the doors of that chapel are closed once more they will prevent anything undead from entering the tomb within.' A cruel smile appeared on the Red Duke's face. 'Entering... or leaving.'

Terror crawled onto Baron de Gavaudan's misshapen face. 'No master! I have been faithful! I have carried out your orders!' He was still protesting his loyalty when the grave guard slammed the lid of his coffin in place. Sternly, they bore the casket back into the chapel. The Red Duke watched them depart. Baron de Gavaudan would have a long time to contemplate his faithless treachery.

And a long time to think about how much he would give to taste blood again.

The Red Duke turned away from the chapel. A flicker of annoyance entered the vampire's countenance as he noticed one of the bodies still unmoving upon the ground. The Red Duke motioned to Sir Corbinian. The wight-lord marched to the offending corpse, lifting it from the ground. The armoured body groaned in pain. The Red Duke recognized this not-quite-corpse now. It was the knight who had fought so vainly and so valiantly to deny him access to the chapel.

'Bring him to me,' the Red Duke commanded Sir Corbinian. The wight-lord bowed its head and dragged the mortally wounded knight towards the vampire. The Red Duke stared down at the dying Maraulf. He reached down and tore the helm from the knight's head, smiling cruelly as he saw the haggard face of his enemy, the bloodless colour of his skin. Despite his fast approaching death, there was still a look of defiance in the knight's eyes.

The Red Duke could have snapped Maraulf's neck like a twig, but another idea had occurred to him. With Baron de Gavaudan consigned to an unquiet grave, the vampire would need someone to lead his army into battle. Someone with more stomach for the job than a peasant like Renar and more wits than a wight or banshee.

Coldly, the Red Duke pulled back the mail coif around Maraulf's head, exposing the man's neck. Realising what the vampire intended, the knight struggled feebly to pull away.

'You have squandered your life defending these peasants,' the Red Duke declared. 'Now you shall serve a more noble master.'

Maraulf screamed as the vampire's fangs tore into his throat.

CHAPTER XI

'To oars ye scugs! This scupper's headed straight ta Mannan's casket!'

The deck of the Bretonnian carrack was a confusion of activity as sailors scurried about trying to follow the frantic commands of the ship's mates. The loudmouthed seaman who pronounced the ship's doom was struck in the nose by his furious captain. He crashed to the crazily leaning deck, his nose a red smear across his face.

For the passengers of the carrack, there seemed no doubt that the vessel was doomed. Three days out from Lashiek the ship had started to founder, water rushing into her hold. In the space of an hour, the carrack had started to list badly to port, defying the efforts of the crew to correct the tilt by shifting cargo and ballast.

Marquis Galafre d'Elbiq stood upon the quarter deck and surveyed the desperate attempt by the crew to save their ship. He was no seaman, but he knew their efforts were useless. He knew their efforts were useless because he knew what had happened to their ship.

The nobleman cursed Baron de Gavaudan under his breath. The scheming baron had betrayed them all. He wasn't content to allow the poison and sickness afflicting the Duke of Aquitaine to run its course. He was too impatient to see his liege dead. Marquis Galafre had been taken into the baron's confidence before the carrack had left Araby. The promise of increased rank and lands had been made if Galafre would ensure the duke never reached Aquitaine.

Galafre felt shame that he had accepted the baron's offer. He had been a loyal vassal to the duke, following El Syf into battle across Estalia and Araby. But he was also a practical man. The duke would never recover from the dastardly poison his Arabyan ambushers had used on him. There was no dishonour in breaking allegiance with a corpse. He had his future to think about and that of his family. Baron de Gavaudan would be Steward of Aquitaine under the new duke. He would be the most powerful man in the dukedom, and there was no sense offending him needlessly.

Even so, Galafre could not still the sense of guilt that nagged at him. This latest display of the baron's naked ambition only heightened his distaste for the entire plot. The baron's agents had drilled holes into the hull and sealed them with salt plugs. After a few hours with the sea eroding them, the plugs dissolved enough that they crumbled away entirely, letting the sea rush into the hold.

Galafre could see the plot quite plainly in his head, for it had been suggested to him by the baron before the carrack set sail. It was a plan that offended the knight's sensibilities. He had vowed to find another way to deal with the dying duke. Clearly, Baron de Gavaudan had been fond enough of his idea to sink the carrack that he'd found another agent to put his plan into action.

It was the act of a base villain! Galafre clenched his fist at his side. Whatever the baron had promised him, there was no honour in the knave! Why, he could almost believe the baron had sent the Arabyans to ambush the duke in the desert!

'We must get his grace off this ship.' The statement was

made by the man standing beside Galafre. The marquis barely shifted his gaze. Earl Durand du Maisne's first thought would be the welfare of the duke. It was small wonder the baron had not approached Durand with his offer. Father-in-law to King Louis or no, Durand would have cut the dog down before he finished describing his plot.

'The crew may yet keep this tub afloat,' Galafre said, but he made no especial effort to make the words sound convincing. It occurred to him that Baron de Gavaudan had intended to drown him along with the duke by this act of sabotage. He wasn't as inclined to further the rogue's ambitions now as he had been a few hours ago.

Durand shook his head. 'We should prepare for the worst. "Trust in the Lady, but hobble your horse." We should lower the longboats and put over provisions. If the sailors can save the ship, we can always put his grace aboard again.'

The ship's captain, in between bellowing orders to his crew, had been paying attention to the exchange between his noble passengers. 'If you will pardon my impertinence, my lords,' the captain said, his voice both grim and apologetic. 'I think Earl Durand has the right of it. Mannan's got one hand around this ship already. A little tug from him and she goes to the bottom.' The seaman grinned, displaying his blackened teeth. 'A captain's honour is to go down with his ship, but a duke is made for better things. Please, save his grace if you can. I'd find a poor place in the gardens of Morr with the death of a hero on my hands.'

'Have your men lower the longboats,' Durand told the captain. 'We shall attend to his grace.'

Galafre shrugged. It was a plan of action at least and a part of him wanted to see Baron de Gavaudan's face

*when they brought the duke back to Aquitaine despite his
efforts to kill them all.*

AIMEE COULD FEEL her little heart pounding like a
blacksmith's hammer in her chest. It hurt to breathe,
her tiny lungs felt like they were burning each time
she drew air into them. Her legs were almost numb
from the pain in her muscles, her skirt torn and tattered by brambles and thorns. But worst of all was
the icy fear that made her body feel as though all the
strength had been drawn out of it.

'Run, Aimee! Run, and for Shallya's sake, don't look
back!'

The terrified words of her mother still rang in her
ears. She stifled a sob as she thought of her mother,
lying sprawled across the gravestones, her leg caught
in the splintered lid of a rotten coffin. There had been
no thought of checking the ground when the monsters
had broken into the chapel and they had been forced
to flee into the cemetery. Her mother's foot had broken
through the surface of a shallow grave, ending her dash
for freedom.

Aimee would have stayed with her mother. The
thought of leaving her behind had been scarier than
the monsters, but her mother had shouted at her and
pushed her away. There was anger in her mother's voice
as she ordered the little girl to run.

She did cry as she thought of her mother being so
angry with her. But it was better than thinking about
those other sounds. She didn't want to think they had
come from her mother, those anguished shrieks. Almost,
Aimee had turned to look back, but her mother's warning kept her from doing so. She knew deep inside that if
she looked back she would see something so terrible…

Aimee's red-rimmed eyes went wide with fright as she heard running feet racing through the underbrush. She scrambled for the shelter of an old oak tree, nuzzling her small body down among the roots. She clapped a small hand across her mouth to stifle her whimpers. Her other hand covered one of her ears. She pressed the other side of her head against the tree, trying to block out the sound of running feet.

Since entering the forest, Aimee had heard the sound of running feet almost continuously. Some were the sounds of other people trying to get away. Some were the sounds of the things chasing after them. Sometimes the things caught the people. Then the night was ripped apart by horrible screams. Aimee didn't want to hear any more of the screams.

The little girl crouched among the roots, her wide eyes peering into the dark. She didn't want to hear what was going on in the forest, but she wouldn't close her eyes. She didn't know where she would go without her mother and father; in all her short life she had only once been beyond the borders of Mercal, and that was to attend a festival at the lord's castle. She didn't really know where that was, only that it had big rock walls and that knights lived there.

A tiny flicker of hope flashed through the child's heart. If she could find the castle she could get the knights to help her! They would ride to the village on their white horses, their armour shining in the sun! They would make all the monsters go away and save her mother and everybody else!

Aimee removed her hands from her ear and from her mouth. She leaned away from the roots and listened to the sounds of the forest. It was important for her to be brave now, because the knights would only listen to a brave girl. She closed her eyes, wiping at her tears. She didn't know how she would find the castle, but she knew that she had to.

From overhead, Aimee heard a sharp, hissing sound, like her old granny sucking air through her cracked teeth. The little girl turned her face upwards. Instantly, she was paralysed with fear.

Looking down at her, crouched upon the largest of the roots like some huge toad, was a fanged ghoul, his yellow eyes peering at her hungrily. The ghoul's claws dug into the root, tearing into the pulp. A string of spittle dripped from his teeth, a famished growl rumbled from his belly.

Aimee screamed and leaped from her shelter. The ghoul dropped down from his perch, landing where the girl had been only a second before. His claws slashed at the fleeing child, ripping shreds of home-spun from her dress. Growling angrily, the monster took off after her, scrambling across the ground on all fours.

The little girl raced through the black forest, feeling the stagnant breath of the ghoul at her back. Wild yells and bestial howls rose from the darkness, the sound of naked feet slapping against the dirt. Drawn by her screams and the hungry growls of her pursuer, other ghouls were rushing through the shadows, eager to rend and tear and chew the dainty morsel fleeing through the woods. Aimee could hear their lank bodies crashing through the brush, their sharp claws slashing at branches as they tore their way closer.

Horror kept her running when every muscle in her body told her to lay down and die. Terror sent the blood pumping through her shivering body, fear forced breath into her burning lungs. The screams of her mother echoed inside her skull.

The claws of the ghoul behind her slashed out, whipping through her hair. Other monstrous cannibals came loping out from the trees, converging upon Aimee's course from either side. The girl screamed, crying out to the gods.

The back of the first ghoul's hand slammed into the small of Aimee's back, knocking her to the ground. The monster leered at her, licking his fangs as he saw blood oozing up from the girl's skinned knee. Other ghouls closed in upon her, forming a cordon around their helpless prey.

'Foul varlet!' a fierce voice cried out. 'Here's a supper of steel for your foul heart!'

The lead ghoul shrieked as two feet of steel was thrust into its chest. The creature wilted upon the sword, collapsing as the blade was withdrawn. Aimee looked up with wonder as a towering knight stepped out from the darkness, placing himself between her and the monsters.

Sir Leuthere glared at the skulking ghouls, watching as the cowardly creatures cringed away from his sword. Like a pack of starving mongrels, the cannibals circled warily around the knight. 'Base villains!' Leuthere spat. 'You have stomach to chase a little girl, but no spleen for fighting a grown man!'

The ghouls spat and snarled at Leuthere, but made no move to close upon him. At the same time, the knight did not press forwards. He knew the monsters were only waiting for one of their number to occupy his sword. Then the whole pack would set upon him.

If such was their plan, the cannibals were in for a ghastly surprise. So fixated were they upon Leuthere and Aimee, they did not notice Count Ergon until the second knight lashed out with his sword, the weapon's keen edge hewing through the neck of one ghoul and sending its head bouncing into the bushes.

The unexpected attack broke the feeble courage of the ghouls. Whining like whipped curs, the degenerate cannibals fled, scattering back into the forest. Count Ergon made to chase after the fleeing monsters.

'No,' Leuthere said. 'Let them go. They're not important and you'd never catch them on foot.'

Count Ergon gazed down at the shivering little girl clinging to Leuthere's armoured leg. 'Then by the Lady I'll ride the vermin down!' he swore. 'Where's your man with the horses! Bring up my destrier, you craven knave!'

The clatter of hooves and the nervous whinny of horses sounded from the darkness. Vigor strode out from behind the trees, leading a small herd of animals. To his own pony and Leuthere's destrier had been added a pair of fleet-footed coursers and a heavy-limbed packhorse taken from the du Maisne stables, as well as the enormous black warhorse bearing the arms of the count himself. Count Ergon wiped the blood from his blade and sheathed his sword as he marched towards his steed.

'We can't leave the girl,' Leuthere protested as Count Ergon climbed into his destrier's saddle.

'Let your man take care of her,' the count answered, his voice bristling with impatience. 'By the grail, don't you realize this scum may put us back on the vampire's trail!'

Leuthere glowered at the count. 'I'll not abandon a child to the night for sake of vengeance,' he said. Turning his back to the bristling count, Leuthere focused his attention on Aimee. 'What are you doing alone in the woods, little one?' he asked. 'Where is your home?'

Aimee stifled her tears. She had to be brave now, because the knights wouldn't listen to her if she was afraid. Stiffening her back, choking back her fear, the little girl answered Leuthere. 'I'm from Mercal, but nobody's there now. The holy knight said we should all go to the chapel because bad monsters were coming. But when they came they got into the chapel too and everybody had to run away.' Despite her effort at control, fresh tears began to stream down her cheeks. 'Please, you have to go help my mummy! She's in the graveyard and the monsters will get her!'

Count Ergon bit his lip, fury filling his face. 'By the Lady, I'll cut down every last grave-cheating abomination and leave its bones for the crows!' He spurred his horse forwards, marching it so that he loomed over Leuthere. Aimee cringed away from the fearsome destrier, hiding behind the younger knight.

'Leave the girl to your man, d'Elbiq,' Count Ergon said. 'We have to catch these animals while the trail's still hot.'

Leuthere slowly rose. Gently he led Aimee towards Vigor and the horses. The little girl was uncertain of the crook-backed servant, but after an injunction from Leuthere to be brave, she allowed the man to lift her up onto the back of his pony.

'Don't worry about the trail going cold,' Leuthere told Count Ergon as he climbed into the saddle of his own warhorse. 'I know where the Red Duke is going. This holy knight she speaks of must be Sir Maraulf, guardian of the Chapel Sereine. He told me the Red Duke would strike at Mercal. He said the vampire left something in the chapel, something he was going to come back for.'

'Then we ride for the chapel,' Count Ergon snarled.

'The two of us? Alone?' Leuthere asked. 'I know you want to avenge your family. I know you want to take revenge for your son's death…'

'You have no idea how I feel, d'Elbiq!' Count Ergon snapped.

Leuthere's gaze was like ice as he glared at the nobleman. 'Yes I do. I know what it means to lose a son because I watched that poison eat away at my uncle everyday. I watched Earl Gaubert's mind become more and more twisted until there was nothing left but the thought of revenge. And I saw where that terrible bloodlust led him.'

'Then you know better than to try and stop me.'

Leuthere waved his hands in exasperation. 'Think!' he pleaded. 'We can't fight the Red Duke and his army alone! However many of them we destroy, they will overwhelm us in the end!'

Count Ergon sneered at the younger knight. 'I only need to kill the vampire,' he said. 'Stay behind with the peasants if your courage fails you. The d'Elbiqs were ever a pack of yellow-bellied cowards.' The nobleman did not spare further words on Leuthere. Digging his spurs into the flanks of his steed, he set off at a gallop along the forest path.

Leuthere cursed under his breath. 'Stay here with the girl,' he told Vigor. 'If we're not back before dawn or if you hear anything moving among the trees that isn't a horse, then get out of here and take her someplace safe.'

Vigor waved at the knight as he galloped off into the darkness in pursuit of Count Ergon. The peasant felt a pang of disappointment at being left behind. He knew Leuthere was riding into certain death and he knew it was not concern for Count Ergon that drove him to such desperation. He knew, because the same mix of shame and guilt burdened his own heart.

A CRUEL SMILE twisted the lean features of Renar's face as he looked out across the ranks of undead cavalry marching behind the Red Duke's banner. The black knights were fearsome apparitions, their skeletal bodies draped in mouldering burial shrouds, rusting breastplates and corroded helmets clinging to their bones, crumbling scraps of barding dangling about their fleshless steeds. Here, the necromancer thought, was a force that would pay the arrogant knights of Aquitaine back in their own coin. He was almost eager to see the Red Duke unleash his mounted wights upon Duke Gilon's army.

The necromancer glanced nervously at the black clad knight riding beside the Red Duke. Somehow, he had expected the knight's aura of menace to lessen after he became a vampiric thrall of the Red Duke. Instead, Renar found himself even more anxious around the fledgling vampire. In life, the knight's purpose had been to kill men like Renar. The necromancer couldn't shake the impression that even as one of the undead, the same idea was fixed in the dark knight's mind.

Renar bit down on his anxiety and pushed his way through the decayed ranks of zombie foot soldiers to join the Red Duke and his entourage. He cursed for the thousandth time the loss of the horse he had taken from the Chateau du Maisne. His steed now was a shivering old plough horse from Mercal, an animal so decrepit it could only become more limber as a zombie.

'Your grace,' the necromancer addressed the Red Duke as he rode up alongside the vampire. He was careful to place the Red Duke between himself and the dark knight. 'If we continue along this road we shall reach the barrow mounds of the horse lords. The ancient kings were buried with their entire households. Horses, chariots, entire companies of warriors, all walled up inside the mounds by the old druids.'

Renar smiled, imagining the bones of the ancients marching alongside their army. With the horse lords summoned from their barrows the Red Duke would be in command of an undead horde such as Bretonnia had never seen. The vampire would be able to extend his Kingdom of Blood beyond Aquitaine. He could conquer Quenelles and Brionne, perhaps even Bordeleaux and Carcassonne. He could seize the graves of the vanquished Cuileux and summon those bold knights from their crypts. With such a host they would be able to sweep every noble in Bretonnia into the sea.

It was a plan that had inspired the necromancer as he watched the dead of Mercal rise from their graves. The very presence of the Red Duke seemed to augment Renar's own powers. Never before had he been able to summon and maintain so many skeletons and zombies. This, he thought, was what true power felt like.

As they marched from the Chapel Sereine, he had broached his plan to the Red Duke. Then, the vampire had been pleased by the plan, almost excited by the prospect of smashing Duke Gilon with a legion of the ancient dead.

Now, the vampire only scowled at Renar.

'I do not need the hoary dead to march under my banner,' the vampire snarled. 'When I have the support of the Prophetess Isabeau, every able man in Aquitaine will be forced to recognize me as their rightful lord. The Usurper King will have no claim upon my lands. He cannot question the word of the prophetess. To do so would be to deny the Fay Enchantress and the Lady of the Lake herself. Even a treacherous king like Louis would not dare such an outrage.'

Renar sagged in the saddle, all the air draining out of him in a long sigh. 'Your grace, Isabeau has been dead three hundred years and more. Iselda is now the Prophetess of the Tower.'

The vampire sneered at Renar, displaying his fangs. 'What does a mere peasant know of such matters?' The Red Duke raised an eyebrow as he noted that the necromancer was mounted. 'And why do you ride beside your betters?'

'The horse was distempered, your grace,' was Renar's snide reply. 'It would be unseemly to risk injury to a noble by having them ride an unbroken beast.'

The Red Duke waved aside Renar's reply. 'See that the horse is returned to its owner when its disposition improves,' the vampire said. Suddenly he sat straight in his saddle, staring with some confusion at the road ahead. 'This is not the way to Lake Tranquil and the Tower of Wizardry!'

'It is a short cut, your grace,' Renar said.

'Don't you think I know the lay of my own domain?' the Red Duke snarled. He raised his armoured hand, motioning the column to halt. The clatter of fleshless bones on rusty armour was almost deafening as the marching undead came to rest.

The Red Duke studied the fields and forest around them, his supernaturally keen vision piercing the veil of night as though the land were lit by the noonday sun. The vampire pointed his fist towards the north-east. 'The tower lies in that direction,' he declared, spurring El Morzillo forwards. With blind obedience, the rest of the undead left the road and followed their master across the dusty fields.

Renar rolled his eyes but urged his horse to follow the vampire. Later, when the Red Duke was capable of listening to reason, he'd be able to steer the vampire back towards the barrow mounds and Renar's plan. Until then, Renar would have to just make the best of the situation and wait for this fit of madness to pass.

At least there would be no lack of opportunity to practise his black art, the necromancer reflected. When the Red Duke was like this, he had the endearing habit of razing any village they passed which he did not recognize, decrying the inhabitants as intruders and trespassers. And after nearly five hundred years, there were few villages in Aquitaine the vampire would still recognize.

Sir Leuthere tethered Gaigun to a withered tree at the edge of the forest. Count Ergon's huge black destrier was similarly tied only a few feet away. Cautiously, Leuthere drew his sword and crept out from the trees.

The cemetery was eerily silent. All across the grave-yard Leuthere could see the marks of battle: the trenches and earthworks built by the peasants, pools of blood, severed limbs, and the chewed remains of those caught beneath the teeth of the ghouls. But of a whole body there was no sign, despite the evidence of what must have been a horrible fray. The knight didn't like to think about why the bodies had been removed. Or how.

Sounds rose from behind the lonely marble façade of the chapel itself. Leuthere circled warily around the structure, bracing himself for any manner of monstrous foe. He breathed a little easier when he saw that the pounding noise came from Count Ergon. The nobleman was banging upon the heavy stone doors of the chapel with his sword, trying to force his way inside. The scrape of Leuthere's boot on a gravestone brought the older knight spinning around in alarm.

'No sign of the Red Duke, I take it?' Leuthere asked.

Count Ergon shrugged his shoulder towards the stone doors. 'Not unless he's down there.' He turned and squinted at the horizon. 'Sun will be coming up soon. The graveworm may have gone to ground.'

Leuthere pointed to a patch of black clouds away to their south. 'The old stories say the Red Duke could cloak himself inside a storm so the sun wouldn't harm him.'

'I want to check this place just the same,' Count Ergon said, returning his attentions to the heavy doors. Already the blows from his sword had chipped away the grail carved into the stone panels. 'I need to be sure,' he added between grunts as he began hammering away again.

'Let me help you,' Leuthere said, sheathing his blade and walking over to join Count Ergon.

'I need no charity from a d'Elbiq,' Count Ergon snapped.

'And I have none to give a du Maisne,' Leuthere returned. 'Sir Maraulf said the Red Duke wanted something inside the chapel. Before we leave here, I want to find out what it was.'

The younger knight pressed his back against the heavy door and exerted his full strength. It began to shift. A sour expression came upon Count Ergon's face. He slammed his sword back into its sheath with a frustrated oath, then helped Leuthere push against the door.

Slowly, with jerks and shudders, the door began to swing inwards, its bottom grinding against the marble floor of the chapel. Chips of stone clattered into the darkness, echoing from the chapel's cold walls.

As soon as the doorway swung open, both knights were bowled over as a tremendous force slammed into them. The two men crashed to the ground, the breath driven from their lungs by the furious impact. A bestial voice snarled down at them.

'My gratitude, fools! My master left me to starve, but instead I find two succulent morsels to quench my thirst!'

Leuthere looked up to see the grisly creature looming over them. It was pale and withered, the blackened armour of a knight hanging loose about its shrivelled husk. One arm was curled against its chest, even more scrawny than the rest of its wasted frame. Half of the creature's face was contorted into a hungry leer, the other half dripped in idiot fashion.

'Vampire!' Leuthere decried the creature.

'But not the Red Duke!' cursed Count Ergon.

A tittering giggle rasped from the vampire's withered face. 'The Red Duke,' the vampire repeated. 'His enemies gather all around him.' The creature pointed its emaciated claw at Leuthere. 'A d'Elbiq,' it pronounced. 'And a du Maisne,' it added, gesturing at Count Ergon. The vampire tapped its own chest. 'And the Baron de Gavaudan. All the old enemies.

The Red Duke is doomed to fight his past.'

'Where is he?' Count Ergon demanded.

Baron de Gavaudan laughed, a sound as sinister and cruel as the crack of a torturer's whip. 'Let's find him together!' the vampire hissed, lips pulling away from glistening fangs.

Like a panther, Baron de Gavaudan pounced upon Count Ergon, crushing the nobleman to the ground. The vampire's claw smashed down upon his sword-arm, bruising it to the very bone. The old knight cried out in pain, his entire arm going numb from the blow.

Baron de Gavaudan twisted his opponent's head around, snarling as Leuthere rose from the ground in a lunging dive, his outswept arms catching the vampire and driving it from Count Ergon's chest. The crazed creature writhed from Leuthere's grip, turning the knight's dive into an uncontrolled roll into the cemetery. The monster's claw tore at Leuthere, tearing the gorget from around his neck, shredding the mail coif beneath.

Leuthere's fingers closed about the dagger hanging from his belt. Desperately he pulled the blade free and stabbed it into the vampire's body. Again and again he drove the steel into the baron's withered carcass. The angle of attack was too low to threaten the monster's black heart, all Leuthere's efforts could do was annoy his foe. But it was enough to distract the vampire and keep its fangs from his throat.

Hissing in anger, the baron seized the top of Leuthere's helm and savagely drove the knight's head into one of the gravestones. The marker cracked apart under the impact, even with the quilt padding under his coif, Leuthere felt his brains rattling inside his skull. Stunned, he flopped helpless beneath the vampire.

Baron de Gavaudan grinned and leaned down to worry the throat of his victim.

'You forgot to break both my arms,' Count Ergon roared. His battered arm hanging limp at his side, the nobleman gripped his sword in his left hand and delivered a brutal slash across the vampire's spine.

The vampire shrieked in agony, skin blistering around the cut. Baron de Gavaudan fell to the ground, his one good hand pawing at his back, trying to reach his burning wound.

Count Ergon kicked the crippled monster, snapping its head back with enough force to kill anything that could still call itself human. The vampire's head lolled obscenely upon its broken neck. The creature struggled to pull itself upright, but its broken back left it writhing on the ground.

Count Ergon glared down at the monster. He gestured at the vampire with his sword, displaying the bulb of garlic he held against the hilt, the same bulb of garlic he had rubbed against the edge of his blade. 'One of the peasants must have dropped this during the battle,' he told the vampire. 'I decided to put it to good use.' Count Ergon stabbed the point of his sword into one of the baron's knees, the vampire's flesh blistering from the garlic-stained steel.

'I'll ask this again, bloodworm; where's the Red Duke?' Count Ergon pressed home his question by pressing his sword deeper into the baron's flesh. The vampire answered him with a spiteful hiss. The nobleman shrugged and cast his gaze skyward. 'Suit yourself. Dawn's breaking anyway.'

Baron de Gavaudan's eyes were wide with terror

as he heard the count's words. The crippled vampire thrashed about, trying to free himself from the knight's sword, but every exertion only caused him more pain. In a matter of moments, the first light of day blazed across the roof of the chapel, bathing the vampire in its purifying light. The baron opened his mouth to shriek, but already his flesh was crumbling into dust. The vampire's eyes melted into his collapsing skull, his hair shrivelling as though set beneath a flame. The rest of the creature quickly followed, disintegrating as completely as salt plugs dumped into the sea. In a matter of minutes, the only trace of Baron de Gavaudan was a stench in the air.

Count Ergon watched every moment of the vampire's dissolution, wishing every second that it was the Red Duke rather than one of the monster's slaves. When the last of Baron de Gavaudan was gone, the count turned and looked towards the south. He could see the black clouds Leuthere had mentioned. It was there he would find the Red Duke.

Holding his injured arm, Count Ergon began to walk back to his horse. The painful moans of Leuthere stopped him. He glanced at the young knight and clenched his fist.

As much as it offended him, the d'Elbiq had saved his life. Feud or no feud, revenge or no, Count Ergon knew he couldn't leave Leuthere like this.

Bitterly, the count turned a last longing gaze at the black clouds receding into the south.

CHAPTER XII

A cloud of smoke rose from the burning villages, a black pall of death that rolled out over the crystal waters of Lake Tranquil. The sound of axes felling timber rang from the forest as tree after tree collapsed to the earth. Fields and pastures were trampled underfoot as the Red Duke's army scoured the land.

The vampire watched from the top of a rocky knoll as his troops, living and undead, carried out his orders. Not a single inhabitant of the region would be spared, be it man, child or beast. When he was finished, the land about the Tower of Wizardry would be a desolation to match the most abhorrent desert in Araby. The wasteland would be a monument of terror, a testament of his power and authority.

In the fields, the Red Duke's engineers set about constructing the siege machines he would need to bring down the ancient fortress. Great towers of timber covered in hides ripped from the flesh of slaughtered livestock, giant trebuchets armed with masonry plundered from the rubble of grail chapels and shrines to the Lady, huge battering rams and immense mangonels, spear-hurling ballistae and corkscrew-shaped bores. It was an arsenal the likes of which had never been seen before in Aquitaine.

There was something else in the fields never seen before in Aquitaine. The Red Duke shifted his gaze from his living vassals to his undead slaves. He watched as gangs of zombies lifted great wooden stakes into the air. Upon the point of each, a captured peasant writhed. The zombies had already erected a small forest of impaled prisoners. By the time they finished the Red Duke's grove would stretch all the way to the shores of Lake Tranquil. It would dwarf the vampire's garden at the Crac de Sang.

From her balcony, the Prophetess Isabeau would have a fine view of the vampire's forest. It would take many days for the impaled peasants to die and the faithless witch would be able to enjoy every excruciating moment. The cries and moans of the dying would sing to her as she slept and welcome her when she awoke. She would be able to watch as the crows and jackdaws flitted about the forest, indifferent whether they supped upon the dead or the dying.

The Red Duke grinned up at the tower, sneering as he saw the lone woman upon the high balcony. She had brought this upon these people, not he. She had refused to acknowledge his right to rule Aquitaine. She had refused to bestow upon him the favour of the Lady. Isabeau had thrown her lot in with that of the usurper, the treacherous cur who dared call himself Louis the Righteous.

The witch had tried to kill him when he had ridden to the tower to ask for her support and the Lady's blessing. Her spells had seared his flesh, scorched his armour. If he had still been mortal, she would have succeeded where all of Baron de Gavaudan's assassins had failed. But the Red Duke was more than mortal now, and he had endured. The best the witch could do was drive him from her tower.

Now he was back, and with his army, the Red Duke would break Isabeau's fortress. He would see the witch

*grovel at his feet, begging him for mercy. Gladly would
she bestow upon him the Lady's favour before he allowed
her to die.*

*Aquitaine was his! It belonged to him, now and forever!
Neither the Lady nor her treasonous servants would deny
the Red Duke his birthright!*

*The vampire's eyes narrowed with hate as he glared at
the tower. 'When this is over, you will regret betraying me,
witch! I'll tear this place down stone by stone and drag your
carcass from the rubble! There are fates worse than death
and, woman, you shall know them all!'*

'YOU HAVE NOT told me how it was that you happened
to be following this monster.'

Sir Leuthere had dreaded the question, dreaded it
ever since Count Ergon had decided to join him on his
hunt to destroy the Red Duke. He leaned back in his
saddle, his hands folded across the horn. He stared at
the long mane of the courser Count Ergon had given
him, not seeing the horse, seeing instead the body of
his uncle twitching above the Red Duke's tomb. Seeing the Countess du Maisne butchered in the courtyard
of her home. Seeing the cruelty inflicted upon Sir
Armand du Maisne. There was no way he could tell the
old knight the truth – that he rode to atone for Earl
Gaubert's evil, that it was his uncle who had called this
horror from its grave.

Leuthere turned and looked back at Vigor, willing the
peasant to silence. Astride his pony, the little arms of
the girl wrapped about his middle, the huge warhorses
following behind, Vigor had enough to worry about
without adding the fury of Count Ergon to his woes.
He gave Leuthere a slight nod of understanding. Whatever the knight said, Vigor would not contradict him.

'I followed the vampire after he killed Earl Gaubert,' Leuthere said, voicing what small part of the truth he felt able.

Count Ergon nodded his head in grim understanding. 'We both seek out this fiend so we may avenge our dead.' A flicker of pain crept onto his face. 'I must thank you for saving my life in the cemetery.' Count Ergon winced as each word left his mouth. 'It comes hard to me to speak kindly to a d'Elbiq.'

'The balance is even,' Leuthere sighed. 'You saved me from de Gavaudan too, remember. I won't ask a du Maisne to accept my gratitude, but you have it just the same.'

'The balance is even,' Count Ergon repeated, mulling the words over. He fixed Leuthere with an imperious gaze. 'See that you remember that. You don't owe me any courtesy. I don't owe you any.'

Slowly, Leuthere let his right hand drop from the horn of his saddle so it would be in easy reach of his sword. He watched Count Ergon carefully. The nobleman was still favouring his left arm after the fight with Baron de Gavaudan. It was an advantage Leuthere intended to remember.

'We agreed to set the feud aside,' Leuthere said.

'And so it is,' Count Ergon told him. 'But I will say one other thing. I do not know what regard you held Earl Gaubert in, but I will say it can only pale beside the love I had for my son. When we find the vampire, he is mine to slay.'

Leuthere did not flinch as he met Count Ergon's stern gaze. 'A d'Elbiq has just as much right to honour as a du Maisne,' he said, his voice cold and firm. 'If my chance comes, I will not stand aside for any man.'

Count Ergon pulled back on the reins of his courser,

stopping the horse in the middle of the dirt road they had been following. 'I will avenge my son,' he warned Leuthere.

'And I will redeem my honour,' the younger knight retorted. A dangerous tension filled the air. Leuthere's hand closed about the hilt of his sword. Count Ergon awkwardly reached for his own weapon with his left hand.

Vigor spurred his pony forwards, trying to get between the two knights before they came to blows. 'Don't you think we should catch the vampire first, my lords?' the peasant asked, putting on his most ingratiating expression.

'We have only to follow the vultures,' Count Ergon answered, nodding his head at a circle of carrion birds wheeling in the distance. The knight tightened his hold on his reins, leaving his sword sheathed. 'This will wait, Sir Leuthere,' he told the other knight. 'But it will not wait long.'

Leuthere felt the threat of Count Ergon's words, all the old hate of the feud rising under the nobleman's provocation. He knew it was more than prideful arrogance that made the count so obdurate, but that knowledge did not lessen the anger growing within him. Only the oath he had given the count kept Leuthere from drawing his sword. Leuthere's honour had been impinged enough by the deeds of his uncle, it did not need to suffer further indignity.

'As you say, du Maisne,' Leuthere hissed. 'This will wait.' The knight let his hand fall back to the horn of his saddle. He stood in his stirrups, using the extra height to peer over the thick hedges that bordered the road. They had entered a region of bocage, rolling fields separated by winding ridges and sunken lanes bordered by thick hedgerows which acted as living fences.

The bocage country made travel slow, the lanes curling like serpents through the fields, twisting first one way and then another. Leuthere considered themselves fortunate it was not raining, for it seemed the farmers had engineered the sunken lanes to double as drainage ditches during the rainy season. The knight considered that things were bad enough without navigating a mire of mud and agricultural runoff.

Following the Red Duke's army had been easy enough. As Count Ergon had said, all one needed to do was follow the vultures. The vampire's horde had left a swathe of destruction behind it, burnt out villages and manors, not a living soul left in them. In some villages, the Red Duke's viciousness had been especially pronounced, the entire population impaled upon stakes or lynched and hung from trees. In others, the vampire's army had displayed a restrained, almost delicate touch. Porridge still smouldered over flickering embers, flagons of mead sat untouched in the taverns, bundles of wheat were piled outside the mills. Leuthere wondered if the people in these villages had been forewarned of the Red Duke's advance and fled before his army, hiding in the wilds until they decided it was safe to return.

The vampire's march displayed neither rhyme nor reason as far as Leuthere could tell. First the undead had been heading south, plundering graveyards along the way. Then the horde had abruptly turned northwards. Why the sudden change, Leuthere did not know, but it was certain there seemed an element of haste behind their march now. While the undead continued to despoil villages, they no longer stopped to loot the cemeteries. For a time, the knight dared to hope that Duke Gilon's army was pursuing that of the vampire; however, if any force gave chase to the undead it left no trace of its presence.

A troubling thought occurred to Leuthere as he gazed out across the hedgerows. Perhaps the Red Duke was not being pursued. Perhaps instead the reason for the vampire's haste was that he was himself pursuing something. The knight turned his eyes northward where a murder of crows circled above the smoking ruins of a farm. It came to Leuthere that he recognized that farm, indeed all of the surrounding terrain. This was the way to Lake Tranquil and the Tower of Wizardry. He had ridden this way many times to seek the serenity of the lake's quiet shore.

The Prophetess Iselda! Leuthere could curse himself for not thinking of it before!

'Perhaps we do not need to play hare and hound with the vampire,' Leuthere told Count Ergon. He smiled as he saw the doubt on the nobleman's face. The younger knight pointed with his armoured hand towards the northeast, beyond the burning farmstead. 'If we strike in this direction we will reach the Tower of Wizardry and the Prophetess Iselda. Her magic is great. I have seen it for myself firsthand. If we appeal to her, she may use her powers to guide us to the Red Duke.'

'But would she aid us?' Count Ergon frowned. 'She is a servant of the Lady. Of what concern to her the affairs of men?'

'Iselda has given me aid once,' Leuthere said, 'I think she will help me again. The Red Duke is a danger to all Bretonnia, not just the lords of Aquitaine. I cannot think that the Lady would abandon her people to such evil.' The knight watched the crows circling above the farm. 'No, Iselda will help us,' he said. 'She knows the threat the Red Duke poses.'

Count Ergon nodded in agreement. 'Then let us seek out the wisdom of the prophetess. My sword is eager to taste a vampire's heart.'

FOR THE REST of the day the two knights followed a meandering trail across fields and through gaps in the hedgerows. These were the same paths used by the farmers when tending their fields, a roundabout course that allowed the peasants to avoid the sunken lanes in times of flood. Progress through the bocage was slow but steady. If Leuthere had not travelled by these same paths dozens of times in the past, Count Ergon knew they would never have found their way. Even with the younger knight leading them, Count Ergon was sore pressed to make any kind of sense of where they were going.

'You are sure you know the way?' the nobleman asked for the hundredth time since they had left the sunken lanes.

Leuthere gave vent to an exasperated sigh. 'If you'd like me to get us lost, keep distracting me,' he grumbled. Standing in the stirrups, he peered over the hedgerows, studying the layout of the adjoining fields and matching them to the map locked inside his memory.

At once Leuthere dropped back into the saddle, his hand flying to his sword. He had other things to worry him now besides Count Ergon's surly chatter. There were men on the other side of the hedgerow – armed men.

'Someone's on the other side of these hedges,'

Leuthere whispered to Count Ergon.

'Undead?' the nobleman asked, reaching left-handed for his own weapon.

'No,' Leuthere answered. 'Living men, but bearing spears and bows. I don't think they've seen us.'

The young knight turned around in his saddle to hiss a warning to Vigor. As he did so, he found that it was too late to tell Vigor about the men. He already knew. Seven scruffy-looking men in threadbare cloaks and dirty hoods were arrayed all around Vigor and the horses. One of the men held the pony's reins in his hand, two others held the reins of the destriers. The other four held bows in their hands, arrows nocked to the strings and aimed at the two knights.

'You can come out now, Robert,' one of the bowmen called out. 'We've gotta bead on these fine gen'lemen. They's so much as look cross-eyed and they'll be sproutin' more feath'rs 'n a old tuck gobbler.'

It was not an idle threat. The strength of the Bretonnian longbow was infamous, capable of piercing a coat of plates from a hundred yards away. These bowmen were much closer and their broadhead arrows would easily tear through the armour the two knights wore at such a short range.

A mob of dirty, unkempt men pushed their way through the hedgerow. Most of the men bore a crude spear with a flame-hardened wooden point, but several carried the same deadly longbows as the men who had ambushed the knights and a few even carried iron swords and axes. They cast ugly looks at the knights as they emerged from the hedges, several of them pausing to spit at the ground as they passed by.

'Lo 'n behold, th' gallant nob'ty deigns take int'rest in th' 'fairs o' th' comm'n folk.' The words came as little more than a guttural snarl from a bearded, bear-like peasant bearing a battered buckler and a bent sword in his huge, ham-like hands. 'Where were ya' lot when our homes were burnin' 'n our fam'lies bein' run threw! All high 'n lordy, gettin' fat off'n our sweat! But when we needs ya, where's our mighty nob'ty then!'

'Have a care, 'bert,' one of the other peasants warned. 'Mind y'r place 'r they'll string y'r neck!'

One of the bowmen sneered at the frightened speech. 'I don't see no rope. All I see is two nob pigeons waitin' to be plucked.' He drew back on the arrow nocked to his bow. 'A groat says I put this one right in the old one's eye!'

'And a groat will get you very far, Pierre, when you're hiding in the woods with all the other animals.' The admonition came from an older peasant, his lean face still bearing dark soot-stains. By the quality of his clothes, he was probably a village hetman, burned out of his farm by the marauding undead.

'Stay out of this, Otker!' the bowman snarled.

Vigor straightened up as best he could and glared down at the murderous Pierre. 'Sure, don't listen to the one fellow talking sense!' He snorted derisively. 'You won't have to wait for the vampire to kill you. Murder these nobs and they'll send a hundred knights looking for you. Believe me they will. The nobs have a way of finding out about things and they avenge their own.' He stared pointedly at Sir Leuthere, then shifted his gaze to Count Ergon. 'They go crazy when they have kinfolk to avenge and even common sense won't get in their way. Loose that arrow and you better hightail it for the Forest of Châlons. You might be able to hide out there for a year or so as an outlaw.'

Vigor shrugged, a gesture made somehow unsettling because of his deformity. 'That is, if you don't starve first or get eaten by beastmen.'

Fear crawled into Pierre's eyes. Slowly the man lowered his bow, his shoulders slumping in defeat. Leuthere saw the doubt on the faces of the other peasants. These men weren't really murderers, they were just angry and frightened, looking for someone to blame their misfortune on. Someone to lash out at.

'I sympathize with your plight,' the knight addressed the mob. 'But trying to kill us isn't going to bring back your dead or rebuild your farms. It most certainly won't stop the Red Duke.'

Leuthere watched the reaction as he invoked the fearsome name of the legendary fiend. Gasps rose from the peasants, several men dropping to their knees and making the sign of Shallya, calling on the goddess of mercy for protection against this nightmarish monster.

'The Red Duke,' Otker repeated with a shudder, leaning heavily on the scythe he carried. 'It was the Red Duke who destroyed our homes, killed our folk?' He shook his head and grimaced. 'After all these years, the Red Duke has returned.'

'His stay will be a short one,' Count Ergon vowed, his voice a venomous growl.

The bear-like Robert scoffed at the nobleman's boast. 'It'd take 'n army to reach th' monster, 'n th' Green Knight hi'self to lay him 'n his grave! What're two lone knights suppos'd to do agin'st such a fiend!' An angry murmur swept among the peasants as Robert voiced his scornful doubt.

Leuthere raised his hand, motioning the mob to silence. Long years of deference and servitude made the peasants respond almost instinctively. 'You are right to be doubtful, but if there is a way to stop this monster before he can hurt anyone else, then it is our obligation to try.'

'They're mad,' Pierre exclaimed. 'The both of 'em! No need to stick 'em with arrows, they're gonna do the job for themselves!'

'Damn your churlishness!' Count Ergon growled. 'The vampire killed my son, my wife and my servants! Anything worth calling himself a man would hunt down this scum if he were the Blood God himself!'

'We intend to seek guidance from the prophetess,' Leuthere said. 'Perhaps her magic can show us a way to destroy the Red Duke.'

An uneasy silence fell upon the peasants. They glanced anxiously at one another, each hoping for one of his fellows to speak first. It was Otker the hetman who finally broke the silence.

'You intend to go to the tower?' he asked.

'That is our plan,' Count Ergon said, irritation in his tone. The nobleman was growing irritated at wasting time with these men.

Otker nodded. 'Then you'd better leave your horses here,' he said. He smiled as he saw the suspicion that flashed across the faces of the two knights. 'We'll take care of them for you,' he promised. 'Every man here knows the only thing more stupid than killing a knight is stealing his horse.'

Slowly, with some reluctance, Leuthere and Count Ergon dismounted.

'What about the girl, my lord?' Vigor asked. Aimee continued to cling to the man's waist, making the prospect of dismounting even more awkward for the crippled peasant.

'Is there someone who could look after the girl?'
Leuthere asked Otker. 'She doesn't have any kinfolk,
her village was wiped out by the Red Duke.'

'I'll see she gets the best of care,' Otker promised.
One of the bowmen slung his weapon over his shoulder and lifted the little girl from the pony's back. The
child resisted, trying to maintain her grip on Vigor's
back. Gently, Vigor worked her hands loose and the
bowman took her away.

'A word of warning, my lords,' Otker told the
knights. 'We'll have to be careful where we're going.
If you want to get close enough to see the tower, then
stay quiet and keep your head down.'

OTKER AND TWO of the bowmen led Sir Leuthere,
Count Ergon and Vigor into a dense stand of trees
several fields from where the peasant mob had
ambushed them. The trees ran along one side of the
bocage country, eventually connecting with a forest. The going was rough, the ground uneven and
overgrown with brambles. It was a strange sort of
journey, for the woods were entirely silent, devoid of
the rustling and scurrying of small animals, absent of
the whistles and chirps of birds. Even the flies, a persistent nuisance in Aquitaine this time of year, were
gone. It was as though every living thing in the forest
had fled or was in hiding.

Darkness found the men several hours into their
woodland hike. Several times Count Ergon com-
plained about leaving the horses behind. It would
have been quicker to skirt the edge of the forest and
dismount closer to where they were going. After a
time, even Leuthere began to echo the nobleman's .
sentiment. Otker, however, insisted that the woods

offered the only cover from spying eyes. If the knights wanted to see the tower, then their only hope was to remain unseen.

When the sounds of axes chopping wood reached their ears, it seemed like the roar of thunder after the silence they had become accustomed to. Otker raised a warning finger to his lips, motioning for the knights to stay close behind him. The bowmen nocked arrows to their strings and spread out, warily watching the shadows.

Count Ergon did not need to be told when they drew near the enemy. He was the first to recognize the rancid stink in the air, the sickly scent of decaying flesh and dark magic. At once, the old knight grew tense, his right arm reflexively moving towards his sword until a spasm of pain stopped the motion. He scowled at his injured arm and used his left hand to draw his blade.

'Woodcutters,' Otker whispered. He pointed three fingers to their left. Dimly, through the darkness, the men could see a trio of grisly creatures awkwardly felling timber, their fleshless bones almost seeming to glow in the moonlight. 'The woods are full of them.'

'Soon there will be a few less,' Count Ergon promised. He started towards the walking skeletons. Otker dashed after the knight, gripping him by the arm.

'They're only after timber,' Otker said. 'They won't even look our way if we don't bother them.'

Count Ergon ripped his arm free from the peasant. 'Coward,' he cursed the man.

'We're not here to destroy the vampire's slaves,' Leuthere reminded the nobleman. 'It's the Red Duke we're after, and our best chance to get him is to speak with Iselda.'

Reluctantly, Count Ergon nodded his head and turned back.

'Perhaps once you've seen the tower you will change your mind, my lord,' Otker said.

Another hour found the men at the northernmost edge of the woods. They had been forced to follow a circuitous route through the forest to avoid the undead woodcutters, which seemed to increase in number the farther they went. Several times, loping ghouls had come scuttling through the trees, but the loathsome scavengers had passed the lurking men by without noticing them.

Ahead, through the trees, the knights could see the Tower of Wizardry, the walls of the fortress standing stark in the moonlight. They could also see the fields around the tower, fields that now swarmed with activity. Pale, fleshless shapes were at work in the fields, not to till crops but to shape the timber that gangs of zombies and skeletons dragged from the forest. Hundreds of the undead were at work with saw and hammer, taking the logs and rendering them down into flattened planks and beams. Other skeletons worked to assemble the planks and beams into more complex constructions.

Before the knights' eyes, the first siege tower rose above the field. The reason for the Red Duke's journey north was now explained.

The vampire was besieging the Tower of Wizardry!

CHAPTER XIII

'I will not ask you to stay. I know your pride and your honour are too great for that. I know there is nothing that would make you forsake your duty to the king, nothing that would keep you from giving your sword to a just and righteous cause.' Duchess Martinga closed her arms around her husband, pressing her soft lips against his neck. 'Only promise me, promise me you will come back to me.'

'The Lady herself could not keep me from your side,' the duke said, hugging Martinga close to him. 'We shall rout this villain Jaffar and drive his thieving corsairs out of Estalia and back into their deserts. I'll be back before the harvest.'

The duchess pulled away from him. She lifted her face and smiled at his optimistic assurances, but the smile did not reach her eyes.

The duke noted Martinga's unease. He bent his knee, kneeling before his wife. He took her little hand in his own, turning it over so that he could kiss the palm. 'The king needs me. I am the best swordsman in Aquitaine, and that means in all of Bretonnia. He will need good fighting men if we are to free Estalia from the heathen.'

'I know,' Martinga assured him, but there was still a note of fear in her voice.

The duke rose to his feet, laughing at his wife's anxiety, making a great display of nonchalant bravado. 'Why carry on so?' he asked. 'I've been away before on far more perilous quests. Remember last summer when I helped Duke Chararic campaign against the orcs raiding his lands along the Upper Grismerie? Or when I joined Duke Arnulf to hunt down the dragon Gundovald? Or when I spent a month at the court of Duke Ballomer and had to endure the raw seafood diet of Lyonesse?' He tried to tickle his wife's throat as he made the last jest. Defiantly, she drew back.

'Be serious,' she said, trying to suppress a shudder. 'I know you have done many bold and reckless things…'

'Some would call them heroic,' the duke quipped. 'Most certainly anyone who has stared at a Lyonesse lobster lying sprawled in its enormity across his plate.' He saw that his levity had not lightened Martinga's mood. Contritely, he clapped a hand over his mouth and waved his hand in apology.

Martinga began to pace across the lush carpets of her sitting room, collecting her thoughts, trying to put into words the nameless dread that clutched her heart. Her steps carried her to the narrow window that allowed light and air into the chamber. She stared out the opening, watching the guards patrolling the castle walls, seeing the craftsmen and merchants navigating the narrow streets of the town beyond the castle as they brought their wares to market. Everything seemed so peaceful, so normal, that she could not help but think her fears to be childish and unfounded. But however she tried to rationalize them away, she could not rid herself of them.

'There's something… some dark force I don't understand,' she told the duke. 'Every night I wake up and I can see it, a black shape looming over you. Reaching down to take you from me!'

'You sound like the Prophetess Isabeau,' the duke told her. 'The next time you think you see this phantom, wake me so that I can see it too.'

Martinga's face went pale. She rushed to her husband, taking his hands in hers. 'I don't ever want you to see it,' she gasped. 'It's an omen, a warning! Something evil is waiting for you if you ride with the king!'

'I can no more abandon the king than he would abandon me,' the duke told her, his voice carrying a painful note, knowing his words would cause his wife hurt. 'I have to join his crusade against the sultan.'

Martinga turned away. 'I know you do,' she said. 'But be careful. Remember a foolish woman's nightmares. 'Don't let the darkness take you from me.'

THE RED DUKE watched as his engineers began to assemble the first of the trebuchets that would batter the Tower of Wizardry into rubble. When he was finished here, he would leave no trace that a fortress had ever stood here. He would cast the ruins of the tower into Lake Tranquil stone by stone. He would raze the very foundations, undermine the crypts and cellars from below and send them crashing down into the very pits of hell. A hundred years and no man would be able to say where the tower had stood or dare to speak the name of the treacherous witch who was its mistress.

He thought of Martinga's warning, that last day before he set out for Carcassonne and the Estalian frontier. She had spoken of a dark phantom, a black shadow reaching down to take him from her. He had always thought of the duchess as a calm, practical and iron-nerved woman. He had loved her because of her strong personality, the dignified courage only a member of the fair sex could ever lay claim to. She was not someone given to premonitions and nightmares. Perhaps that is why he hadn't listened to her warning, had allowed himself to be unmoved by her dread.

But she had been right. Something evil had been waiting for him, to inflict upon him a fate worse than dragon's breath and troll's belly. A fate that had taken him from her, taken him away for all eternity. He would never enter the Gates of Morr, never see the peaceful gardens where his wife's spirit had gone.

He was now the Red Duke, now and forever.

How was it that his wife, a woman without the arcane powers of a prophetess, had foreseen the horrible doom waiting for him at the end of his crusade? How was it that Isabeau, with all the magic and mystery of the grail damsels behind her, with the divine grace of the Lady flowing through her, how was it that she had failed to sense the Red Duke's damnation?

There was only one answer: she had. Perhaps it was she who had turned the ear of King Louis. Perhaps it was Isabeau who had plotted the whole sordid plan to wrest the dukedom from its rightful lord and pass it to a usurping king.

The Red Duke glared up at the tower, watching as the prophetess walked about the balcony. She had changed her appearance, looking more youthful and dark than when she had cast him out from the tower. Her dress was of a sheer, body-hugging cut that he had never seen before, her long conical hat draped with ribbons of silk and feathered tassels. The vampire did not know what Isabeau was playing at, but if she thought a change of clothes and a bit of magic to alter her face would hide her from him, then she was sorely mistaken.

The Red Duke laughed grimly as he watched gangs of skeletons dragging long slender poles out into the field below the balcony. He knew how to break the woman's spirit. Like all women, she would have little stomach for violence and barbarity. The vampire had learned much of both when he made war against the Arabyans. For now, the sharpened stakes lay upon the ground, but soon they would rise high over the fields, burdened with the screaming bodies of villagers and farmers. He would break the witch's defiance.

The vampire growled irritably, snapping an order for Baron de Gavaudan to attend him. He was annoyed at the lack of progress being shown by his army. They should have captured hundreds of peasants by now. His skeleton warriors should already be well into planting a forest of the impaled before the tower walls. Instead they stood idle beside their piles of stakes, drawing the fire of the few bowmen hidden inside the fortress.

'Where is de Gavaudan!' the Red Duke roared, kicking at the zombie polishing his boots. The creature toppled back, its jaw broken by the vampire. Mindlessly, the rotting corpse crawled back to its seated master and resumed its duties, oblivious to the shattered bone piercing its cheek.

'Where is that slinking cur!' the vampire snarled again.

Renar, like the others of the Red Duke's inner circle, stood in attendance upon the vampire within his shadowy pavilion. The necromancer groaned. It was almost on his tongue to tell his master that he had left Baron de Gavaudan locked inside the chapel at

Mercal, but he knew no good would come of bringing that up. Instead he nudged the dark knight standing beside him, the thrall the Red Duke had created to replace de Gavaudan. 'I think you'd better be the baron,' Renar told the dark knight.

Confused, the dark knight approached the seated Red Duke, bowing low before his master.

'Where have you been, de Gavaudan? Out filling your belly with the blood of peasant girls?' The Red Duke glared at his thrall. 'I am displeased with the progress my troops are making. I dispatched my knights to burn all the villages and bring back every prisoner they could catch.' He gestured angrily at the empty fields. 'That was yesterday and they still have not returned! I want my prisoners, baron! If those louts can't find a rabble of illiterate peasants, I'll have their spurs! I'll lay each of them across an open fire and cook them in their own armour!'

Renar shook his head as he heard the Red Duke's fury. The delusion was upon him again, the sickness that made him think he was still making war against King Louis the Righteous. He'd sent his black knights out to destroy villages that had been razed almost five hundred years ago, to capture people who had been dead and buried for centuries.

Meanwhile, the vampire's army was fixed in place, laying siege to the Tower of Wizardry, as vulnerable as a newborn babe should Duke Gilon's army come charging down upon them. After the trail of destruction they had left behind them, Renar was convinced that Duke Gilon had already sent the clarion call to all his vassals to assemble their knights and men-at-arms. That they had not already given battle to the Red Duke only meant that Duke Gilon was still marshalling his forces.

By the time they faced Duke Gilon's knights, Renar hoped to have three thousand undead horse lords marching with them. He wanted the Barrows of Cuileux ripped open and plundered, the ancient knights drawn from their tombs to fight under their new vampiric lord. Most of all, he wanted the Red Duke rational and sane, his brilliant mind concentrated upon the tactics that would crush Duke Gilon's army. He didn't need the vampire lost within his own world of memory and illusion.

Renar stroked his chin as an idea came to him. He glanced over at the grim, wraithlike form of Jacquetta. The Red Duke's madness was fixed upon visiting revenge upon the long-dead mistress of the tower. What if Renar was able to give him that long-denied vengeance? Just as the Red Duke mistook Maraulf for Baron de Gavaudan, so he might accept Iselda for her predecessor Isabeau. The shock of achieving the victory he had failed to gain five centuries ago might be enough to break the vampire of his delusions.

Jacquetta was the key to Renar's plan. While it could take weeks or months to batter down the tower's thick walls, the banshee needed no breach to effect entrance to the fortress. She could pass right through the stones, find Iselda and kill her. Then there would be no reason for the vampire to maintain his siege.

The necromancer leaned back, only half listening as the Red Duke continued to berate his dark knight for the failures of Baron de Gavaudan. It would take some cunning to broach his plan in a way that would be acceptable to the Red Duke in his present state of mind. The right alchemy of flattery and deference. Fortunately, if there was one thing any intelligent man born into Bretonnia's peasant class quickly learned, it was how to be flattering and deferential when conversing with the nobles who ruled the kingdom.

COUNT ERGON WAS at a loss to understand what the Red Duke was doing. The vampire had set much of his undead army to the chore of felling lumber and assembling siege engines, yet several hundred skeletons stood idle on the field, standing passively as archers inside the tower whittled away at them. The vampire's cavalry had ridden off, scattering in every direction. The count could not speak for the duties entrusted to the other black knights, but those he had seen through the trees were simply galloping between two stretches of lifeless dead ground. Otker suggested that villages might have once stood in these places, long ago. The wights were probably trying to locate the burial grounds that had once served the long vanished communities so that their foul master might resurrect the buried dead as skeleton warriors and swell the ranks of his monstrous army.

The nobleman looked longingly at the vampire's encampment. There was no mistaking the Red Duke's tent, a pavilion of black cloth that looked as though it had been stitched together from burial shrouds. Only a few armoured wights stood guard over their master's lair, but with hundreds of zombies standing at attention all around the tent, there was small need for them. Count Ergon dismissed the thought of trying to fight his way to the Red Duke. Even mounted upon his warhorse, he knew he would never be able to cut his way through the undead soldiers before they could overwhelm him through sheer numbers. The thought that he should die before avenging his son was physically repugnant to the count.

No, he would wait, wait for a chance when he could be certain of crossing swords with the vampire.

'For a brilliant strategist, the Red Duke musters a poor siege,' Sir Leuthere observed. 'I've seen orcs use better tactics.'

Count Ergon turned away from his view of the field, careful to lower the branch of the bush he sheltered behind slowly so as not to make any undue noise. 'He has the tower sealed up well enough,' the count said. 'He doesn't need all of his troops to keep one lone woman and her servants bottled up. In fact, he may have left such glaring gaps in his deployment on purpose, hoping to draw Iselda out then set upon her as she tried to escape.' He nodded sombrely as he considered the cunning of such a tactic. 'The Red Duke's creatures are probably watching for any hint of someone trying to make a break for it.'

Leuthere didn't agree. 'We had an easy enough time getting this close to the tower. That speaks poorly for the vigilance of the Red Duke's troops.'

'Maybe,' Count Ergon said. 'Or maybe it's just that we're headed in the wrong direction to interest them. The Red Duke's monsters seem to need to be told exactly what to do. They don't have any initiative to act beyond their orders. Remember the skeletons standing out in the field, not even lifting a finger while the bowmen inside the tower kept shooting at them? They didn't even have enough motivation to move out of range, just standing there letting themselves be shot, waiting for someone to tell them what to do.'

'Then you think we might be able to get into the tower?' Leuthere wondered. 'Even with the Red Duke's army encamped all around it?'

'If they haven't been told to stop anybody from going *to* the tower,' Count Ergon answered. 'And if we can avoid running into any of the Red Duke's creatures that *can* think for themselves.'

Leuthere pulled back a branch, grimacing as he saw the picket line of zombies staggered about the perimeter of the tower. There were gaps in the line large enough to sail a Tilean war galleon through, but Count Ergon's warning about a trap made him see menace rather than promise from the curious way the vampire had deployed his creatures. If Count Ergon was wrong, they'd be slaughtered.

The young knight cast his eyes upwards, seeing the balcony high atop the tower. He could see the distant figure of a woman dressed in blue leaning against the rail of the balcony. Despite the distance and the shelter of the forest, Leuthere imagined he could feel her looking straight at him.

'We have to try,' Leuthere decided, slamming a fist into an open palm. 'The Red Duke is laying siege to the tower for a reason. Five hundred years ago, the Prophetess Isabeau pitted her magic against him and took a hand in his defeat. Maybe he is trying to make certain that Iselda can't do the same.'

'Then the prophetess must know the secret to destroying this fiend,' Count Ergon hissed, excitement in his voice.

'Even if she doesn't, we can't abandon a woman in such distress,' Leuthere said. 'The laws of chivalry would not allow a knight to behave in such a knavish fashion. Whatever it costs us, we have to rescue her from the Red Duke.' The young knight turned and stared at Vigor, Otker and the bowmen.

'Honour demands that Count Ergon and I give

aid to the Prophetess Iselda,' Leuthere said. 'If we are wrong about our chances of reaching the tower, then we are walking into certain death. As peasants, you have no honour to offend by staying behind. I will understand if you wish to keep out of this.'

Otker nodded his head vigorously. 'Thank you, my lord,' he said. 'What you've talked about sounds as mad as a hatter's ravings. Me and my friends would be just as happy to stay right here.'

Vigor stepped away from the other peasants, bowing awkwardly before Sir Leuthere. 'I may not have a knight's honour, my lord, but there is a burden upon my soul for which I must atone. Please, allow me to accompany you. If it means death, then at least I may die opposing the evil I helped set loose.'

Leuthere went cold as he heard Vigor speak. He was touched by the peasant's display of fortitude, but horrified by his lapse in judgement. He looked aside at Count Ergon, watching the nobleman's reaction to Vigor's speech, but the count merely raised an eyebrow at Vigor's talk of loosing evil upon the land. The chill running down Leuthere's spine merged with the sick feeling rising in his belly. He knew Count Ergon would remember what Vigor had said. The count might not demand an explanation now, with them preparing to mount a possibly suicidal dash for the tower, but that demand would come. When it did, Leuthere would have to confess the role Earl Gaubert had played in freeing the Red Duke from his tomb. If that did not rekindle the feud between d'Elbiq and du Maisne, nothing would.

The three men took their leave of Otker and crept to the very edge of the forest. They could see the nearest gang of skeletons only a few hundred yards away, the undead labouring to smooth timber into poles and beams for assembly into a trebuchet. The sound of hammers and saws drowned out the noise of their own pounding hearts.

An ashen-faced Vigor turned to address Leuthere. 'Let me go first, my lord,' the crippled peasant asked. 'If they... if they come after me, you can figure out another way into the tower.'

There was logic behind Vigor's offer, logic that made Leuthere agree to the scheme even while feeling shame that he was allowing a peasant to embrace danger on his behalf. Desperate times, however, often demanded unusual measures. It would be a greater shame to fail and allow Iselda to fall into the Red Duke's hands.

The knights watched as Vigor walked out onto the field with slow, faltering steps. The peasant's crooked body trembled with fear, a soft moan of terror escaping him as he drew closer to the grisly gang of skeletons. Once or twice, Vigor stopped, standing completely still except for the tremor that shivered through his limbs. Not once, however, did the peasant turn and look back. With a resolution worthy of a knight, the guilt-ridden man kept going forwards.

Leuthere kept watching the skeletons, waiting for them to react to Vigor's presence. The undead never even lifted their heads, intent upon the task set for them by their sinister master. Before long, the peasant was past the work crew and making his way towards one of the gaps in the picket line.

'He's through,' Leuthere breathed, his shoulders slumping in relief.

'The real test will be if he can get past the pickets,' Count Ergon said. 'That will tell us if this mad idea is going to work or not.'

Both men watched in silence as Vigor drew close to the unmoving formations of zombie soldiers. Even from the cover of the forest, the knights could smell the rotten stink of the creatures, could see the decaying flesh peeling away from their putrid bodies. Vigor paused as he approached the gap between the zombies, wiping his sweaty palms on his breeches, making the sign of Shallya in the air with his fingers.

Then the peasant was moving forwards again, his pace even and unhurried. Several times he stumbled, awkwardly reaching out with his arms to correct his balance. Leuthere guessed the reason for Vigor's strange advance. The peasant had closed his eyes lest he be overwhelmed with horror at the sight of the zombies. If the undead pickets were to take notice of him, the man didn't want to know. He didn't want to see death coming for him.

After what seemed an eternity, Vigor was well ahead of the line of rotting sentries. The zombies had not so much as moved a single muscle, one of them even had a crow picking maggots from its scalp without making any sign it was aware of the hungry bird. Vigor was going to make it! He was going to reach the tower! The zombies weren't going to stop him!

Leuthere's jaw dropped open as a sudden realisation hit him. The undead might not keep Vigor from reaching the tower, but the men inside could! There were archers inside that fortress, watching from every window. They had no way of knowing Vigor was a friend, no way of knowing he was anything but another of the Red Duke's slaves. Indeed, with his stumbling, blind advance, they might even mistake him for one of the undead!

Leuthere expressed his worry to Count Ergon. The

older knight cursed himself for not considering this problem, angrily slapping his left hand against his injured right arm, using the flare of pain as a physical admonishment to his mistake.

'We have to get out there,' Count Ergon told him. 'If those men in the tower see a pair of knights coming towards them, they might hold back.'

'Unless they think we're more of the Red Duke's creatures,' Leuthere pointed out.

Count Ergon grimaced at the suggestion. 'We'll just have to make sure we march across the field with our eyes open,' he said.

The two knights quit the forest, striding out into the open. Their gait was bold, stiffened with a confidence neither man really felt. It was the resignation that they were probably going to die that bolstered their courage. If they were to die, then they would at least do so with the dignity of a true knight of Bretonnia.

They passed the skeletons building the trebuchet without even glancing at the monsters. The eyes of both men were locked on the tower, watching as Vigor blindly stumbled closer to the fortress. Every moment the knights expected the crippled peasant to wither under a volley of arrows, but yard-by-yard Vigor was able to proceed without a single shot protesting his advance.

The knights were crossing the open ground between the skeleton labourers and the picket line when they saw Vigor finally reach the base of the tower. They saw the peasant stumble against the rock foundation of the fortress. He picked himself off the ground a moment later. His eyes must have been open at that point, for the knights could hear a distant yelp of triumph and see Vigor's fist strike out into the air. The peasant glanced about, sighting the barred entryway into the tower. He scrambled over the uneven jumble of stones arrayed around the tower's base and made for the massive steel door.

Leuthere had no time to see how Vigor progressed from that point. A sharp whisper from Count Ergon drew his attention back to the picket line. The men were within twenty yards of the closest zombies. The undead soldiers stood stiffly at attention, their decayed faces staring straight towards the tower. Each of the zombies held a crude spear or a rusty halberd in its rotting hand; many of them even wore battered kettle helms or strips of mail. Leuthere was shocked to find that not all of the zombies were men, but that a large number of them were women and children. When the Red Duke inducted the dead into his army, the vampire took everything that could lift a weapon.

Unconsciously, the knights slowed their pace as they passed the menacing ranks of the undead. Each man clenched his sword tightly, wary of any move on the part of the zombies. But the creatures paid them no notice, staring with unblinking eyes at the tower they had been told to guard.

The knights vented a sigh of relief as they passed the picket line without being challenged. As Count Ergon had predicted, the creatures had been ordered to keep people from leaving the tower. No provision had been given them about what to do if somebody tried to get inside.

That changed all too soon. A sharp cry rose from behind the picket line. Simultaneously, Leuthere and Count Ergon turned their heads to find the source of the shout. What they saw was a gaunt, cadaverous man dressed in a long black coat. He was stamping his foot in fury, waving his hands over his head.

This was no mindless creature of the vampire's, but rather a living man who had damned his soul by allying himself to the Red Duke.

'IDIOTS! WORM-CRAWLING CARRION!' Renar raged, shaking his fists at the still unmoving zombies. 'They're walking right into the tower!' The necromancer cursed the still-unmoving zombies, quickly guessing the reason for their lethargy. He closed his eyes, drawing into himself the dark power of Dhar, weaving the fell energy into a spell that would place the zombies under his direct control.

The knights did not wait around to see how successfully Renar would rouse the undead from their stupor. Breaking into a run, the men dashed towards the tower. The possibility of being struck down by the archers inside the fortress was one that plagued them at every step, but at least it would be a quicker death than being butchered by a hundred zombies.

Behind them, Renar continued to rage and curse. The necromancer could see that the pickets he had seized control over would never catch the fleeing knights. Exerting more of his dark power, he forced the lumbering zombies into a magically-charged run, driving them to greater and greater effort. Some of the most rotten of the sentries collapsed as their decayed bodies broke from the strain, wormy legs snapping, brittle bones cracking, bloated organs ripping through desiccated skin. But enough of the zombies were whole enough to withstand the sorcerous punishment.

Enough to drag down the knights and make them regret their heroics. A cold smile was on Renar's face as he thought about what he would do to the knights once they were in his power. He would take his time about killing them, of that he was determined. He would make the men die a little for every year he had grovelled at the feet of their kind. He would make them suffer as he had suffered and when they could suffer no more, he would infuse their dead carcasses with a semblance of life so that they might wait upon *him* and serve *him* as he had once been forced to serve.

Distracted by his vengeful daydream, Renar failed to bolster his zombies for the last sprint that would allow them to close with the knights. He scowled when he noticed his error, watching as the zombies reverted to their usual lumbering shuffle and the knights dashed ahead of them to the base of the tower.

Renar was about to infuse the zombies with a fresh burst of magical energy when he noticed something amusing. The steel door of the tower was still shut. There was a crook-backed peasant standing their arguing with the warden inside, but it seemed the man inside wasn't about to be swayed. The door remained shut.

A cruel smile worked itself onto Renar's face. No reason to waste his energy now. Let the knights reach the tower. Let them beg and plead and cry trying to get inside. They'd be trapped out there, trapped against the wall when Renar's zombies came for them. Inches from safety, their destruction would be all the more crushing.

The necromancer chuckled to himself and raised his eyes to the tower itself. Safety? Perhaps it was wrong to use that word. Indeed, if the knights knew what he had unleashed inside the tower, they might prefer to stay outside and be mauled by Renar's zombies!

CHAPTER XIV

'Your grace.'

The voice trembled with sorrow, the words choked and strained. Somehow they fought their way through the crimson oblivion that had seized the duke's mind. He struggled up from the bloody dreams, grasping desperately at every word.

'I do not know if you hear me,' the voice was saying. 'I do not know if you can hear me. But I must tell you, your grace. I must tell you.'

The voice was that of Earl Durand du Maisne. The vassal who had disobeyed his orders to leave him behind in the Arabyan desert. The duke felt a flush of admiration for Earl Durand, the man whose loyalty had made him stand fast beside his stricken lord. He could not remember now why he had wished to die. Dimly he remembered a dark figure leaning over him, doing something to him as he lay helpless upon the sand.

The duke brushed aside the errant thought, concentrating as Durand's pained voice spoke again.

'We are back, your grace. Back in Castle Aquin. We have returned.'

Emotion flared through the duke's heart. Castle Aquin! Aquitaine! He had despaired of ever seeing his home again. Furiously he struggled to open his eyes, but they felt as though iron weights had been chained to each lid. Then he suddenly remembered the emotion in Earl Durand's voice. He sounded anything but jubilant. His was hardly the voice of a soldier returned in triumph from a long crusade. The duke wondered what horror he would see if he did manage to open his eyes.

'Your grace,' Durand said, choking back a sob. The duke felt a tremor of fear course through him, trying to imagine what kind of tragedy could so unman a brave knight of Bretonnia.

'Your grace, the Duchess Martinga is dead.'

The words pierced the duke's mind like a red-hot knife. There was more; Durand was talking about how news had reached Aquitaine that the duke had died in battle. He spoke of how Martinga had at first disbelieved such tales, but how, in the end, as all the other crusading lords returned, she had at last accepted the truth of her husband's death. Refusing to live without him, she had climbed to the highest tower in the castle and thrown herself over the parapet.

Agony, pain like nothing he'd felt even with the Arabyan poison burning in his veins, flared through the duke's body. He would have screamed, thrashed his limbs against the torment, but his sickened muscles refused to obey him. Instead, he cast his mind afield, trying to retreat into memory from the horror assailing his senses.

In his mind, the duke raced through the dreary halls of his castle, passing by rooms rendered cheerless and forlorn without Martinga's presence. He saw her sitting room, that happy chamber high above the outer wall. Was it from here she had watched for his return? And was it from here that despair had at last claimed her?

The duke imagined he could see two men standing in

*the abandoned chamber. He recognized them, saw the
faces of Baron de Gavaudan and Marquis Galafre d'Elbiq.
He could hear them talking, discussing the invalid corpse
Marquis Galafre had brought back from Araby. Their talk
turned to accusations of sabotage and treachery. Marquis
Galafre blamed the baron for sinking the ship bearing
them back to Bretonnia. The baron, in turn blamed Marquis Galafre for not completing their compact.*

*The duke's mind retreated from the treacherous words,
recoiling back into his paralysed body.*

*Earl Durand was still speaking to him, telling him of
his wife's suicide. But El Syf knew better now. His wife's
despair had been born from a lie. A lie fathered by Baron
de Gavaudan and the one man who would profit from the
Duke of Aquitaine's death.*

*The man all of Bretonnia knew as King Louis the Right-
eous.*

SIR LEUTHERE AND Count Ergon raced to the massive
steel door that offered the only entrance to the Tower
of Wizardry. Behind them, they could hear the horde
of zombies awkwardly climb the rocky mound upon
which the tower had been reared. Though some of
them had fallen in their pursuit of the two knights,
hundreds remained. The unexpected and unnatural
speed the creatures had displayed seemed to have
abated, reducing their pursuit of the men to a steady,
relentless shamble.

There was some hope, if the knights could gain
entry to the tower in time. But as the two men drew
closer, they saw that such would be easier said than
done. Vigor was engaged in a vigorous argument with
the warder on the other side of the steel door. The
wart-nosed man peered out from a small window in

the centre of the portal, studying Vigor intently.

'How do I know you're not some creature of the vampire's?' the warder demanded to know. 'A spy trying to slither his way into the tower so he can kill milady?'

Vigor slammed his hand against the unyielding door. 'We've been over that!' he cursed. 'You've had a good look at my neck. Does it look like the vampire bit me?'

The warder shook his head. 'Maybe the vampire didn't need to bite you. Maybe you're working for him to earn some silver. There's lots of wretches would do worse for less.'

'I'll do worse to you!' Vigor snarled, bashing his hand against the door again. He turned a hopeful look towards Leuthere and Count Ergon as the two men came running towards the door. 'If you don't believe me, maybe you'll believe my noble lords,' the peasant announced. He gestured Leuthere towards the door. 'Tell this idiot why we're here.'

'We need to get inside to see the prophetess,' Leuthere said, gasping for breath. 'Open this door and conduct us to your mistress.'

The warder sneered back at him. 'How do I know you're a real knight?' he demanded. 'Seems awful strange all those fiends would just let you march right in here.' His eyes narrowed with suspicion. 'How do I know you're not vampires yourselves?' He drew back from the window. 'Show me your neck,' he ordered in a frightened voice.

Count Ergon watched as the first of the zombies reached the top of the mound. Their brief respite was almost over. 'Look, we're friends,' he growled at the warder. 'But in a minute, we'll just be a pile of

butchered meat if you don't open that door!' The
count shook his head in frustration. 'Ask your archers
if we're part of the Red Duke's army!' he exclaimed.
'If we were, don't you think they would have shot us
down before we could reach this door?'

Leuthere turned from the door, looking back at
the zombies climbing the foundations of the tower.
'That's right,' he told Count Ergon. 'But why aren't
they loosing arrows into that mob?'

An uneasy feeling gripped the three men who had
risked their lives to cross the battlefield. Count Ergon
pressed his face against the little window in the door.

'Something's wrong,' he told the warder. 'Something's wrong inside the tower!' As he spoke, a
piercing shriek echoed through the guardroom, a
deafening wail that set the very flesh crawling. The
warder cast terrified eyes to the ceiling, wondering
what was going on in the halls above.

The colour drained from Count Ergon's face. His
body trembled. 'I know that sound,' he muttered,
oblivious to who heard him. It was the shriek that
had presaged the Red Duke's attack on the Chateau
du Maisne. The wail of the banshee.

'What is it?' Leuthere asked, noting the nobleman's
fright.

Count Ergon ignored him, facing the warder
instead. 'Let me in, man! I tell you I know what has
been set loose in the tower!'

The warder stared back at Count Ergon, paralysed
with fear. On the small rise around the base of the
tower, a full score of zombies had finished their climb
and were shuffling slowly towards the gateway and the
three men trapped on the wrong side of the door. The
knights could hear the creak of dry bones grinding

against one another, the rattle of loose armour against decaying flesh, the drip of unclean juices from burst organs. As the zombies advanced, they clumsily hefted the crude spears and rusty glaives they bore, presenting the trapped men with a fence of splintered wood and sharp iron.

Leuthere and Vigor turned away from the door, both men brandishing their own weapons, prepared to meet the lumbering horde. Count Ergon continued to pound on the door, trying to spur the terrified warder into action.

It was nothing Count Ergon did that finally had the man scrambling forwards to unbar the gate. It was the keening wail of the banshee echoing once more down from the tower that broke through to the frightened man. Fairly leaping for the door, the warder threw back the heavy bolts and pulled down the heavy beam.

Count Ergon scrambled through the door as soon as it started to open. Vigor hurried after him, Leuthere following last of all. The three men threw their weight against the door once they were inside the guard room, slamming it in the very faces of the oncoming zombies. The rotten hand of one of the creatures was caught in the slamming portal, decayed fingers spilling to the floor as the edge of the closing door sliced them off.

The door closed with a metallic boom. The knights continued to press their armoured weight against it while Vigor and the warder hefted the heavy beam back into place and drove home the half-dozen bolts that secured the door into the stone wall.

'I'm… I'm sorry, my lords…' the warder apologized. Vigor spoke for all of them when he planted his fist in the man's stomach.

'We're in, what do we do now?' Vigor asked as he turned away from the retching warder.

The ghastly shriek of the banshee sounded once more, piercing each of the men to the very core of his being. Like a thousand nightmares, the eerie sound set their bones shivering.

'We go up there and find what's making that noise,' Count Ergon declared, the intense look in his eyes telling his companions he would brook no argument.

Leuthere nodded in agreement. 'What do we do when we find it?'

Count Ergon rolled his left hand, letting the light play across the sharp edge of his sword.

'We make it stop,' he said.

CLIMBING THE CENTRAL stair that wound upwards through the tower, it was not long before the three men found the first of the bowmen. Dressed in the grubby raiment of a peasant, the archer was slumped against the inward column to which the narrow steps had been set. Blood stained his ears, trails of gore running from eyes and nose. As Vigor pressed a hand to the bowman to check him for any sign of life, the body shifted, crashing to the stairs and slowly sliding down the steps. A grotesque thumping noise echoed through the stairway as the corpse gradually rolled down the steps.

The bowman had been one of many to flee to the tower for protection against the Red Duke's attack. He had trusted the thick stone walls and the magic of the prophetess to protect him. Instead, he had found a strange and horrible death.

'Be vigilant,' Count Ergon warned. 'The banshee does not need to see you to kill you. Her wail is enough.' The nobleman removed a silk ribbon from the sleeve of his gauntlet, then took the steel helm from off his head. Pulling back the mail coif and padded quilting which he wore under the helmet, he began to wind the ribbon around his head, binding his ears. Sir Leuthere noted the faint scent of perfume on the ribbon and the heraldry of the du Maisnes embroidered upon it.

'Cover your ears,' the count advised the other men. 'It may help against the banshee's scream.'

The count drew ahead of his companions, carefully mounting the winding stairs. The atmosphere about the stairwell was icy and lifeless, the knight's breath turning to frost before his face. A splash of blood upon the centre wall had crystallized, shimmering weirdly in the flickering torchlight.

Count Ergon's thoughts turned back to the horror that had descended upon his own castle, his men-at-arms and knights slaughtered by a nightmarish apparition that could kill merely with the sound of her hideous voice. Against such a spectral fiend, he did not know if courage and steel were enough to cause harm. All that he did know was that an effort had to be made to stop the ghastly ghost before she could accomplish whatever malignant purpose the Red Duke expected of her.

The body of another bowman lay crumpled across the steps, his face frozen in an expression of agony and terror. Count Ergon hesitated, staring down at the dead man, picturing how he had died. He imagined the same fate lurking in wait for him just beyond the next turn. In his mind he could see his own face, dead and terrified, blood seeping from his lifeless eyes.

The knight summoned his faltering courage,

whispering a quiet prayer for the Lady to preserve his valour in this, his moment of need. Carefully, Count Ergon stepped over the dead archer. He gazed anxiously at the winding climb ahead of him. The silk favour bestowed upon him by his wife had bound his ears in such a way that he was almost deaf. A good defence against the banshee's wail, but now the count found himself wishing he could hear just a little more, detect some sound that would betray the presence of the malignant spirit.

Firming his resolve, Count Ergon continued up the stairs. Another dead bowman was slumped across the steps, this one with his hands still locked about the shaft of an arrow. The peasant had sought to escape the torment of the banshee's scream by driving the head of the arrow through his ear. The knight hoped the dead man had achieved some small measure of peace through his desperate act.

As Count Ergon raised his eyes from the dead bowman, a gasp of horror exploded from his lungs. He staggered back, almost tripping over the legs of the corpse at his feet.

Only a few feet from him, unearthly in her terrible beauty, was the pale figure of a woman, her voluptuous body clad only in the billowy rags of a burial shroud. The lissom ghost drifted rapidly towards the knight. As she closed upon him, her gorgeous face withered, collapsing into a leering skull. The banshee's jaws opened in a hateful shriek.

Count Ergon staggered, feeling the power of the banshee's wail tearing at his body, clawing at his soul. Even with his ears deafened to sound, the pitch of the spectral scream was penetrating into his brain. Pain shot through his entire being, pain like a thousand tiny fires burning beneath his flesh. Still, the knight counted his blessings. Without the precaution of binding his ears, he knew the banshee's wail would have killed him outright.

Jacquetta's fury swelled, intensified by the knight's refusal to die. She swung the short sword clutched in one of her slender hands, chopping down at the staggered nobleman, intending to separate his head from his shoulders.

If Count Ergon had been uninjured, the banshee's sword would have finished him then and there. Pressed close to the supporting column, there was little room for a man climbing the steps to wield a blade in his right hand, certainly not enough for the knight to intercept the descending blow of Jacquetta's sword.

But Count Ergon had been injured. Clenched in his left hand, his sword had room enough to strike out, slashing across the banshee's blade. The short sword was torn from Jacquetta's spectral clutch by the nobleman's desperate parry, the blade clattering off down the stairway.

Hateful fires blazed in the sockets of Jacquetta's skull. The shrieking banshee swept down upon Count Ergon, clawing at him with ghostly fingers. The nobleman could feel her hands like icy knives digging at him, shivering through flesh and armour. He lashed out furiously with his sword, the steel passing harmlessly through the wispy essence of the spirit. Overcome by pain, he fell to his knees, swatting at Jacquetta as the banshee began to pull the helm from his head. The ghost had guessed how he had survived her killing shriek and was now intent upon removing his defence.

Leuthere and Vigor came running up the stairs, alerted to Count Ergon's peril by the sword he'd knocked from the banshee's hand. The younger knight paused awkwardly as he struggled to work his way around Count Ergon so that he could strike at Jacquetta. The banshee turned her head, shrieking at the knight, her fury swelling as she saw that he, too, was defended against her killing wail.

While the banshee faced Leuthere, Vigor dove in to attack her from behind. Squirming around Count Ergon, the crook-backed peasant stabbed the point of his sword through the phantom. Jacquetta spun about, howling malignantly at the man. Set upon from all sides now, the banshee's face filled out, her beautiful features growing outwards to replace the decayed skull. She smiled coyly at the men, then in a flicker she was away, sinking into the very wall of the tower.

Leuthere lunged at the fading banshee, his sword drawing sparks from the wall as it scraped against the cold stone. Count Ergon gripped his arm and shook his head. It was impossible to hurt the ghost that way. He pointed up towards the higher levels of the tower. His meaning was clear. If they couldn't hurt the banshee, then at least they could find Iselda and get the prophetess to safety.

Hurriedly, the knights raced up the stairs. They watched the corridors that branched off from the stairway, expecting at any instant to run into the ethereal killer again. The men kept away from the walls as much as possible, fearful that the banshee would reach out from the very stones to claw at them with her ghostly fingers.

Everywhere they found evidence of death and

C. L. Werner

destruction. The bodies of peasant bowmen and servants in the livery of the tower were everywhere, sprawled in attitudes of abject horror or curled into little balls of pain. The chill of black magic and the supernatural was all around them, sucking the warmth from their bodies, draining the very vitality from their bones.

It was near the top of the tower that Leuthere noted a change. One of the corridors branching off from the winding stairway felt different: cold, but without the debilitating taint that had assaulted them throughout their climb. He held his arm out, blocking the progress of his comrades. Firmly, he gestured towards the hallway. Count Ergon nodded in understanding, stepping aside so the younger knight could lead the way.

The cold hallway was positively inviting after the supernatural chill they had experienced. The corridor was appointed in lavish style, with marble columns and gilded sculptures of the grail affixed to each of the white oak doors set into the walls. Here there were no signs of violence, no splashes of spilled blood and pain-wracked corpses. A sense of peace and security suffused the three men as they traversed the hall, drawn to the oaken double doors at the end of the corridor.

Without hesitation, Leuthere opened the doors. Beyond them was a room that was ablaze with light. A flaming brazier stood at the centre of the chamber, an aromatic white smoke rising from the golden coals. The walls of the chamber were covered in mirrors of every description and size, from humble panes of polished tin to enormous sheets of crystal bound in frames of silver.

A huddle of frightened humanity cowered against the far wall of the mirror room, peasant women and children for the most part, though with a few shame-faced men among them. A few servants in the livery of the tower were there too, doing their best to keep the refugees calm.

Standing apart from them all was Iselda. The prophetess stood a little way from the brazier, staring intently into one of the mirrors on the wall. She looked away when Leuthere stepped into the room. The suggestion of a smile played at the corner of her pursed lips. She waved the men forwards, then gestured for them to remove the coverings that deafened them.

'Your arrival is most timely,' Iselda told them. 'I had expected you, but not quite so soon.'

'You expected us?' Count Ergon asked, his voice conveying both surprise and doubt.

Iselda smiled at him. 'I sent Sir Leuthere to find you, Count Ergon du Maisne,' she told him. 'Your family has an important part to play in destroying the Red Duke.' The prophetess let her smile fade into a frown. 'We can discuss all of this later,' she said. 'For now, could I please ask you all to stand beside these good people.' She waved her hand towards the huddle of peasants.

'Lady Iselda,' Leuthere protested. 'It is not safe for you, for any of us to stay here.'

'The banshee?' Iselda asked, a light laugh punctuating her question. 'I'm afraid that nasty ghost can't find us here. The magic of the oracle confounds her dead senses. She can't even see this room on her own. That's why I needed you to let her follow you.'

Leuthere turned around in alarm as Iselda spoke.

Count Ergon was already trying to restore the silk binding to his ears. Vigor lunged towards the doorway, vainly hoping that he could shut out the ghost by sealing the doors.

In the hallway, her face once again nothing but a leering skull, Jacquetta's spectral figure glided towards the scrying chamber, her jaws open in a keening wail.

'No!' Iselda snapped at the men who would defend her. 'Let the creature come! I cannot destroy her unless she enters this room! Five of my servants have given their lives trying to lure her to me! I will not have their sacrifice wasted.'

Leuthere and the others drew back, joining Iselda beside the smoking brazier. They could feel the banshee's cry clawing at their brains, but the pain was far less even than when they had deafened themselves. The sickly chill of black magic was lessened too, barely evoking a single goose pimple. The white magic of Iselda and the divine power of the Lady was retarding the murderous power of the banshee.

But would it be enough to destroy the nightmarish horror?

Jacquetta noticed the resistance of those within the mirrored room to her wail. The banshee laughed, a sound more sinister and terrible than her scream. She displayed a fresh sword gripped in her bony hand. The meaning was clear. She didn't need her shriek to kill.

Like a fell wind, the banshee streaked across the hallway and into the chamber, her sword raised to cleave Iselda's beautiful face in two. The prophetess remained impassive, not even flinching as the vengeful spectre came hurtling towards her. Leuthere prepared to lunge between Iselda and the undead witch, but before he could start to move, the trap was sprung.

As Jacquetta crossed the threshold from the hallway, the mirrors blazed with a brilliant flare of light. Leuthere shielded his eyes, peering through his fingers to see the banshee engulfed in the white light. Like shreds of rotten cloth, the ghost's ethereal body was torn apart, streamers of her ghastly essence drawn into a dozen separate mirrors. This time, when the banshee screamed, it was a shriek of pain that heralded no death except her own.

In an instant, the white light was gone again, and with it the horrifying banshee. Jacquetta's sword, the only thing of solidity the ghost had carried, fell to the floor with a loud crash.

Iselda leaned her hand against the brazier and used it to support her suddenly weakened body. Leuthere rushed to her side, helping her back to her feet.

'Thank you,' the prophetess said. 'That thing was becoming a nuisance.'

'WE MUST GET you to safety,' Sir Leuthere argued. The knight was hard-pressed to keep up with Iselda as she marched down the long hallway. 'The Red Duke has sent one of his creatures to kill you. He will try again.'

Iselda shook her head. 'The Red Duke doesn't even know I exist,' she told Leuthere. 'He's too busy trying to kill my honoured predecessor Isabeau to care about me.'

Leuthere's brow knitted in confusion. 'That doesn't make any sense,' he observed.

'No, it doesn't,' she told him. 'That is why it took me so long to understand what the vampire is doing.' Iselda stared hard into Leuthere's face, then shifted her gaze to Count Ergon, who had followed them into the hall.

'You see, my lords, the Red Duke is insane,' Iselda told them. 'Isabeau sealed him away inside the monument King Louis unwisely raised to honour the man the vampire had once been. For almost five hundred years, the Red Duke has been trapped inside his own tomb. Unable to escape. Unable to die. That's enough to drive even a vampire to madness.'

Count Ergon shook his head, striking his fist against his side. 'I don't care about any of that,' he told the prophetess, annoyance in his voice. 'I only want to know how to destroy this monster.'

'Come with me, and I will show you,' Iselda said. The prophetess led the two knights further down the hall. Throwing open one of the oak doors, she beckoned them out onto the high balcony which overlooked Lake Tranquil and the field upon which the Red Duke's army was encamped. The two knights drew in a horrified gasp. From this height, they could see the magnitude of the army the vampire had assembled. Not hundreds, not even thousands, but tens of thousands of skeleton warriors were arrayed across the fields. Nor were these the only troops under the Red Duke's command. Hundreds of zombies remained in the picket line, hundreds more stood in statuesque silence about the vampire's black pavilion. Packs of flesh-eating ghouls roamed through the undead camp like hungry curs. The trees near the Red Duke's encampment were covered in black, leathery shapes – bats drawn from their cavern lairs by the vampire's dark sorcery.

Iselda ignored all of these, directing the attention of the two men to the grisly undead knights who served the Red Duke. These were scattered across the plains, prowling about in a disordered manner. From this height, the confusion of the black knights was obvious.

Before, Leuthere had imagined the wights were seeking old graves their master could plunder, but now he was not so sure. It seemed to him as if the monsters were busy trying to find something else. Something that wasn't where they had expected – or been told – it would be found.

'They seek villages to slaughter in the name of their loathsome master,' Iselda explained. 'They have been ordered to raze the same villages the Red Duke destroyed when he made war against Lady Isabeau centuries ago. Those villages were never rebuilt, the land abandoned by those few who escaped. In time, even the ruins were obliterated by the elements. The dark riders hunt for something that no longer exists.'

'The Red Duke is doomed to fight his past,' Leuthere said, a shiver in his voice. He saw the questioning look Iselda and Count Ergon turned upon him. 'Something the vampire we destroyed in Mercal said,' he explained. 'It was listening to us talk as we tried to force our way into the Chapel Sereine. When it learned our names, the creature said something about all of the "old enemies" and that the Red Duke was "doomed to fight his past". It didn't make much sense to me then,' Leuthere confessed with a shrug.

Iselda swept forwards, taking the knight's hands in hers. 'It is the only thing that does make sense,' she said excitedly. 'Long have I gazed in the scrying pools, trying to predict the Red Duke's plans. Nothing I did would allow me to see the monster's intentions, his plans for the future. It is because of the vampire's madness. I can not predict his future because the Red Duke's mind is locked in his own past. Except for brief spells of lucidity, the Red Duke truly believes he is in the past, not merely recreating the battles of long ago, but actually refighting them!'

'Then by following history, we can do what your magic cannot,' Count Ergon said. 'We can predict where the vampire is going and what he plans to do!'

'If we can get this information to Duke Gilon, we can strike the vampire when he is at his most vulnerable!' Leuthere exclaimed. The young knight's jubilation quickly turned to a scowl. He slammed his fist against the rail. 'But we can't do a thing while the Red Duke has us trapped inside this tower! And we can't fight our way through his army!'

'We won't have to,' Iselda assured Leuthere. 'Eventually the Red Duke will become lucid again. Something will snap his mind back to the present. When that happens, he will realize how vulnerable his army is here and he will break the siege off on his own.'

'And what if the vampire remains locked in his delusion?' asked Count Ergon.

Iselda shrugged. 'The original siege lasted only a few weeks before the Red Duke pulled his army away to deal with the invasion of the wine country by King Louis. At some point, the vampire will believe he must leave to respond to the king's attack.'

The prophetess gestured to the sinister army below. 'We must be patient, my lords. Time is our ally now… and it will betray the Red Duke one way or another.'

THE RED DUKE scowled as Sir Maraulf strode into his pavilion. The vampire regarded his dark knight with open contempt. 'Where are my prisoners?' he hissed. 'I need them to break the will of that witch Isabeau. When she sees her peasant friends slowly dying beneath her very window, she will throw open her gates and beg my mercy.'

Renar leaned back against one of the posts that supported the heavy tent cloth. This was going to be somewhat amusing. If he had to suffer the Red Duke's insanity, then at least he would be entertained by it. The necromancer had sensed the destruction of Jacquetta. He wasn't sure how Iselda had managed to vanquish a banshee, but it did make him quite determined to leave breaking into the tower entirely up to the Red Duke.

For now, Renar would just sit back and watch Sir Maraulf squirm under the Red Duke's thumb.

'We have scoured the countryside, your grace,' the dark knight reported. 'There is no trace of a single village. No one has lived in this area in generations.'

The Red Duke's face contorted into a mask of fury, lips pulling away from serpent-like fangs. The vampire crossed to where his thrall stood, his hand poised to strike the undead knight. Suddenly, he stopped, bewilderment in his expression. The Red Duke stared keenly into Maraulf's pale face, then shifted his gaze to the knight's left arm.

Renar's interest in the scene suddenly became one of more than amusement. He studied every flicker of emotion that crossed the Red Duke's face. *He realizes Maraulf isn't Baron de Gavaudan*, Renar thought. If that was true, then perhaps more of the vampire's madness would fade away.

'My knights have found… no one?' the Red Duke repeated, confusion still in his eyes.

'There is no one to find, your grace,' Maraulf answered.

Renar saw the confusion continue to grow in the Red Duke's face. Quickly, the necromancer stepped forwards, determined to seize the opportunity before it could pass.

'Your army has caused the wretches to flee, your grace,' Renar declared. 'They go to hide with Duke Gilon, knowing that the Prophetess Iselda is powerless to oppose you and cannot protect them.'

The vampire turned and regarded Renar. At first the Red Duke's expression was harsh and imperious, but as the necromancer continued to speak, the vampire began to soften. The names 'Gilon' and 'Iselda' had no meaning to the vampire's delusion of the past, but they were links to the present. A present the Red Duke's mind was gradually returning to.

'The roads will be choked with refugees,' Renar continued. 'All of them heading for Castle Aquitaine and Duke Gilon's protection. Even if the duke has assembled his army, they will be forced to slow their progress while dealing with the refugees. That will give us time to bolster our own forces.'

'My forces,' the Red Duke snapped. 'Do not forget your place, deathmaster!' He turned, snarling orders at Sir Maraulf and Sir Corbinian. 'Gather the troops. We break camp at once.'

Renar smiled despite the reprimand the Red Duke had given him. At least the vampire appreciated his value in this state of mind. 'You should head south and east, your grace,' Renar suggested. 'Dragon Hill and the barrows of the horse lords are in that direction. We can plunder the mounds at our leisure while Duke Gilon is still trying to move his knights out of the wine country.'

'With the horse lords and the knights of Cuileux under my command, I will sweep away this Duke Gilon like an insect,' the Red Duke vowed. The vampire's eyes blazed with bloodlust. 'Then all Aquitaine shall be mine again! A Kingdom of Blood that shall last a thousand years!'

CHAPTER XV

The smell of fire intruded upon El Syf's dreams. The Duke of Aquitaine struggled to keep his mind from rising out of the comforting darkness, but his senses refused to submit to his desire for oblivion. Shouts and snarls, the crash of metal against metal, the sickening crunch of steel hewing through bone, the screams of dying men, these were sounds the duke's ears refused to deafen themselves to.

Slowly, El Syf opened his eyes. The hot light of the sun seared into his face like the touch of a torch. He cried out in pain, wincing against the sharp stab of agony pulsing through his body.

'The duke lives!'

The voice was that of Earl Durand du Maisne, ringing out clearly above the crash of battle. El Syf was not surprised that his stout-hearted vassal was here, fighting to defend his debilitated lord. Durand's loyalty was the stuff of song and ballad, a fiery determination to sacrifice himself in the name of chivalry. Dim memories flickered through the duke's mind, images of Durand lowering his paralysed body from the sinking ship, visions of Durand bursting into his tent to save him from the claws and fangs of the ratmen. What danger was it that Durand would now protect him from? Could it be any worse than the menace

303

he feared was even now coursing through his veins?

'*He won't be for long! None of us will be!*'

The despairing shout was given by Marquis Galafre d'Elbiq. El Syf found it strange to hear the cool, calculating Galafre abandoned to such a bleak humour. Even in the heat of battle against the heathen, Galafre had always been the one to see a way to turn disaster to his benefit. He was a man with a keen sense of how to trick fate when it seemed the odds were stacked against him. Galafre was a man who always could find a way to escape the toils of doom.

El Syf determined to discover what it was that could make the opportunistic marquis give voice to despair. Despite the pain the sun caused him, he forced his eyes open again. At first, everything was just a white blur, but gradually, as the duke forced himself to suffer the stinging pain, shapes began to resolve themselves.

He was resting upon a wooden bier, his body swaddled in heavy blankets. All around him he could see craggy grey mounds of rock, their summits crowned with clumps of brown brambles and thorny cactus. El Syf had seen this sort of terrain before, on the long march south to free Magritta from the armies of Jaffar. Wherever he was, it was someplace in the dry, desolate hinterlands of Estalia.

The small patch of level ground between the rocky hills was littered with the tattered scraps of tents, the bright heraldry of Aquitaine's nobility lying torn and bloodied in the Estalian dust. The duke could see the ragged remnants of his own pavilion sagging brokenly from a few poles, several bodies strewn about its perimeter. He felt a pang of remorse for these men, both peasant and noble. The manner of their death was obvious. They had died defending the pavilion while Durand and Galafre moved his paralysed husk out, making a desperate gambit to get their lord to safety.

Brutal barks and bestial grunts drowned out even the crash of swords. El Syf knew those inhuman voices well. Any man who had fought in the Massif Orcal could not fail to have that sound burned upon his memory. There was no reason to speculate on who had attacked his small retinue or why. Only orcs could possess such deep, bellowing voices, and orcs needed no more reason to attack than a fish needs a reason to swim.

The duke focused his eyes on the inhuman attackers. There were at least two dozen of the monsters, the smallest a full head taller than himself and each possessing the bullish bulk of an Argonian boar. The orcs were roughly human in shape, covering their leathery green hides with piece-meal armour scavenged from those they had slain in battle or crudely forged by goblins deep below the earth. Each of the greenskins wielded a massive axe-like blade, something neither meat cleaver nor falchion, but possessing all the uglier aspects of both. Many of the orcs bore fresh wounds, nasty gouges that wept syrupy green-black treacle, rancid-smelling filth that served them in place of blood.

Only a few men yet stood against the orcs. Besides Durand and Galafre, the duke could see only six men-at-arms, a few unarmoured valets and a pair of knights in battered plate. As he watched, a hulking brute of an orc smashed his cleaver-like blade into the breastplate of one of the knights, the impact denting the steel armour so badly that he could hear the knight's ribs crack. Before the wounded knight could even stagger away from the crippling blow, the orc grabbed him by the helm with his free hand. With a savage wrench, the orc twisted the helmet, snapping the neck of the man within the armour.

A surge of raw fury blazed through El Syf's body as he saw the orc warlord throw back his head and heard the beast's bellowing laughter echo over the battlefield. For a knight of Bretonnia to die in such a manner was insult enough, for him to be killed by such inhuman vermin after surviving an entire crusade against a mighty enemy was tragic. For the man's killer to mock his death was unendurable.

Before he was aware of what he was doing, the duke threw back the heavy blankets. Despite the long months of sickness and immobility, he felt strength pouring through his limbs, a raw power like nothing he had ever known. He did not charge the orc warlord, he covered the dozen yards between them in a single bound, pouncing on the monster like a springing panther.

The orc's beady red eyes widened with shock, his lantern-like jaw fell open to gawp in amazement as the sickly duke attacked him. The orc's amazement became disbelief as El Syf's fist smashed into his face, cracking his iron-capped tusk and splitting his leathery lip. With a bellow of rage, the orc warlord drew his arm back, intending to cut the crazed human in half with one sweep of his oversized blade.

Twenty-pounds of butchering iron slashed down at El Syf, propelled by the ox-like strength of the orc's arm. The threatened blow was such that would cleave through an armoured warhorse, much less a man whose only protection was a thin woollen shift.

For the second time, the warlord blinked in wonder, but this time there was fear crawling into his eyes. The monstrous blade had failed to cleave his enemy in half. It had failed to even touch the man. It had failed because the duke had latched onto the orc's fist with his hand and arrested the sweep of the blade. The orc grunted in horror as the duke began prying his fingers from the hilt of his own sword, a feat that even the orc's primitive brain understood was impossible!

Bellowing in fright-fuelled fury, the orc drove his fist at the duke. The human released the warlord's arm and ducked beneath the knobby mass of leathery flesh. The warlord's freed arm swung around, slashing a deep furrow across the knuckles of his other hand. Unbalanced, the warlord staggered backwards.

The duke rushed upon the reeling monster. Like some beast of the dark jungle, he pounced upon the orc, driving his knee into the brute's belly, forcing him downwards as the wind was driven out of him in an agonized gasp. Before the warlord could react, El Syf seized the orc's lower jaw in his clawed fingers.

A gargled scream rasped across the battlefield as, with a single pull, the Duke of Aquitaine ripped the orc's jaw from his face.

Green blood sprayed from the monster's mutilated face, raw terror filled the red eyes. The warlord threw down his oversized sword, casting aside his brutish bravado as pure fear consumed his brain. The orc turned to his heels, his only thought being to flee this crazed human who fought with the strength of a daemon.

The orc took only a few steps before the duke leapt onto his back, straddling his midsection with his legs. The warlord pawed at the man, trying to rip him off, but the duke defied his efforts. Coldly, Elf Syf gripped either side of the orc's thick skull. With a savage twist, the duke broke the monster's neck.

The warlord took a few more steps, then his massive body slammed into the stony ground, twitching as death slowly stole upon it. The duke disengaged himself from the carcass. He peered through dazed eyes at the battlefield. Men and orcs alike had stopped fighting so they could watch the feral battle between warlord and nobleman. Men and orcs alike gazed upon him with expressions of dread and awe.

The orcs gave voice to a cacophony of disillusioned yells, scattering as they fled from this gruesome man who had slaughtered their leader with his bare hands. The monsters abandoned weapons and plunder in their fear, kicking and punching each other as they fled, none wanting to be left behind to share their warlord's fate.

The duke's vassals were slow to approach their lord. Fear was in their faces, a frightened doubt that claimed even Earl Durand. El Syf could guess their thoughts. They wondered if some dread spirit had claimed the body of their master, some malign entity that would set upon them with the same brutality it had the orc.

They were right to fear.

El Syf looked down upon his hands, hands coated in the orc's greasy blood. He felt a terrible longing burning inside him, a loathsome hunger that thundered inside his brain. Shivering, he began to raise his hand towards his face. He fought against the compulsion, revolting against the hideous impulse that would have him lick the filth from his fingers.

The duke's will won out. Uttering a sharp cry of pain, he fell to the earth, the awful hunger retreating unsated into the black corridors of unconsciousness.

The last thing he heard was Durand's voice urging his retainers to help their stricken lord.

Again, the Duke of Aquitaine prayed his loyal vassal would leave him to die.

Then the nightmare would be over.

THE SICKLY LIGHT of Morrslieb cast eerie shadows upon the land. The air had a dead quality about it, heavy and smothering like the folds of a burial shroud. Through the darkness, the rustle of leather wings and the titter of hunting bats made a sinister accompaniment to the low, guttural chanting of the man who crouched upon the barren earth.

The Red Duke stood beside Renar as the necromancer practised his grisly craft, feeding the mortal the dark power needed to fuel his black magic. The vampire felt his strength being drawn from him, leeched from his body by Renar's parasitic spell.

The Red Duke stared out into the darkness. Arrayed behind him was his army, the skeletons and zombies scavenged from a hundred peasant villages, the ghouls and wights from the catacombs of the Crac de Sang, the black knights from the Chapel Sereine. The vampire scowled as he considered his loathsome legion. They would not be enough, not when the current king brought his army to Aquitaine. He needed more, he needed a force that would crush any living army the Bretonnians could bring against him. Only then could he make the land pay for all it had taken from him. Only then could he build his Kingdom of Blood.

Immense hills surrounded the Red Duke's army, grassy mounds raised by the primitive horse lords to honour their fallen dead. The ancient barrows were a source of strength the Red Duke had not dared to exploit when he had fought against King Louis. Now he knew better. He knew there could be no limits to his ambition and what he would do to achieve it. If the bones of Giles Le Breton were lying before him, he would call upon them to rise and march under his banner!

Renar's incantation ended upon a snarled epithet, a name so ancient and foul it made even a vampire shudder. He could feel an electric charge in the air, a chill seeping into the atmosphere, drawn from a realm beyond the aether. The Red Duke peered anxiously at the mounds, waiting for the necromancer's spell to loose the ancient dead.

For long minutes, there was only silence. Renar glanced nervously at his master, frightened by what the Red Duke would do to him if the spell had failed. The vampire gave no notice to Renar's anxiety. He could feel the change, smell the power in the air, the profane energy being drawn into the cold earth, drawn to the things buried beneath.

There came a distant patter, the soft sound of pebbles shifting and dirt trickling through grass. The Red Duke followed the noise, his face splitting in a fierce grin.

From one of the mounds, a steady stream of soil was rolling down one side, pushed up by the efforts of something digging its way through the side of the barrow. Soon the trickle became a cascade of dirt, rock and grass as dozens of holes began to appear in the face of the mound. A knobby grey stone pushed its way into the feeble moonlight, dirt clinging to its surface, roots draped about its sides. As the stone was thrust higher, it revealed itself to be a thing of bone, the calcified shell of a skull.

Skeletal talons soon followed the skull, gripping the edges of the hole, straining to pull the rest of the fleshless body free from the barrow. The rotted remains of a harness of bronze scales enclosed the wight's ribs, a cleaver-like falchion swung from its waist, fastened to its body by a rusty iron chain.

The Red Duke beckoned to the ancient horse lord. The wight's skull rotated upon its neck with a sharp click, the witchfires smouldering in the sockets of its leering face fixing upon the vampire. Slowly, with the awkward stiffness of a thing two thousand years in its grave, the wight strode towards the Red Duke, dirt and weeds dripping from it as it walked. Other wights followed the first, forming a regiment of the ancient dead.

Renar flinched, cringing away as two hundred resurrected horse lords marched towards him. The necromancer darted behind the imposing bulk of El Morzillo, cowering in the shadow of the spectral warhorse.

The Red Duke remained unmoved, immobile, as the sinister procession of reanimated skeletons advanced upon him. The vampire lifted his hand, motioning for the hoary revenants to stop. As though composed of a single body, the entire regiment came to a halt, their glowing eyes staring expectantly at their new master.

'Now,' the Red Duke hissed, gazing out across the ranks of undead warriors, 'my revenge begins.' He closed his armoured hand into a fist, the plates grinding against each other as the vampire exerted his hideous strength in a display of rage.

'First the usurper Duke Gilon,' he snarled. 'Then the king and all who pray to the treacherous Lady!'

'It seems Duke Gilon got your message,' Sir Leuthere told Count Ergon.

The knights had just crested the vine-covered hills overlooking Castle Aquitaine. Behind them, riding ponies and leading the massive warhorses, Vigor and the Prophetess Iselda brought up the rear of their small procession. It had taken three days of hard travel to reach Duke Gilon's castle. They had not dared to tarry in their journey to draw supplies and remounts from the castles they passed. There was no saying how much time they had to stop the Red Duke. Worse, there was no saying where the vampire's madness would send his undead legions next. Every castle they passed might already have fallen to the Red Duke and be held by his skeleton warriors as a bastion against the living.

Despite Iselda's assurances that she had seen Duke Gilon assembling his army in her reflecting pool, the two knights felt better seeing the muster for themselves. It was an impressive force, a gathering of knights such as neither of the men had ever seen before. Even the most opulent tournaments paled beside the numbers of warriors gathered in the fields beyond the village of Aquitaine. Every speck of open ground seemed to have sprouted a tent or pavilion, the brightly coloured pennants of dozens of noble houses snapping in the wind. Coats of arms emblazoned with the heraldry of a hundred families shone from shields and surcoats arrayed upon wooden stands outside the tents. Destriers of every colour and pattern marched anxiously about in a thousand improvised stalls and stables, their bold spirits aroused by the smell of war.

If he had not seen the Red Duke's army for himself, Leuthere would have said nothing could stand against so vast a gathering of knights. But he had seen the vampire's legions, the hideous horde of walking corpses that knew neither fear nor fatigue. What could even this mighty host do against such a foe?

'You must be brave and not allow your spirit to falter,' Iselda said, riding up beside him atop the hill.

Leuthere shifted uncomfortably in his saddle. He didn't like to think that Iselda would use her magic to read his thoughts, though he knew such a thing would be simple for a woman endowed with the magic of the Lady.

Iselda smiled in apology to him. 'I must know the minds of the men who would defend the land,' she said. She turned in the saddle, sweeping her gaze to include Count Ergon. 'More than anyone, it is you who must stand resolute before the Red Duke's evil. For in you burns the only hope of destroying him.' A haunted look crept into her eyes, a troubled frown crossing her face. She glanced at the two knights, not quite hiding the worry in her gaze.

Count Ergon patted the hilt of his sword. 'The monster will die,' he vowed. 'For what he has already done as much as for what he would still do.'

'Do not allow revenge to overcome your honour,' Iselda chastised the nobleman. 'Without a pure heart, you will not prevail. Vengeance is a contagion of the soul.' She peered at Leuthere, studying him intently. 'The lust for glory is no better,' she warned.

The prophetess's words surprised Leuthere, hurting him more deeply than he thought mere words could. His was a noble purpose, the quest to atone for what his uncle had done, to redeem the honour of the d'Elbiqs. There was no shame in such a pursuit. Certainly it was no vainglorious enterprise, a thing built upon a foundation of pride and arrogance.

Iselda continued to look at him. Subtly, she glanced aside at Count Ergon. Leuthere at once guessed her meaning. He still hadn't told the nobleman why the Red Duke had attacked the Chateau du Maisne and killed his household.

Leuthere shook his head, casting his eyes downward. No, there were some things he would not discuss. Not with a du Maisne. Too much depended on them now for them to fall out over the feud. Certainly there was no reason to let du Maisne know of the great shame that tarnished the d'Elbiqs.

Iselda's expression became stern. She gestured to the towers of Castle Aquitaine. 'We should hurry,' she said, casting one last disapproving glance at Sir Leuthere. 'Duke Gilon is meeting with his generals as we speak. It would be best if we had words with him before they have turned his ear with their own strategies and tactics.

'After all, we know the enemy better than the duke's generals,' Iselda said, still looking at Leuthere.

'THERE IS NO mistake. Our enemy is the Red Duke himself, not some pretender to his horrors. He intends to conquer all Aquitaine and remake it into his own Kingdom of Blood.' Iselda's voice echoed through the great stone hall, reverberating off the cavernous walls, ringing off the ancient armour and tarnished shields arrayed throughout the immense chamber.

The men sitting around the huge oak table in the middle of the room had been a bickering mass of egos before the entrance of the prophetess. Now they were silent, attentive, and subdued. They hung off her every word as though it were holy in itself. Barons and counts, earls and marquis, even Duke Gilon himself, the men set aside their own authority to hear the wisdom offered by this servant of the Lady.

'The Red Duke has already ravaged much of the north country. Entire villages have been slaughtered, their graveyards plundered for recruits to swell the ranks of the vampire's army.' Iselda paused, locking eyes with Duke Gilon. 'He plans even worse horrors, your grace. Even now, the Red Duke marches to the barrows of the horse lords to stir the ancient dead from their tombs.'

'If he should reach Dragon's Hill...' muttered Sir Roget, the old knight's face turning pale.

Iselda nodded grimly. 'There are thousands of ancient warriors buried inside Dragon's Hill. With these marching under his banner, the Red Duke will have an army to threaten all of Bretonnia.'

'The king has been made aware of our peril,' Duke Gilon said. He looked to have aged ten years since the day he had cast Sir Leuthere from his presence, his features drawn and haggard, his eyes dark with fatigue. A nervous tremor tugged at his left cheek, causing half his face to twitch sporadically. 'It will take time for the king to raise an army, time for word to reach the other dukedoms. Until then, we have only Sir Richemont and those who rode with him from Couronne.'

The duke indicated the knight sitting at his right hand. Sir Richemont favoured his father's looks, though not his father's dour humour. Richemont fairly exuded an excited energy, his martial spirit eager to cross blades with so formidable an enemy. Like all young knights, he was impatient to earn his name and to heap glory upon his family.

'If the Red Duke tarries among the barrows, he gives us time to prepare our campaign against him,' Richemont said. 'A single knight is worth a dozen of his walking skeletons. Let the vampire call his bags of bones to battle. Every hour he delays his attack is another hour the king's army grows.'

'You do not appreciate the scope of his army,' Count Ergon warned, rising from his chair. 'I have seen it for myself. Already the Red Duke's legion outnumbers us. If he can plunder the graves of the horse lords, he will have a force great enough to smash even this muster like a flea. It will not be a question of twelve to one, it will be fifty, a hundred to one against us!'

'And do not forget, my lord,' Leuthere said. 'While our army must provision itself and rest between battles, the Red Duke's horde is driven by nothing more than the vampire's evil. They need neither food nor sleep nor shelter. They can maintain the attack until every man in Aquitaine lies dead.'

Duke Gilon slammed his mailed fist against the heavy oak table, drawing all eyes to him. 'The vampire must be kept from reaching Dragon's Hill,' he declared. 'We cannot allow his army to grow any more vast than it already is.'

'Fine and good, your grace,' objected a bewigged baron from the wine country, 'but how do we stop him? It will take days to decamp the troops here and intercept the Red Duke. We'd have to leave behind the foot soldiers and the baggage train. The only supplies we could take would be whatever could fit across a saddle.'

Duke Gilon slumped back in his chair, his cheek twitching as he considered the logistical problem. 'Supplies could be floated down river,' he proposed, then shook his head. 'No, that would require gathering enough barges to carry everything and we simply don't have them.'

'My lords,' Iselda addressed the generals. 'There is another way. If we can divert the Red Duke from his purpose, make him abandon his plan to violate the barrows of his own accord...'

'Why would the vampire do such a thing?' Richemont asked. 'By all accounts he was a masterful strategist when he was alive. Becoming one of the undead may have made him evil, but I think it is too much to hope that it has made him stupid as well.'

'Not stupid,' Iselda corrected Richemont. 'Mad.' She let the word linger in the room before explaining. 'The vampire's mind is disordered, unable to focus fully upon the present. He drifts between today and yesterday, unable to make the distinction. When he laid siege to the Tower of Wizardry, it was Isabeau he made battle against, not her humble successor Iselda.' The prophetess scowled, clenching her delicate hands into frustrated fists. 'The Red Duke's madness makes it impossible for my powers of foresight to predict what he will do next. I can see how he *might* act, but not how he *will* act.'

'Then you are saying we are lost?' Duke Gilon asked, a hint of fear behind his words. 'The Lady is powerless to help us against this monster?'

'No, your grace,' Leuthere said. 'What Lady Iselda is saying is that her magic cannot help us predict what the vampire will do. However, we do not need her magic to do that.'

'What is your meaning?' demanded one of the seated generals. 'How can we predict what the Red Duke will do without the prophetess and her foresight?'

Count Ergon leaned over the table, tapping his armoured finger against the vellum map of Aquitaine spread out upon its surface. 'We know how the Red Duke made war against King Louis the Righteous,' he stated, casting his firm gaze across the generals. 'We know the battles he fought and where he fought them. When the vampire laid siege to the Tower of Wizardry, he did so in slavish repetition to the way he conducted the campaign the first time. He even sent his undead cavalry to attack the sites of villages he razed centuries ago.'

Duke Gilon clapped his hands together, his face brightening to the theme of Count Ergon's proposal. 'We can fight the Red Duke as King Louis did!' he beamed. 'The chronicles of Aquitaine recount every battle fought against the vampire and his forces. We can see where the Red Duke will attack ahead of time!' The duke slammed his fist down against the map, smashing his hand against the ancient mounds of the horse lords. 'We can make our plans and crush this monster where he will be at his most vulnerable!'

'Ceren Field!' Sir Roget exclaimed. 'The open space there will offer an excellent vantage for our knights to ride down the vampire's infantry and smash them to bits!'

'There are also the hills to consider,' remarked a scar-faced marquis. 'We can position bowmen on two sides of the battlefield and soften up the vampire's legion before sending in our knights.' The marquis bobbed his head in contrition as he saw the surly looks the other noblemen directed at him. 'I am not doubting the valour of our knights, but I feel we must look at things prudently. There is the possibility the Red Duke will vastly outnumber us. I ask which is the greater shame: to accept the value of a peasant's bow or to allow a vampire to conquer Aquitaine because the land's champions were prideful and arrogant?'

The chastising words of the marquis had their effect, silencing the offended hubris of the knights.

'We can also take comfort in the presence of Duke Galand's tomb. Galand drank from the grail and the divine power of the Lady still endows his grave with tremendous power.' A fervent, almost worshipful light was in Iselda's eyes as she spoke of the great hero of

Aquitaine. Few of the men at the table noticed the slight flush that came into her cheeks and grim smile that spread across her lips. 'The grace of the Lady saturates Duke Galand's tomb. The holy power will repulse the Red Duke's creatures, perhaps even the vampire himself will be unable to endure the Lady's blessing. In any effect, I know that the Red Duke will be weakened if he is forced to fight on such hallowed ground.

'Then there is another point to consider,' Iselda added, raising one of her slender fingers. 'We know that the Red Duke's madness will eventually lead him back to Ceren Field.' She sighed, frowning as the most troubling thought of them all forced itself onto her tongue. 'The only thing we do not know is when that madness will lead him there. By the time the Red Duke turns to Ceren Field, he may already have plundered the graves of the horse lords and opened the cromlechs around Dragon's Hill.'

Leuthere turned towards the prophetess, a desperate idea forming in his brain. 'Maybe we can provoke the vampire's madness somehow,' he offered. He stared out over Duke Gilon and his advisors, the same men who had mocked his warning before. Now these men watched him with rapt, hopeful expressions. 'If the Red Duke thought he needed to attack Isabeau when he saw the Tower of Wizardry, then maybe that is the key to bringing him to Ceren Field. If we can somehow provoke his madness, make him think King Louis is waiting to do battle with him…'

Richemont leapt to his feet. With quick strides the bold knight crossed the hall, advancing to the rows of armour and weaponry lining the wall. He paused before a tattered old banner bearing a quartered field and the heraldry of a crowned lion rampant opposed by a leopard rampant wearing the crescent-topped helm of an Arabyan sultan. Richemont bowed his head reverently, then pulled the standard away from the wall, holding it over his head by its bronze cross-beam.

'The banner of King Louis the Righteous,' Richemont declared, displaying the colours so that all the assembled generals could see it. 'The same banner that rode beside him at the first battle of Ceren Field! If anything will provoke that undead bastard into facing us in open battle, this is what will do it!'

Duke Gilon beamed at his son, inspired by the cleverness and imagination of Richemont's plan as much as the knight's theatrical oratory. He motioned for the excited murmur of his generals and advisors to quiet. 'A small company of riders can be sent to intercept the Red Duke without any of the logistical concerns that prevent moving against him with the full might of Aquitaine. It will be a perilous mission; the men who ride before the Red Duke must draw near enough to his host that the vampire can see the banner of King Louis, yet stay far enough away that they can withdraw at leisure. They must lead the Red Duke across Aquitaine, drawing him out, goading him into the mad grip of his own past. They must bring the vampire to Ceren Field where the army will await to destroy him and all his monstrous legion.'

'Father,' Richemont said, bending his knee before Duke Gilon. 'I volunteer myself for this task.'

Duke Gilon grew pale. For a moment, the twitch returned to his cheek. 'I cannot allow that,' he said. 'I need you here to help organize the defences at Ceren Field.'

Richemont stood, his face flushed with anger. 'It was my plan, your grace,' he stated, not quite keeping the emotion from his voice.

'Begging your pardon,' Leuthere interrupted. 'But the plan to trick the Red Duke was mine. If anyone should risk his neck, then it is me.'

'We can't trust this mission to a mere household knight,' Count Ergon challenged, stepping forward. 'I offer myself to act as bait for the vampire.'

Leuthere rounded on the older knight, glaring at him. 'You care nothing about luring the Red Duke to Ceren Field! Your only thought is to keep anyone else from destroying the vampire before you get your chance for revenge!' He sneered at Count Ergon, gesturing at the nobleman's stiff right arm. 'Besides which you are wounded, physically unfit.'

Count Ergon grimaced and gripped his right arm as Leuthere spoke. 'I've recovered quite a bit since I saved your life in Mercal,' he said, taking extreme delight in watching Leuthere wince in pain at mention of his rescue. 'As for the Red Duke, I have sworn by the Lady to kill the fiend. That is truth.' He bowed before Duke Gilon, laying his sword upon the floor at his feet. 'But now I swear this oath. I vow that I shall bring the vampire to Ceren Field, whatever it costs me. I will take no move to avenge my family until the Red Duke has fallen into your trap.'

Duke Gilon smiled at the intensity of Count Ergon's oath. 'I have known your family a long time, du Maisne. I have never known one of them to break his word. You may lead the "bait" as you call it.' The duke pointed sternly at the kneeling count. 'But I add this condition. You will take Sir Leuthere d'Elbiq with you. If, in the heat of the moment, you should be tempted to forget your vow to me, then Leuthere will be there to remind you of your promise.'

Count Ergon scowled as he rose to his feet, directing an acid look at Leuthere. 'As you command, your grace.'

'Choose your companions,' Duke Gilon directed. 'No more than a dozen men. Take the finest horses that have been brought to the muster, choose animals known for the stoutness of their hearts and the fleetness of their legs.' The duke's expression became dour.

'Lady be with you, Count Ergon,' the duke said. 'The fate of Aquitaine rests upon the success of your mission.'

CHAPTER XVI

'I thought you said you knew how to ride!'

The mocking laughter of Duchess Martinga rolled back through the orchard. For the duke, the sound was as enchanting as the faerie music of the Athel Loren. There was a mixture of enticement and warmth in her voice that made his heart quicken whenever he heard her speak. Even in her angriest moods, his wife fascinated him.

Today, she was far from angry.

'Someone insisted I buy her the fastest horse in Quenelles,' the duke retorted. 'A rider can't be responsible if his horse is outmatched!'

Martinga turned her steed about, a reproving pout on her pretty face. 'That is a churlish thing to say,' she scolded him. 'Blaming your poor mount for your own failure.'

A mischievous grin crept onto the duke's face. With a sudden burst of speed, he charged his horse forwards. Before Martinga could spur her own mount into action, he had her reins in his hand.

'That was cheating,' she scolded him.

'That was strategy,' he winked back at her. 'Battles are not won by bravery and bullheadedness. You have to trick the enemy into making a mistake.'

Martinga arched an eyebrow at him. 'Oh, so I'm the

enemy now?'

The duke laughed and pressed her hands to his lips. *'The Lady forbid!'* he exclaimed. *'I can think of no more perilous a foe than the one who holds my heart in her soft hands.'*

Still laughing, he threw his leg over the neck of his horse and slid down from the saddle. He reached up to help his wife extricate herself from the complicated, ladylike contrivance lashed to the back of her own steed.

'We should be getting back,' she warned him. Despite the admonition, she made no effort to resist as he lowered her to the ground.

'I'm the duke,' he smiled back at her. *'They won't dare start the feast until I get back.'*

'And what about the duchess?' Martinga asked.

He licked his lips and pursed his mouth as he made a show of considering the question. *'They probably won't wait if it's only you,'* he said at last. *'What is a duchess more or less when there is eating and drinking to be done?'*

Martinga rolled her eyes at him. *'To think I might have been Queen of Bretonnia instead of simply Duchess of Aquitaine!'*

Instantly she regretted the flippant words. Meant in jest, she saw the flash of pain in her husband's eyes. Quickly she took his hand in hers, squeezing it tight, letting him know there had been no malice intended.

The duke stared at her, his eyes heavy with pain and not a little guilt. *'You could have been queen,'* he said. *'Louis always favoured you. By the grail, there were days when I gave up all hope, when I was sure he would win your affection. When he came back from his quest glowing with the grace of the Lady, I was certain I had lost you.'*

Martinga hugged him to her. *'My dear, sweet knight,'* she whispered. *'He could never move my heart as you do. Even if he is king, I would still choose my noble duke.'*

He let her slip free from his grip, reassured by the love in her voice. The moment of doubt and pain passed and the mischievous twinkle was back in his eye. 'He's my junior by two years, you know. He'd have been a much better catch than this tired old warhorse.'

Martinga smiled at him, nodding in agreement. 'Louis was always the spry one. You'd hardly believe he shared the same parents as the clumsy, worn-out ogre I married.'

Without warning, the duke caught her around the waist, pulling her with him as he fell onto the grass. 'Worn-out ogre?' he challenged. 'You shall rue those words!'

Martinga giggled in feigned terror. 'Not here! What if someone is watching!'

The duke leaned over her, staring into her eyes. 'These are the king's orchards. Nobody is supposed to be in them. So if there are any spies about, I'll have their eyes put out.'

'If nobody is supposed to be in the orchard, doesn't that mean we're in the wrong too?' Martinga objected, fending off her husband's kiss.

'Oh we'll be fine,' the duke assured her with assumed severity. 'My little brother has always been a bit afraid of me.'

THICK STORM CLOUDS choked the leaden sky, blotting out the sun like a murderer's cloak. The woods were silent, undisturbed by the song of bird or the scamper of deer. Nothing living dared stir within the forest, nothing save the degenerate ghouls that ranged ahead of the monstrous army and the swarm of bats that circled above the rotting zombies.

One other living creature braved the presence of the Red Duke's army, riding alongside his vampiric master on the rigid back of a zombified horse. The heart of Renar's living steed had quit long ago, frightened into bursting by the swelling numbers of undead marching under the Red Duke's banner. Renar had accepted the animal's defection with a pragmatic shrug, using one of his spells to force the horse's carcass to serve him more faithfully than before. He only wished the creature had retained some of the resiliency of life. His arse was beginning to chafe from contact with the animal's bony back.

The necromancer rubbed his sores and scowled at the grim procession of wights and skeletons shambling through the forest. The undead did not tire, they had no need for rest or provision the way mortal soldiers did. The Red Duke could march his legion to the end of the earth and there would never arise from them the slightest murmur of discomfort. It was inspiring, really, until one noted the worms wriggling through the flesh of the zombies, or the rusty bits of harness crumbling off the grey bones of the wights.

Ahead, the forest began to thin out, the trees becoming sickly runts of their breed, clawing at the darkened sky with naked branches, their trunks peeling from the ravages of fungus and beetle. The ground, so lush before, became a lifeless stretch of dun-hued dirt, as withered in its fashion as the trees sprouting from it. Legend held that the ground had been poisoned by the venomous blood of a mighty dragon slain by some now forgotten hero centuries before Giles le Breton was born.

Unfit for crops or pasture, the pragmatic horse lords had employed the region to entomb their dead. Through the dead trees, Renar could see the barren hillocks within which the bones of the Bretonni tribesmen had rested down through the ages. There were dozens of the barrows, each raised to honour

an ancient king. The druids of those times had practised horrific rites and most ghastly of all had been
the ceremonies made to consecrate the graves of
their kings. Heroic warriors would be massacred and
entombed beside their king that the sovereign might
have a fitting bodyguard to accompany him into the
world of shadow. Fine steeds, the favourite consorts
of the king, even cooks and artisans would be chained
inside the barrow to follow the spirit of their master
into the land of death. Even a member of the cruel
druidic order would stay to attend the dead sovereign,
sealing the barrow from within at the conclusion of
the burial.

The necromancer rubbed his hands together in sardonic glee. The bloody rituals of the druids had left
the barrows choked with dead horse lords. Each tomb
would offer dozens, if not hundreds of bodies to
reanimate. There would be no stopping the Red Duke
once such a force was bound to his will.

Renar looked over at his vampiric master. The Red
Duke sat astride his ghastly horse, staring hungrily at
the rows of barrows. The vampire seemed most keen
to investigate the sprawling mound called Dragon's
Hill. The necromancer could easily guess why. From
the size of the mound, the king entombed within
must have had an entire nation buried with him. Or,
and the thought brought a tremor of excitement to
him, perhaps the site was the tomb of that forgotten
hero who had slain the venomous wyrm so long ago.
It was possible the druids had buried hero and beast
together.

Might the bones of a dragon lie inside Dragon's
Hill? It was a fascinating question. Renar had read of
necromancers who had restored such mighty beasts

to the simulacrum of life, resurrecting their reptilian bones as mammoth zombies. He wondered if his knowledge of the black arts was sufficient to create such a monster should they uncover a real dragon buried under the mound.

'There is much work for you here, sorcerer,' the Red Duke hissed, turning his savage gaze upon Renar. 'The ground is obscene with the smell of death.'

Renar nodded his head in fawning agreement. 'Quite so, your grace,' he told the vampire. 'It will tax both our powers to call so many from their graves, but when we are finished here, your army shall be the mightiest Bretonnia has ever seen!'

'No,' the Red Duke corrected him. 'It will not be finished here. I will not be content until I have a legion great enough to scour Aquitaine clean.' The Red Duke's gaunt face pulled back in a feral snarl. 'Why– I have finished with Aquitaine, not a bird, not a rabbit, not a mouse will be left to draw breath. The land shall suffer for rejecting its master. I shall make of Aquitaine a charnel house that shall make the Lady tremble and cower! The blood of Aquitaine will be exterminated, burned away like a noxious pestilence!'

The vampire's oath made Renar shiver, his pasty features becoming pale with fear. There was no doubt the Red Duke meant what he said. In his moments of madness, he sought to refight lost battles. In his lucid state, the vampire's ambition was to satiate his long-denied bloodlust, to avenge the centuries of torment he had endured within his own tomb. The agony of all he had lost, the pain of his wife's suicide, the betrayal of his king, these he would wash from his soul by unleashing a tidal wave of slaughter upon the land. It was enough to horrify even Renar's twisted morality.

'When we are done here, we shall march to the tombs of the knights of Culieux,' the Red Duke continued. 'Then I shall be ready to ride against Duke Gilon and the other traitor-lords who have usurped my dominion. I will rebuild the ruins, recast the land into my Kingdom of...'

The vampire's voice trailed off, a haunted light coming into his eyes. Renar watched as the Red Duke's imperious snarl drooped into an expression of shock mingled with fear. The necromancer followed the direction of the vampire's gaze. Through the dead trees he could see a small mob of knights standing atop one of the nearby barrows.

In the feeble light of Morrslieb, Renar could make out only the outlines of men and horses, the faint gleam of moonlight upon polished armour. He sneered in contempt at the small number of riders. There was no threat to the Red Duke's formidable host from so few men. Even if each of them were Giles Le Breton reborn, they could never hope to overcome the undead legions arrayed behind the vampire's banner. These men could only observe and report back to Duke Gilon what they had seen. That would actually serve the necromancer's cause quite nicely. Only despair and terror could greet any report these men could give. The knowledge that the Red Duke was swelling the ranks of his horde with the wights of Dragon's Hill would hardly bring cheers to the nobles of Aquitaine. It pleased Renar to think of those bold and haughty lords cowering on their thrones, knowing that their doom was marching down upon them, unstoppable and unrelenting. Yes, Renar was disposed to allow these men to escape, to make their heroic ride back to Duke Gilon and announce that the nobles had no hope of stopping the Red Duke. Let them, for once, appreciate what it was to feel helpless and at the mercy of a being who cared nothing for their welfare.

Renar turned to suggest the Red Duke spare the scouts when he noticed the vampire's agitation. The vampire's shock had been replaced by a mask of pitiless hate, hate that made Renar's own loathing of the nobility farcical by comparison.

'I… I will send the ghouls to chase those men off,' Renar said.

'King Louis…' the Red Duke whispered, his eyes blazing as he spoke the name.

FROM THE TOP of the barrow mound, Sir Leuthere stared for the first time upon the monster his vengeful uncle had called from its grave. An aura of violent evil surrounded the ghastly creature, a palpable sense of malevolent menace that made the young knight's flesh crawl in revulsion and his heart quiver in fear. The courser he sat upon nickered nervously, stamping its hooves, impatient for its rider to quit this place of horrors.

The Red Duke. This then was the fiend Leuthere had journeyed so far to destroy, the monster who would drown all Aquitaine in a sea of blood. This was the terrible power Earl Gaubert had called upon to pursue his vendetta against the du Maisnes. It was bitterly ironic that by his ruthless prosecution of the feud, Earl Gaubert had instead forced the two families into alliance. Du Maisne and d'Elbiq together, united against the common foe.

Count Ergon's eyes were moist as he looked down from the hillock, watching as the vampire's undead legion marched out from the trees. The nobleman's fist tightened about the hilt of his sword, knuckles cracking from the intensity of his grip. His legs grew tense, poised to dig spurs into the flanks of his steed, to drive the frightened animal straight down into the skeleton horde. Leuthere saw the same obsessed desire for revenge written across Count Ergon's face as had been on that of his uncle. The observation brought a new anxiety to the young knight's mind, reopening his concern that Count Ergon would cast aside everything, his fealty to Duke Gilon, his personal honour, the plan to save Aquitaine – all of these he would sacrifice in order to soothe the pain inside him.

Count Ergon slowly relaxed his body. He turned and gave Leuthere a sombre nod of understanding. The older knight was not blind to what was at stake here. His revenge would wait. He would keep to his word.

'Raise the king's standard high,' Count Ergon told Leuthere. 'Make sure that blackguard sees our colours.'

Leuthere lifted the tattered banner of King Louis high over his head, waving it through the air like an Estalian matador goading a bull with his cape.

The Red Duke's reaction was as violent as that of any bull. The vampire quivered with rage, drawing his sword and sweeping it through the air before him. In answer to the Red Duke's howls, the undead host surged forwards, wights mounted upon bony steeds galloping towards the barrows.

'Time to leave,' Leuthere advised Count Ergon. The other knights with them shared Leuthere's anxiety, yet their valour would not permit a withdrawal until their commander gave the order.

Count Ergon glared down at the Red Duke, unable to tear his gaze from that hateful countenance. Only the whinny of terror that sounded from the horse beneath him snapped him back to the immediacy of the situation. The foremost of the wights had reached the base of the mound and their deathly steeds were beginning the arduous climb. Count Ergon watched them for a moment, then reluctantly slashed his hand through the air, motioning for the knights to retreat.

'To Ceren Field!' Count Ergon shouted, driving his spurs into his steed. 'And Lady grant this abomination is mad enough to chase us!'

'BARON DE GAVAUDAN! Sir Corbinian!' the Red Duke's voice was like the lash of a whip as he called out his sub-officers. The vampire didn't look aside as the wight-lord and the dark knight who had replaced the baron rode forwards to join him. His eyes were fixed upon the banner he had seen the knights display so boldly upon the top of the barrow. It was a challenge, a gesture of contempt and defiance from King Louis! The usurper was taunting him, mocking him in his own domain! But the king would soon learn that there was only one Duke of Aquitaine, and he did not hold court in Couronne!

'I want those men,' the Red Duke snarled at Sir Corbinian and Sir Maraulf. 'Alive or dead, I want them. Bring them to me!'

'It will be a hard ride, your grace,' Maraulf said, bowing his head in deference to his master. 'The enemy has chosen ground it will be difficult to cross.'

The Red Duke glared at Maraulf. 'Their steeds will tire, yours will not,' he reminded his thrall. 'Bring those men to me! I will find out where my treacherous brother has encamped.' The vampire bared his fangs in a hateful grimace. 'There is much the good king has to answer for before I allow him the luxury of death.'

Maraulf bowed again, turning away to gather up some of the undead cavalry not already rushing the ancient graves. The Red Duke dismissed the vampire from his thoughts, shifting his attention instead to the skeletal frame of Corbinian.

Before the Red Duke could issue orders to the wight-lord, a shouted protest erupted from Renar.

'It's a trick!' the necromancer shrieked, unable to contain himself. 'King Louis is dead and has been for centuries! That's not his men up there! It's all a trick to lead you into a trap!'

The Red Duke glowered at the necromancer. 'Speak about matters that concern you, peasant,' he warned. 'Leave war to those who know how to fight it.'

Renar rolled his eyes, laughing derisively, the absurdity of the situation overcoming his prudence. 'Know how to fight! You damn fool, you're fighting battles against men who have been dead almost five hundred years!' He waved his hands indicating the barrow mounds before them and the imposing bulk of Dragon's Hill. 'This is where we need to be, not chasing phantoms! We can raise every horse lord in these mounds, then do the same to the vanquished knights of Cuileux! As you said, we can build an army that no lord in all Bretonnia would dare oppose!'

The Red Duke's armoured hand lashed out, cracking against Renar's jaw. The necromancer was thrown from his saddle, landing in a tangle of limbs on the ground. Spitting blood, he reared up from the barren earth, drawing upon the dark energies of the barrow mounds to empower a spell that would send the vampire back to his grave.

Before Renar could unleash his spell, bony claws closed about him, pinning his arms to his sides. The necromancer looked about in terror, finding himself in the embrace of Corbinian's fleshless hands.

'You dare not kill me!' Renar shouted at the Red Duke. 'You need me! You need my magic and my counsel!' The necromancer cringed as he saw the piti-less evil behind the vampire's eyes. 'You're making a mistake! Try to be sane!' he pleaded.

The Red Duke's cold flesh drew back in a grin of cruel amusement. 'Take this peasant away,' he ordered Corbinian. 'But first remove his rebellious tongue. It tires me.'

Renar's screams collapsed into a wet gurgle as the wight-lord carried out its master's command. The Red Duke had already dismissed the necromancer from his thoughts, turning his gaze back to the place he had seen Leuthere display the colours of King Louis. He closed his eyes in murderous reverie, imagining the hundred ways he would visit revenge upon his brother. The king would answer for everything the Red Duke had lost to his treachery. Lands and title, honour and fame. But most of all, the king would answer for Martinga's death.

The Red Duke opened his eyes again and stared out across his silent legion. There was no need to chase after the king's banner. He knew where he was destined to face the king's army. He could see it in his mind as clearly as if the battle had already been fought.

The vampire raised his sword, stabbing it high into the air.

'We march!' the Red Duke roared. 'We march to Ceren Field!'

THREE DAYS' HARD ride brought Sir Leuthere and Duke Gilon to the River Morceaux. It had been a perilous journey, and made at such a pace that taxed both man and beast. Without the remounts sent by Duke Gilon, staggered across their return route in relays, the knights knew they would never have managed. The Red Duke's unholy forces pursued them both night and day. Swarms of bats tormented them by night and by day, swooping out of the shadows to slap at their faces with leathery wings or snap at their eyes with needle-sharp teeth. So regular had become these attacks that the knights had been forced to keep the visors of their helmets lowered despite the almost unendurable heat and discomfort.

The bats had been the least of their worries however. Soon after quitting the region of Dragon's Hill and the barrows of the horse lords, their small band had been beset by a new foe – undead knights upon skeletal steeds. Leading them was a monster Leuthere was horrified to find himself recognizing: Sir Maraulf, the holy knight of Mercal. The once noble champion of Aquitaine had been corrupted by the evil of the Red Duke, restored to a villainous mockery of life as a vampire. It was this dark knight who led the chase, driving his prey before him like a country lord hounding foxes across his estate.

Two of the valiant knights who had accompanied Leuthere and Count Ergon were lost to the vampire's blade, cut down by the undead monster from ambush. While the rotting steeds of Maraulf's wights could not match the speed of living horses, some profane vitality burned within the vampire's horse, allowing him to overtake them whenever the sun retreated from the sky. Only by force of arms and invoking the name of the Lady had they been able to drive the vampire off. Though it pained them to do so, they had left their dead behind, not daring even the brief respite required to attend their comrades.

At last, the River Morceaux appeared before them, stretching from behind the forest like a shimmering ribbon of crushed sapphire. A sense of triumph swelled the hearts of the knights as they drove through the last of the trees, spurring their coursers down towards the stone bridge that spanned the river. They were surprised when the formerly ferocious bats abandoned them, flittering back into the dark of the forest.

Another surprise awaited them as they drew closer to the bridge. A large body of knights, over a hundred strong, were arrayed about the end of the bridge. As Leuthere rode closer, he could see that the knights bore no devices upon their shields, instead sporting the plain coloured fields of men who had not yet won their coat of arms. These were knights errant, young warriors eager to prove themselves upon the field of battle. Leuthere had never seen so many of the fledgling knights gathered in one place before. The sheen from their bare steel armour was almost blinding and the colourful pennants fitted to their lances seemed like a field of blooming flowers as they snapped in the breeze.

One of the knights guarding the bridge rode forwards as Leuthere and his comrades advanced towards the river. A half-dozen knights quickly formed up around the lone rider. Leuthere was surprised to see the fleur-de-lys emblazoned upon their shields and the caparisons clothing their horses. These were no humble knights errant, but knights who had forsaken their titles and positions to take up the grail quest. They would wander the land, righting wrongs and fighting monsters whatever their foul shape in hopes that through such chivalrous deeds they might be led to the grail by the Fay Enchantress and be deemed worthy of sipping from that holy vessel.

Their leader, the man around whom the questing knights had formed, had not taken up the grail quest. He still wore the heraldry of his family, the colours of Duke Gilon's own household. Sir Richemont raised a hand in salutation as Leuthere rode towards him. His eyes lingered up on the banner of King Louis, then shifted to Leuthere. There was no missing the question in his gaze.

'The plan worked,' Leuthere told him. 'The Red Duke's minions have been at our heels for three days and three nights.'

'If we had kicked our boots into a beehive, we could not have received a more violent reception,' Count Ergon said, riding up beside Leuthere. 'The vampire went wild when he saw the king's standard.'

Richemont scratched his chin, sighing as he heard the news. 'I had hoped the Red Duke might show some caution,' he stated. 'Every hour he marches gives us more time for help to arrive. After you left, Duke Gilon received messages from Quenelles and Brionne. Knights from both dukedoms are riding to help in the battle against the Red Duke. Within a fortnight, we could have another thousand swords at our side.'

Leuthere shook his head. 'I fear we did not have the time to dally,' he told Richemont. 'We reached the Red

Duke just as his army was advancing upon Dragon's Hill. There can be no question that if he'd been left to his own devices, he would have called all of the ancient dead entombed within the barrows to fight for him.'

'There are other ways of holding the vampire back,' Richemont declared. He gestured over his shoulder to the bridge behind him. 'The prophetess tells us that this is the bridge the Red Duke used to cross the Morceaux before. She is not certain if he will use it again,' here the knight clapped a hand against his chest, 'but I am betting that he will.'

'What do you have planned?' Count Ergon asked, a note of concern in his voice.

Richemont smiled, clearly pleased to explain the merits of his plan. 'I intend to hold the bridge and prevent the Red Duke from crossing. If he is as obsessed by the past as you say, then he will stay and fight for this bridge and no other. We can hold him here until reinforcements are in place at Ceren Field.'

Count Ergon shook his head. The nobleman was showing the effects of three days in the saddle, but he refused to leave his doubts unspoken. 'It might be dangerous to expect the vampire to follow the exact pattern he did before. He might be drawn to the same places, but do not rely upon him slavishly doing what he did before.'

'I'm not,' Richemont said. He gestured once again to the bridge. 'We only need to hold the bridge for a few more hours. My father has dispatched teams of sappers to demolish the bridge and they will be here before nightfall.'

Leuthere frowned as he heard Richemont describe the destruction of the bridge. 'If the Red Duke can't cross, he may snap back to reality.'

Count Ergon gave the worried knight a tired slap on the back. 'If that happens, we'll just have to ride back out to him and wave the standard under his nose again.'

The grim jest brought a few feeble chuckles from the men who had survived the journey to Dragon's Hill. Brave as they were, none of them wanted to repeat the experience.

'You can rest your horses on the other side of the river,' Richemont declared. He looked over the exhausted men. 'And you'd better get some sleep for yourselves. As run down as you are now, I doubt you could account for a dozen zombies if the Red Duke were to attack.'

Leuthere was in accord with Richemont's sentiment. Even Count Ergon did not naysay the young knight's words. For once, the old nobleman's prodigious endurance had been taxed beyond its limits. Not even his thirst for revenge could sustain him. Solemnly, the small band of knights rode their haggard steeds across the old stone bridge.

IT WAS NOON when the undead arrived at the river. The mounted wights that had pursued Leuthere and the others from Dragon's Hill emerged from the forest, a ghastly wall of bleached bone and rusty armour. The skeletal monsters stared at Sir Richemont and his knights, silent and unmoving as a phalanx of gravestones.

The quiet was broken when a sinister rider pushed his way through the skeletal cavalry. The dark knight's black armour and surcoat seemed like a piece of midnight that refused to be vanquished by the sun. A faint wisp of smoke rose from Sir Maraulf's armour, carrying with it the sickly smell of burnt flesh. So recently inducted into the ranks of the undead, the dark knight did not need the powerful sorceries of the Red Duke to sustain him by day. There was still enough of an echo of life about him that the dark knight wasn't condemned to hide in his grave until nightfall. But the vampire could not entirely ignore the hostile gaze of the sun. If the purifying light was not enough to destroy him, it was enough to scorch his unclean flesh and fill his unholy body with pain.

Tormented by the sun, compelled to accomplish the commands of his master, the dark knight glared in fury at the knights who defended the bridge. He could see the banner of King Louis on the far shore, standing above the tent in whose shade Sir Leuthere and Count Ergon rested. The Red Duke wanted that banner and the men who bore it. Maraulf would let nothing, not even his own agony, stop him from meeting that obligation.

Without preamble or warning, the dark knight drew his sword and charged towards the bridge. The undead cavalry surged after him without hesitation, a galloping horde of grinning skulls and corroded spears. The wights were a mixture of the Red Duke's black knights, their bones encased in pitted armour and tattered mail, and the ancient horse lords who bore only the fragments of bronze helmets and shields. Whatever they had been in life, the wights were now united in undeath.

Richemont watched the undead cavalry bear down upon the bridge. The wights vastly outnumbered his own force, but their vampire commander had not spared any thought to forming them into a proper battleline. The undead charged towards the

Bretonnians in a disorganized rabble. A rabble Richemont intended to sweep aside as quickly as possible.

'Men of Aquitaine!' Richemont cried out. 'Your hour of glory is at hand! For the Lady and the king!'

Richemont spurred his powerful destrier towards the enemy, the questing knights forming up around him, their massive swords at the ready. To either side of his small squadron, great wedges of knights errant assumed their flanking positions, their lances lowered.

With a crash of steel and the thunder of hooves, the two forces collided three hundred yards from the bank of the river. The steel-tipped lances of Richemont's knights smashed through the corroded shields and brittle armour of the undead, shattering the bony fiends with the sheer impact of the assault. The huge swords of the questing knights crushed those wights unfortunate enough to come against them, cleaving through rider and steed alike in the fury of their attack.

In a matter of moments, the knights were through the broken ranks of their undead enemies. Richemont gazed in amazement at his men as they emerged from the shattered mass of the enemy. The entire attack had cost him only a dozen men, yet there were hundreds of skeleton horsemen shattered across the battlefield. He felt his heart swell with pride at the bravery of these men who had followed him into battle.

Richemont's jubilation quickly turned to horror as he cast his eyes back towards the bridge. Only a handful of knights had been left to guard the crossing, Richemont believing a solid attack being the only way to deal with the undead charge. The counter-charge had worked better than he had expected, but

Richemont had failed to fully appreciate the kind of foe he faced.

Any mortal army would have been routed by the havoc Richemont and his knights had visited upon it. The undead, however, had no hearts to fill with fear or minds in which to render doubt. Even as Richemont watched, the survivors from his attack continued to push for the bridge. Even after the toll he had exacted from them, there were still hundreds of the skeletal horsemen. At their head, smoke still rising from his armour, the dark knight raced towards the river.

'Back! Back into the fray!' Richemont cried out, waving his sword overhead, striving to rally his men for another attack. Most of the knights errant threw aside their splintered lances and drew an assortment of swords, axes and maces from their belts, hurrying to follow their leader back into battle.

Again, Richemont was due to be surprised by his enemy. Against orcs or Northmen, an attack on the rear would set the enemy into confused panic. These horrors, however, seemed indifferent to their fate, striking back at their attackers when able, but otherwise ignoring them in their reckless drive for the bridge.

One of the questing knights tore his way to the very front of the battle, spurring his steed towards the vampire in his smoking armour. Many of those who had been killed in the first charge had been claimed by the vampire's sword. Now this lone knight challenged the fiend's blade. It was an uneven contest. The knight's heavy sword was caught by the vampire's shield while the monster's own sword stabbed out, piercing the eye of the knight's steed. As the animal crumpled beneath him, the knight was smashed to the ground.

The vampire did not deign to end the contest with a slash of his sword, instead ending the knight's quest for the grail by crushing his skull beneath the flailing hooves of his skeletal horse.

Richemont's heart blazed at the sight of such a dastardly act. Frenziedly, he fought his way through the press of combatants around him, determined to close with the vampire.

Maraulf noted the impetuous knight's effort to reach him. He raised his blade in a sardonic salute and prepared to receive Richemont's charge.

Duke Gilon's son drove his warhorse straight at the gruesome dark knight. The animal whinnied in terror, its every sense offended by the vampire's profane aura, but years of careful training kept it plunging forwards. Richemont's steed crashed into Maraulf's bony charger with the impact of a battering ram.

Richemont had seen such an assault shatter the skeletal steeds of the wights, but the vampire's mount was barely jostled by the attack. The dark knight drove his spurs against the nightmare's exposed ribs. The creature reared back, its hooves flashing out. The knight was forced to raise his shield to protect himself from the undead beast's assault. As he did so, Maraulf brought his monstrous blade slashing downwards.

It was luck more than skill that enabled Richemont to intercept the vampire's sword. There was a ghastly crashing sound as Maraulf's blade smashed into his shield. Wood splintered, metal twisted beneath that superhuman blow. Richemont heard his arm snap an instant before the red rush of pain roared through his body.

Somehow, the knight found the strength to stay in his saddle, lashing out at Maraulf with his sword. The blade rasped across the vampire's armour and as the steel edge came into contact with the dark knight it seemed to blaze with a sapphire flame.

The vampire recoiled from Richemont, a cry of torment echoing from behind the steel mask of his helmet. Maraulf drove his nightmare steed away from the wounded knight, abandoning his injured foe. Richemont could only grind his teeth in helplessness as the vampire fled the field, his remaining wights galloping away with him, back into the forest.

Richemont stared in surprise at his sword, for it again seemed like any other blade forged for a Bretonnian knight. Then a grim chuckle forced its way through the pain gripping him. When he had visited the Great Chapel of the Lady in Couronne, he had anointed his sword in the font just within the doors of that holy place. The Lady's grace must have entered the blade, blessing it against unholy vermin like the vampire.

The ducal heir was still laughing at his miraculous escape from the undead fiend when one of the surviving questing knights rode up to take the reins of his horse and lead the injured lord from the battlefield.

As he crossed the bridge, a broad smile spread over Richemont's face. He could see the sappers and their wagons arriving on the far side of the river. With them were a hundred bowmen who lost no time readying their weapons. A few yeomen in the heraldry of Duke Gilon shouted orders to the men, getting them into positions from which they would be able to shoot down any attack from the forest.

The battle had been won. The dark knight had withdrawn with only a few hundred wights left. His force was too weak to take the bridge now. Within a handful of hours, the sappers would demolish the bridge and the Red Duke would be trapped.

Richemont rode past the tent where Sir Leuthere and Count Ergon were resting. He smiled down at the two men, pointing to his broken left arm.

'Between us, we make a full knight,' Richemont told Count Ergon.

The count gave a half-hearted laugh, caressing his injured right arm. 'There's a certain amount of foolishness getting that close to a vampire,' he agreed. A cold light crept into his eyes. 'Just the same, I intend to do it again.'

'By the time the Red Duke can cross that river, perhaps both our wounds shall have healed,' Richemont said. He turned about in his saddle, stifling a grunt of pain as his arm brushed against the saddle horn. 'These sappers will soon have the bridge down,' he observed as the mob of leather-aproned specialists began to attack the bridge with pick and hammer. 'They'll be quick about it too. Nothing like a vampire's army of the damned to motivate peasants to be speedy in their labours.'

'I just pray the Red Duke follows the plan,' Leuthere said.

'If we trust him to come to Ceren Field, then we can trust him to come here,' Richemont stated. He frowned as he looked across the Morceaux. The dark knight had emerged from the trees. With him was one of the wights, a hoary-looking revenant wearing the crumbling tatters of a crown about its skull. Upon the wight's arm, a grisly creature was perched, the skeletal husk of a falcon.

While the men watched, the dark knight took a small roll of vellum and tied it about the bird's leg.

Impossibly, despite the absence of feathers or flesh, the skeletal falcon took wing. The carrion bird circled twice over the vampire, then turned eastward.

'You can stop worrying,' Count Ergon told Richemont and Leuthere. 'The Red Duke will come here when he receives that message from his creature.

'The question is, will he stay on the other side of the river?'

CHAPTER XVII

The Red Duke gazed across the trudging ranks of his infantry, scowling as he considered the slowness of their march. Far beyond, just where the road lost itself in the forest, he could see the front of the baggage train bringing up the rear. His face pulled back in a snarl of contempt. King Louis the Usurper was wreaking havoc across his domain and he was stuck here, burdened by the weight of his army.

'We must make greater haste, Earl Maryat,' the vampire hissed in a low voice.

The knight beside him muttered anxiously under his breath, catching himself before he gave voice to the name of the Lady. Of late, the Red Duke had grown intolerant of such sentiments, adding blasphemy to the long catalogue of his sins. Earl Maryat regretted the oath he had given this creature, the word of honour that bound him to the vampire's fate. If he could, he would have taken back his loyalty. But such was an impossibility for a knight of Aquitaine. Once given, a nobleman did not betray his word.

'We cannot drive the men more than we already are,' Earl Maryat said. 'They are already about to drop from exhaustion. They'll be in no condition to fight when we reach the king.'

The Red Duke was unmoved by his general's protest. 'If

347

the peasant scum cannot do what I need of them, then they are worthless to me.'

'You ask too much of them, your grace,' the knight objected. 'These men are loyal. They will not betray you. They would not dare.'

The vampire gripped Earl Maryat beneath the chin, forcing the knight's head to turn. He forced the general to watch the silent ranks of skeletons and zombies filing down the road. 'These are the sort of troops who will not betray me. They have none of the failings of flesh. Whatever I demand of them, they do.'

Earl Maryat's face became like a graven image as all the colour drained out of it. 'But they are just dead things. Unholy…'

The Red Duke turned away, his cape billowing about him in the wind. 'The peasants are slowing us down,' he said. 'That I will not allow.'

The horrified general hurried after his liege. 'You cannot mean to…'

'See that they are disposed of,' the Red Duke told him. 'I shall attend them later and restore them to a state better able to defend my realm.' He noted the stunned disbelief in Earl Maryat's pallid face.

'Do as I command,' the vampire told his general with a snarl. 'You do not want me to begin questioning the loyalty of my noble retainers.'

DARKNESS BLACKER THAN night fell across the banks of the Morceaux. From the canopy of the forest, a grim procession of ghastly creatures marched. The ancient dead of the barrow mounds, the armoured husks of Bretonnian knights, the decaying wreckage of slaughtered peasants. Overhead, snarling blood bats circled, their leathery wings fanning the corpse-stench of the zombies across the river. Packs of slinking ghouls crawled through the shadows, their ravenous eyes fixed upon the bodies strewn across the battlefield.

Against the bare bones, rusty armour and decayed flesh of his hideous army, the crimson armour of the Red Duke shone like a beacon blazing in the very pit of hell. The vampire's skeletal steed marched unhindered through the horde of walking corpses, the undead parting before their master like wheat before the scythe. Regal and terrible, the Red Duke made his way through the ranks of his army, pressing forwards until he stood upon the edge of the battlefield.

The vampire's eyes blazed as he studied the havoc visited upon his cavalry by Sir Richemont's force. His tactical mind could appreciate the disposition of the dead knights, extrapolating from the wreckage of war the strategies of the combatants. His own dark knight would have much to answer for.

The Red Duke turned his attention to the river itself and the bridge that spanned it. He nodded grimly when he saw the dilapidated condition of the bridge, its destruction wrought by neither time nor element, but by the deliberate hand of man. On the far side of the Morceaux he could see Richemont's knights, could see the sappers and bowmen watching him with rapt fascination. Even over the stench of his zombies and the musky stink of the swarming bats, the vampire could smell the terror dripping from the Bretonnians.

Deciding to test the magnitude of the fear gripping his enemy, the Red Duke urged El Morzillo into a canter. With a grace made loathsome by its deathly shape, the warhorse pranced across the battlefield, daring the watching archers to shoot it and the monster in its saddle. Not an arrow flew over the river, not a man dared loose a shaft at this fiend risen from story and legend to make war against their land.

The Red Duke's lip curled back in a sneer. He had been prepared to admire the valour of these men after their bold display against his cavalry, but now he found their courage a thing for contempt. Mockingly, he drew his sword in challenge to the watching knights. A fearsome laugh tore through the darkness as the vampire turned his warhorse about and galloped back to his own waiting army.

'They have torn down the bridge,' the vampire told those of the undead with enough reason and willpower left to them to serve him as generals and commanders. 'They think to balk me, to keep me from riding against King Louis.' The Red Duke displayed his gleaming fangs in a scowl of inhuman hate. 'They play for time, so the usurper can flee back to the safety of his castle.'

The Red Duke looked out over his army and his scowl became a cruel smile. 'The fools forget our strength and their weakness.' He raised his hand, pointing his finger at several of the wights. 'Take your troops. Cross the river. Kill anything stupid enough to still be there when you reach the other side.'

In a feeble echo of their mortal lives, the wights saluted the Red Duke in the discordant fashion of chivalrous Bretonnian knight and primitive barbarian horse lord. The vampire paid them no notice, already turning his attention to other problems. He glared at the packs of ghouls creeping about the fringes of his army.

'Earl Maryat,' the Red Duke hissed, addressing his words to the black shape of Sir Maraulf. The dark knight was accustomed to his master's confused mind, accepting the role of Earl Maryat as easily as he had that of Baron de Gavaudan.

'The peasants will slow us down,' the Red Duke told his thrall. 'See that they are disposed of. I shall attend them later and restore them to a state better able to defend my realm.'

FROM THE FAR shore of the river Morceaux, Sir Leuthere and Count Ergon watched with mounting horror as hundreds of skeletal infantry began to march. Where Sir Richemont's bowmen had shown hesitancy to shoot at the Red Duke, they loosed arrows into the advancing skeletons with frantic abandon. Many of the skeletons fell, their skulls splintered by the impact of an arrow, but for each that fell it seemed there were three others still moving towards the river.

'They cannot think to use the bridge.' The remark was made by Sir Richemont. His arm bound up in a sling, the young general had joined the two knights to watch the arrival of the Red Duke and his horde. 'It would take weeks to repair and I can assure you that my archers will not relent in their persecution of these monsters! The Red Duke will lose thousands before he can span the gap.'

A cold chill ran down Count Ergon's spine. The nobleman's voice was heavy with dread when he spoke. 'I do not think the fiend means to use the bridge.' He pointed to the edge of the forest. The zombies and wights had turned upon the ghouls, setting on them from every direction, cutting them down with hayforks and bill-hooks. The agonized wails of the betrayed monsters were piteous and horrible to hear.

'The vampire truly is mad!' Leuthere exclaimed. 'He

sets his own troops against each other!'

Count Ergon shook his head. 'Insane he may be, but the monster still has a daemon's cunning.' He gestured again to the river where the march of skeletons had been thinned by relentless bowfire, but was hardly brought to a stop. It was apparent to those watching that the skeletons were making no move towards the bridge, but were intent upon the reaching the river itself.

'The ghouls were the only part of his army that was truly alive,' Count Ergon explained. 'Because of that, they were no longer useful to the Red Duke. Living soldiers would need a bridge to cross the Morceaux.'

The meaning of the count's words was quickly apparent. The marching skeletons reached the river. Without hesitation the undead continued their grim procession, plunging full on into the current. They trudged through the water, eventually sinking completely from view.

'Impossible!' Richemont cried. 'They cannot swim against such a current! The Morceaux has never been so violent! The Lady herself fights to keep the vampire at bay! They cannot swim the river!'

Leuthere shook his head, understanding the terrible truth of what they were witnessing. 'The undead aren't swimming across the Morceaux. They're walking along the bottom, using their spears and claws to brace themselves against the current. What Count Ergon says has the right of it. The Red Duke doesn't need the bridge.'

Richemont stared with disbelief at the marching skeletons vanishing beneath the water. The failure of his plan to stop the Red Duke and buy time for his father's allies to arrive was a bitter taste in his mouth.

Instead of days or weeks, the best he had bought Duke Gilon was a few hours. He told as much to his companions.

'I think you've bought us at least a day, maybe two,' Leuthere corrected him. He pointed to the far side of the river. The Red Duke and a few ghastly skeletons wearing the tatters of ancient druid robes were prowling among the slaughtered ghouls, lingering over each body. The vampire and his liches gestured with their claws above the face of each ghoul, muttering some vile incantation which the observers could not hear. As the monsters performed their necromancy, the corpses began to twitch and rise, fresh zombies to join the decaying ranks of the Red Duke's infantry.

'It will take them time to raise all the dead left on the far shore,' Leuthere continued. 'And they will need to recover after invoking such dark powers.'

'The hours of darkness will bolster their vitality,' Count Ergon said. 'We've seen as much during our pursuit of the Red Duke. I think we can depend on only a single day's respite. When the sun falls, the vampire's army will again be on the march.'

Richemont digested the words of the two knights, the men who had the most firsthand experience with the Red Duke. Reluctantly, he accepted the wisdom of their council. 'My father's allies will not reach Ceren Field in time then,' he said. 'It was in my mind to fight a holding action here, to cut down the undead as they emerge from the river. We could destroy many of them, but to what end? We would only squander our strength here. Eventually sheer numbers would confound our valour and drive us from the field. In triumph, the Red Duke would simply raise his vanquished slaves and add to them our own noble dead.'

Richemont cast his gaze again at the crimson figure of the Red Duke, feeling the malignant evil rising from the vampire's body. 'Duke Gilon will need every sword he can get when this fiend is across the river.' Turning away from the river, Richemont shouted to his captains to muster their commands and begin the withdrawal.

'HE IS COMING,' Sir Richemont reported to his father. The Duke of Aquitaine had established his command tent upon the hill overlooking Ceren Field, right beside the cemetery where it had all began. Whether the placement of his headquarters would prove poetic justice or cruel irony, only the outcome of the coming battle would tell.

'He is coming and in numbers even greater than we feared,' Richemont continued. 'We must consider that to his existing forces he will add those who were killed fighting to hold the bridge against his vanguard.'

Duke Gilon shook his head, saddened by the thought that men who had died valiantly defending his domain should now be enslaved by the vampire. He could not fault Richemont's decision to leave the bodies, however. It would have cost more lives to recover them and, as his son had correctly said, Duke Gilon needed every able-bodied man he could get.

'We've taken precautions against any further depredations by the Red Duke,' Duke Gilon said, his voice hard as steel. He gestured to the opening of his tent. In the brisk coolness of the morning, gangs of peasants could be seen labouring throughout the old cemetery. They were a motley collection of elderly men, haggard women and malnourished children, scarcely the most able-bodied work crew Aquitaine had ever seen. These were the peasants deemed too weak to take up arms against the vampire and his horde. Instead, Duke Gilon had found another way for these people to help defend their land.

With shovel and hammer, the peasants were breaking open the tombs. Noble and commoner, no grave was left inviolate. Every corpse was pulled out into the sun, dragged to the great bonfire which blazed at the heart of the graveyard. Grail damsels and priests of Morr conducted rites over the bodies as they were cast into the flames, begging the forgiveness of the dead and the understanding of the gods for the sacrilege necessity had forced upon them.

'All across Aquitaine, in every hamlet and thorpe, the same scene is being played out. Everywhere my messengers could reach has been given the order to burn their dead,' Duke Gilon said. His eyes dropped and a red flush of shame spread over his face. 'Even the crypts of Castle Aquitaine have been broken open. I would rather the bones of our forefathers were rendered into ash than that their bodies should be violated by the Red Duke's sorcery. Only the tomb of Duke Galand has been left unbroken. The prophetess worries that if the tomb is disturbed then Duke Galand's spirit will depart and with it, the Lady's blessing. All other graves must be destroyed.'

The assembled generals of Aquitaine nodded in sombre support of Duke Gilon's desperate act. They knew how hard it had been for their liege to make such a decision and the terrible burden it placed upon his personal honour.

'We must stop him here!' Duke Gilon snarled, pounding his fist against the oak table.

'Victory or defeat, we must keep our hearts firm and

our heads cool,' Iselda scolded him. The prophetess rose from the velvet-trimmed chair in which she sat and cast her gaze across the assembled knights. 'Do not rely upon the Red Duke to walk slavishly into our trap, as Sir Richemont did at the river. In life he was the greatest of King Louis's warlords. You must be ready for the vampire's trickery.'

'Cannot our prophetess foretell the monster's battleplan?' Sir Roget demanded, speaking the impious thought that was on every knight's mind.

Iselda looked sternly at the old knight until he turned away from her. 'The Red Duke's madness is his shield against my powers. From present to past, his insanity leads him down paths only he can see. Leading him back to Ceren Field is in itself a small triumph, but whether it will bring final victory, only the Lady herself could say.'

As she spoke the last, Iselda turned her eyes upon Sir Leuthere and Count Ergon. The old enemies stood side-by-side now, united by their quest to destroy a still greater foe. Yet she could sense the tension still lurking beneath the surface, the suspicion and resentment engendered by the ancient feud.

'We must stay true to our purpose and never forget that we fight not only for Aquitaine, but for the Lady,' Iselda said, keeping her eyes on the two knights whose destinies offered her the only substantial link to the vampire's future. No, not the only one, she reflected with a shudder. There was another possibility – one that had haunted her ever since the vampire was set loose. A possibility that promised her own doom.

Duke Gilon drew his sword, laying the blade across the table. 'My steel shall be sheathed no more unless it be in the vampire's black heart,' he vowed. His words brought protests from his assembled nobles. Angrily, he brushed aside their objections, shouting them down. 'Am I Duke of Aquitaine?' he growled. 'Or has that monster already assumed my authority? It is my land this fiend despoils!'

'But you must not risk yourself, your grace,' insisted one of the barons from the winelands. 'You are the heart of Aquitaine. Without you, who is there to guide us?'

'Without victory over this monster, there is no Aquitaine!' Duke Gilon snapped back. 'Do you expect me to hide up here, watching as others fight for my lands! No, far better to die on the battlefield than know such shame! I may be an old man, but there is at least one more fight left in me!'

'Then I will fight too,' Richemont announced. The young knight's broken arm was tied against his chest, encircled by stout wooden splints. Even the oldest of Aquitaine's nobles had never seen such a thoroughly shattered arm. Many of them thought the limb would eventually mortify and need to be amputated, though they were too wise to speak of such to Duke Gilon. The idea that Richemont would ride into battle with such an injury was one that struck them as morbidly absurd.

Duke Gilon did not share their sentiment. He could see the determination on his son's face. Tears of admiration rolled down his cheeks that he should sire a man with such courage and conviction. 'You will command the left flank,' he told Richemont. 'Be my shield, my son. And if today sees the end of our line, then let it be an ending that shall live on after us in ballad and chanson.'

Richemont bowed his head in gratitude for the

honour his father paid him. Turning away from Duke Gilon, he addressed Leuthere and Count Ergon. 'I know your hearts are stout and your valour great. I will not command you to ride at my side, but if you will consent to follow me into battle, I promise you will find no lack of work for your swords.'

Leuthere knelt before the ducal heir. 'My lord, it is my honour to serve you in whatever way I am able.'

Count Ergon was less effusive in his acceptance of Richemont's request. 'If it gets me close to the Red Duke, I'll ride with you into the maw of Chaos.'

THE BEACON LIGHTS burning from castle towers announced the advance of the Red Duke's army long before the first scouts returned to the Bretonnian camp. The undead were still marching towards Ceren Field and thus far were acting in accordance to Iselda's prediction and Duke Gilon's hope. How long they could count upon the vampire's delusion to work in their favour, none of the Aquitainians wanted to consider.

As the brightness of day began to fade, as sinister black clouds swelled from nothingness to choke the sky, the Bretonnians took their positions upon the field. A sense of dread coursed through each man's heart as he considered the immense power of the Red Duke's magic, the power to turn day into night and to smother the sun itself with his evil. Courage faltered in the face of such a display of supernatural might.

Even as fear began to take root, a blazing brilliance erupted from the centre of the field. The tomb of Duke Galand was engulfed in a warm white radiance that seemed to reach out to each man, filling him with a sense of peace and serenity. Iselda stood before the tomb, a slender branch of yew clutched in her dainty hand. As the prophetess waved the branch before the door of the tomb, the radiance grew even more brilliant, spreading out to encompass the whole of the field and bring comfort to the bowmen mustered upon the flanking hills.

The knights of Aquitaine took to the centre of the field, awaiting the coming of the foe, the pennants fixed to their lances snapping in the wind, the banners of their households forming a riotous array of colour and heraldry. Some distance behind them came their men-at-arms, spears and halberds at the ready. The peasant-soldiers would exploit any gaps in the enemy line caused by the charge of the knights, making it impossible for the enemy to reform ranks after their assault. In the event the knights were forced to retreat, the men-at-arms would form a defensive bulwark and prevent the cavalry from being overrun by the pursuing enemy.

On the left flank of the main block of knights was a second gathering of cavalry composed of the surviving knights errant and questing knights who had taken part in the battle at the bridge. Their numbers were swollen by large groups of mounted squires and yeomen, unarmoured horse-troops drawn from the households of Aquitaine's noble lords.

Sir Leuthere and Count Ergon took their positions behind Sir Richemont's mighty destrier. With them was Vigor, the crook-backed peasant overjoyed to take part in the battle, determined to atone for his own guilt by taking the fight directly to the Red Duke's unholy warriors.

Upon each of the flanking hills hundreds of bowmen moved into position. The vantage points chosen for them presented a great field of fire for their long-bows. Before the vampire's army could come to grips with the defenders of Aquitaine, they would be forced to cross four hundred yards of punishment from the archers on the hills.

Duke Gilon strode from his campaign tent and buckled his helmet to his head, the golden crown of Aquitaine shining above the hinged visor. Sternly he crossed to the covered stable his servants had erected beside the tent. Looking like the oversized hutch of some monstrous hare, the strange stable had been hastily constructed to hold Duke Gilon's favourite steed.

The duke's grooms emerged from the stable leading a magnificent creature. At first glance, the beast looked like a mighty destrier, larger even than the warhorses of Richemont and the other knights. Snowy white in colour, the great horse was clothed in a colourful caparison of red and blue. Upon its head, the animal wore a winged crown of gold that matched the crest of Duke Gilon's helm. Fierce, intelligent eyes gleamed from behind the silk mask the steed wore, betraying a wisdom greater than that of any common horse.

This steed was Fulminer, and as it emerged from the hutch-like stable, it spread the great pinions attached to its shoulders and removed any doubt that it was but a common horse. Twenty-foot wings folded out-wards, fluttering as Fulminer eased the stiffness from its limbs. The great feathered wings, of a barred white and brown colour, fanned the air in a bold display of strength and power.

Duke Gilon stroked the muzzle of the pegasus, greeting the creature like an old friend. Fulminer had been a gift from the Duke of Parravon, given to him when the pegasus had been a foal. No more valiant or noble steed was to be found in all Aquitaine.

The current ordeal, however, would test the courage of both knight and steed. Duke Gilon's intention was to circle above the battlefield, to seek out and find the Red Duke himself. Once he was certain of reaching the vampire, he would descend upon the fiend from the sky.

With the Red Duke destroyed, the vampire's army would crumble away. At least such was the account of the first Battle of Ceren Field.

Now, Duke Gilon would put the legend to the test.

If the Lady was merciful, the old tales would be proven true.

As Fulminer took to the sky, Duke Gilon was afforded a more complete view of Ceren Field than any of his generals could hope for. He could see his troops moving into position. It sent a thrill of pride through him to see the fine discipline of even the peasants as they set their minds to the labour of war. The white light of Galand's tomb cast brilliant reflections from the armour worn by the Bretonnian knights, making the entire battlefield shine like a tapestry woven from stars.

The growing confidence in Duke Gilon's breast faltered as Fulminer whinnied anxiously. He turned his flying steed about, watching as a cloud of giant bats swarmed towards the battlefield, their bodies bloated with blood. Beneath the flocks of bats marched a seemingly numberless horde of skeletons and zombies. Duke Gilon could make out the Red Duke's abominable cavalry leading the way, not a scrap of flesh to be found on either riders or steeds. They were a vile mockery of knighthood, wasted husks of chivalry stolen from their graves and enslaved by the black sorcery of a merciless monster.

Soon, their profane existence would be ended. Duke Gilon felt some of his confidence return as he watched the undead lumber out onto the field. For all his vaunted tactical prowess, the Red Duke was behaving exactly as he had against King Louis. In only a matter of moments, the archers would begin loosing volleys of arrows into the rotten horde. Before the vampire could reach the centre of the field where Aquitaine's knights awaited him, half his army would be destroyed.

By the Lady, the salvation of Aquitaine would soon be realised!

CHAPTER XVIII

Mehmed-bey's cavalry came charging down the narrow neck of the wadi, pursuing the crusader horsemen as they retreated. Mad with hate, arrogant with pride, the Arabyan knights came pouring down the valley like a flood of steel and fury. These were the terrors of the desert, the warriors who had kept a land twice the size of Bretonnia beneath the cruel fist of Sultan Jaffar. They would not suffer the insult paid to them by this miserable little company of infidel cowards!

And upon the hills, hidden beneath cloaks coloured to match the sands, El Syf's bedouin scouts watched as Mehmed-bey's great army plunged headlong into the duke's trap. Once the siphais were far enough into the wadi, enclosed upon each side by the rocky cliffs, once the numberless horde of Mehmed's mamelukes and janissaries were choking the mouth of the wadi and cutting off all chance for escape, the scouts sprang into action. One after another, the vengeful bedouins placed horns to their lips and blew a single note.

Behind the dunes, hidden from sight, rank upon rank of Bretonnian bowmen drew back their strings and loosed volley after volley into the wadi. The iron-tipped arrows fell upon the Arabyan cavalry in a withering hail, piercing armour and flesh and bone. The arrogant charge of the siphais disintegrated into a panicked route, and still the arrows came. Broken and bloodied, the heavy cavalry turned to escape the punishment of the unseen archers, trampling their own infantry in their desperate attempt to flee.

With the great horde of Mehmed-bey falling into confusion, the scouts blew a second call upon their horns. The volleys of arrows suddenly stopped. In their place came the thunder of hooves. Hundreds of crusading knights charged into the wadi, striking like a burning spear through the disordered ranks of the Arabyan army.

At the head of the crusaders rode the Duke of Aquitaine, El Syf, his golden sword striking out at the panicked Arabyans. He cut through the enemy, slaughtering them by their dozens, unstoppable as a desert sandstorm. Always his eyes remained fixed on the banner of the Black Lizard, the flag of Mehmed the Butcher.

There could be no victory this day unless Mehmed-bey was dead. El Syf kissed his sword and vowed to the Lady that he would not leave the field unless it was with the head of his enemy hanging from his saddle.

THE RED DUKE'S cold lips pulled back in a sardonic smile as he observed the disposition of the king's forces. He saw in the Bretonnian battleline the echo of the tactics he himself had employed to work the ruin of Mehmed-bey. The cavalry offered as tempting bait, the bowmen arrayed to either flank to act as the deadly jaws of the trap.

The vampire sneered at the crudity of his enemy. His brother would have known, of course, how Mehmed-bey had been defeated. He himself had instructed the king in the strategy used against the Arabyans. It was insulting to find the ploy so crudely and poorly executed here. He found it even more audacious than the fact the king thought he could use one of the vampire's own strategies against him. It was further proof, if the Red Duke needed any, of the perfidy of the Lady that the goddess should consider such an inept fool worthy of drinking from the grail. He would take great delight in defiling her shrines and massacring her damsels when this battle was over.

Lifting his hand, the vampire motioned his army to halt. He ran an armoured thumb along his cheek as he considered the defences that had been prepared to destroy him. He remembered the destruction of the Arabyans and how it had been brought about. Hateful flames blazed in the Red Duke's eyes as inspiration came upon him. He would turn King Louis's poorly chosen strategy against him. The jaws of the trap would sit unsprung, the chivalrous bait would be drawn out to act as the vampire's shield.

Ghastly laughter hissed through the Red Duke's fangs as he summoned his captains to him and told them what they must do.

SIR LEUTHERE WATCHED as the undead horde came onwards. The knight made a quiet prayer of thanksgiving to the Lady. For long minutes, the undead had stood frozen in place at the edge of Ceren Field, exciting a despair in the breasts of every man. Doubt crept into each mind, the fear that the Red Duke would withdraw without pressing his attack. There would be no better ground upon which to face the vampire, no better place to crush the mighty undead horde.

As Leuthere saw the skeletons and zombies surge into motion again, he felt such relief that he was oblivious to the horror of the situation for the moment. Then the awfulness came screaming back into his body, sending goose pimples along his arms. The stink of death and unholy magic, the hideous aspect of thousands of corpses stalking the land, the clatter of fleshless bones against rusted armour and the profane chants of the undead druids. This was different than fighting a mortal foe, of riding forth to battle orcs or to slay an ogre. This was like making war against the one foe no man could ever overcome: Death itself.

Warmth and peace flowed back into the knight's body and Leuthere was thankful for the caress of Iselda's white magic. He had need of her power to sustain his courage. They all did. Duty and obligation could only drive a man so far before his very flesh rebelled against him. Even the onerous burden of his family shame was not enough to steel his heart against the terrifying aspect of the Red Duke's warhost. It needed more than mortal courage to stand before the legions of the dead.

High over the battlefield, Duke Gilon could be seen, the pegasus Fulminer circling above the Aquitainian positions. Coloured flags fluttered from the duke's hand, strips of white that signified the knights were to hold their ground. A complex series of signals had been arranged by the duke with his generals, allowing him to exploit his fantastic steed to his best advantage. The view from the sky gave Duke Gilon an unparalleled appreciation of the battlefield. He could see events develop much more rapidly than the commanders on the ground. Advance warning of the undead tactics would be essential if the Bretonnians were to carry the day.

'Duke Gilon makes a great sacrifice,' Count Ergon observed, his voice ringing with admiration. 'He chooses to lead his army instead of provoking the contest he so greatly desires. With Fulminer, he could strike into the heart of the undead horde and cross swords with the vampire.'

'My father may yet do just such a thing,' Sir Richemont said. 'But he will not risk the outcome of the battle to confront our enemy.'

Leuthere shook his head, not understanding. 'If Duke Gilon can kill the Red Duke, the vampire's army will be broken. Iselda has stressed that fact in every war council.'

Richemont fixed Leuthere with a reproving glower. 'And if my father should fail? If he should be cut down by the Red Duke deep within the enemy lines? We would lose the benefit of his command and the vantage Fulminer's wings gives him. We would be fighting like blind men.' Richemont clenched his teeth, all the colour rising in his face. 'Worse, my father knows his careful strategy would be lost. We would rush upon the undead in a reckless charge, determined to recover his body from the vampire's vile hands. There would be no more thought given to victory. Only revenge.'

Overhead, Duke Gilon displayed yellow flags, waving them from right to left. These were commands to the bowmen on the hills, motioning them to adopt new positions. Suddenly the duke's flags fell still. Then, in a frantic gesture, the white flags appeared again. Duke Gilon waved them in a frenzy, the effect striking the watching knights and their commanders like a fierce shout, an imploring demand for the knights to hold their ground.

'Duke Gilon seems to think it is urgent we stay here,'

Count Ergon said.

'It is almost as though he fears we will disobey his orders,' Leuthere agreed.

Richemont's expression became troubled with doubt. 'Something is wrong, that much is obvious. But why does he think we would...'

As he spoke, the ducal heir had risen in the stirrups of his saddle, peering across the field at the advancing skeletons. Like the Bretonnians, they marched with their cavalry to the fore, a solid wall of equine bones and rusted barding, skull-faced riders grinning at their distant foes. It seemed to Richemont that the Red Duke was behaving exactly as his father had hoped, walking right into the trap prepared for him. Then there was a flurry of motion within the lines of the undead. Ghastly figures rose above the marching skeletons.

'Good Lady preserve us!' Richemont gasped in horror as he beheld the obscenity.

The knights of Aquitaine knew they had left the bodies of fallen comrades behind them at the Morceaux. They had resigned themselves to the fact that the vampire would have performed his abominable magic upon the corpses, that in this battle they would likely face the reanimated husks of dead friends and kinsmen. This horror the men had accepted, steeling their hearts against crossing swords with their former comrades.

The abomination they now witnessed was more hideous than any they could have imagined. The Red Duke had indeed worked his filthy magic upon their dead comrades, but they did not march with his unholy army. Instead, they were raised above them, impaled upon great poles, carried aloft like ghastly standards. As if the corpses of knights being subjected to such barbarous and obscene treatment was not enough, the Red Duke had inflicted another atrocity.

Like the body of Earl Gaubert, the Red Duke had animated the impaled corpses of his foes. They writhed and twitched upon their stakes like insects skewered on a pin.

Shrieks of outrage and hate welled up from the ranks of the knights as they recognized some of the tortured corpses. Overhead, Duke Gilon's signals became more frantic. A volley of arrows streaked overhead, the bowmen shooting at the undead even though they were still out of range. It was a last, desperate effort by the duke to remind his soldiers of the plan and the trap and their role in it.

The reminder was not enough to stem the fury that now gripped the knights. A few cool-headed captains were not enough to enforce the order to hold their ground.

Richemont's fist tightened about his lance. More than any of the men around him, he felt the shame of leaving the bodies behind. Shame became rage and a determination to make the Red Duke pay for this obscenity. Richemont was a dishonoured man, and his pride would only be restored when he saw the vampire's head spitted on a spike above the gates of Castle Aquitaine.

'A cask of gold and a blade of silver to the man who brings me that monster's black heart in his hand!' Richemont shouted. Count Ergon made a grab for the ducal heir's reins, trying to prevent what would come next. It was a last effort to save Duke Gilon's battleplan, and it was doomed to failure.

'For Aquitaine! For the Lady!' Richemont fairly

screamed as he led the charge against the undead.

THE RED DUKE'S cold smile had a suggestion of amusement about it as he watched the Aquitainians mount their charge. They had acted just as he had predicted. Just like Mehmed-bey's troops, they were rushing headlong to their own destruction. The vampire might have been moved to pity them, if that emotion had been more than just an empty word to him.

The knights were doomed as soon as they put spurs to their horses. On the hills, the bowmen were frantically trying to reposition themselves, trying to out race the galloping warhorses and put themselves in a position where they could shoot into the undead before their lines were hopelessly confused with those of the charging knights.

Although he thought little of the archers' chances to outrun charging cavalry, the Red Duke decided to ensure the bowmen wouldn't get the chance to loose arrows into his horde. Exerting his black will, the vampire set the great flocks of blood bats swooping down at the peasants. Great swarms of leather-winged rodents descended upon the men, at once breaking their dash along the hills.

Hissing his cruel laughter, the Red Duke returned his attention to the charging knights. They made an awesome spectacle, proud and noble, a peerless fusion of man and steed into a single, deadly whole. The vampire felt bitter resentment as he turned his eyes from the magnificent sight of Aquitaine's knights and stared across the decaying mass of his own cavalry. Spiteful hate boiled up inside him. If he could not lead men such as those who now rode against him, then he would obliterate their kind from the face of the earth.

'Half-march,' the Red Duke snarled. At his command, the skeletal horsemen and black knights pulled back on the reins of their grisly mounts. As the cavalry slowed, ranks of skeleton infantry crept forwards between the closely packed horsemen. Now hurtling towards his army at a full charge, the vampire doubted if his foes would notice the reduced pace of the undead. Even if they did, the Bretonnians could never halt their attack in time.

The Red Duke grinned, licking his fangs in bloodthirsty anticipation as the knights thundered across Ceren Field. He gave a mocking salute with his golden sword to the frantic King Louis, still circling the battlefield overhead. He could imagine the terror surging through his little brother's heart as he watched his army rushing to embrace its own ruin.

Snarling in sadistic anticipation, the Red Duke returned his eyes to the charging enemy. He could see their bright surcoats and ornate helmets now, could smell the blood pounding in their veins. The vampire trembled with excitement, picturing the slaughter to come.

At fifty yards, the Red Duke gave the command. 'Spearmen forward.'

The Aquitainains would have only a second to appreciate that theirs was no longer the only trap on Ceren Field.

After that second, they would be much too busy dying to care why.

ACROSS CEREN FIELD, the knights charged, oaths of vengeance falling from their lips, prayers to the Lady ringing in their ears. Sir Leuthere could see the grimly silent ranks of the Red Duke's cavalry arrayed before them. Every moment, he expected the skeletal riders to spring into motion, to sally forth and meet the coming attack. Each time his destrier's hooves smashed against the earth, he expected the undead to surge forwards.

Closer and closer the knights were drawn and still there came no reaction from the Red Duke's army. Not a single arrow, not a single outcry, only the deathly silence of the grave.

Then Leuthere saw them, marching out from between the Red Duke's undead cavalry. Hundreds of skeletons armed with long spears of oak as thick around as the stakes upon which the zombies twitched and writhed. The skeletons took five steps, then dropped into a crouch, planting the butt of the spears into the earth and bracing it with their bony knees. In only a few moments, a jagged fence of corroded iron and bronze spikes girded the enemy's position. To Leuthere, it looked like nothing less than the jaws of some great beast opening to devour the warriors of Aquitaine.

There was no time to turn the charge, the momentum of the horses was already committed. The only reduction was in the readiness of the men who sat in the saddles. Lances were raised, shields were lowered as the knights instinctively tried to halt their headlong drive into the Red Duke's spears.

A deafening roar, like the death-cry of a mountain, boomed across Ceren Field as the knights smashed into the undead. Men screamed, horses shrieked as spears stabbed into their flesh and their own momentum spitted them upon the weapons. The same furious momentum drove the dying warhorses onwards, crushing the brittle skeletons that bore the spears, scattering their splintered bones in a wave of destruction.

Onwards the charge was driven, the hooves of the destriers smashing all in their path. The fence of spears was obliterated, the skeletal skirmishers pulverized. At the same time, wounded Bretonnians were crushed into the blood-spattered soil by the remorseless tide of their own comrades, their screams lost in the chaos of battle.

The undead cavalry held before the surging knights, using shield and sword to defend against the Aquitainians. The Red Duke's spearmen had not stopped the attack. They had done something worse. They had broken the cohesion of the Bretonnian knights and blunted the impetus of their assault. Instead of smashing through the undead line and reforming on the other side, the knights were caught in a quagmire of individual fights. The men no longer fought as a group, but as lone warriors filled with a furious sense of outrage tempered by an equal measure of mortal terror.

Leuthere smashed his lance full into the face of a leering wight, watching as the creature's jawbone shattered and sprayed rotten teeth at him. He brought the broken lance back around, plunging it through the skeletal horseman's chest, letting the weight of the heavy mass of wood and iron drag the grisly creature from its saddle. The wight toppled to the ground, snapping one of its legs as it struck. For an instant, the creature tried to rise, then the plunging hooves of Leuthere's horse cracked down upon its spine and the monster moved no more.

Beside him, Count Ergon fought with the madness

of a daemon. Sweeping his sword left-handed, the nobleman hacked down skeletons with ferocious abandon. Leuthere knew the count's purpose. Battle had been joined. Now there was nothing to hold him back. He would carve his way through the entire undead legion if need be to come to grips with the Red Duke and exact revenge for his slaughtered family.

Leuthere ground his teeth together. He could not allow Count Ergon to cheat him of his only chance to atone for his uncle's evil. If Count Ergon struck down the vampire, the only chance to restore the honour of the d'Elbiqs would be lost.

'Vigor!' Leuthere cried out. Another of the undead horsemen pressed against the knight, forcing him to focus upon fending off its lethargic swordarm and the corded bronze blade it held. The crook-backed peasant rushed forwards, forcing his timid steed into the face of the mounted skeleton. Vigor's mace crashed against the fleshless skull, tearing it from the spindly neck.

'Vigor!' Leuthere shouted again, gesturing with his sword towards Count Ergon. 'Stay close to the count! Don't let him reach the Red Duke! I must be the one to destroy the vampire! It is the only way to make amends for the shame Earl Gaubert has brought upon us!'

The peasant nodded grimly. Leuthere felt his gorge rise when he saw Vigor grasp the dagger thrust beneath the belt the peasant wore. Every chivalrous bone in his body railed against the idea, but the despair in his heart was enough to silence his misgivings. 'Don't kill him,' was the only remonstration he gave Vigor as the peasant urged his steed after Count Ergon.

Lady forgive him, but he could not risk Count Ergon destroying the Red Duke!

SIR RICHEMONT'S HORSE faltered beneath him. A proud and noble beast, the destrier had refused to accept its pending death, plunging on into the undead lines with two spears piercing its body. The knight wept as the valiant animal stumbled and its legs buckled beneath it. The warhorse threw back its head, neighing loudly, as though railing against the weakness that prevented it from wreaking further havoc upon the enemy.

The destrier kept itself upright long enough for Richemont to clear the saddle, then crashed down upon its side, blood streaming from its many wounds. The knight stared down sadly at his dying steed and saluted the horse's fierce spirit with his raised sword.

Around him, Richemont had cleared a great circle in the ranks of the undead. Splintered and broken skeletons were strewn everywhere, some of them still struggling to move with broken arms and shattered legs. A few fellow knights, veterans bearing the fleur-de-lys upon their surcoats, stood by the dismounted heir, using their great two-handed swords to hold back the undead as they began to close the gap.

Richemont cursed his foolishness. He had led these men into battle with no more thought than that of an angry child. He had spoiled his father's carefully laid plan. The Red Duke would have no need to run the gauntlet of Ceren Field now. The vampire could happily massacre the knights on his own terms and never expose his own horde to the bowmen on the hills.

Guilt fuelled Richemont's anger still further. There was no way to undo what had been done, but there was still a chance to break the Red Duke's army. If they could fight their way clear to the undead commanders and destroy them, the rest of the horde would be vanquished. Almost lethargic in their movement, there was a good chance of exploiting any gap in their lines. Despite their greater numbers, the undead were too slow to stop brave and determined men.

Richemont slashed his sword across the legs of a skeletal horse as it galloped towards him, spilling beast and rider to the ground. As the skeleton knight started to rise from the tangled wreckage of its steed, Richemont's blade severed its spine, leaving the bisected creature writhing in the dirt.

Richemont thrust his sword into the earth and removed his helmet to wipe the sweat from his eyes. It was an awkward manoeuvre, made more complicated by the use of only one hand. The broken wreck of his left arm was curled behind the padded interior of an over-sized jousting shield tied against his chest. The knight grimaced as he remembered the awful strength of the vampire he had fought at the bridge. He felt a tremor of fear as he considered that the creature he now sought was that which the dark knight called master.

Yet he had to try. Richemont prayed to the Lady for the courage to face his foe. Through the ranks of the undead, he could see the gleam of the vampire's crimson armour, stark and blazing against the decay all around it. The Red Duke himself, commanding his undead horde as they cut down the knights of Aquitaine. Only a few hundred yards were between Richemont and the monster. A few hundred yards, and a few hundred undead corpses that existed only to destroy the living.

The ducal heir cast his eyes skyward, watching as his father circled over the battlefield, waving his flags desperately at the knights below. Duke Gilon was signalling for Richemont to withdraw, for the knights to retreat back across Ceren Field. But it was already too late for that. The undead were overlapping the flanks, slowly encircling the knights. There was no way back. The only path was forward.

Forward to victory or death!

THE PROPHETESS ISELDA watched as the Red Duke's warriors lapped around the embattled knights. The vampire and his liches were empowering their undead fighters with unholy energies, driving them with a speed and surety beyond their decayed frames. More quickly than any of the knights could have expected, rank upon rank of zombies and skeletons were surrounding them, locking them inside a cage of spears.

The men were doomed. Iselda did not need her powers of foresight to know there was no escape from the trap the Red Duke had laid for them. It would need a miracle to free them from the destruction that now threatened them.

She closed her eyes, her heart pounding in terror. The holy power of Duke Galand's tomb flowed through her, pulsing through her body like fingers of lightning and flame. She could harness that power, harness it to far greater effect than she had been. She could give the knights the miracle that would save them.

Tears glistened in Iselda's eyes as she gazed out over the battlefield. The screams of dying men and horses echoed back to her. On the hills, she could see the archers, their formations in disarray as the Red Duke's bats swarmed about them. Below, on the field proper, she could see ancient chariots emerge from the flanks of the vampire's army. Grisly constructions of rotten leather and yellowed bone, drawn by fleshless steeds and crewed by grinning skeletons, the chariots rolled towards the slopes of the hills. It did not need imagination to picture what the scythe-like blades fitted to the wheels of the chariots would do to the embattled bowmen once they crested the hills.

Fighting down the despair and terror that burdened her heart, Iselda allowed her mind to focus upon the sacred image of the Lady and the grail. She knew what she had to do. She had known from the first what her fate must be. She had hoped that by guiding Sir Leuthere and Count Ergon into an early confrontation with the Red Duke she would be able to escape the doom she had foreseen for herself in that dark hour when the vampire was freed.

Iselda could not remain passively emboldening the Aquitainians with the power of Duke Galand's tomb. She had to fashion the holy energies of the grail into a weapon, a lance of divine power that would strike down the profane undead. She had the power at her fingertips to burn away the vampire's army with the cleansing purity of the Lady's justice.

A chill crawled down Iselda's spine and doubt tugged at her mind once more. Only the least of the vampire's creatures would be repulsed by the holy light. Others would endure, enraged by the sacred flame, driven into crazed fury by the magical assault. By saving the knights, she would draw the Red Duke's vengeance upon herself.

The prophetess shook her head. Now, in the moment of her doom, she wished with all her being to cling to life, no matter the consequences. She could not say what would happen after she was gone, whether Duke Gilon would be able to escape with his army back to Castle Aquitaine, whether the Red Duke could still be stopped by Leuthere and Count Ergon.

She only knew that the vampire would find her.

'FOR ARMAND! FOR the pride of the du Maisnes!' Count Ergon roared, driving his sword into the face of an ancient horse lord. With a twist of his wrist, he bisected the monster's skull, leaving fragments of bone and rotted helm to crumble into its bony shoulders.

The count caught the sweep of another undead rider's axe against his shield, feeling the sting of the impact throb up through his injured arm. Gritting his teeth against the pain, he drove his horse sidewards, upsetting the lighter undead steed and sending both it and its rider crashing to the ground.

A moment's respite allowed the count to fully appreciate his situation. He was completely surrounded by the undead now, caught within a circle of fleshless faces and rusted iron blades. Despite the vigour with which he had fought, he seemed no closer to reaching the Red Duke. The vampire's crimson armour was visible but distant, as tantalizingly close and mockingly unattainable as a desert mirage.

To come so close yet fail in the end was more than Count Ergon could accept. Anger boiled over in his veins. He surged forwards once more, taking the fight to the deathly enemy. His sword slashed outwards, taking the forearm of a mounted skeleton, splitting its ulna and radius like dry kindling.

Suddenly there was another fighter beside him,

battering away at the closing skeletons with a footman's mace. Count Ergon was surprised to find that
the lone comrade who had joined him was Leuthere's
valet, the crook-backed peasant Vigor. The peasant
was slashed and bleeding from dozens of cuts, his
hair matted with blood from an ugly scalp wound.
The broken tip of a spear protruded from the peasant's side.

Count Ergon nodded in admiration of Vigor's persistence and bravery. 'Your courage shames better
men,' the knight told Vigor.

The peasant smiled at him crookedly. 'I must…
atone,' he wheezed, forcing each word from his rasp-
ing chest. It was then that Count Ergon noticed the
dagger clenched in Vigor's other hand.

'I must atone!' Vigor repeated in a fierce shriek.
Before Count Ergon could react, the peasant lunged at
him with the dagger. Years of attending Earl Gaubert
made Vigor know exactly where to strike. The dagger
slipped past the join between thigh and waist, stabbing deep into the knight's leg.

'Varlet!' the knight snarled, smashing his shield into
Vigor's side. The peasant recoiled, leaving the dagger
stuck in the count's leg. The next instant, a scream
of agony burst from Vigor's body. A skeleton's spear
transfixed the man, lifting him from the saddle.

'I… must… atone…' Vigor gasped, blood bubbling
from his mouth.

Count Ergon spurred his horse towards the skeletal spearman, smashing it down with a sweep of his
blade. Skeleton and victim both crashed to the earth,
sprawled beneath the hooves of the knight's warhorse.

Other skeletons surged towards Count Ergon, ringing him around with a circle of spears and bill-hooks.

The nobleman lashed out at them, seeking to drive them back and gain room to effectively use his sword. Spears glanced against his armour or grated along the painted face of his shield, but the only hurt he suffered was from the dagger embedded in his thigh.

Just as Count Ergon began to despair of fending off his attackers, a blinding white light engulfed him. His entire body was suffused by a sensation of peace and security such as he had never known. It was like the warm embrace of the Lady herself. For an instant, the knight wondered if he had been killed and drawn into the presence of his goddess.

Then the light passed and the world reassumed its dark and dreary hues. Instead of finding himself dead, Count Ergon saw his enemies wilting to the ground, their bony bodies collapsing into a mush of ash and cinder. All across Ceren Field, he could see similar scenes, entire swathes of the undead army disintegrating before the amazed eyes of the beleaguered Bretonnians. Shouts of triumph and prayers of thanksgiving rose from the battered knights.

The battle was far from over, however. The undead army had been crippled by the miraculous light, but it still vastly outnumbered the jubilant Aquitainians. Count Ergon could see dozens of rattling chariots ascending the hills to assault the peasant bowmen. He could see new formations of zombies and skeletons racing forwards to assault the knights once more. Beyond them, a great company of black knights was thundering away from the fight, driving past the embattled Bretonnians and towards the tomb of Duke Galand.

Count Ergon had the impression that the tomb had been the source of the divine fire, that somehow

Iselda had brought that purifying flame searing across Ceren Field to rescue the doomed knights. It was an impression that was shared by at least one other combatant.

At the forefront of the black knights, Count Ergon could see the crimson figure of the Red Duke. The vampire was leading the charge against Iselda and the tomb!

All injury and fatigue was banished from the Count's mind as he saw his enemy galloping away. He knew it would be his death to chase after the Red Duke, but his life was a price he was willing to pay if he could cross swords with the fiend and end his evil forever. After that, the vampire's black knights could avenge their master. The count's vengeance would be complete.

Other knights were already rushing after the Red Duke, charging their steeds across the crumbling husks of the vanquished undead. Count Ergon set his spurs to the flanks of his own destrier, determined to be the first to reach the vampire.

The horse whinnied in protest, then collapsed. Count Ergon rolled away from the animal as it slumped to the ground, managing to keep his foot from being pinned under the brute's side. He stifled the curse that was on his lips when he saw the magnitude of the animal's injuries. That it had bore him so far for so long was evidence of its stout heart.

Count Ergon turned away from his dying steed and looked to the fleeing Red Duke. The other knights seemed certain to reach the monster before he could gain the tomb. There were only a handful of knights to face the vampire and the three dozen wights riding alongside him, but perhaps one might break through to face the Red Duke. He smiled as he noted the colours of Leuthere among the riders. If he could not destroy the vampire himself, it was fitting that it should be the young d'Elbiq.

'I… must… atone…' a garbled voice croaked. Count Ergon turned his gaze downwards, discovering the body of Vigor crushed beneath the warhorse. The peasant's eyes were glazed with blindness, his breath coming in ragged gasps. Death was only a matter of moments from taking him into its fold.

Suspicion flared in the count's mind, the old animosity between du Maisne and d'Elbiq rising once more to the fore. It was the second instance when Leuthere's valet had mentioned atoning for something. What, the knight wondered, was the misdeed that so plagued Vigor? What drive was it that could move a peasant to murder a nobleman in the midst of battle?

Count Ergon knelt beside the dying peasant, speaking to him in soft, soothing tones.

Determined to find out Vigor's secret while there was still time.

CHAPTER XIX

El Syf lay upon the sand, the Arabyan poison burning through his veins. The black-robed nomads circled about him like a pack of hungry hyenas, eager to claim the kill as soon as they were satisfied their prey lacked the strength to strike back.

Suddenly a black shape was among the Arabyans, hewing right and left with a monstrous sword. The murderous nomads were cleft asunder by the shadow's blade, their bodies butchered like swine at a slaughterhouse. The shrieks of the nomads resonated with terror, a horror beyond simply the fear of death. They did not even consider standing their ground against the dark intruder, but turned to flee into the dunes.

The black stranger did not allow them the luxury of flight. With amazing speed, he swept down upon them, catching each man in his turn. The nomads were cut to ribbons by the razored edge of the lone warrior's giant sword, their blood spraying across the sands in great gleaming arcs.

The Duke of Aquitaine smiled a bitter smile. He might die, but at least he had been avenged. No Arabyan would slip back to his tent and boast that he had murdered the great El Syf. No nomad would cut off his ears and bear them back to his tribe as a keepsake.

He closed his eyes, whispering am entreaty to the Lady that she would keep Duchess Martinga safe and watch over her when he was gone. A feeling of peace began to close about El Syf's heart as death drew him into its embrace.

The duke's eyes opened again, round with fright, his skin prickling with a crawling fear. Standing over him, staring down at him, was the black stranger.

Arabyan blood dripped from the stranger's ornate, fat-bladed sword, forming little streams in the yellow sand. The man wore a suit of plates, its steel enamelled with some pigment that made it impossibly dark, as though a piece of midnight had been torn from the sky and hammered into armour. The breastplate and greaves were richly gilded with symbols and letters strange to Bretonnian eyes, as unlike the swirling script of Araby as the sharp runes of the dwarfs. The open-faced helmet was both ornate and archaic; if it had been crafted of leather instead of steel, the duke might have thought it had been looted from the barrow of a horse lord.

A cold smile was on the stranger's pale face as he regarded the dying knight. The man's features were as exotic as his armour, fine and precise, yet with a stamp of arrogance and pride. The man's flesh was almost colourless, reminding the duke of a corpse laid out for a wake. The eyes, however, were far from dead. Great dark pools, depthless and sinister, they bored into the duke's with a predatory intensity, probing down into the dying man's very soul.

'You are of the Bretonni?' the stranger asked, his voice a deep growl, his accent possessing a curious nasal inflection. The duke was too weak to answer, but his interrogator seemed to divine the answer just the same. 'It is many, many years since I last visited those shores,' he said, his face growing contemplative. 'Such times they were. I should visit your land, someday. I imagine Giles is long dead and my word to him satisfied.'

El Syf heard the stranger's words only vaguely, his attention focused upon the ground at the warrior's feet. Despite the brilliance of the sun, the man cast no shadow upon the sand.

The vampire took note of the duke's observation. He smiled, and in that smile was all the malice and pride of his many-centuried existence. 'Yes,' he said. 'I have conquered many of the weaknesses of my condition since leaving my vanished homeland, but some remain.' A gleam of cruel amusement crept into the vampire's eyes. 'Perhaps, in time, you will conquer these weaknesses too.'

The words sent a thrill of terror surging through the duke's body. He struggled to crawl away, to flee this ghastly vulture that had descended upon him, promising a fate worse than a shameful death. In the vampire's cold voice, El Syf heard the threat of damnation eternal.

The vampire watched his prey squirm in the sand. When he tired of the sport, he set his steel boot upon the duke's shoulder and held him still. 'Your battle with the Arabyans was magnificent,' the monster announced. 'I watched you from the dunes. I am something of a connoisseur of war, you might say. It has given me purpose down these many centuries, the pursuit of excellence in arms. The Bretonni were always a fierce people. You do your ancestors proud.' The vampire's lips curled back in a regretful expression. 'A pity to allow such skill to end upon the knives of cowards.'

Before El Syf's horrified eyes, the vampire drew off one of his ornate gauntlets, baring his pallid hand. The creature leaned his head down and sank his fangs into the exposed palm. Dark blood bubbled from the wound. Crouching down over the dying duke, the vampire pressed his bleeding palm against the knight's mouth, holding it there until some of his blood dripped past the man's lips.

'I do not know if you will survive,' the vampire said as he rose from the shuddering knight. 'It may be that the Arabyan poison has already done its work and you will die. It may be that the influence of the sun will oppose the gift I have bestowed upon you and you will shrivel up and perish.'

The vampire's smile tightened and his voice became a malignant hiss. 'I do not think you will die,' he said. 'The warrior spirit inside you will fight to survive, even if your mind begs for death. Even for one who has lived since the days of Alcadizzar and Lahmizzash, I have seldom seen a warrior with a greater affinity for the sword. You were destined to ascend from the frailty of mortal flesh and become something greater.

'To become the get of Abhorash.'

The vampire laughed as he mounted his mummified steed and vanished back into the dunes. Behind him, he left the Duke of Aquitaine to live or die as fate and the knight's defiant spirit decreed.

THE SMALL GROUP of knights urged their horses onwards, determined to reach the vampire's cavalry before the undead could defile the tomb of Duke Galand or bring harm to the Prophetess Iselda. Both tomb and damsel were sacred to the Lady of the Lake, and their faith in the goddess fired their hearts as even the defence of their homes had failed to stir them.

Sir Leuthere was among the foremost of the knights, spurring his destrier towards the evil his uncle had loosed from its tomb. The Red Duke's destruction would redeem the honour of the d'Elbiqs and even the thought of serving the Lady herself did not make him forget the terrible sin Earl Gaubert had committed.

The Red Duke took note of the pursuit halfway across the field. The vampire snarled as he twisted about in the saddle, glaring at the few men desperately trying to intercept him. For an instant, his eyes locked with Leuthere's, then the vampire raised his armoured hand, snapping orders to his undead slaves.

A third of the black knights followed the Red Duke's gesture, wheeling away to confront the pursuing Bretonnians. Leuthere was horrified to see the black figure of Sir Maraulf leading the wights. In life, Maraulf had been a formidable warrior, but as a vampire, his strength had become monstrous. Leuthere felt a shudder pass through him as he recalled the awful might of Baron de Gavaudan at the Chapel Sereine and the terrible prowess of Maraulf during the frantic retreat from Dragon's Hill.

Maraulf spurred his nightmarish steed into a charge, outpacing the slower wights and their skeletal horses. The dark knight was upon the foremost of the Bretonnians in an instant, his sword sweeping out in a deadly arc before the Aquitainian could even begin to raise his shield to ward off the blow. The blade caught the Bretonnian in the neck, shearing clean through in a burst of gore. The dead knight's head leapt from his shoulders as though it had been flung by a catapult. Leuthere watched in horror as the grisly wreckage bounced across the field.

The second knight ahead of Leuthere fared just as poorly against the supernatural power of the vampire. One of the questing knights equipped with a massive two-handed sword, the knight thrust his blade ahead of him as he forced his horse into a frenzied charge, thinking to use the heavy sword as an improvised lance. Against a normal foe, the tactic would have worked, but Maraulf displayed unnatural speed as he twisted his nightmare from the charging Bretonnian's path. As the knight passed him, the vampire's blade lashed out, tearing through the neck of the warhorse then driving upwards to split the armoured belly of the rider. Man and beast collapsed in a jumble of broken flesh and spurting blood.

Leuthere's mouth hung open, the young knight awestruck by Maraulf's grisly display of power and speed.

The vampire lifted his eyes from the wreckage of his last victim. Stabbing his spurs into the black flesh of his mount, the dark knight galloped towards Leuthere.

ISELDA'S BODY SAGGED against the door of the tomb. She felt as though every muscle in her body had become cold as ice. Frost rasped past her lips every time she exhaled, stinging her throat. Her limbs trembled with a nervous ague and she found that she could only focus her vision with a conscious effort. When she reached a quivering hand to her head, five strands of golden hair came away at her touch.

The power divine was not a thing to be called upon with impunity, even for a sacred prophetess of the grail.

The woman turned her head with a weariness such as she had never known. A bitter smile crossed her face as she saw the damage she had wrought upon the vampire's army. Hundreds of the undead had been scorched, reduced to ash by the magic she had turned upon them, but it was less than a tenth of the host the Red Duke had called from their graves.

Now, Iselda knew, the vampire would come for her.

She laid her palm against the frigid door of Duke Galand's tomb. Even with Duke Gilon's plan foiled, there was still a chance to break the Red Duke upon Ceren Field. Perhaps it was why Isabeau had advised Duke Galand to erect his tomb upon the battlefield. Perhaps it was why Galand had agreed.

As the black knights charged towards the tomb, Iselda felt the terror of her own impending destruction seize her once more. She knew that she had already lived beyond the years allotted to a normal woman; the magic of the Lady had sustained her for almost two centuries. Even so, she was greedy for more. She did not want to die. Whatever she had foreseen in her pools and mirrors, she did not want to die.

Iselda reached down inside herself, drawing upon her own tremendous will. She pictured the marble effigy of Duke Galand inside his tomb, imagined her hand closing about that of the heroic grail knight. She felt her energies uniting with his own, her spirit joining with the ghost of the long-dead hero. Together, they called out with their souls, called out to the Lady to bestow once more the holy essence of her being, to unleash the light of purity and burn away the undead corruption charging across Ceren Field.

Her prayer was answered. Iselda's body jerked upright, stiff and rigid as the magic of the Lady burned through her body once more. Blazing light erupted from every pore of her skin, flaring across Ceren Field in a wave of coruscating luminance. The purifying light smashed into the Red Duke and his obscene knights. The undead riders were engulfed in the divine energies, their corrupt bodies flayed by the rage of the goddess. Iselda could see the black knights being incinerated by the light, their bones shattering, their armour crumbling as the evil sustaining them was obliterated.

Iselda collapsed in a pile at the foot of the tomb, beads of ice covering her body where the sweat had frozen. Blood trickled from the corners of her eyes, her heart throbbed unevenly within her breast, her stomach coiled into a painful knot. Focusing her eyes, she saw that her fingernails were split and blackened where the power had erupted from them. Her body felt like a single open wound, but Iselda rejoiced in the pain. She was alive! She had destroyed the Red Duke and she was alive!

The sound of hooves continued to assail her. At first she refused to acknowledge the sound, refused to accept this portent of doom. Reluctantly, she turned her head and forced her vision into focus.

Galloping furiously down the field were two riders, two undead monstrosities of such malignance and power that their terrible wills had sustained them through even the cleansing flame of the Lady's judgement. One was the ghastly wight of a Bretonnian knight, baleful flames blazing in the sockets of its skull. The other... the other was that figure which promised doom to the prophetess, the crimson shape of the Red Duke himself.

Iselda moved her hands feebly as the vampire and his seneschal came charging towards her. She could still feel the holy power of Duke Galand's tomb, but she was far too weak to draw upon it again. She had thrown every ounce of her strength into those two, desperate efforts to destroy the vampire.

As the Red Duke drew back on the reins of El Morzillo, as the vampire glared down at her with his fiery eyes, as his pale lips pulled back to expose gleaming fangs, Iselda knew she had lost her frantic struggle to escape the doom she had foreseen.

THE RED DUKE gloated as the wretched prophetess cowered before him. For all of her magic, all her vaunted foresight, all the blessings the Lady had supposedly bestowed upon her, Isabeau trembled before him just like any other woman.

She would suffer, this treasonous bitch who had conspired to steal everything he possessed and bestow it upon a fratricidal usurper! She would pay for every ounce of pain the Red Duke had endured, for the ghastly loss of his beloved wife. She would know what it was to be truly damned.

The vampire dismounted. He would savour the destruction of the prophetess. Her ruin would be no hasty affair, but a plague that would see her bound to him forever in the darkness. He scowled at the whimpering, weary thing cringing against the door of the tomb. Amusement hissed through the Red Duke's fangs. If the woman sought to join the dead, she was going to get her wish.

At least for a time.

Stalking towards the tomb, the Red Duke shielded his eyes against the hateful glare that emanated from the marble walls. He could feel the holy energies straining to repulse him, to force him from the sacred ground. If Isabeau had not tapped the power of this place so recklessly, perhaps the protective aura would have been enough to overpower even the vampire's fierce determination. As it was, all the emanations evoked was a snarl of anger from the Red Duke.

'We meet again,' the Red Duke growled at the prostrate woman. 'Your goddess has deserted you. Your king has abandoned you. Now you belong to me.' The vampire stood above her, reaching out with his clawed hand.

Isabeau raised her head, looking up at him with wide, terrified eyes. She fought to look away, but it was too late. She had already been trapped by the Red Duke's hypnotic gaze. If the world were to crack open at her feet, still she would be gripped by those fiery eyes.

At the vampire's gesture, the woman rose to her feet, drawing upon reserves of strength she did not know she possessed. The Red Duke grinned evilly at her, his fangs parted, his wolfish tongue licking his colourless lips hungrily. He started to lean towards her, intent on sinking his fangs into her soft white throat. The vampire caught himself, hurling himself back.

'No,' he hissed. 'For you, it will not be so easy. You will share my curse fully, not as some half-witted vermin like de Gavaudan! You will know the horror that has claimed you, you will appreciate everything you have lost!' The Red Duke's hand closed about his steel breastplate, tearing it open as though it were nothing but sackcloth, exposing the pallid chest beneath. With his thumb, he gouged the cold flesh, opening a vein from which stagnant blood bubbled.

'You will drink of me,' the Red Duke said. 'You will drink my curse and become one of the damned!'

The vampire reached for the woman's neck, to force her lips to his scarred chest. As he reached for her, he hesitated. A faint smile had appeared on Isabeau's lips, a coy, almost sneering expression of triumph.

An instant later, a dark shadow fell across the Red Duke. Powerful wings smashed against him, battering him to the ground.

'Unhand that lady, filth!' a furious voice roared. 'By the sacred sword of King Giles, I'll cut you down like the crawling graveworm you are!'

The Red Duke rolled across the ground as the mighty wings continued to beat at him. The vampire snarled up at his attacker. King Louis the Usurper had deigned to challenge him after all. He was not impressed. His brother had lost all of the elegance and command he'd possessed during those long years campaigning in the desert. He looked like a shabby old man sitting there on the back of his pegasus. Killing him, the Red Duke reflected, might almost be considered an act of charity.

'You should have stayed a coward, brother,' the vampire's hate-ridden voice rasped. 'That the Lady should choose a maggot such as you to be king is all the evidence I need that she is a false goddess.'

The eyes of King Louis blazed with righteous outrage behind the visor of his helm. 'I claim no kinship to you, tomb-rat! Nor do I claim the crown of our good king! Know that you face Duke Gilon, mad varlet! Duke Gilon, true lord of Aquitaine!'

Duke Gilon's outburst caused the vampire to stagger momentarily. The Red Duke clutched at his head, trying to squeeze the confusion from his brain, vainly attempting to silence the voices screaming within his mind.

Chivalry would have demanded Duke Gilon to wait until his foe had recovered enough to defend himself, but the laws of chivalry could hardly be extended to a butchering monster risen from the grave. With a great shout, the knight urged Fulminer forwards and raised his sword overhead, both hands closed about it. He would bring that blade cleaving down through the vampire's skull and end the horror that had haunted Aquitaine for so long.

Before Duke Gilon could strike, Fulminer stumbled and shrieked in pain. The staggering pegasus managed to stay standing, awkwardly turning about to face the creature that had assaulted it. Duke Gilon could see that its hind leg had been hideously gashed, cleft down to the bone, bits of corroded metal sinking maliciously into the grisly wound. Fulminer's attacker leered before the stricken pegasus, the animal's blood dripping from his rusty sword.

Fixating upon destroying the Red Duke and protecting Iselda, Duke Gilon had forgotten the vampire's seneschal. The wight-lord glared at the knight, the unholy lights glowing from the sockets of its skull. Grimly, Sir Corbinian struck out with his mouldering sword, slashing one of Fulminer's mighty wings.

The pegasus shrieked in agony as the wight's blade shattered its wing. Duke Gilon urged Fulminer forwards, trusting that the natural ferocity of the pegasus would make it lash out at its attacker. The great beast reared back, angrily flailing its hooves and its uninjured wing. The flailing hooves cracked against the wight-lord's chest, collapsing the undead champion's ribs and spilling the monster to the earth.

Sir Corbinian started to rise despite the hideous damage visited upon him by the enraged Fulminer. But now the wight-lord was within reach of Duke Gilon's vengeful sword. The knight's blade came whistling down in a murderous arc, crunching through the wight-lord's decayed helm and splitting his skull down to the jawline. For an instant, the angry flames blazing in the sockets of Corbinian's skull flared even more malignantly, then they cooled, evaporating into a wisp of foulness that was borne away by the autumn breeze.

Duke Gilon spared only a momentary glance at the vanquished monster. Gently, he urged the injured Fulminer to turn back around. There was still another fiend he had to destroy.

The Red Duke stood before the tomb, awaiting Duke Gilon's return. The vampire saluted the knight. 'You may not be King Louis, the man who stole my title and my lands,' the vampire hissed, 'but you bear the rewards of his treachery. For that, Gilon, you will die.'

Without further preamble, the Red Duke lunged at his foe. Duke Gilon had never seen anything move so swiftly. In the blink of an eye, the vampire was upon him. Fulminer lashed out at the fiend with its hooves. The pegasus shrieked as the Red Duke's sword slashed clean through its flailing limb, sending its foreleg spinning away across the field. Duke Gilon chopped down at the malignant undead, but the pained panic of his steed made him miss his foe entirely.

Neighing in agony, Fulminer tried to quit the battlefield, its single wing beating frantically at the air as it vainly tried to return to the sky. Duke Gilon desperately tried to recover some control of the pegasus, to turn it about so he could face his enemy. What success he might have had was undone when the Red Duke's flashing sword clove into the animal's flank. Fulminer reared back with such violence that its rider was hurled from the saddle.

Duke Gilon landed in a jangle of armour. He felt a sharp stab of pain rush through him as one of his legs snapped beneath his thrown body. Furiously he struggled to draw breath back into his winded lungs, then groped about in the dirt for the sword that had been knocked from his grasp.

A pale, lifeless visage glared down at the prostrate knight. Duke Gilon looked up helplessly as the Red Duke bared his fangs in an ugly leer.

'No quarter for a traitor,' the vampire declared, burying his sword in Duke Gilon's chest, skewering the knight like a boar upon a spit.

SIR LEUTHERE KNEW he was about to die. As the dark knight charged towards him upon his ghastly nightmare, Leuthere knew he faced a foe he could not defeat. The gory spectacle of Sir Maraulf's first victims left him with no delusions that he could overwhelm the vampire through force of arms and a stout heart.

Then, before the dark knight could close upon Leuthere, a blinding blast of light emanated from the tomb of Duke Galand. Leuthere felt a wave of warmth and peace engulf him and knew that this was the holy light of the Lady, called forth again by the Prophetess Iselda. His faith in the goddess reached out to the light, drawing it inside him, filling his body with the Lady of the Lake's divine power.

The effect upon the undead was instantaneous and dramatically different. The black knights following Maraulf crumbled even as they charged towards the Bretonnians, the skeletons of both steeds and riders flaking apart like clots of dried mud. As their decaying bodies struck the ground, they exploded into clouds of rancid dust.

Where a dozen wights had been there was now only piles of ash. Alone of the undead, Maraulf remained, the vampire's terrible will strong enough to defy the purifying rays of the Lady's light. Yet even the vampire was not untouched by the holy firestorm that swept about him. His armour was charred, his surcoat hanging from his body in scorched strips. The nightmare he rode no longer galloped across Ceren Field in search of blood, but limped about in a crippled fashion.

Bolstered by the grace of the Lady, emboldened by the dark knight's weakened state, Leuthere urged his warhorse to the attack.

Maraulf met the young knight's charge. The vampire's sword crashed against Leuthere's shield, denting the wood but failing to wreak the havoc he had dealt Sir Richemont at the river. The dark knight's strength was still formidable, but it was no longer superhuman.

The vampire's reflexes proved slower as well. Slashing his sword at the dark knight's throat, Leuthere was able to cleave through the gorget, sending the twisted scrap of armour glancing off into the darkness. Maraulf twisted his sword around to intercept the blow too late to parry the attack. Dark blood began to stream from the vampire's gashed neck.

The smell of his own blood seemed to drive Maraulf into a bestial fury. He leapt from the saddle, pouncing upon Leuthere like some beast of the forest. Knight and vampire tumbled across the earth, the rattle of steel against stone drowning out the pained grunts and growls of the two combatants.

The tumble across the ground ended with both fighters locked in a deadly embrace. In his fall, Maraulf had lost his sword while Leuthere retained his. Each warrior struggled for control of the sword, striving to turn it against the breast of his enemy.

A momentary horror gripped Leuthere as he met the malignant, inhuman gaze of Maraulf's eyes. There was nothing left of the hermit knight who had tended his uncle's body and advised Leuthere how he might atone for the evil Earl Gaubert had unleashed. The thing glaring at him from inside the black steel helmet was nothing human, however much it claimed a human shape.

The vampire hissed in triumph as Leuthere's grip slackened and the sword began to turn towards the knight's chest. Leuthere clenched his eyes shut, blocking out the hateful glare of Maraulf's gaze. He prayed to the Lady, drawing upon the divine warmth that he could still feel coursing through him.

A shriek split the darkness, then a low, gasping moan.

Leuthere stared at the now truly lifeless shape sprawled on the ground beside him. The sword had been turned about at the last, driven through the dark knight's side to pierce his black heart. The monster was gone. When Leuthere looked into the dead eyes behind the black helmet, he saw no trace of the inhuman hate that had smouldered there before. All he saw was an expression of peace and gratitude.

THE RED DUKE stalked away from Duke Gilon's twitching corpse. He licked the dead knight's blood from his blade, savouring the taste of terror and despair that permeated it. He grinned as he drew towards the woman still crumpled against the door of the tomb.

Iselda tried not to scream as the vampire fell upon her, but despite all her magic, all the holy secrets that had been entrusted to her, she was still mortal and suffered all of a mortal's fear.

The Red Duke seized her long blonde hair in his mailed fist, twisting it about his fingers as he savagely jerked Iselda to her feet. 'Not Isabeau, but one of her sister-witches,' he growled. 'Tell me where that traitorous harlot is and I will make your death a quick one.'

Iselda struggled to turn her face from the Red Duke's terrifying visage, his gleaming fangs, his mouth smeared with blood, his eyes burning like balefires. Never in all her life had she really understood true fear.

'Tell me where she is!' the vampire demanded, forcing Iselda to face him by tightening his hold upon her.

'Dead,' the prophetess told him. As the word was forced from her lips, a feeling of defiance blazed up within her. She knew what her fate would be. She had seen it. There was no escaping it now, so why should she fear this monster. The certainty of her impending death lent her a grim courage.

'She is dead,' Iselda repeated. 'Dead these three hundred years. She is not here to seal you back in your tomb! To wall you up alone with the dark and the thirst!'

The Red Duke's face contorted into a vision of rage. He raised his sword. Almost he brought the blade crashing down into the defiant woman's sneering face. The vampire's lip curled in a snarl. Brutally, he forced Iselda to turn and face the battlefield.

'Your magic has weakened my army,' the Red Duke confessed. 'But see! There are still enough left to vanquish these gallant fools! And when they are all slain, I will use them to build my army anew. You have not stopped me, witch! You have only delayed the inevitable. Every grave, every tomb, every barrow in Aquitaine will give up its dead. I shall build an army such as Bretonnia has never known and with it I shall crush the Lady and her duplicitous cult.' The vampire's smile became icy, an inhumanly cruel glint shining in his eye.

'I will rebuild my army,' the Red Duke said. He turned his head, glaring at the door of Duke Galand's tomb. 'And I will start with your precious champion. How fitting that one of the Lady's grail knights should be the first of my new slaves.'

Contemptuously, the Red Duke threw Iselda aside. The prophetess smashed against the marble wall of the tomb with such force that she could hear one of her ribs snap inside her. Pain flared through her body, threatening to drive consciousness from her. Only by force of will was she able to stay on her feet. Only through sheer determination was she able to force words past her blood-flecked lips.

'Go, then, monster,' she snarled at the vampire. 'Go and profane the grave of your kin.'

The Red Duke spun about, his eyes gleaming with a strange and terrible light. Iselda quailed before that look, but she knew the secret must be told. The secret that had been hidden for so long. The secret that would be enough to break the Red Duke.

'You thought Martinga threw herself from the tower because of you,' Iselda stated, mockery in her tone. 'She died to preserve the life of her son... the son she bore nine months after you departed on the crusade. She had hidden him when she became aware of Baron de Gavaudan's ambitions for the dukedom. By her death, she ensured that the baron and his agents could never find the ducal heir.'

The vampire's face twitched with fury. 'You lie,' he snarled, his fist clenching about the grip of his sword. 'The boy's name was Galand and he was entrusted to the keeping of Lady Isabeau,' Iselda continued. 'The secret of his parentage was kept from him, but it was known to a few. Among them was King Louis. The king watched over Galand, ensuring he would become a good and noble knight, that his nephew might atone for the evil his father had committed. After many heroic feats, Galand encountered the Lady and was allowed to drink from the grail. With this final proof of Galand's goodness, King Louis consented to his marriage to his daughter, thereby restoring to his brother's bloodline the dukedom Baron de Gavaudan had thought to usurp.'

'Lies!' the Red Duke roared. 'Baron de Gavaudan was my creature! My slave! He would have told me this!'

'He was your creature,' Iselda said. 'You brought him back from the dead as a half-crippled thing, broken in body… and in mind. Your thrall told you only what you wanted him to tell you. His twisted mind could not separate your suspicions from his own confused memories.'

'No!' the Red Duke raged. 'King Louis wanted my lands for his own! He plotted treachery against me! He wanted Aquitaine as a birthright for his children!'

'A birthright he handed back to his brother's bloodline. He even told Duke Galand who his father had been before he died. Why else do you think Galand was buried here instead of the family crypt beneath Castle Aquitaine? He wanted to be near the resting place of his father.'

The vampire shook his head, his entire body trembling with emotion. 'No! No! No!' he howled. Gripped by fury, he drove towards Iselda, his blade slashing out. The golden sword smashed into the prophetess's shoulder, ripping down until it had torn through her lung. Iselda gave a hollow gasp, then sank against the side of the tomb. The Red Duke glared down at her, even the sight of the blood pooling about her body was not enough to stir his mind from the mocking revelations she had made.

None of it could be true! None of it! King Louis had cheated and betrayed him! Galand was nothing, just some vagabond knight who had used his status as a grail knight to marry into the royal family! Martinga had died for love of him! Everything that had been stolen from him... all of it was still his to take!

Growling like a crazed wolf, the Red Duke turned back to the door of the tomb. Raising his bloodied sword, he brought it smashing down upon the holy seals that bound the door. The stone plaque with its depiction of the grail was shattered by the fierceness of his strike, falling in splinters to the ground. The vampire could feel the holy energies of the tomb dissipate, drawn off into the aether as he profaned the sacred symbols.

With inhuman strength, the Red Duke pushed open the stone doors of the tomb. He stared into the musty darkness, his sharp eyes picking out the marble effigy of the dead knight which stood guard above Duke Galand's sarcophagus. Drawing the dark forces of his unholy magic into himself, the Red Duke called out to the dead man's spirit...

An instant later, the Red Duke was fleeing from the tomb, his eyes wide with horror. Frantically he seized the reins of El Morzillo, leaping into the spectral steed's saddle. Lashing his undead warhorse, the Red Duke galloped away from the tomb, fleeing into the darkness as though all the daemons of Chaos were upon his heels.

Lying in her own blood, Iselda managed a strained smile as she watched the vampire flee.

They had won. Aquitaine was saved.

THE RED DUKE'S sudden desertion was the breaking point in the battle. The lesser undead, drawing their very existence from the vampire's hideous will, collapsed where they stood. Battalions of skeletons and zombies that only a moment before stood ready to massacre the knights of Aquitaine became only so much carrion in the blink of an eye.

Some of the more powerful undead endured. The wights called from Dragon's Hill, the liches of the ancient druids, the grave guard that had once defended the Crac de Sang against King Louis, these were able to maintain their unholy vitality despite the flight of their master. But they fought without coordination or cohesion, becoming easy prey for the vengeful knights who prowled Ceren Field.

Sir Richemont broke away from the battle the instant victory was assured. Securing a horse from one of his captains, he rode at once towards the tomb of Duke Galand. No knight on the battlefield had failed to see Duke Gilon swoop down to confront the Red Duke. No knight on the battlefield had failed to notice that Fulminer never rose back into the sky.

The ducal heir jumped from his saddle as soon as he came to the tomb. He knelt down beside the body of his father, cradling the dead man's head in his lap. Tears streamed down Richemont's face.

'Do not weep for him, Duke Richemont.'

The voice was little louder than a whisper, but it caught Richemont's attention just the same. He turned about, finding the speaker lying against the side of Duke Galand's tomb. The Prophetess Iselda was a ragged mess, her dress caked in blood, her face drawn and pale. Sir Leuthere crouched beside her, trying to staunch the flow of blood rising from the ghastly wound she had suffered. One glance told Richemont that the young knight's efforts were futile. The wound was a mortal one.

'Your father died to save his people,' Iselda continued. A haunted expression came over her and Richemont had the impression that she was gazing somewhere deep inside herself rather than at anything which anyone else could see. 'There is no greater honour than to sacrifice one's own life to save others.'

Richemont bowed his head, knowing that Iselda's words were true. He found it hard to hold the dying woman's gaze, however. His grief was too great and too personal to spare any for the prophetess. 'The questing knights have already set out in pursuit of the vampire. They will avenge my father and bring that fiend's head back to Castle Aquitaine on a spike.'

Iselda shook her head. 'No, Duke Richemont,' she told him. 'They will not catch the vampire.' She raised her hand slowly, closing it about that of Leuthere. 'I have seen the men who can destroy the Red Duke.' Her expression darkened, dropping into a frown. 'If they can set aside their hate and guilt to work together.'

Leuthere stared at the ground, colour rushing into his face. His thoughts were of Vigor and the terrible thing the peasant had intended during the battle. 'Lady Iselda, we do not even know if Count Ergon survived the battle.'

'If he has, I will find him,' Richemont swore. 'You shall both have the finest armour, the best horses, the sharpest blades Aquitaine can bestow upon you.' The new duke clenched his fist. 'Only bring me that monster's head!'

DUKE RICHEMONT WAS true to his word. He dispatched a hundred men to scour Ceren Field in search of Count Ergon. When the old knight was found, he was brought before the new duke and told of the quest he must undertake. It was an easy matter for Count Ergon to agree to hunt down the Red Duke, but his gaze was cold when he stared at Sir Leuthere. More than an echo of the old feud, there was a cold hate in the nobleman's eyes that caused Leuthere's blood to shiver in his veins.

Iselda was not there to see the two men outfitted for their mission. The prophetess had died of her wound an hour before. Whatever last words or advice and guidance she might have given the knights went unspoken.

As dusk began to fade into night, the two men set out on the trail of the Red Duke. They rode in silence, the clatter of their horses' hooves the only sound that passed between them. With the bright orb of Mannslieb shining across the land, the journey was far easier than the desperate race from Dragon's Hill.

It was almost midnight when Leuthere finally broke the brooding silence. He could suffer the unspoken disdain of his companion no longer. 'How can you follow the fiend's trail?' he asked Count Ergon. 'I can see nothing in this light.'

'There is no need to follow the vampire,' Count Ergon replied, his voice low and icy. 'He will seek out his old fortress in the Massif Orcal.'

'How can you be so sure?' Leuthere demanded.

'Most of the men in Duke Richemont's camp seemed to think the vampire would flee into the Forest of Châlons knowing few men would pursue him there.'

'I would pursue that monster into the maw of Chaos,' Count Ergon growled. For the first time since they had set out, he turned in his saddle and set his cheerless eyes on Leuthere. 'He may seek to lose the questing knights in the forest, but he will return to his fortress. And I will be there waiting for him.'

'We will be there,' Leuthere corrected him.

Count Ergon laughed, but it was a mirthless sound. 'I ride to avenge my family, slain by the vampire's hand. Why do you pursue the vampire? Glory? Honour?' The nobleman's voice dropped into a hiss of loathing. 'Shame?'

Suddenly there was a dagger in Count Ergon's fist. Leuthere might have avoided the older man's thrust had he not been frozen with horror. He recognized that weapon, had seen it last in Vigor's belt. He'd assumed the peasant had been killed by the undead before he could reach the count. Now, the agonising truth thrust itself into his gut.

Leuthere dropped from the saddle, crashing to the ground, Vigor's dagger buried to the hilt in his belly. He writhed weakly, struggling to reach his horse, but Count Ergon had already seized the animal's reins and drawn it away.

'The chivalry of the d'Elbiqs,' Count Ergon scoffed, spitting on the ground. 'I had a talk with your assassin before he died. He confessed everything to me. It was no accident that the Red Duke attacked my home, slaughtered my family. Your uncle freed him to destroy my kinfolk!'

Leuthere stretched his hands towards the glowering

nobleman. 'I tried to make amends. I tried to warn you, but it was too late. All... all I had left was... to atone. To set things right.'

'Atone?' Count Ergon scoffed. 'You do not deserve that chance! You and your vile family can fester with the guilt and shame of the horror you've brought upon Aquitaine!'

Leuthere's face contorted in pain as he tried to move. He could feel blood and bile bubbling from his wound. He lifted a bloodied hand imploringly to Count Ergon. 'I have wronged you... wronged you in a way for which I cannot ask forgiveness... but you must help me. Lady Iselda said only the two of us could destroy the Red Duke! We must face him together!'

Count Ergon turned his back on the wounded knight. 'The prophetess is dead and her prophecy with her,' he said. 'I will hunt down the Red Duke and I will destroy him. Alone.'

'Don't leave me like this!' Leuthere cried as Count Ergon started to ride away. 'Don't defy the prophecy! We must face the vampire together!'

'Die in the dirt or crawl to a healer,' the count called back without turning to look upon the stricken knight. 'It is all the same to me.'

Leuthere continued to cry out, begging the count not to abandon him, pleading with him to heed the words of Iselda. But the nobleman was deaf to his entreaties. His mind was fixated upon the memory of his son's mutilated body and the courtyard of his castle heaped with his slain household. He would find the Red Duke.

Lady willing he would have his revenge.

EPILOGUE

The Circle of Blood was closed when the Red Duke was again defeated upon Ceren Field. The vampire fled, pursued by the bravest of Aquitaine's knights, but though they searched for many years, the final fate of the monster was never certain.

Sir Leuthere d'Elbiq survived long enough to be discovered by one of the knights hunting the Red Duke. The mortally wounded Leuthere was returned to the Chateau d'Elbiq, where he related his tale to others of his clan, and in so doing reignited the ancient feud against the du Maisnes. To this day, the feud persists, becoming known as the most bloodthirsty and bitter of all Aquitaine's querulous nobles.

Count Ergon du Maisne, after striking down Leuthere, held true to his word and pursued his trail of vengeance alone. He was seen by a shepherd riding up into the hills overlooking the Forest of Châlons, that haunted region where the Red Duke's fortress had been built. It was the last time any trace of Count Ergon was ever found. To this day, the fate of the avenging knight remains a mystery.

Many different tales are told of the Red Duke, stories that he continues to haunt the Forest of Châlons, lurking hidden in the shadows, awaiting his chance for revenge against the people of Aquitaine. Certainly his is the darkest and most savage account of vampirism in a land that has been largely free of the depredations of nosferatu.

One of the most striking accounts of the Red Duke's survival into modern times comes from the famed troubadour Jacques le Thorand who claimed to have been visited by the vampire while staying at an inn bordering the Forest of Châlons. According to Jacques, the Red Duke spent the night relating to him the true facts of his atrocities. Certainly, when Jacques afterwards rewrote his Ballad of the Red Duke, the tale little resembled that expounded by historians and songsters. Accepted history would have the Prophetess Iselda killed at the Tower of Wizardry long before the Second Battle of Ceren Field and Sir Richemont's deeds at the River Morceaux were far more successful than those claimed by Jacques.

Still, there is a disturbing veracity in Jacques's account, whether it really came from the Red Duke himself or no. It is an easily confirmed fact that a determined effort has been made by the lords of Aquitaine to efface the name of the Red Duke from all histories, monuments and records, such that it becomes impossible to verify if he was indeed the brother of King Louis the Righteous. The idea that he was also the father of Duke Galand of Aquitaine is one that is violently rejected by the knights of that land – often at the point of a sword. The thought that the ruling family of a Bretonnian dukedom could share their heritage with the infamous vampire would be akin to claiming Emperor Karl-Franz was descended from the Reikerbahn Butcher.

Jacques le Thorand never recovered from whatever dark epiphany claimed him that night on the border of the forest. From a healthy, robust traveller renowned for his handsome looks and gentle mien, he became pale, listless and reclusive, shutting himself in a garret in Quenelles. Never *more would he wander the green fields of Bretonnia or visit the grand courts of the kingdom. It was whispered that a curious madness had taken hold of the once renowned troubadour, a peculiar malady that caused him to slowly waste away, unable to stir from his squalid lodgings. To the end, Jacques spent what small coin he possessed on copious supplies of candles and his garret could always be seen fairly glowing with light from dusk until dawn until the day when he finally succumbed to his illness and died.*

I present this volume, drawn from the Ballad of the Red Duke as revised by Jacques le Thorand before his death and make no assertions as to its truth or lack thereof. The events described occurred in the year 1932 of the Imperial reckoning, over five hundred years ago, yet the legend of the Red Duke persists. A wise man wonders if this grim tale could remain so fresh in the minds of illiterate peasants if there were not some current and persistent influence still acting upon them.

There are things in the night. Things which are to be feared.

Ehrhard Stoecker

Parravon

I. C. 2506

ABOUT THE AUTHOR

C. L. Werner was a diseased servant of the Horned Rat long before his first story in *Inferno!* magazine. His Black Library credits include the Chaos Wastes books *Palace of the Plague Lord* and *Blood for the Blood God, Mathias Thulmann: Witch Hunter, Runefang* and the *Brunner the Bounty Hunter* trilogy. Currently living in the American south-west, he continues to write stories of mayhem and madness set in the Warhammer World.

Visit the author's website at
www.vermintime.com

The next Warhammer Heroes novel

LUTHOR HUSS

CHRIS WRAIGHT

WARHAMMER

OUT FEBRUARY 2012